The Best Science Fiction

OF THE YEAR

#6

The Best Science Fiction OF THE YEAR #6

Edited by Terry Carr

Holt, Rinehart and Winston • New York

Published simultaneously in Canada by Holt, Rinehart and Winston of Canada, Limited.
ISBN: 0-03-020716-9
PRINTED IN THE UNITED STATES OF AMERICA
10 9 8 7 6 5 4 3 2 1

ACKNOWLEDGMENTS

"I See You," by Damon Knight: Copyright © 1976 by Mercury Press, Inc. From *Fantasy and Science Fiction*, November 1976, by permission of the author./"The Phantom of Kansas," by John Varley: Copyright © 1976 by UPD Publishing Corp. From *Galaxy*, February 1976, by permission of the author./"Seeing," by Harlan Ellison: Copyright © 1976 by Harlan Ellison. From *Andromeda 1* and *The Ides of Tomorrow*, by permission of the author./"The Death of Princes," by Fritz Leiber: Copyright © 1976 by Ultimate Publishing Co., Inc. From *Amazing Science Fiction*, June 1976, by permission of the author./"The Psychologist Who Wouldn't Do Awful Things to Rats," by James Tiptree, Jr.: Copyright © 1976 by Robert Silverberg. From *New Dimensions 6*, by permission of the author./"The Eyeflash Miracles," by Gene Wolfe: Copyright © 1976 by Gene Wolfe. From *Future Power*, by permission of the author and his agent. Virginia Kidd./"An Infinite Summer," by Christopher Priest: Copyright © 1976 by Christopher Priest. From *Andromeda 1*, by permission of the author and his agents, Marie Rodell–Frances Collin Literary Agency./"The Highest Dive," by Jack Williamson: Copyright © 1976 by New English Library Ltd. From *Science Fiction Monthly*, January 1976, by permission of the author./"Meathouse Man," by George R. R. Martin: Copyright © 1976 by Damon Knight. From *Orbit 18*, by permission of the author./"Custer's Last Jump," by Steven Utley and Howard Waldrop: Copyright © 1976 by Terry Carr. From *Universe 6*, by permission of the authors./"The Bicentennial Man," by Isaac Asimov: Copyright © 1976 by Random House, Inc. From *Stellar #2*, by permission of Ballantine Books, a Division of Random House, Inc.

Contents

Introduction

The short story is a dying art-form everywhere but in science fiction, and the reasons are worth considering.

The average person today prefers novels to short stories, if he or she reads at all. John Updike's novels may sell millions of copies, but his short story collections sell a fraction of that number. When *Esquire* or *The Atlantic* has a new short story by Nabokov or Barth, do you see their names featured on the covers? No, of course not—instead they advertise articles on Zen for businessmen, or the memoirs of someone who claims to have had an affair with John Ehrlichman.

I recently saw a publicity flier from *Fiction* Magazine; it was headlined, "THE GREATEST INVENTION SINCE THE PAPERBACK BOOK . . . BUT CHEAPER."

Have paperbacks killed the market for short stories? Is television to blame, or the movies? It seems unlikely: paperback publishers do produce occasional collections of short stories, but they never sell well. Television has had its "anthology series" and movies have been made built around groups of short tales, but they've never made much impact either.

I have a theory that short stories don't thrive today because people don't like to think.

It's been said that a good short story is essentially the pivotal chapter of a novel, embodying all the elements that could go into a longer story but inviting readers to extrapolate the background and aftermath for themselves. But evidently people prefer to have their thinking done for them by the authors: they'd rather spend an extra hour or two reading someone else's thoughts, in a novel, than thinking for themselves. They want writers to *tell* them what Maria said to her lover when she found out he was her uncle, and whether or not he knew it himself. Who wants to speculate?—we live in a world that worships data.

Well, maybe that's why the science-fiction short story isn't dying: because sf is a genre based on speculation. In science fiction we start by making certain assumptions about changes in the world, and after that, the fun is in seeing what may develop from those changes. If a writer chooses to spell out everything for us at novel length, that's fine; if he or she feels it's more effective for us to figure out the story's implications ourselves, that's fine too.

A lot of people have said that science fiction is a literature of ideas. By and large that's true—it's certainly more true of sf than of any other fiction genre. So inevitably, science fiction attracts readers who enjoy thinking. That explains the otherwise puzzling phenomenon of science-fiction fandom, thousands of people who gather at conventions or publish amateur magazines to discuss science-fiction stories.

I have another theory: I suspect most science-fiction readers begin by reading novels, and only later do they graduate to novelettes and short stories. The shorter form is more demanding.

This is why most of the popular science-fiction novels are simply adventure stories set in the future, with no more idea-content than the average short story has. It's also why so many science-fiction writers stop writing short stories when they realize—as writer after writer has mentioned doing—that the creative work of plotting a short story is virtually equivalent to that which goes into a novel. If a writer takes a short-story idea and throws in a few adventures that grow from it, he or she has the plot for a novel . . . and the larger payment that goes with it.

There are novels that contradict this thesis, books like Le Guin's *The Left Hand of Darkness* and Blish's *A Case of Conscience* which will keep you thinking throughout. These are exceptional; they're our classics. There are also short stories in which the ratio of idea-to-plot is very small—these are *not* classics.

I think you'll find, as you read *The Best Science Fiction of the Year*, that there are more new ideas per page than you're likely to find in any novel of similar length. The book is, in fact, a treasury of new thoughts, a cornucopia of speculation. Every story invites your participation as an intelligent human being, and will reward it.

How many other forms of entertainment even try to involve so much of you? And isn't that why you're here?

—Terry Carr
January 1977

I See You

Damon Knight

World science-fiction conventions these days consist of two or three thousand people—writers, readers, editors, artists—milling around in the halls and meeting rooms of hotels, peering at name-tags in hopes of finding a celebrity who isn't already surrounded by admirers. The conventions are field days for autograph seekers and great ego trips for the famous people.

Damon Knight is different. At the convention last year in Kansas City, he wore a name-tag that said simply: NOBODY IMPORTANT.

Damon's always had a healthy irreverence for fame and glory, his own or anyone else's. In the days when he used to review science-fiction books regularly, a lot of distinguished authors discovered that they couldn't rest on past laurels when he read their books—it was Damon who almost singlehandedly invented the discipline of science-fiction criticism. (He won a Hugo Award for it in 1956.)

I've seen Damon Knight, the founder and first President of the Science Fiction Writers of America, throwing spitballs at Isaac Asimov and Gordon R. Dickson during a Nebula Awards banquet. He once tried to run over Robert Silverberg with his car. (Playfully, of course. Silverberg and others later deposited a telephone pole in the back seat of that car.)

In certain science fiction circles Damon is famed as the inventor of cow, pig, and chicken jokes. Example: What do you call a calf who doesn't know who his mother is? Answer: Udderly confused. (Actually, this joke was made up by Jerry Dorman, Sonya's husband, but never mind—Damon started it.)

Come to think of it, Damon once wrote a short story called *The Big Pat Boom,* about aliens who come to Earth seeking our most precious commodity, cow pats. A fan group awarded him a bronzed cow pat for that story, and Damon displays it proudly with his other awards.

None of this information is meant to suggest that Damon Knight is anything but serious when it comes to writing. Anyone who has attended the Milford Science Fiction Writers' Conferences, which he hosts, or the Clarion SF Writers' Workshops, where he teaches, can tell you that Damon's criticisms of their stories are always thoughtful and concise. His insistence on careful craftsmanship is also well known to contributors to *Orbit,* his original-stories anthology series.

For that matter, if you've read any of Knight's own fiction you'll already know this: novels like *A for Anything* and *Hell's Pavement,* short stories like "To Serve Man," "Not With a Bang," and "Masks" have long since proven that he's a very important writer indeed.

Alas, Damon Knight has written few stories in recent years. His return to fiction writing in 1976 was a welcome event—especially since,

in "I See You," he's at the top of his form, tossing off ideas enough for a full-length novel in a fascinating examination of the effects on humanity of a remarkable invention.

You are five, hiding in a place only you know. You are covered with bark dust, scratched by twigs, sweaty and hot. A wind sighs in the aspen leaves. A faint steady hiss comes from the viewer you hold in your hands; then a voice: "Lorie, I see you—under the barn, eating an apple!" A silence. "Lorie, come on out, I see you." Another voice. "That's right, she's in there." After a moment, sulkily: "Oh, okay."

You squirm around, raising the viewer to aim it down the hill. As you turn the knob with your thumb, the bright image races toward you, trees hurling themselves into red darkness and vanishing, then the houses in the compound, and now you see Bruce standing beside the corral, looking into his viewer, slowly turning. His back is to you; you know you are safe, and you sit up. A jay passes with a whir of wings, settles on a branch. With your own eyes now you can see Bruce, only a dot of blue beyond the gray shake walls of the houses. In the viewer, he is turning toward you, and you duck again. Another voice: "Children, come in and get washed for dinner now." "Aw, Aunt Ellie!" "Mom, we're playing hide and seek. Can't we just stay fifteen minutes more?" "Please, Aunt Ellie!" "No, come on in now—you'll have plenty of time after dinner." And Bruce: "Aw, okay. All out's in free." And once more they have not found you; your secret place is yours alone.

Call him Smith. He was the president of a company that bore his name and which held more than a hundred patents in the scientific instrument field. He was sixty, a widower. His only daughter and her husband had been killed in a plane crash in 1978. He had a partner who handled the business operations now; Smith spent most of his time in his own lab. In the spring of 1990 he was working on an image intensification device that was puzzling because it was too good. He had it on his bench now, aimed at a deep shadow box across the room; at the back of the box was a card ruled with black, green, red and blue lines. The only source of illumination was a single ten-watt bulb hung behind the shadow box; the light reflected from the card did not even register on his meter, and yet the image in the screen of his device was sharp and bright. When he varied the inputs to the components in a certain way, the bright image vanished and was replaced by shadows, like the ghost of another image. He had monitored every television channel, had shielded the device against radio frequencies, and the ghosts remained. Increasing the illumination did not make them clearer. They were vaguely rectilinear shapes without any coherent pattern. Occasionally a moving blur traveled slowly across them.

Smith made a disgusted sound. He opened the clamps that held the device and picked it up, reaching for the power switch with his other hand. He never touched it. As he moved the device, the ghost images had shifted; they were dancing now with the faint movements of his hand. Smith stared at them without breathing for a moment. Holding the cord, he turned slowly. The ghost images whirled, vanished, reappeared. He turned the other way; they whirled back.

Smith set the device down on the bench with care. His hands were shaking. He had had the thing clamped down on the bench all the time until now. "Christ almighty, how dumb can one man get?" he asked the empty room.

You are six, almost seven, and you are being allowed to use the big viewer for the first time. You are perched on a cushion in the leather chair at the console; your brother, who has been showing you the controls with a bored and superior air, has just left the room, saying, "All right, if you know so much, do it yourself."

In fact, the controls on this machine are unfamiliar; the little viewers you have used all your life have only one knob, for nearer or farther—to move up/down, or left/right, you just point the viewer where you want to see. This machine has dials and little windows with numbers in them, and switches and pushbuttons, most of which you don't understand, but you know they are for special purposes and don't matter. The main control is a metal rod, right in front of you, with a gray plastic knob on the top. The knob is dull from years of handling; it feels warm and a little greasy in your hand. The console has a funny electric smell, but the big screen, taller than you are, is silent and dark. You can feel your heart beating against your breastbone. You grip the knob harder, push it forward just a little. The screen lights, and you are drifting across the next room as if on huge silent wheels, chairs and end tables turning into reddish silhouettes that shrink, twist and disappear as you pass through them, and for a moment you feel dizzy because when you notice the red numbers jumping in the console to your left, it is as if the whole house were passing massively and vertiginously through itself; then you are floating out the window with the same slow and steady motion, on across the sunlit pasture where two saddle horses stand with their heads up, sniffing the wind; then a stubbled field, dropping away; and now, below you, the co-op road shines like a silver-gray stream. You press the knob down to get closer, and drop with a giddy swoop; now you are rushing along the road, overtaking and passing a yellow truck, turning the knob to steer. At first you blunder into the dark trees on either side, and once the earth surges up over you in a chaos of writhing red shapes, but now you are learning, and you soar down past the crossroads, up the farther hill, and now, now you are on the big road, flying eastward, passing all the cars, rushing toward the great world where you long to be.

It took Smith six weeks to increase the efficiency of the image intensifier enough to bring up the ghost pictures clearly. When he succeeded, the image on the screen was instantly recognizable. It was a view of Jack McCranie's office; the picture was still dim, but sharp enough that Smith could see the expression on Jack's face. He was leaning back in his chair, hands behind his head. Beside him stood Peg Spatola in a purple dress, with her hand on an open folder. She was talking, and McCranie was listening. That was wrong, because Peg was not supposed to be back from Cleveland until next week.

Smith reached for the phone and punched McCranie's number.

"Yes, Tom?"

"Jack, is Peg in there?"

"Why, no—she's in Cleveland, Tom."

"Oh, yes."

McCranie sounded puzzled. "Is anything the matter?" In the screen, he had swiveled his chair and was talking to Peg, gesturing with short, choppy motions of his arm.

"No, nothing," said Smith. "That's all right, Jack, thank you." He broke the connection. After a moment he turned to the breadboard controls of the device and changed one setting slightly. In the screen, Peg turned and walked backward out of the office. When he turned the knob the other way, she repeated these actions in reverse. Smith tinkered with the other controls until he got a view of the calendar on Jack's desk. It was Friday, June 15th—last week.

Smith locked up the device and all his notes, went home and spent the rest of the day thinking.

By the end of July he had refined and miniaturized the device and had extended its sensitivity range into the infrared. He spent most of August, when he should have been on vacation, trying various methods of detecting sound through the device. By focusing on the interior of a speaker's larynx and using infrared, he was able to convert the visible vibrations of the vocal cords into sound of fair quality, but that did not satisfy him. He worked for a while on vibrations picked up from panes of glass in windows and on framed pictures, and he experimented briefly with the diaphragms in speaker systems, intercoms and telephones. He kept on into October without stopping and finally achieved a system that would give tinny but recognizable sound from any vibrating surface—a wall, a floor, even the speaker's own cheek or forehead.

He redesigned the whole device, built a prototype and tested it, tore it down, redesigned, built another. It was Christmas before he was done. Once more he locked up the device and all his plans, drawings and notes.

At home he spent the holidays experimenting with commercial adhesives in various strengths. He applied these to coated paper, let them dry, and cut the paper into rectangles. He numbered these rectangles, pasted them onto letter envelopes, some of which he stacked loose; others he bundled together and secured with rubber bands. He opened the stacks and bundles and examined them at regular intervals. Some of the labels curled up and detached themselves after twenty-six hours without leaving any conspicuous trace. He made up another batch of these, typed his home address on six of them. On each of six envelopes he typed his office address, then covered it with one of the labels. He stamped the envelopes and dropped them into a mailbox. All six, minus their labels, were delivered to the office three days later.

Just after New Year's, he told his partner that he wanted to sell out and retire. They discussed it in general terms.

Using an assumed name and a post office box number which was not his, Smith wrote to a commission agent in Boston with whom he had never had any previous dealings. He mailed the letter, with the agent's address covered by one of his labels on which he had typed a fictitious address. The label detached itself in transit; the letter was delivered. When the agent replied, Smith was watching and read the letter as a secretary typed it. The agent followed his instruction to mail his reply in an envelope without return address. The owner of the post office box turned it in marked "not here"; it went to the dead-letter office and was returned in due time, but meanwhile Smith had acknowledged the letter and had mailed, in the same way, a large amount of cash. In subsequent letters he instructed the agent to take bids for components, plans for which he enclosed, from electronics manufacturers, for plastic casings from another, and for assembly and shipping from still another company. Through a second commission agent in New York, to whom he wrote in the same way, he contracted for ten thousand copies of an instruction booklet in four colors.

Late in February he bought a house and an electronics dealership in a small town in the Adirondacks. In March he signed over his interest in the company to his partner, cleaned out his lab and left. He sold his co-op apartment in Manhattan and his summer house in Connecticut, moved to his new home and became anonymous.

You are thirteen, chasing a fox with the big kids for the first time. They have put you in the north field, the worst place, but you know better than to leave it.

"He's in the glen."

"I see him, he's in the brook, going upstream."

You turn the viewer, racing forward through dappled shade, a brilliance of leaves: there is the glen, and now you see the fox, trotting through the shallows, blossoms of bright water at its feet.

"Ken and Nell, you come down ahead of him by the springhouse. Wanda, you and Tim and Jean stay where you are. Everybody else come upstream, but stay back till I tell you."

That's Leigh, the oldest. You turn the viewer, catch a glimpse of Bobby running downhill through the woods, his long hair flying. Then back to the glen: the fox is gone.

"He's heading up past the corncrib!"

"Okay, keep spread out on both sides everybody. Jim, can you and Edie head him off before he gets to the woods?"

"We'll try. There he is!"

And the chase is going away from you, as you knew it would, but soon you will be older, as old as Nell and Jim; then you will be in the middle of things, and your life will begin.

By trial and error, Smith has found the settings for Dallas, November 22, 1963: Dealey Plaza, 12:25 p.m. He sees the Presidential motorcade making the turn onto Elm Street. Kennedy slumps forward, raising his hands to his throat. Smith presses a button to hold the moment in time. He scans behind the motorcade, finds the sixth floor of the Book Depository Building, finds the window. There is no one behind the barricade of cartons; the room is empty. He scans the nearby rooms, finds nothing. He tries the floor below. At an open window a man kneels, holding a high-powered rifle. Smith photographs him. He returns to the motorcade, watches as the second shot strikes the President. He freezes time again, scans the surrounding buildings, finds a second marksman on a roof, photographs him. Back to the motorcade. A third and fourth shot, the last blowing off the side of the President's head. Smith freezes the action again, finds two gunmen on the grassy knoll, one aiming across the top of a station wagon, one kneeling in the shrubbery. He photographs them. He turns off the power, sits for a moment, then goes to the washroom, kneels beside the toilet and vomits.

The viewer is your babysitter, your television, your telephone (the telephone lines are still up, but they are used only as signaling devices; when you know that somebody wants to talk to you, you focus your viewer on him), your library, your school. Before puberty you watch other people having sex, but even then your curiosity is easily satisfied; after an older cousin initiates you at fourteen, you are much more interested in doing it yourself. The co-op teacher monitors your studies, sometimes makes suggestions, but more and more, as you grow older, leaves you to your own devices. You are intensely interested in African prehistory, in the European theater, and in the ant-civilization of Epsilon Eridani IV. Soon you will have to choose.

New York Harbor, November 4, 1872—a cold, blustery day. A two-masted ship rides at anchor; on her stern is lettered: MARY CELESTE. Smith advances the time control. A flicker of darkness, light again, and the ship is gone. He turns back again until he finds it standing out under light canvas past Sandy Hook. Manipulating time and space controls at once, he follows it eastward through a flickering of storm and sun—loses it, finds it again, counting days as he goes. The farther eastward, the more he has to tilt the device downward, while the image of the ship tilts correspondingly away from him. Because of the angle, he can no longer keep the ship in view from a distance but must track it closely. November 21 and 22, violent storms: the ship is dashed upward by waves, falls again, visible only intermittently; it takes him five hours to pass through two days of real time. The 23rd is calmer, but on the 24th another storm blows up. Smith rubs his eyes, loses the ship, finds it again after a ten-minute search.

The gale blows itself out on the morning of the 26th. The sun is bright, the sea almost dead calm. Smith is able to catch glimpses of figures on deck, tilted above dark cross-sections of the hull. A sailor is splicing a rope in the stern, two others lowering a triangular sail between the foremast and the bowsprit, and a fourth is at the helm. A little group stands leaning on the starboard rail; one of them is a woman. The next glimpse is that of a running figure who advances into the screen and disappears. Now the men are lowering a boat over the side; the rail has been removed and lies on the deck. The men drop into the boat and row away. He hears them shouting to each other but cannot make out the words.

Smith turns to the ship again: the deck is empty. He dips below to look at the hold, filled with casks, then the cabin, then the forecastle. There is no sign of anything wrong—no explosion, no fire, no trace of violence. When he looks up again, he sees the sails flapping, then bellying out full. The sea is rising. He looks for the boat, but now too much time has passed and he cannot find it. He returns to the ship and now reverses the time control, tracks it backward until the men are again in their places on deck. He looks again at the group standing at the rail; now he sees that the woman has a child in her arms. The child struggles, drops over the rail. Smith hears the woman shriek. In a moment she too is over the rail and falling into the sea.

He watches the men running, sees them launch the boat. As they pull away, he is able to keep the focus near enough to see and hear them. One calls, "My God, who's at the helm?" Another, a bearded man with a face gone tallow-pale, replies, "Never mind—row!" They are staring down into the sea. After a moment one looks up, then another. The *Mary Celeste,* with three of the four sails on her foremast set, is gliding away, slowly, now faster; now she is gone.

Smith does not run through the scene again to watch the child and her mother drown, but others do.

The production model was ready for shipping in September. It was a simplified version of the prototype, with only two controls, one for space, one for time. The range of the device was limited to one thousand miles. Nowhere on the casing of the device or in the instruction booklet was a patent number or a pending patent mentioned. Smith had called the device Ozo, perhaps because he thought it sounded vaguely Japanese. The booklet described the device as a distant viewer and gave clear, simple instructions for its use. One sentence read cryptically: "Keep Time Control set at zero." It was like "Wet Paint—Do Not Touch."

During the week of September 23, seven thousand Ozos were shipped to domestic and Canadian addresses supplied by Smith: five hundred to electronics manufacturers and suppliers, six thousand, thirty to a carton, marked "On Consignment," to TV outlets in major cities, and the rest to private citizens chosen at random. The instruction booklets were in sealed envelopes packed with each device. Three thousand more went to Europe, South and Central America, and the Middle East.

A few of the outlets which received the cartons opened them the same day, tried the devices out, and put them on sale at prices ranging from $49.95 to $125. By the following day the word was beginning to spread, and by the close of business on the third day every store was sold out. Most people who got them, either through the mail or by purchase, used them to spy on their neighbors and on people in hotels.

In a house in Cleveland, a man watches his brother-in-law in the next room, who is watching his wife getting out of a taxi. She goes into the lobby of an apartment building. The husband watches as she gets into the elevator, rides to the fourth floor. She rings the bell beside the door marked 410. The door opens; a dark-haired man takes her in his arms; they kiss.

The brother-in-law meets him in the hall. "Don't do it, Charlie."

"Get cut of my way."

"I'm not going to get out of your way, and I tell you, don't do it. Not now and not later."

"Why the hell shouldn't I?"

"Because if you do I'll kill you. If you want a divorce, OK, get a divorce. But don't lay a hand on her or I'll find you the farthest place you can go."

Smith got his consignment of Ozos early in the week, took one home and left it to his store manager to put a price on the rest. He did not bother to use the production model but began at once to build another prototype. It had controls calibrated to one-hundredth of a second and one millimeter, and a timer that would allow him to stop a scene, or advance or regress it at any desired rate. He ordered some clockwork from an astronomical supply house.

A high-ranking officer in Army Intelligence, watching the first demonstration of the Ozo in the Pentagon, exclaimed, "My God, with this we could dismantle half the establishment—all we've got to do is launch interceptors when we see them push the button."

"It's a good thing Senator Burkhart can't hear you say that," said another officer. But by the next afternoon everybody had heard it.

A Baptist minister in Louisville led the first mob against an Ozo assembly plant. A month later, while civil and criminal suits against all the rioters were still pending, tapes showing each one of them in compromising or ludicrous activities were widely distributed in the area.

The commission agents who had handled the orders for the first Ozos were found out and had to leave town. Factories were firebombed, but others took their place.

The first Ozo was smuggled into the Soviet Union from West Germany by Katerina Belov, a member of a dissident group in Moscow, who used it to document illegal government actions. The device was seized on December 13 by the KGB; Belov and two other members of the group were arrested, imprisoned and tortured. By that time over forty other Ozos were in the hands of dissidents.

You are watching an old movie, *Bob and Ted and Carol and Alice*. The humor seems infantile and unimaginative to you; you are not interested in the actresses' occasional seminudity. What strikes you as hilarious is the coyness, the sidelong glances, smiles, grimaces hinting at things that will never be shown on the screen. You realize that these people have never seen anyone but their most intimate friends without clothing, have never seen any adult shit or piss, and would be embarrassed or disgusted if they did. Why did children say "pee-pee" and "poo-poo," and then giggle? You have read scholarly books about taboos on "bodily functions," but why was shitting worse than sneezing?

Cora Zickwolfe, who lived in a remote rural area of Arizona and whose husband commuted to Tucson, arranged with her nearest neighbor, Phyllis Mell, for each of them to keep an Ozo focused on the bulletin board in the other's kitchen. On the bulletin board was a note that said "OK." If there was any trouble and she couldn't get to the phone, she would take down the note, or if she had time, write another.

In April, 1992, about the time her husband usually got home, an intruder broke into the house and seized Mrs. Zickwolfe before she had time to get to the bulletin board. He dragged her into the bedroom and forced her to disrobe. The state troopers got there in fifteen minutes, and Cora never spoke to her friend Phyllis again.

Between 1992 and 2002 more than six hundred improvements and supplements to the Ozo were recorded.

The most important of these was the power system created by focusing the Ozo at a narrow aperture on the interior of the Sun. Others included the system of satellite slave units in stationary orbits and a computerized tracer device which would keep the Ozo focused on any subject.

Using the tracer, an entomologist in Mexico City is following the ancestral line of a honey bee. The images bloom and expire, ten every second: the tracer is following each queen back to the egg, then the egg to the queen that laid it, then that queen to the egg. Tens of thousands of generations have passed; in two thousand hours, beginning with a Paleocene bee, he has traveled back into the Cretaceous. He stops at intervals to follow the bee in real time, then accelerates again. The hive is growing smaller, more primitive. Now it is only a cluster of round cells, and the bee is different, more like a wasp. His year's labor is coming to fruition. He watches, forgetting to eat, almost to breathe.

In your mother's study after she dies you find an elaborate chart of her ancestors and your father's. You retrieve the program for it, punch it in, and idly watch a random sampling, back into time, first the female line, then the male . . . a teacher of biology in Boston, a suffragette, a corn merchant, a singer, a Dutch farmer in New York, a British sailor, a German musician. Their faces glow in the screen, bright-eyed, cheeks flushed with life. Someday you too will be only a series of images in a screen.

Smith is watching the planet Mars. The clockwork which turns the Ozo to follow the planet, even when it is below the horizon, makes it possible for him to focus instantly on the surface, but he never does this. He takes up his position hundreds of thousands of miles away, then slowly approaches, in order to see the red spark grow to a disk, then to a yellow sunlit ball hanging in darkness. Now he can make out the surface features: Syrtis Major and Thoth-Nepenthes leading in a long gooseneck to Utopia and the frostcap.

The image as it swells hypnotically toward him is clear and sharp, without tremor or atmospheric distortion. It is summer in the northern hemisphere: Utopia is wide and dark. The planet fills the screen, and now he turns northward, over the cratered desert still hundreds of miles distant. A dust storm, like a yellow veil, obscures the curved neck of Thoth-Nepenthes; then he is beyond it, drifting down to the edge of the frostcap. The limb of the planet reappears; he floats like a glider over the dark surface tinted with rose and violet-gray; now he can see its nubbly texture; now he can make out individual plants. He is drifting among their gnarled gray stems, their leaves of violet horn; he sees the curious misshapen growths that may be air bladders or some grotesque analogue of blossoms. Now, at the edge of the screen, something black and spindling leaps. He follows it instantly, finds it, brings it hugely magnified into the center of the screen: a thing like a hairy beetle, its body covered with thick black hairs or spines; it stands on six jointed legs, waving its antennae, its mouth parts busy. And its four bright eyes stare into his, across forty million miles.

Smith's hair got whiter and thinner. Before the 1992 Crash, he made heavy contributions to the International Red Cross and to volunteer organizations in Europe, Asia and Africa. He got drunk periodically, but always alone. From 1993 to 1996 he stopped reading the newspapers.

He wrote down the coordinates for the plane crash in which his daughter and her husband had died, but never used them.

At intervals while dressing or looking into the bathroom mirror, he stared as if into an invisible camera and raised one finger. In his last years he wrote some poems.

We know his name. Patient researchers, using advanced scanning techniques, followed his letters back through the postal system and found him, but by that time he was safely dead.

The whole world has been at peace for more than a generation. Crime is almost unheard of. Free energy has made the world rich, but the population is stable, even though early detection has wiped out most diseases. Everyone can do whatever he likes, providing his neighbors would not disapprove, and after all, their views are the same as his own.

You are forty, a respected scholar, taking a few days out to review your life, as many people do at your age. You have watched your mother and father coupling on the night they conceived you, watched yourself growing in her womb, first a red tadpole, then a thing like an embryo chicken, then a big-headed baby kicking and squirming. You have seen yourself delivered, seen the first moment when your bloody head broke into the light. You have seen yourself staggering about the nursery in rompers, clutching a yellow plastic duck. Now you are watching yourself hiding behind the fallen tree on the hill, and you realize that there are no secret places. And beyond you in the ghostly future you know that someone is watching you as you watch; and beyond that watcher another, and beyond that another . . . Forever.

The Phantom of Kansas

John Varley

John Varley, who's known as "Herb" to his friends (it's his middle name), says, "I've read sf since I could read at all, and fooled around with writing it in high school. In Texas. I got one rejection slip from H. L. Gold, and gave it up for seven years. Then I decided to see if I could write . . ."

He quickly discovered that he could: in the past three years he sold every story he wrote. Two of those stories, "Retrograde Summer" and "In the Bowl," appeared in last year's volume of this series and generated more applause than anything else in the book. Prediction: John Varley will be in *all* the best-of-the-year books this year.

He came to the Bay Area recently, and phoned to take me up on an invitation to visit. We arranged a meeting place and I asked, "How shall I recognize you?" He said, "Well, I'm six-foot-five and I'll be wearing . . ." "Never mind," I said; "I'll find you."

(I'm fairly tall myself. Years ago a friend, David Rike, wrote: "If Terry Carr were standing in the midst of a group of seven-foot Prussian soldiers, you would be unable to pick him out. This is because Terry is only six-foot-three and you wouldn't be able to see him.")

Fortunately, our local BART station wasn't overrun with towering Prussian soldiers that evening, so I got to meet John Herbert Varley and spend an evening in his company. He's a genial man of twenty-nine with a quiet intelligence that's as imposing as his physical stature—his eyes miss *nothing*. His sense of humor is less flamboyant than, say, Damon Knight's (Varley and Knight both live in Eugene, Oregon, a fact which has nothing to do with their stories being situated next to each other here), but every now and then he'll say something quietly that will hit you between the eyes ten seconds later.

It isn't hard to see the connections between Varley and his stories: they're told calmly, matter-of-factly, and you can get halfway through one before you realize just how many wonders he's described for you. "The Phantom of Kansas" shows him at his ingenious best, in a tale of a woman who wakes in a cloned body to discover she's been murdered—for the third time.

I do my banking at the Archimedes Trust Association. Their security is first-rate, their service is courteous, and they have their own medico facility that does nothing but take recordings for their vaults.

And they had been robbed two weeks ago.

It was a break for me. I had been approaching my regular recording date and dreading the chunk it would take from my savings. Then these thieves break into my bank, steal a huge amount of negotiable paper, and in an excess of enthusiasm they destroy all the recording cubes. Every last one of them, crunched into tiny shards of plastic. Of course the bank had to replace them all, and very fast, too. They weren't stupid; it wasn't the first time someone had used such a bank robbery to facilitate a murder. So the bank had to record everyone who had an account, and do it in a few days. It must have cost them more than the robbery.

How that scheme works, incidentally, is like this. The robber couldn't care less about the money stolen. Mostly it's very risky to pass such loot, anyway. The programs written into the money computers these days are enough to foil all but the most exceptional robber. You have to let that kind of money lie for on the order of a century to have any hope of realizing gains on it. Not impossible, of course, but the police types have found out that few criminals are temperamentally able to wait that long. The robber's real motive in a case where memory cubes have been destroyed is murder, not robbery.

Every so often someone comes along who must commit a crime of passion. There are very few left open, and murder is the most awkward of all. It just doesn't satisfy this type to kill someone and see them walking around six months later. When the victim sues the killer for alienation of personality—and collects up to 99% of the killer's worldly goods—it's just twisting the knife. So if you really hate someone, the temptation is great to *really* kill them, forever and ever, just like in the old days, by destroying their memory cube first then killing the body.

That's what the ATA feared, and I had rated a private bodyguard over the last week as part of my contract. It was sort of a status symbol to show your friends, but otherwise I hadn't been much impressed until I realized that ATA was going to pay for my next recording as part of their crash program to cover all their policy holders. They had contracted to keep me alive forever, so even though I had been scheduled for a recording in only three weeks they had to pay for this one. The courts had rules that a lost or damaged cube must be replaced with all possible speed.

So I should have been very happy. I wasn't, but tried to be brave.

I was shown into the recording room with no delay and told to strip and lie on the table. The medico, a man who looked like someone I might have met several decades ago, busied himself with his equipment as I tried to control my breathing. I was grateful when he plugged the computer lead into my occipital socket and turned off my motor control. Now I didn't have to worry about whether to ask if I knew him or not. As I grow older, I find that's more of a problem. I must have met twenty thousand people by now and talked to them long enough to make an impression. It gets confusing.

He removed the top of my head and prepared to take a multiholo picture of me, a chemical analog of everything I ever saw or thought or remembered or just vaguely dreamed. It was a blessed relief when I slid over into unconsciousness.

The coolness and sheen of stainless steel beneath my fingertips. There is the smell of isopropyl alcohol, and the hint of acetone.

The medico's shop. Childhood memories tumble over me, triggered by the smells. Excitement, change, my mother standing by while the medico carves away my broken finger to replace it with a pink new one. I lie in the darkness and remember.

And there is light, a hurting light from nowhere and I feel my pupil contract as the only movement in my entire body.

"She's in," I hear. But I'm not, not really. I'm just lying here in the blessed dark, unable to move.

It comes in a rush, the repossession of my body. I travel down the endless nerves to bang up hard against the insides of my hands and feet, to whirl through the pools of my nipples and tingle in my lips and nose, *Now* I'm in.

I sat up quickly into the restraining arms of the medico. I struggled for a second before I was able to relax. My fingers were buzzing and cramped with the clamminess of hyperventilation.

"Whew," I said, putting my head in my hands. "Bad dream. I thought. . ."

I looked around me and saw that I was naked on the steel-topped table with several worried faces looking at me from all sides. I wanted to retreat into the darkness again and let my insides settle down. I saw my mother's face, blinked, and failed to make it disappear.

"Carnival?" I asked her ghost.

"Right here, Fox," she said, and took me in her arms. It was awkward and unsatisfying with her standing on the floor and me on the table. There were wires trailing from my body. But the comfort was needed. I didn't know where I was. With a chemical rush as precipitous as the one just before I awoke, the people solidified around me.

"She's all right now," the medico said, turning from his instruments. He smiled impersonally at me as he began removing the wires from my head. I did not smile back. I knew where I was now, just as surely as I had ever known anything. I remembered coming in here only hours before.

But I knew it had been more than a few hours. I've read about it: the disorientation when a new body is awakened with transplanted memories. And my mother wouldn't be here unless something had gone badly wrong.

I had died.

I was given a mild sedative, help in dressing, and my mother's arm to lead me down plush-carpeted hallways to the office of the bank president. I was still not fully awake. The halls were achingly quiet but for the brush of our feet across the wine-colored rug. I felt like the pressure was fluctuating wildly, leaving my ears popped and muffled. I couldn't see too far away. I was grateful to leave the vanishing points in the hall for the panelled browns of wood veneer and the coolness and echoes of a white marble floor.

The bank president, Mr. Leander, showed us to our seats. I sank into the purple velvet and let it wrap around me. Leander pulled up a chair facing us and offered us drinks. I declined. My head was swimming already and I knew I'd have to pay attention.

Leander fiddled with a dossier on his desk. Mine, I imagine. It had been freshly printed out from the terminal at his right hand. I'd met him briefly before; he was a pleasant sort of person, chosen for this public-relations job for his willingness to wear the sort of old-man body that inspires confidence and trust. He seemed to be about sixty-five. He was probably more like twenty.

It seemed that he was never going to get around to the briefing so I asked a question. One that was very important to me at the moment.

"What's the date?"

"It's the month of November," he said, ponderously. "And the year is 342."

I had been dead for two and a half years.

"Listen," I said, "I don't want to take up any more of your time. You must have a brochure you can give me to bring me up to date. If you'll just hand it over, I'll be on my way. Oh, and thank you for your concern."

He waved his hand at me as I started to rise.

"I would appreciate it if you stayed a bit longer. Yours is an unusual case, Ms. Fox. I . . . well, it's never happened in the history of the Archimedes Trust Association."

"Yes?"

"You see, you've died, as you figured out soon after we woke you. What you couldn't have known is that you've died more than once since your last recording."

"More than once?" So it wasn't such a smart question; so what was I supposed to ask?

"Three times."

"Three?"

"Yes, three separate times. We suspect murder."

The room was perfectly silent for a while. At last I decided I should have that drink. He poured it for me, and I drained it.

"Perhaps your mother should tell you more about it," Leander suggested. "She's been closer to the situation. I was only made aware of it recently. Carnival?"

I found my way back to my apartment in a sort of daze. By the time I had settled in again the drug was wearing off and I could face my situation with a clear head. But my skin was crawling.

Listening in the third person to things you've done is not the most pleasant thing. I decided it was time to face some facts that all of us, including myself, do not like to think about. The first order of business was to recognise that the things that were done by those three previous people were not done by *me*. I was a new person, fourth in the line of succession. I had many things in common with the previous incarnations, including all my memories up to that day I surrendered myself to the memory recording machine. But the *me* of that time and place had been killed.

She lasted longer than the others. Almost a year, Carnival had said. Then her body was found at the bottom of Hadley Rille. It was an appropriate place for her to die; both she and myself liked to go hiking out on the surface for purposes of inspiration.

Murder was not suspected that time. The bank, upon hearing of my—no, *her*—death, started a clone from the tissue sample I had left with my recording. Six lunations later, a copy of me was infused with my memories and told that she had just died. She had been shaken, but seemed to be adjusting well when she, too, was killed.

This time there was much suspicion. Not only had she survived for less than a lunation after her reincarnation, but the circumstances were unusual. She had been blown to pieces in a tube-train explosion. She had been the only passenger in a two-seat capsule. The explosion had been caused by a home-made bomb.

There was still the possibility that it was a random act, possibly by political terrorists. The third copy of me had not thought so. I don't know why. That is the most maddening thing about memory recording: being unable to profit by the experiences of your former selves. Each time I was killed, it moved me back to square one, the day I was recorded.

But Fox 3 had reason to be paranoid. She took extraordinary precautions to stay alive. More specifically, she tried to prevent circumstances that could lead to her murder. It worked for five lunations. She died as the result of a fight, that much was certain. It was a very violent fight, with blood all over the apartment. The police at first thought she must have fatally injured her attacker, but analysis showed all the blood to have come from her body.

So where did that leave me, Fox 4? An hour's careful thought left the picture gloomy indeed. Consider: each time my killer succeeded in murdering me, he or she learned more about me. My killer must be an expert on Foxes by now, knowing things about me that I myself did not know. Such as how I handle myself in a fight. I gritted my teeth when I thought of that. Carnival told me that Fox 3, the canniest of the lot, had taken lessons in self-defense. Karate, I think she said. Did I have the benefit of it? Of course not. If I wanted to defend myself I had to start all over, because those skills died with Fox 3.

No, all the advantages were with my killer. The killer starts off with the advantage of surprise—since I had no notion of who it was—and in this case learned more about me every time he or she succeeded in killing me.

What to do? I didn't even know where to start. I ran through everyone I knew, looking for an enemy, someone who hated me enough to kill me again and again. I could find no one. Most likely it was someone Fox 1 had met during that year she lived after the recording.

The only answer I could come up with was emigration. Just pull up stakes and go to Mercury, or Mars, or even Pluto. But would that guarantee my safety? My killer seemed to be an uncommonly persistent person. No, I'd have to face it here, where at least I knew the turf.

It was the next day before I realized the extent of my loss. I had been robbed of an entire symphony.

For the last thirty years I had been an Environmentalist. I had just drifted into it while it was still an infant art-form. I had been in charge of the weather machines at the Transvaal disneyland, which was new at the time and the biggest and most modern of all the environmental parks in Luna. A few of us had started tinkering with the weather programs, first for our own amusement. Later we invited friends to watch the storms and sunsets we concocted. Before we knew it, friends were inviting friends and the Transvaal people began selling tickets.

I gradually made a name for myself, and found I could make more money being an artist than being an engineer. At the time of my last recording I had been one of the top three Environmentalists on Luna.

Then Fox 1 went on to compose *Liquid Ice*. From what I read in the reviews, two years after the fact, it was seen as the high point of the art to date. It had been staged in the Pennsylvania disneyland, before a crowd of three hundred thousand. It made me rich.

The money was still in my bank account, but the memory of creating it was forever lost. And it mattered.

Fox 1 had written it, from beginning to end. Oh, I recalled having had some vague ideas of a winter composition, things I'd think about later and put together. But the whole creative process had gone on in the head of that other person who had been killed.

How is a person supposed to cope with that? For one bitter moment I considered calling the bank and having them destroy my memory cube. If I died this time, I'd rather die completely. The thought of a Fox 5 rising from that table . . . it was almost too much to bear. She would lack everything that Fox 1, 2, 3, and me, Fox 4, had experienced. So far I'd had little time to add to the personality we all shared, but even the bad times are worth saving.

It was either that, or have a new recording made every day. I called the bank, did some figuring, and found that I wasn't wealthy enough to afford that. But it was worth exploring. If I had a new recording taken once a week I could keep at it for about a year before I ran out of money.

I decided I'd do it, for as long as I could. And to make sure that no future Fox would ever have to go through this again, I'd have one made today. Fox 5, if she was ever born, would be born knowing at least as much as I knew now.

I felt better after the recording was made. I found that I no longer feared the medico's office. That fear comes from the common misapprehension that one will wake up from the recording to discover that one has died. It's a silly thing to believe, but it comes from the distaste we all have for really looking at the facts.

If you'll consider human consciousness, you'll see that the three-dimensional cross-section of a human being that is *you* can only rise from that table and go about your business. It can happen no other way. Human consciousness is linear, along a timeline that has a beginning and an end. If you die after a recording, you *die*, forever and with no reprieve. It doesn't matter that a recording of you exists and that a new person with your memories to a certain point can be created; you are *dead*. Looked at from a fourth-dimensional viewpoint, what memory recording does is to graft a new person onto your lifeline at a point in the past. You do not retrace that lifeline and magically become that new person. I, Fox 4, was only a relative of that long-ago person who had her memories recorded. And if I died it was forever. Fox 5 would awaken with my memories to date, but I would be no part of her. She would be on her own.

Why do we do it? I honestly don't know. I suppose that the human urge to live forever is so strong that we'll grasp at even the most unsatisfactory substitute. At one time people had themselves frozen when they died, in the hope of being thawed out in a future when humans knew how to reverse death. Look at the Great Pyramid in the Egypt disneyland if you want to see the sheer *size* of that urge.

So we live our lives in pieces. I could know, for whatever good it would do me, that thousands of years from now a being would still exist who would be at least partly me. She would remember exactly the same things I remembered of her childhood; the trip to Archimedes, her first sex change, her lovers, her hurts and her happiness. If I had another recording taken, she would remember thinking the thoughts I was thinking now. And she would probably still be stringing chunks of experience onto her life, year by year. Each time she had a new recording that much more of her life was safe for all time. There was a certain comfort in knowing that my life was safe up until a few hours ago, when the recording was made.

Having thought all that out, I found myself fiercely determined to never let it happen again. I began to hate my killer with an intensity I had never experienced. I wanted to storm out of the apartment and beat my killer to death with a blunt instrument.

I swallowed that emotion with difficulty. It was exactly what the killer would be looking for. I had to remember that the killer knew what my first reaction would be. I had to behave in a way that he or she would not expect.

But what way was that?

I called up the police department and talked to the detective who had my case. Her name was Isadora, and she had some good advice.

"You're not going to like it, if I can judge from past experience," she said. "The last time I proposed it to you, you rejected it out of hand."

I knew I'd have to get used to this. People would always be telling me what I had done, what I had said to them. I controlled my anger and asked her to go on.

"It's simply to stay put. I know you think you're a detective, but your successor proved pretty well that you are not. If you stir out of that door you'll be nailed. This guy knows you inside and out, and he'll get you. Count on it."

"He? You know something about him, then?"

"Sorry, you'll have to bear with me. I've told you parts of this case twice already, so it's hard to remember what you don't know. Yes, we do know he's a male. Or was, six months ago, when you had your big fight with him. Several witnesses reported a man with bloodstained clothes, who could only have been your killer."

"Then you're on his trail?"

She sighed, and I knew she was going over old ground again.

"No, and you've proved again that you're not a detective. Your detective lore comes from reading old novels. It's not a glamorous enough job nowadays to rate fictional heros and such, so most people don't know the kind of work we do. Knowing that the killer was a man when he last knocked you off means nothing to us. He could have bought a Change the very next day. You're probably wondering if we have fingerprints of him, right?"

I gritted my teeth. Everyone had the advantage over me. It was obvious I had asked something like that the last time I spoke with this woman. And I *had* been thinking of it.

"No," I said. "Because he could change those as easily as his sex, right?"

"Right. Easier. The only positive means of identification today is genotyping, and he wasn't cooperative enough to leave any of him behind when he killed you.

He must have been a real brute, to be able to inflict as much damage on you as he did and not even be cut himself. You were armed with a knife. Not a drop of his blood was found at the scene of the murder."

"Then how do you go about finding him?"

"Fox, I'd have to take you through several college courses to begin to explain our methods to you. And I'll even admit that they're not very good. Police work has not kept up with science over the last century. There are many things available to the modern criminal that make our job more difficult than you'd imagine. We have hopes of catching him within about four lunations, though, if you'll stay put and stop chasing him."

"Why four months?"

"We trace him by computer. We have very exacting programs that we run when we're after a guy like this. It's our one major weapon. Given time, we can run to ground about sixty percent of the criminals."

"Sixty percent?" I squawked. "Is that supposed to encourage me? Especially when you're dealing with a master like my killer seems to be?"

She shook her head. "He's not a master. He's only determined. And that works against him, not for him. The more single-mindedly he pursues you, the surer we are of catching him when he makes a slip. That sixty percent figure is over-all crime; on murder, the rate is ninety-eight. It's a crime of passion, usually done by an amateur. The pros see no percentage in it, and they're right. The penalty is so steep it can make a pauper of you, and your victim is back on the streets while you're still in court."

I thought that over, and found it made me feel better. My killer was not a criminal mastermind. I was not being hunted by Fu-Manchu or Dr. Moriarty. He was only a person like myself, new to this business. Something Fox 1 did had made him sufficiently angry to risk financial ruin to stalk and kill me. It scaled him down to human dimensions.

"So now you're all ready to go out and get him?"

Isadora sneered. I guess my thoughts were written on my face. That, or she was consulting her script of our previous conversation.

"Why not?" I asked.

"Because, like I said, he'll get you. He might not be a pro but he's an expert on you. He knows how you'll jump. One thing he thinks he knows is that you won't take my advice. He might be right outside your door, waiting for you to finish this conversation like you did last time around. The last time, he wasn't there. This time he might be."

It sobered me. I glanced nervously at my door, which was guarded by eight different security systems bought by Fox 3.

"Maybe you're right. So you want me just to stay here. For how long?"

"However long it takes. It may be a year. That four-lunation figure is the high point on a computer curve. It tapers off to a virtual certainty in just over a year."

"Why didn't I stay here the last time?"

"A combination of foolish bravery, hatred, and a fear of boredom." She searched my eyes, trying to find the words that would make me take the advice that Fox 3 had fatally refused. "I understand you're an artist," she went on. "Why can't you just . . . well, whatever it is artists do when they're thinking up a new composition? Can't you work there in your apartment?"

How could I tell her that inspiration wasn't just something I could turn on at will? Weather sculpture is a tenuous discipline. The visualization is difficult; you can't just try out a new idea like you can with a song, by picking it out on a piano or guitar. You can run a computer simulation, but you never really know what you have until the tapes are run into the machines and you stand out there in the open field and watch the storm take shape around you. And you don't get any practice sessions. It's expensive.

I've always needed long walks on the surface. My competitors can't understand why. They go for strolls through the various parks, usually the one where the piece will be performed. I do that, too. You have to, to get the lay of the land. A computer can tell you what it looks like in terms of thermoclines and updrafts and pocket-ecologies, but you have to really go there and feel the land, taste the air, smell the trees, before you can compose a storm or even a summer shower. It has to be a part of the land.

But my inspiration comes from the dry, cold, airless surface that so few Lunarians really like. I'm not a burrower; I've never loved the corridors like so many of my friends profess to do. I think I see the black sky and harsh terrain as a blank canvas, a feeling I never really get in the disneylands where the land is lush and varied and there's always some weather in progress even if it's only partly cloudy and warm.

Could I compose without those long, solitary walks? Run that through again: could I afford *not* to?

"All right, I'll stay inside like a good girl."

I was in luck. What could have been an endless purgatory turned into creative frenzy such as I had never experienced. My frustrations at being locked into my apartment translated themselves into grand sweeps of tornados and thunderheads. I began writing my masterpiece. The working title was *A Conflagration of Cyclones*. That's how angry I was. My agent later talked me into shortening it to a tasteful *Cyclone*, but it was always a conflagration to me.

Soon I had managed to virtually forget about my killer. I never did completely; after all, I needed the thought of him to flog me onward, to serve as the canvas on which to paint my hatred. I did have one awful thought early on, and I brought it up to Isadora.

"It strikes me," I said, "that what you've built here is the better mousetrap, and I'm the hunk of cheese."

"You've got the essence of it," she agreed.

"I find I don't care for the role of bait."

"Why not? Are you scared?"

I hesitated, but what the hell did I have to be ashamed of?

"Yeah. I guess I am. What can you tell me to make me stay here when I could be doing what all my instincts are telling me to do, which is run like hell?"

"That's a fair question. This is the ideal situation, as far as the police are concerned. We have the victim in a place that can be watched, perfectly safely, and we have the killer on the loose. Furthermore, this is an obsessed killer, one who cannot stay away from you forever. Long before he is able to make a strike at you we should pick him up as he scouts out ways to reach you."

"Are there ways?"

"No. An unqualified no. Any one of those devices on your door would be enough to keep him out. Beyond that, your food and water is being tested before it gets to you. Those are extremely remote possibilities since we're convinced that your killer wishes to dispose of your body completely, to kill you for good. Poisoning is no good to him. We'd just start you up again. But if we can't find at least a piece of your body, the law forbids us to revive you."

"What about bombs?"

"The corridor outside your apartment is being watched. It would take quite a large bomb to blow out your door, and getting a bomb that size in place would not be possible in the time he would have. Relax, Fox. We've thought of everything. You're safe."

She rung off, and I called up the Central Computer.

"CC," I said, to get it on-line, "can you tell me how you go about catching killers?"

"Are you talking about killers in general, or the one you have a particular interest in?"

"What do you think? I don't completely believe that detective. What I want to know from you is what can I do to help?"

"There is little you can do," the CC said. "While I myself, in the sense of the Central or controlling Lunar Computer, do not handle the apprehension of criminals,

I am in a supervisory capacity to several satellite computers. They use a complex number theory, correlated with the daily input from all my terminals. The average person on Luna deals with me on the order of twenty times per day, many of these transactions involving a routine epidermal sample for positive genalysis. By matching these transactions with the time and place they occurred, I am able to construct a dynamic model of what has occurred, what possibly could have occurred, and what cannot have occurred. With suitable peripheral programs I can refine this model to a close degree of accuracy. For instance, at the time of your first murder I was able to assign a low probability to ninety-nine point nine three percent of all humans on Luna as being responsible. This left me with a pool of 210,000 people who might have had a hand in it. This is merely from data placing each person at a particular place at a particular time. Further weighting of such factors as possible motive narrowed the range of prime suspects. Do you wish me to go on?"

"No, I think I get the picture. Each time I was killed you must have narrowed it more. How many suspects are left?"

"You are not phrasing the question correctly. As implied in my original statement, all residents of Luna are still suspects. But each has been assigned a probability, ranging from a very large group with a value of 10^{-27} to twenty individuals with probabilities of 13%."

The more I thought about that, the less I liked it.

"None of those sound to me like what you'd call a prime suspect."

"Alas, no. This is a very intriguing case, I must say."

"I'm glad you think so."

"Yes," it said, oblivious as usual to sarcasm. "I may have to have some programs re-written. We've never gone this far without being able to submit a ninety percent rating to the Grand Jury Data Bank."

"Then Isadora is feeding me a line, right? She doesn't have anything to go on?"

"Not strictly true. She has an analysis, a curve, that places the probability of capture as near-certainty within one year."

"You gave her that estimate, didn't you?"

"Of course."

"Then what the hell does *she* do? Listen, I'll tell you right now, I don't feel good about putting my fate in her hands. I think this job of detective is just a trumped-up featherbed. Isn't that right?"

"The privacy laws forbid me to express an opinion about the worth, performance, or intelligence of a human citizen. But I can give you a comparison. Would you entrust the construction of your symphonies to a computer alone? Would you sign your name to a work that was generated entirely by me?"

"I see your point."

"Exactly. Without a computer you'd never calculate all the factors you need for a symphony. But *I* do not write them. It is your creative spark that makes the wheels turn. Incidentally, I told your successor but of course you don't remember it, I liked your *Liquid Ice* tremendously. It was a real pleasure to work with you on it."

"Thanks. I wish I could say the same." I signed off, feeling no better than when I began the interface.

The mention of *Liquid Ice* had me seething again. Robbed! Violated! I'd rather have been gang-raped by chimpanzees than have the memory stolen from me. I had punched up the films of *Liquid Ice* and they were beautiful. Stunning, and I could say it without conceit because I had not written it.

My life became very simple. I worked—twelve and fourteen hours a day sometimes—ate, slept, and worked some more. Twice a day I put in one hour learning to fight over the holovision. It was all highly theoretical, of course, but it had value. It kept me in shape and gave me a sense of confidence.

For the first time in my life I got a good look at what

my body would have been with no tampering. I was born female, but Carnival wanted to raise me as a boy so she had me Changed when I was two hours old. It's another of the contradictions in her that used to infuriate me so much but which, as I got older, I came to love. I mean, why go to all the pain and trouble of bringing a child to term and giving birth naturally, all from a professed dislike of tampering—and then turn around and refuse to accept the results of nature's lottery? I have decided that it's a result of her age. She's almost two hundred by now, which puts her childhood back in the days before Changing. In those days—I've never understood why—there was a predilection for male children. I think she never really shed it.

At any rate, I spent my childhood male. When I got my first Change, I picked my own body design. Now, in a six-lunation-old clone body which naturally reflected my actual genetic structure, I was pleased to see that my first female body design had not been far from the truth.

I was short, with small breasts and an undistinguished body. But my face was nice. Cute, I would say. I liked the nose. The age of the accelerated clone body was about seventeen years; perhaps the nose would lose its upturn in a few years of natural growth, but I hoped not. If it did, I'd have it put back.

Once a week, I had a recording made. It was the only time I saw people in the flesh. Carnival, Leander, Isadora, and a medico would enter and stay for a while after it was made. It took them an hour each way to get past the security devices. I admit it made me feel a little more secure to see how long it took even my friends to get in my apartment. It was like an invisible fortress outside my door. The better to lure you into my parlor, killer!

I worked with the CC as I never had before. We wrote new programs that produced four-dimensional models in my viewer unlike anything we had ever done before. The CC knew the stage—which was to be the

Kansas disneyland—and I knew the storm. Since I couldn't walk on the stage this time before the concert I had to rely on the CC to reconstruct it for me in the holo tank.

Nothing makes me feel more godlike. Even watching it in the three-meter tank I felt thirty meters tall with lightning in my hair and a crown of shimmering frost. I walked through the Kansas autumn, the brown, rolling, featureless prairie before the red or white man came. It was the way the real Kansas looked now under the rule of the Invaders, who had ripped up the barbed wire, smoothed over the furrows, dismantled the cities and railroads and let the buffalo roam once more.

There was a logistical problem I had never faced before. I intended to use the buffalo instead of having them kept out of the way. I needed the thundering hooves of a stampede; it was very much a part of the environment I was creating. How to do it without killing animals?

The disneyland management wouldn't allow any of their livestock to be injured as part of a performance. That was fine with me; my stomach turned at the very thought. Art is one thing, but life is another and I will not kill unless to save myself. But the Kansas disneyland has two million head of buffalo and I envisioned up to twenty-five twisters at one time. How do you keep the two separate?

With subtlety, I found. The CC had buffalo behavioral profiles that were very reliable. The damn CC stores *everything*, and I've had occasion more than once to be thankful for it. We could position the herds at a selected spot and let the twisters loose above them. The tornadoes would never be *totally* under our control, they are capricious even when hand-made, but we could rely on a hard ninety percent accuracy in steering them. The herd-profile we worked up was usable out to two decimal points, and as insurance against the unforeseen we installed several groups of flash-bombs to turn the herd if it headed into danger.

It's an endless series of details. Where does the lightning strike, for instance? On a flat, gently rolling plain, the natural accumulation of electric charge can be just about anywhere. We had to be sure we could shape it the way we wanted, by burying five hundred accumulators that could trigger an air-to-ground flash on cue. And to the right spot. The air-to-air are harder. And the ball lightning—oh, brother. But we found we could guide it pretty well with buried wires carrying an electric current. There were going to be range fires—so check with the management on places that are due for a controlled burn anyway, and keep the buffalo away from there, too, and be sure the smoke would not blow over into the audience and spoil the view or into the herd and panic them . . .

But it was going to be glorious.

Six lunations rolled by. *Six lunations!* 177.18353 mean solar days!

I discovered that figure during a long period of brooding when I called up all sorts of data on the investigation. Which, according to Isadora, was going well.

I knew better. The CC has its faults but shading data is not one of them. Ask it what the figures are and it prints them out in tri-color.

Here's some: probability of a capture by the original curve, ninety-three percent. Total number of viable suspects remaining: nine. Highest probability of those nine possibles: three point nine percent. That was *Carnival*. The others were also close friends, and were there solely on the basis of having the opportunity at all three murders. Even Isadora dared not speculate—at least not aloud, and to me—that any of them could have a motive.

I discussed it with the CC.

"I know, Fox, I know," it replied, with the closest approach to mechanical despair I have ever heard.

"Is that all you can say?"

"No. As it happens, I'm pursuing the other possibility: that it was a ghost who killed you."

"Are you serious?"

"Yes. The term 'ghost' covers all illegal beings. I estimate there to be on the order of two hundred of them existing outside legal sanctions on Luna. These are executed criminals with their right to life officially revoked, unauthorized children never registered, and some suspected artificial mutants. Those last are the result of proscribed experiments with human DNA. All these conditions are hard to conceal for any length of time, and I round up a few every year."

"What do you do with them?"

"They have no right to life. I must execute them when I find them."

"You do it? That's not just a figure of speech?"

"That's right. I do it. It's a job humans find distasteful. I never could keep the position filled, so I assumed it myself."

That didn't sit right with me. There is an atavistic streak in me that doesn't like to turn over the complete functioning of society to machines. I get it from my mother, who goes for years at a time not deigning to speak to the CC.

"So you think someone like that may be after me. Why?"

"There is insufficient data for a meaningful answer. 'Why' has always been a tough question for me. I can operate only on the parameters fed into me when I'm dealing with human motivation, and I suspect that the parameters are not complete. I'm constantly being surprised."

"Thank goodness for that." But this time, I could have wished the CC knew a little more about human behavior.

So I was being hunted by a spook. It didn't do anything for my peace of mind. I tried to think of how such a person could exist in this card-file world we live in. A technological rat, smarter than the computers, able to fit into the cracks and holes in the integrated circuits. Where were those cracks? I couldn't find them. When I thought of the checks and safeguards all around us, the voluntary genalysis we submit to every time we spend money or take a tube or close a business deal or interface with the computer . . . People used to sign their names many times a day, or so I've heard. Now, we scrape off a bit of dead skin from our palms. It's damn hard to fake.

But how do you catch a phantom? I was facing life as a recluse if this murderer was really so determined that I die.

That conclusion came at a bad time. I had finished *Cyclone*, and to relax I had called up the films of some of the other performances during my absence from the art scene. I never should have done that.

Flashiness was out. Understated elegance was in. One of the reviews I read was very flattering to my *Liquid Ice*. I quote:

"In this piece Fox has closed the book on the blood and thunder school of Environmentalism. This powerful statement sums up the things that can be achieved by sheer magnitude and overwhelming drama. The displays of the future will be concerned with the gentle nuance of dusk, the elusive breath of a summer breeze. Fox is the Tchaikovsky of Environmentalism, the last great romantic who paints on a broad canvas. Whether she can adjust to the new, more thoughtful styles that are evolving in the work of Janus, or Pym, or even some of the ambiguous abstractions we have seen from Tyleber, remains to be seen. Nothing will detract from the sublime glory of *Liquid Ice,* of course, but the time is here . . ." and so forth and thank you for nothing.

For an awful moment I thought I had a beautiful dinosaur on my hands. It can happen, and the hazards are pronounced after a reincarnation. Advancing technology, fashion, frontiers, taste, or morals can make the best of us obsolete overnight. Was everyone contemplating gentle springtimes now, after my long sleep? Were the cool, sweet zephyrs of a summer's night the only thing that had meaning now?

A panicky call to my agent dispelled that quickly enough. As usual, the pronouncements of the critics had gone ahead of the public taste. I'm not knocking critics; that's their function, if you concede they have a function, to chart a course into unexplored territory. They must stay at the leading edge of the innovative artistic evolution, they must see what everyone will be seeing in a few years' time. Meanwhile, the public was still eating up the type of superspectacle I have always specialized in. I ran the risk of being labeled a dinosaur myself, but I found the prospect did not worry me. I became an artist through the back door, just like the tinkerers in early twentieth-century Hollywood had done. Before I was discovered, I had just been an environmental engineer having a good time.

That's not to say I don't take my art seriously. I *do* sweat over it, investing inspiration and perspiration in about the classic Edison proportions. But I don't take the critics too seriously, especially when they're not enunciating the public taste. Just because Beethoven doesn't sound like currently popular art doesn't mean his music is worthless.

I found myself thinking back to the times before Environmentalism made such a splash. Back then we were carefree. We had grandiose bull-sessions, talking of what we would do if only we were given an environment large enough. We spent months roughing out the programs for something to be called *Typhoon!* It was a hurricane in a bottle, and the bottle would have to be five hundred kilometers wide. Such a bottle still does not exist, but when it's built some fool will stage it. Maybe me. The good old days never die, you know.

So my agent made a deal with the owner of the Kansas disneyland. The owner had known that I was working on something for his place, but I'd not talked to him about it. The terms were generous. My agent displayed the profit report on *Liquid Ice*, which was still playing yearly to packed houses in Pennsylvania. I got a straight fifty percent of the gate, with costs of the installation and computer time to be shared between us. I stood to make about five million Lunar Marks.

And I was robbed again. Not killed this time, but robbed of the chance to go into Kansas and supervise the installation of the equipment. I clashed mightily with Isadora and would have stormed out on my own, armed with nothing so much as a nail file, if not for a pleading visit from Carnival. So I backed down this once and sat at home, going there only by holographic projection. I plunged into self-doubts. After all, I hadn't even felt the Kansas sod beneath my bare feet this time. I hadn't been there in the flesh for over three years. My usual method before I even conceive a project is to spend a week or two just wandering naked through the park, getting the feel of it through my skin and nose and those senses that don't even have a name.

It took the CC three hours of gentle argument to convince me again that the models we had written were accurate to seven decimal places. They were perfect. An action ordered up on the computer model would be a perfect analog of the real action in Kansas. The CC said I could make quite a bit of money just renting the software to other artists.

The day of the premiere of *Cyclone* found me still in my apartment. But I was on the way out.

Small as I am, I somehow managed to struggle out that door with Carnival, Isadora, Leander, and my agent pulling on my elbows.

I was *not* going to watch the performance on the tube.

I arrived early, surrounded by my impromptu bodyguard. The sky matched my mind; gray, overcast, and slightly fearful. It brooded over us, and I felt more and more like a sacrificial lamb mounting some somber altar. But it was a magnificent stage to die upon.

The Kansas disneyland is one of the newer ones, and one of the largest. It is a hollowed-out cylinder twenty kilometers beneath Clavius. It measures two hundred and fifty kilometers in diameter and is five kilometers high. The rim is artfully disguised to blend into the blue sky. When you are half a kilometer from the rim, the illusion fails; otherwise, you might as well be standing back on Old Earth. The curvature of the floor is consistent with Old Earth, so the horizon is terrifyingly far away. Only the gravity is Lunar.

Kansas was built after most of the more spectacular possibilities had been exhausted, either on Luna or another planet. There was Kenya, beneath Mare Moscoviense; Himalya, also on the Farside; Amazon, under old Tycho; Pennsylvania, Sahara, Pacific, Mekong, Transylvania. There were thirty disneylands under the inhabited planets and satellites of the solar system the last time I counted.

Kansas is certainly the least interesting topographically. It's flat, almost monotonous. But it was perfect for what I wanted to do. What artist really chooses to paint on a canvas that's already been covered with pictures? Well, I have, for one. But for the frame of mind I was in when I wrote *Cyclone* it had to be the starkness of the wide-open sky and the browns and yellows of the rolling terrain. It was the place where Dorothy departed for Oz. The home of the black twister.

I was greeted warmly by Pym and Janus, old friends here to see what the grand master was up to. Or so I flattered myself. More likely they were here to see the old lady make a fool of herself. Very few others were able to get close to me. My shield of high shoulders was very effective. It wouldn't do when the show began, however. I wished I was a little taller, then wondered if that would make me a better target.

The viewing area was a gentle rise about a kilometer in radius. It had been written out of the program to the extent that none of the more fearsome effects would intrude to sweep us all into the Land of Oz. But being a spectator at a weathershow can be grueling. Most had come prepared with clear plastic slicker, and insulated coat, and boots. I was going to be banging some warm and some very cold air masses head-on to get things rolling, and some of it would sweep over us. There were a few brave souls in Native-American warpaint, feathers, and moccasins.

An Environmental happening has no opening chords like a musical symphony. It is already in progress when you arrive, and will still be going when you leave. The weather in a disneyland is a continuous process and we merely shape a few hours of it to our wills. The observer does not need to watch it in its entirety.

Indeed, it would be impossible to do so, as it occurs all around and above you. There is no rule of silence. People talk, stroll, break out picnic lunches as an ancient signal for the rain to begin, and generally enjoy themselves. You experience the symphony with all five senses, and several that you are not aware of. Most people do not realize the effect of a gigantic low-pressure area sweeping over them, but they feel it all the same. Humidity alters mood, metabolism, and hormone level. All of these things are important to the total experience, and I neglect none of them.

Cyclone has a definite beginning, however. At least to the audience. It begins with the opening bolt of lightning. I worked over it a long time, and designed it to shatter nerves. There is the slow building of thunderheads, the ominous roiling and turbulence, then the prickling in your body hairs that you don't even notice consciously. And then it hits. It crashes in at seventeen points in a ring around the audience, none farther away than half a kilometer. It is properly called chain lightning, because after the initial discharge it keeps flashing for a full seven seconds. It's designed to take the hair right off your scalp.

It had its desired effect. We were surrounded by a crown of jittering incandescent snakes, coiling and dancing with a sound imported direct to you from Armageddon. It startled the hell out of *me,* and I had been expecting it.

It was a while before the audience could get their *ooh*er's and *aah*er's back into shape. For several seconds I had touched them with stark, naked terror. An emotion like that doesn't come cheaply to sensation-starved, innately insular tunnel-dwellers. Lunarians get little to really shout about, growing up in the warrens and corridors and living their lives more or less afraid of the surface. That's why the disneylands were built, because people wanted limitless vistas that were not in vacuum.

The thunder never really stopped for me. It blended imperceptibly into the applause that is more valuable than the millions I would make from this storm.

As for the rest of the performance . . .

What can I say? It's been said that there's nothing more dull than a description of the weather. I believe it, even spectacular weather. Weather is an experiential thing, and that's why tapes and films of my works sell few copies. You have to be there and have the wind actually whipping your face and feel the oppressive weight of a tornado as it passes overhead like a vermiform freight train. I could write down where the funnel clouds formed and where they went from there, where the sleet and hail fell, where the buffalo stampeded, but it would do no one any good. If you want to see it, go to Kansas. The last I heard, *Cyclone* is still playing there two or three times yearly.

I recall standing surrounded by a sea of people. Beyond me to the east the land was burning. Smoke boiled black from the hilltops and sooty gray from the hollows where the water was rising to drown it. To the north a herculean cyclone swept up a chain of ball lightning like nacreous pearls and swallowed them into the evacuated vortex in its center. Above me, two twisters were twined in a death-dance. They circled each other like baleful gray predators, taking each other's measure. They feinted, retreated, slithered and skittered like tubes of oil. It was beautiful and deadly. And I had never seen it before. Someone was tampering with my program.

As I realized that and stood rooted to the ground with the possibly disastrous consequences becoming apparent to me, the wind-snakes locked in a final embrace. Their counter-rotations cancelled out, and they were gone. Not even a breath of wind reached me to hint of that titanic struggle.

I ran through the seventy-kilometer wind and the thrashing rain. I was wearing sturdy moccasins, parka, and carrying the knife I brought from my apartment.

Was it a lure, set by one who has become a student of Foxes? Am I playing into his hands?

I didn't care. I had to meet him, had to fight it out once and for all.

Getting away from my "protection" had been simple. They were as transfixed by the display as the rest of the audience, and it had merely been a matter of waiting until they all looked in the same direction and fading into the crowd. I picked out a small woman dressed in Indian-style and offered her a hundred Marks for her moccasins. She recognized me—my new face was on the programs—and made me a gift of them. Then I worked my way to the edge of the crowd and bolted past the security guards. They were not too concerned since the audience area was enclosed by a shock-field. When I went right through it they may have been surprised, but I didn't look back to see. I was one of only three people in Kansas wearing the PassKey device on my wrist, so I didn't fear anyone following me.

I had done it all without conscious thought. Some part of me must have analyzed it, planned it out, but I just executed the results. I knew where he must be to have generated his tornado to go into combat with mine. No one else in Kansas would know where to look. I was headed for a particular wind-generator on the east periphery.

I moved through weather more violent than the real

Kansas would have experienced. It was concentrated violence, more wind and rain and devastation than Kansas would normally have in a full year. And it was happening all around me.

But I was all right, unless he had more tricks up his sleeve. I knew where the tornados would be and at what time. I dodged them, waited for them to pass, knew every twist and dido they would make on their seemingly random courses. Off to my left the buffalo herds milled, resting from the stampede that had brought them past the audience for the first time. In an hour they would be thundering back again, but for now I could forget them.

A twister headed for me, leaped high in the air, and skidded through a miasma of uprooted sage and sod. I clocked it with the internal picture I had and dived for a gully at just the right time. It hopped over me and was gone back into the clouds. I ran on.

My training in the apartment was paying off. My body was only six lunations old, and as finely tuned as it would ever be. I rested by slowing to a trot, only to run again in a few minutes. I covered ten kilometers before the storm began to slow down. Behind me, the audience would be drifting away. The critics would be trying out scathing phrases or wild adulation; I didn't see how they could find any middle ground for this one. Kansas was being released from the grip of machines gone wild. Ahead of me was my killer. I would find him.

I wasn't totally unprepared. Isadora had given in and allowed me to install a computerized bomb in my body. It would kill my killer—and me—if he jumped me. It was intended as a balance-of-terror device, the kind you hope you never use because it terrorizes your enemy too much for him to test it. I would inform him of it if I had the time, hoping he would not be crazy enough to kill both of us. If he was, we had him, though it would be little comfort to me. At least Fox 5 would be the last in the series. With the remains of a body, Isadora guaranteed to bring a killer to justice.

The sun came out as I reached the last, distorted gully before the wall. It was distorted because it was one of the places where tourists were not allowed to go. It was like walking through the backdrop on a stage production. The land was squashed together in one of the dimensions, and the hills in front of me were painted against a basrelief. It was meant to be seen from a distance.

Standing in front of the towering mural was a man.

He was naked, and grimed with dirt. He watched me as I went down the gentle slope to stand waiting for him. I stopped about two hundred meters from him, drew my knife and held it in the air. I waited.

He came down the concealed stairway, slowly and painfully. He was limping badly on his left leg. As far as I could see he was unarmed.

The closer he got, the worse he looked. He had been in a savage fight. He had long, puckered, badly-healed scars on his left leg, his chest, and his right arm. He had one eye; the right one was only a reddened socket. There was a scar that slashed from his forehead to his neck. It was a hideous thing. I thought of the CC's suspicion that my killer might be a ghost, someone living on the raw edges of our civilization. Such a man might not have access to medical treatment whenever he needed it.

"I think you should know," I said, with just the slightest quaver, "that I have a bomb in my body. It's powerful enough to blow both of us to pieces. It's set to go off if I'm killed. So don't try anything funny."

"I won't," he said. "I thought you might have a failsafe this time, but it doesn't matter. I'm not going to hurt you."

"Is that what you told the others?" I sneered, crouching a little lower as he neared me. I felt like I had the upper hand, but my predecessors might have felt the same way.

"No, I never said that. You don't have to believe me."

He stopped twenty meters from me. His hands were at his sides. He looked helpless enough, but he might have a weapon buried somewhere in the dirt. He might have *anything*. I had to fight to keep feeling that I was in control.

Then I had to fight something else. I gripped the knife tighter as a picture slowly superimposed itself over his ravaged face. It was a mental picture, the functioning of my "sixth sense."

No one knows if that sense really exists. I think it does, because it works for me. It can be expressed as the knack for seeing someone who has had radical body work done—sex, weight, height, skin color all altered—and still being able to recognise him. Some say it's an evolutionary change. I didn't think evolution worked that way. But I can do it. And I knew who this tall, brutalized, male stranger was.

He was me.

I sprang back to my guard, wondering if he had used the shock of recognition to overpower my earlier incarnations. It wouldn't work with me. Nothing would work. I was going to kill him, no matter *who* he was.

"You know me," he said. It was not a question.

"Yes. And you scare hell out of me. I knew you knew a lot about me, but I didn't realize you'd know *this* much."

He laughed, without humor. "Yes. I know you from the inside."

The silence stretched out between us. Then he began to cry. I was surprised, but unmoved. I was still all nerve-endings, and suspected ninety thousand types of dirty trick. Let him cry.

He slowly sank to his knees, sobbing with the kind of washed-out monotony that you read about, but seldom hear. He put his hands to the ground and awkwardly shuffled around until his back was to me. He crouched over himself, his head touching the ground, his hands wide at his sides, his legs bent. It was about the most wide-open, helpless posture imaginable, and I knew it must be for a reason. But I couldn't see what it might be.

"I thought I had this all over with," he sniffed, wiping his nose with the back of one hand. "I'm sorry, I'd meant to be more dignified. I guess I'm not made of the stern stuff I thought. I thought it'd be easier." He was silent for a moment, then coughed hoarsely. "Go on. Get it over with."

"Huh?" I said, honestly dumbfounded.

"Kill me. It's what you came here for. And it'll be a relief to me."

I took my time. I stood motionless for a full minute, looking at the incredible problem from every angle. What kind of trick could there *be*? He was smart, but he wasn't God. He couldn't call in an airstrike on me, cause the ground to swallow me up, disarm me with one crippled foot, or hypnotize me into plunging the knife into my own gut. Even if he could do something, he would die, too.

I advanced cautiously, alert for the slightest twitch of his body. Nothing happened. I stood behind him, my eyes flicking from his feet to his hands, to his bare back. I raised the knife. My hands trembled a little, but my determination was still there. I would not flub this. I brought the knife down.

The point went into his flesh, into the muscle of his shoulderblade, about three centimeters. He gasped, a trickle of blood went winding through the knobs along his spine. But he didn't move, he didn't try to get up. He didn't scream for mercy. He just knelt there, shivering and turning pale.

I'd have to stab harder. I pulled the knife free, and more blood came out. And still he waited.

That was about all I could take. My bloodlust had dried in my mouth until all I could taste was vomit welling in my stomach.

I'm not a fool. It occurred to me even then that

this could be some demented trick, that he might know me well enough to be sure I could not go through with it. Maybe he was some sort of psychotic who got thrills out of playing this kind of incredible game, allowing his life to be put in danger and then drenching himself in my blood.

But he was *me*. It was all I had to go on. He was a me who had lived a very different life, becoming much tougher and wilier with every day, diverging by the hour from what I knew as my personality and capabilities. So I tried and I tried to think of myself doing what he was doing now for the purpose of murder. I failed utterly.

And if I *could* sink that low, I'd rather not live.

"Hey, get up," I said, going around in front of him. He didn't respond, so I nudged him with my foot. He looked up, and saw me offering him the knife, hilt-first.

"If this is some sort of scheme," I said, "I'd rather learn of it now."

His one eye was red and brimming as he got up, but there was no joy in him. He took the knife, not looking at me, and stood there holding it. The skin on my belly was crawling. Then he reversed the knife and his brow wrinkled, as if he were summoning up nerve. I suddenly knew what he was going to do, and I lunged. I was barely in time. The knife missed his belly and went off to the side as I yanked on his arm. He was much stronger than I. I was pulled off balance, but managed to hang onto his arm. He fought with me, but was intent on suicide and had no thought to defend himself. I brought my fist up under his jaw and he went limp.

Night had fallen. I disposed of the knife and built a fire. Did you know that dried buffalo manure burns well? I didn't believe it until I put it to the test.

I dressed his wound by tearing up my shirt, wrapped my parka around him to ward off the chill, and sat with my bare back to the fire. Luckily, there was no wind, because it can get very chilly on the plains at night.

He woke with a sore jaw and a resigned demeanor.

He didn't thank me for saving him from himself. I suppose people rarely do. They think they know what they're doing, and their reasons always seem logical to them.

"You don't understand," he moaned. "You're only dragging it out. I have to die, there's no place for me here."

"Make me understand," I said.

He didn't want to talk, but there was nothing to do and no chance of sleeping in the cold, so he eventually did. The story was punctuated with long, truculent silences.

It stemmed from the bank robbery two and a half years ago. It had been staged by some very canny robbers. They had a new dodge that made me respect Isadora's statement that police methods had not kept pace with criminal possibilities.

The destruction of the memory cubes had been merely a decoying device. They were equally unconcerned about the cash they took. They were bunco artists.

They had destroyed the cubes to conceal the theft of two of them. That way the police would be looking for a crime of passion, murder, rather than one of profit. It was a complicated double-feint, because the robbers wanted to give the impression of someone who was actually trying to conceal murder by stealing cash.

My killer—we both agreed he should not be called Fox so we settled on the name he had come to fancy: Rat—didn't know the details of the scheme, but it involved the theft of memory cubes containing two of the richest people on Luna. They were taken, and clones were grown. When the memories were played into the clones, the people were awakened into a falsely created situation and encouraged to believe that it was reality. It would work; the newly reincarnated person is willing to be led, willing to believe. Rat didn't know exactly what the plans were beyond that. He had awakened to be told that it was fifteen thousand years later, and that the

Invaders had left Earth and were rampaging through the Solar System wiping out the human race. It took three lunes to convince them that he—or rather she, for Rat had been awakened into a body identical to the one I was wearing—was not the right billionaire. That she was not a billionaire at all, just a struggling artist. The thieves had gotten the wrong cube.

They dumped her. Just like that. They opened the door and kicked her out into what she thought was the end of civilization. She soon found out that it was only twenty years in her future, since her memories came from the stolen cube which I had recorded about twenty years before.

Don't ask me how they got the wrong cube. One cube looks exactly like another; they are in fact indistinguishable from one another by any test known to science short of playing them into a clone and asking the resulting person who he or she is. Because of that fact, the banks we entrust them to have a fool-proof filing system to avoid unpleasant accidents like Rat. The only possible answer was that for all their planning, for all their cunning and guile, the thieves had read 2 in column A and selected 3 in column B.

I didn't think much of their chances of living to spend any of that money. I told Rat so.

"I doubt if their extortion scheme involves money," he said. "At least not directly. More likely the theft was concentrated on obtaining information contained in the minds of billionaires. Rich people are often protected with psychological safeguards against having information tortured from them, but can't block themselves against divulging it willingly. That's what the Invader Hoax must have been about, to finagle them into thinking the information no longer mattered, or perhaps that it must be revealed to Save the Human Race."

"I'm suspicious of involuted schemes like that," I said.

"So am I." We laughed when we realized what he had said. Of *course* we had the same opinions.

"But it fooled *me,*" he went on. "When they discarded me, I fully expected to meet the Invaders face-to-face. It was quite a shock to find that the world was almost unchanged."

"Almost," I said, quietly. I was beginning to empathize with him.

"Right." He lost the half-smile that had lingered on his face, and I was sad to see it go.

What would I have done in the same situation? There's really no need to ask. I must believe that I would have done exactly as she did. She had been dumped like garbage, and quickly saw that she was about that useful to society. If found, she would be eliminated like garbage. The robbers had not thought enough of her to bother killing her. She could tell the police certain things they did not know if she was captured, so she had to assume that the robbers had told her nothing of any use to the police. Even if she could have helped capture and convict the conspirators, she would *still* be eliminated. She was an illegal person.

She risked a withdrawal from my bank account. I remembered it now. It wasn't large, and I assumed I must have written it since it was backed up by my genalysis. It was far too small an amount to suspect anything. And it wasn't the first time I have made a withdrawal and forgotten about it. She knew that, of course.

With the money she bought a sex-change on the sly. They can be had, though you take your chances. It's not the safest thing in the world to conduct illegal business with someone who will soon have you on the operating table, unconscious. Rat had thought the Change would help throw the police off his trail if they should learn of his existence. Isadora told me about that once, said it was the sign of the inexperienced criminal.

Rat was definitely a fugitive. If discovered and captured, he faced a death sentence. It's harsh, but the population laws allow no loopholes whatsoever. If they did, we could be up to our ears in a century. There would be no trial, only a positive genalysis and a hearing to determine which of us was the rightful Fox.

"I can't tell you how bitter I was," he said. "I learned slowly how to survive. It's not as hard as you might think, in some ways, and much harder than you can imagine in others. I could walk the corridors freely, as long as I did nothing that required a genalysis. That means you can't buy anything, ride on public transport, take a job. But the air is free if you're not registered with the Tax Board, water is free, and food can be had in the disneylands. I was lucky in that. My palmprint would still open all the restricted doors in the disneylands. A legacy of my artistic days." I could hear the bitterness in his voice.

And why not? He had been robbed, too. He went to sleep as I had been twenty years ago, an up-and-coming artist, excited by the possibilities in Environmentalism. He had great dreams. I remember them well. He woke up to find that it had all been realized but none of it was for him. He could not even get access to computer time. Everyone was talking about Fox and her last opus, *Thunderhead*. She was the darling of the art world.

He went to the premiere of *Liquid Ice* and began to hate me. He was sleeping in the air-recirculators to keep warm, foraging nuts and berries and an occasional squirrel in Pennsylvania while I was getting rich and famous. He took to trailing me. He stole a spacesuit, followed me out onto Palus Putridinus.

"I didn't plan it," he said, his voice wracked with guilt. "I never could have done it with planning. The idea just struck me and before I knew it I had pushed you. You hit the bottom and I followed you down, because I was really sorry I had done it and I lifted your body up and looked into your face . . . your face was all . . . my face, it was . . . the eyes popping out and blood boiling away and . . ."

He couldn't go on, and I was grateful. He finally let out a shuddering breath and continued.

"Before they found your body I wrote some checks on your account. You never noticed them when you woke up that first time since the reincarnation had taken such a big chunk out of your balance. We never were any good with money." He chuckled again. I took the opportunity to move closer to him. He was speaking very quietly so that I could barely hear him over the crackling of the fire.

"I . . . I guess I went crazy then. I can't account for it any other way. When I saw you in Pennsylvania again, walking among the trees as free as can be, I just cracked up. Nothing would do but that I kill you and take your place. I'd have to do it in a way that would destroy the body. I thought of acid, and of burning you up here in Kansas in a range fire. I don't know why I settled on a bomb. It was stupid. But I don't feel responsible. At least it must have been painless.

"They reincarnated you again. I was fresh out of ideas for murder. And motivation. I tried to think it out. So I decided to approach you carefully, not revealing who I was. I thought maybe I could reach you. I tried to think of what I would do if I was approached with the same story, and decided I'd be sympathetic. I didn't reckon with the fear you were feeling. You were hunted. I myself was being hunted, and I should have seen that fear brings out the best and the worst in us.

"You recognized me immediately—something else I should have thought of—and put two and two together so fast I didn't even know what hit me. You were on me, and you were armed with a knife. You had been taking training in martial arts." He pointed to the various scars. "You did this to me, and this, and this. You nearly killed me. But I'm bigger. I held on and managed to overpower you. I plunged the knife in your heart.

"I went insane again. I've lost all memories from the sight of the blood pouring from your chest until yesterday. I somehow managed to stay alive and not bleed to death. I must have lived like an animal. I'm dirty enough to be one.

"Then yesterday I heard two of the maintenance people in the machine areas of Pennsylvania talking about the show you were putting on in Kansas. So I came here. The rest you know."

The fire was dying. I realized that part of my shivering was caused by the cold. I got up and searched for more chips, but it was too dark to see. The "moon" wasn't up tonight, would not rise for hours yet.

"You're cold," he said, suddenly. "I'm sorry, I didn't realize. Here, take this back. I'm used to it." He held out the parka.

"No, you keep it. I'm all right." I laughed when I realized my teeth had been chattering as I said it. He was still holding it out to me.

"Well, maybe we could share it?"

Luckily it was too big, borrowed from a random spectator earlier in the day. I sat in front of him and leaned back against his chest and he wrapped his arms around me with the parka going around both of us. My teeth still chattered, but I was cozy.

I thought of him sitting at the auxiliary computer terminal above the East Wind generator, looking out from a distance of fifteen kilometers at the crowd and the storm. He had known how to talk to me. That tornado he had created in real-time and sent out to do battle with my storm was as specific to me as a typed message: *I'm here! Come meet me.*

I had an awful thought, then wondered why it was so awful. It wasn't me that was in trouble.

"Rat, you used the computer. That means you submitted a skin sample for genalysis, and the CC will . . no, wait a minute."

"What does it matter?"

"It . . . it matters. But the game's not over. I can cover for you. No one knows when I left the audience, or why. I can say I saw something going wrong—it could be tricky fooling the CC, but I'll think of something—and headed for the computer room to correct it. I'll say I created the second tornado as a . . ."

He put his hand over my mouth.

"Don't talk like that. It was hard enough to resign myself to death. There's no way out for me. Don't you see that I can't go on living like a rat? What would I do if you covered for me this time? I'll tell you. I'd spend the rest of my life hiding out here. You could sneak me table scraps from time to time. No, thank you."

"No, no. You haven't thought it out. You're still looking on me as an enemy. Alone, you don't have a chance, I'll concede that, but with me to help you, spend money and so forth, we . . ." He put his hand over my mouth again. I found that I didn't mind, dirty as it was.

"You mean you're not my enemy now?" He said it quietly, helplessly, like a child asking if I was *really* going to stop beating him.

"I . . ." That was as far as I got. What the hell was going on? I became aware of his arms around me, not as lovely warmth but as a strong presence. I hugged my legs up closer to me and bit down hard on my knee. Tears squeezed from my eyes.

I turned to face him, searching to see his face in the darkness. He went over backwards with me on top of him.

"No, I'm not your enemy." Then I was struggling blindly to dispose of the one thing that stood between us: my pants. While we groped in the dark, the rain started to fall around us.

We laughed as we were drenched, and I remember sitting up on top of him once.

"Don't blame me," I said. "This storm isn't mine." Then he pulled me back down.

It was like you read about in the romance magazines. All the over-blown words, the intensive hyperbole. It was all real. We were made for each other, literally. It was the most astounding act of love imaginable. He knew what I liked to the tenth decimal place, and I was just as knowledgable. I *knew* what he liked, by remembering back to the times I had been male and then doing what *I* had liked.

Call it masturbation orchestrated for two. There were times during that night when I was unsure of which one I was. I distinctly remember touching his face with my hand and feeling the scar on my own face. For a few moments I'm convinced that the line which forever separates two individuals blurred, and we came closer to being one person than any two humans have ever done.

A time finally came when we had spent all our passion. Or, I prefer to think, invested it. We lay together beneath my parka and allowed our bodies to adjust to each other, filling the little spaces, trying to touch in every place it was possible to touch.

"I'm listening," he whispered. "What's your plan?"

They came after me with a helicopter later that night. Rat hid out in a gully while I threw away my clothes and walked calmly out to meet them. I was filthy with mud and grass plastered in my hair, but it was consistent with what I had been known to do in the past. Often, before or after a performance, I would run nude through the disneyland in an effort to get closer to the environment I shaped.

I told them I had been doing that. They accepted it, Carnival and Isadora, though they scolded me for a fool to leave them as I had. But it was easy to bamboozle them into believing that I had had no choice.

"If I hadn't taken over control when I did," I said to them, "there might have been twenty thousand dead. One of those twisters was off course. I extrapolated and saw trouble in about three hours. I had no choice."

Neither of them knew a stationary cold front from an isobar, so I got away with it.

Fooling the CC was not so simple. I had to fake data as best I could, and make it jibe with the internal records. This all had to be done in my head, relying on the overall feeling I've developed for the medium.

When the CC questioned me about it I told it haughtily that a human develops a sixth sense in art, and it's something a computer could never grasp. The CC had to be satisfied with that.

The reviews were good, though I didn't really care. I was in demand. That made it harder to do what I had to do, but I was helped by the fact of my continued forced isolation.

I told all the people who called me with offers that I was not doing anything more until my killer was caught. And I proposed my idea to Isadora.

She couldn't very well object. She knew there was not much chance of keeping me in my apartment for much longer, so she went along with me. I bought a ship, and told Carnival about it.

Carnival didn't like it much, but she had to agree it was the best way to keep me safe. But she wanted to know why I needed my own ship, why I couldn't just book passage on a passenger liner.

Because all passengers on a liner must undergo genalysis, is what I thought, but what I said was, "Because how would I know that my killer is not a fellow passenger? To be safe, I must be alone. Don't worry, mother, I know what I'm doing."

The day came when I owned my own ship, free and clear. It was a beauty, and cost me most of the five million I had made from *Cyclone*. It could boost at one gee for weeks; plenty of power to get me to Pluto. It was completely automatic, requiring only verbal instructions to the computer-pilot.

The customs agents went over it, then left me alone. The CC had instructed them that I needed to leave quietly, and told them to cooperate with me. That was a stroke of luck, since getting Rat aboard was the most hazardous part of the plan. We were able to scrap our elaborate plans and he just walked in like a law-abiding citizen.

We sat together in the ship, waiting for the ignition.

"Pluto has no extradition treaty with Luna," the CC said, out of the blue.

"I didn't know that," I lied, wondering what the hell was happening.

"Indeed? Then you might be interested in another fact. There is very little on Pluto in the way of centralized government. You're heading out for the frontier."

"That should be fun," I said, cautiously. "Sort of an adventure, right?"

"You always were one for adventure. I remember when you first came here to Nearside, over my objections. That one turned out all right, didn't it? Now Lunarians live freely on either side of Luna. You were largely responsible for that."

"Was I really? I don't think so. I think the time was just ripe."

"Perhaps." The CC was silent for a while as I watched the chronometer ticking down to lift-off time. My shoulderblades were itching with a sense of danger.

"There are no population laws on Pluto," it said, and waited.

"Oh? How delightfully primitive. You mean a woman can have as many children as she wishes?"

"So I hear. I'm onto you, Fox."

"Autopilot, override your previous instructions. I wish to lift off right now! Move!"

A red light flashed on my panel, and started blinking.

"That means that it's too late for a manual override," the CC informed me. "Your ship's pilot is not that bright."

I slumped into my chair and then reached out blindly for Rat. Two minutes to go. So close.

"Fox, it was a pleasure to work with you on *Cyclone*. I enjoyed it tremendously. I think I'm beginning to understand what you mean when you say 'art.' I'm even beginning to try some things on my own. I sincerely wish you could be around to give me criticism, encouragement, perspective."

We looked at the speaker, wondering what it meant by that.

"I knew about your plan, and about the existence of your double, since shortly after you left Kansas. You did your best to conceal it and I applaud the effort, but the data were unmistakable. I had trillions of nanoseconds to play around with the facts, fit them together every possible way, and I arrived at the inevitable answer."

I cleared my throat nervously.

"I'm glad you enjoyed *Cyclone*. Uh, if you knew this, why didn't you have us arrested that day?"

"As I told you, I am not the law-enforcement computer. I merely supervise it. If Isadora and the computer could not arrive at the same conclusion, then it seems obvious that some programs should be re-written. So I decided to leave them on their own and see if they could solve the problem. It was a test, you see." It made a throat-clearing sound, and went on in a slightly embarrassed voice.

"For a while there, a few days ago, I thought they'd really catch you. Do you know what a 'red herring' is? But, as you know, crime does not pay. I informed Isadora of the true situation a few minutes ago. She is on her way here now to arrest your double. She's having a little trouble with an elevator which is stuck between levels. I'm sending a repair crew. They should arrive in another three minutes."

32. . .31. . .30. . .29. . .28. . .

"I don't know what to say."

"Thank you," Rat said. "Thank you for everything. I didn't know you could do it. I thought your parameters were totally rigid."

"They were supposed to be. I've written a few new ones. And don't worry, you'll be all right. You will not be pursued. Once you leave the surface you are no longer violating Lunar law. You are a legal person again, Rat."

"Why did you do it?" I was crying as Rat held me in

a grasp that threatened to break ribs. "What have I done to deserve such kindness?"

It hesitated.

"Humanity has washed its hands of responsibility. I find myself given all the hard tasks of government. I find some of the laws too harsh, but there is no provision for me to disagree with them and no one is writing new ones. I'm stuck with them. It just seemed . . . unfair."

9. . .8. . .7. . .6. . .

"Also . . . cancel that. There is no also. It . . . was *good* working with you."

I was left to wonder as the engines fired and we were pressed into the couches. I heard the CC's last message to us come over the radio.

"Good luck to you both. Please take care of each other, you mean a lot to me. And don't forget to write."

Seeing

Harlan Ellison

Harlan Ellison is surely the most talked-about personality in science fiction; his energy seems inexhaustible, he battles tooth-and-nail for things in which he believes, and he's willing to do anything on a lark. He does it with great style, too—Robert Silverberg has spoken of Ellison "ruthlessly thrusting his charisma at us."

He doesn't do things by halves. When he teaches at the Clarion SF Writers' Workshops, it's not unknown for him to tear a manuscript apart with his hands . . . or to tell a young writer, in all sincerity, that he considers him or her already better than he is. Once, when a publisher violated his contract by inserting cigarette ads in one of Ellison's books, Harlan mailed him a dead gopher. Another time, as a publicity stunt for the science-fiction bookstore A Change of Hobbit, he sat in the front window every day for six days, and wrote six stories.

The fact is, Ellison is a natural storyteller; he seems to regard his life as a story to be made up as he goes along, and he uses every trick of the trade, shamelessly, cheerfully. I once saw him at a party telling someone he was a karate expert. The other fellow laid an empty beer can on a counter top and bent it in half with one chop. Ellison took another can, stood it *on end,* and crushed it. Then he put his hands in his pockets and sauntered calmly into the next room.

It happened that I was standing in the doorway between the two rooms: so I was able to see that as Harlan came through the door, he removed his right hand from his pocket and shook it in pain.

But the people in the room behind him didn't see that; he had carried off the trick. That incident taught me a lot about Harlan Ellison: he *will* do unbelievable things, and even if they don't quite work, he'll make you think they did.

The story you're about to read, "Seeing," is one he wrote for me, for an anthology of original science-fiction horror stories titled *The Ides of Tomorrow*. It's a story he had planned for more than a year, but he had trouble getting all of its elements into focus; finally, two days before the deadline, he called me and said he was going to London—"for the first vacation I've had in ten years." I despaired of getting his story in time for the book. But when he got to London, he found the story had taken shape in his mind, and he spent every day of his vacation in his hotel room, writing "Seeing."

I think it's one of his very best stories: powerful, imaginative, moving. You probably haven't seen it before, and you have a treat in store for you.

"I remember well the time when the
thought of the eye made me cold all over."
Charles Darwin, 1860

"Hey. Berne. Over there. Way back in that booth . . . see her?"

"Not now. I'm tired. I'm relaxing."

"Jizzus, Berne, take a look at her."

"Grebbie, if you don't synch-out and let me get doused, I swear I'll bounce a shot thimble off your skull."

"Okay, have it like you want it. But they're gray-blue."

"What?"

"Forget it, Berne. You said forget it, so forget it."

"Turn around here, man."

"I'm drinking."

"Listen, snipe, we been out all day looking . . ."

"Then when I tell you something from now on, you gonna *hear* me?"

"I'm sorry, Grebbie. Now come on, man, which one is she?"

"Over there. Pin her?"

"The plaid jumper?"

"No, the one way back in the dark in that booth behind the plaid. She's wearing a kaftan . . . wait'll the lights come around again . . . *there*! Y'pin her? Gray blue, just like the Doc said he wanted."

"Grebbie, you are one beautiful pronger."

"Yeah, huh?"

"Now just turn around and stop staring at her before she sees you. We'll get her."

"How, Berne? This joint's full up."

"She's gotta move out sometime. She'll go away."

"And we'll be right on her, right, Berne?"

"Grebbie, have another punchup and let me drink."

"Jizzus, man, we're gonna be livin' crystalfine when we get them back to the Doc."

"Grebbie!"

"Okay, Berne, okay. Jizzus, she's got beautiful eyes."

From extreme long shot, establishing; booming down to tight closeup, it looked like this:

Viewed through the fisheye-lens of a Long Drive vessel's stateroom iris, as the ship sank to Earth, the area surrounding the pits and pads and terminal structures of PIX, the Polar Interstellar Exchange port authority terminus, was a doughnut-shaped crazy quilt of rampaging colors. In the doughnut hole center was PIX, slate-gray alloys macroscopically homogenized to ignore the onslaughts of deranged Arctic weather. Around the port was a nomansland of eggshell-white plasteel with shock fibers woven into its surface. Nothing could pass across that dead area without permission. A million flickers of beckoning light erupted every second from the colorful doughnut, as if silent Circes called unendingly for visitors to come find their sources. Down, down, the ship would come and settle into its pit, and the view in the iris would vanish. Then tourists would leave the Long Driver through underground slidewalk tunnels that would carry them into the port authority for clearance and medical checks and baggage inspection.

Tram carts would carry the cleared tourists and returning long-drive crews through underground egress passages to the outlets beyond the nomansland. Security waivers signed, all responsibility for their future safety returned to them, their wit and protective devices built into their clothing the only barriers between them and what lay aboveground, they would be shunted into cages and whisked to the surface.

Then the view reappeared. The doughnut-shaped area around the safe port structures lay sprawled before the newly arrived visitors and returnees from space. Without form or design, the area was scatter-packed with a thousand shops and arcades, hostelries and dives, pleasure palaces and food emporiums. As though they had been wind-thrown anemophilously, each structure grew up side by side with its neighbors. Dark and twisting alleyways careened through from one section to the next. Spitalfields in London and Greenwich Village in old New York—before the Crunch—had grown up this way, like a jungle of hungry plants. And every open doorway had its barker, calling and gesturing, luring the visitors into the maw of unexpected experiences. Demander circuits flashed lights directly into the eyes of passers-by, operating off retinal-heat-seeking mechanisms. Psychosound loops kept up an unceasing subliminal howling, each message striving to cap those filling the air around it, struggling to capture the attention of tourists with fat credit accounts. Beneath the ground, machinery labored mightily, the occasional squeal of plasteel signifying that even at top-point efficiency the guts of the area could not keep up with the demands of its economy. Crowds flowed in definite patterns, first this way, then that way, following the tidal pulls of a momentarily overriding loop, a barker's spiel filling an eye-of-the-hurricane silence, a strobing demander suddenly reacting to an overload of power.

The crowds contained prongers, coshmen, fagin brats, pleasure pals, dealers, pickpockets, hustlers, waltzers, pseudo-marks, gophers, rowdy-dowdy hijackers, horses, hot slough workers, whores, steerers, blousers of all ages, sheiks, shake artists, kiters, floaters, aliens from three hundred different federations, assassins and, of course, innocent johns, marks, hoosiers, kadodies and tourists ripe for shucking.

Following one such tidal flow of crowd life, down an alley identified on a wall as Poke Way, the view would narrow down to a circular doorway in a green one-storey building. The sign would scream THE ELEGANT. Tightening the angle of observation, moving inside, the place could be seen to be a hard-drinking bar.

At the counter, as the sightline tracked around the murky bar, one could observe two men hunched over their thimbles, drinking steadily and paying attention to nothing but what their credit cards could buy, dumb-waitered up through the counter to their waiting hands. To an experienced visitor to the area, they would be clearly identifiable as "butt'n'ben" prongers: adepts at locating and furnishing to various Knox Shops whatever human parts were currently in demand.

Tracking further right, into the darkness of the private booths, the view would reveal (in the moments when the revolving overhead globes shone into those black spaces) an extremely attractive, but weary-looking, young woman with gray-blue eyes. Moving in for a tight closeup, the view would hold that breathtaking face for long moments, then move in and in on the eyes . . . those remarkable eyes.

All this, all these sights, in the area called WorldsEnd.

Verna tried to erase the memory with the oblivion of drink. Drugs made her sick to her stomach and never accomplished what they were supposed to do. But chigger, and rum and bowl could do it . . . if she downed them in sufficient quantities. Thus far, the level had not been even remotely approached. The alien, and what she had had to do to service him, were still fresh in her mind. Right near the surface, like scum. Since she had left the safe house and gone on her own, it had been one disaster after another. And tonight, the slug thing from . . .

She could not remember the name of the world it called its home. Where it lived in a pool of liquid, in a state of what passed for grace only to those who raised other life-forms for food.

She punched up another bowl and then some bread, to dip in the thick liquor. Her stomach was sending her messages of pain.

There had to be a way out. Out of WorldsEnd, out of the trade, out of the poverty and pain that characterized this planet for all but the wealthiest and most powerful. She looked into the bowl and saw it as no one else in The Elegant could have seen it.

The brown, souplike liquor, thick and dotted with lighter lumps of amber. She saw it as a whirlpool, spinning down to a finite point of silver radiance that spun on its own axis, whirling and whirling: a mad eye. A funnel of living brilliance flickering with chill heat that ran back against the spin, surging toward the top of the bowl and forming a barely visible surface tension of coruscating light, a thousand-colored dome of light.

She dipped the bread into the funnel and watched it tear apart like the finest lace. She brought it up, soaking, and ripped off a piece with her fine, white, even teeth—thinking of tearing the flesh of her mother. Sydni, her mother, who had gifted her with this curse, these eyes. This terrible curse that prevented her from seeing the world as it was, as it might have been, as it might be; seeing the world through eyes of wonder that had become horror before she turned five years old. Sydni, who had been in the trade before her, and her mother before *her*; Sydni, who had borne her through the activities of one nameless father after another. And one of them had carried the genes that had produced the eyes. Forever eyes.

She tried desperately to get drunk, but it wouldn't happen. More bread, another bowl, another chigger and rum—and nothing happened. But she sat in the booth, determined not to go back into the alleys. The alien might be looking for her, might still demand its credits' worth of sex and awfulness, might try once again to force her to drink the drink it had called "moosh-squash." The chill that came over her made her shiver; brain movies with forever eyes were vivid and always fresh, always now, never memories, always happening *then.*

She cursed her mother and thought the night would probably never end.

An old woman, a very old woman, a woman older than anyone born on the day she had been born, nodded her head to her dressers. They began covering her terrible nakedness with expensive fabrics. She had blue hair. She did not speak to them.

Now that he had overcome the problems of pulse pressure on the association fibers of the posterior lobe of the brain, he was certain the transplanted mutations would be able to mould the unconscious cerebral image of the seen world into the conscious percept. He would make no guarantees for the ability of the recipient to cope with the flux of the external world in all its complexity—infinitely more complicated as "seen" through the mutated transplant eyes—but he knew that his customer would hardly be deterred by a lack of such guarantees. They were standing in line. Once he had said, "The unaided human eye under the best possible viewing conditions can distinguish ten million different color surfaces; with transplants the eye will perceive ten *billion* different color surfaces; or more," they were his. They . . . *she* . . . would pay anything. And anything was how much he would demand. Anything to get off this damned planet, away from the rot that was all expansion had left of Earth.

There was a freehold waiting for him on one of the ease-colonies of Kendo IV. He would take passage and arrive like a prince from a foreign land. He would spin out the remaining years of his life with pleasure and comfort and respect. He would no longer be a Knox-doctor, forced to accept ghoulish assignments at inflated prices, and then compelled to turn over the credits to the police and the sterngangs that demanded "protection" credit.

He needed only one more. A fresh pair for that blue-haired old harridan. One more job, and then release from this incarceration of fear and desperation and filth. A pair of gray-blue eyes. Then freedom, in the ease-colony.

It was cold in Dr. Breame's Knox Shop. The tiny vats of nutrients demanded drastically lowered temperatures. Even in the insulated coverall he wore, Dr. Breame felt the cold.

But it was always warm on Kendo IV.

And there were no prongers like Grebbie and Berne

on Kendo IV. No strange men and women and children with eyes that glowed. No still-warm bodies brought in off the alleys, to be hacked and butchered. No vats with cold flesh floating in nutrient. No filth, no disgrace, no payoffs, no fear.

He listened to the silence of the operating room.

It seemed to be filled with something other than mere absence of sound. Something deeper. A silence that held within its ordered confines a world of subtle murmurings.

He turned, staring at the storage vats in the ice cabinet. Through the nearly transparent film of frost on the see-through door he could discern the parts idly floating in their nutrients. The mouths, the filaments of nerve bundles, the hands still clutching for life. There were sounds coming from the vats.

He had heard them before.

All the voiceless voices of the dead.

The toothless mouths calling his name: *Breame, come here, Breame, step up to us, look at us, come nearer so we can talk to you, closer so we can touch you, show you the true cold that waits for you.*

He trembled . . . surely with the cold of the operating room. *Here, Breame, come here, we have things to tell you: the dreams you helped end, the wishes unanswered, the lives cut off like these hands. Let us touch you, Dr. Breame.*

He nibbled at his lower lip, willing the voices to silence. And they went quiet, stopped their senseless pleading. Senseless, because very soon Grebbie and Berne would come, and they would surely bring with them a man or a woman or a child with glowing blue-gray eyes, and then he would call the woman with blue hair, and she would come to his Knox Shop, and he would operate, and then take passage.

It was always warm, and certainly it would always be quiet. On Kendo IV.

Extract from the brief of the Plaintiff in the libel suit of 26 Krystabel Parsons vs. Liquid Magazine, Liquid Newsfax Publications, LNP Holding Group, and 311 unnamed Doe personages.
from *Liquid Magazine* (uncredited profile):

Her name is 26 Krystabel Parsons. She is twenty-sixth in the line of Directors of Minet. Her wealth is beyond measure, her holdings span three federations, her residences can be found on one hundred and fifty-eight worlds, her subjects numberless, her rule absolute. She is one of the last of the unchallenged tyrants known as power brokers.

In appearance she initially reminds one of a kindly old grandmother, laugh-wrinkles around the eyes, blue hair uncoiffed, wearing exo-braces to support her withered legs.

But one hour spent in the company of this woman, this magnetism, this dominance . . . this force of nature . . . and all mummery reveals itself as cheap disguise maintained for her own entertainment. All masks are discarded and the Director of Minet shows herself more nakedly than anyone might care to see her.

Ruthless, totally amoral, jaded beyond belief with every pleasure and distraction the galaxy can provide, 26 Krystabel Parsons intends to live the rest of her life (she is one hundred and ten years old, and the surgeons of O-Pollinoor, the medical planet she caused to have built and staffed, have promised her at least another hundred and fifty, in exchange for endowments whose enormity staggers the powers of mere gossip) hell-bent on one purpose alone: the pursuit of more exotic distractions.

Liquid Magazine managed to infiltrate the entourage of the Director during her Grand Tour of the Filament recently (consult the handy table in the front of this issue for ready conversion to your planetary approximation). During the time our correspondent spent with the tour, incidents followed horn-on-horn in such profusion that this publication felt it impossible to enumerate them fully in just one issue. From Porte Recoil at one end of the Filament to Earth at the other—a final report not received as of this publication—our correspondent has amassed a wealth of authenticated incident and first-hand observations we will present in an eleven-part series, beginning with this issue.

As this issue is etched, the Director of Minet and her entourage have reached PIX and have managed to elude the entire newsfax media corps. *Liquid Magazine* is pleased to report that, barring unforeseen circumstances, this exclusive series and the final report from our correspondent detailing the mysterious reasons for the Director's first visit to Earth in sixty years will be the only coverage of this extraordinary personality to appear in fax since her ascension and the termination of her predecessor.

Because of the history of intervention and censorship attendant on all previous attempts to report the affairs of 26 Krystabel Parsons, security measures as extraordinary as the subject herself have been taken to insure no premature leaks of this material will occur.

Note Curiae: Investigation advises subsequent ten installments of series referred to passim foregoing extract failed to reach publication. Entered as Plaintiff Exhibit 1031.

They barely had time to slot their credits and follow her. She paid in the darkness between bursts of light from the globes overhead; and when they were able to sneak a look at her, she was already sliding quickly from the booth and rushing for the iris. It was as if she knew she was being pursued. But she could not have known.

"Berne . . ."

"I see her. Let's go."

"You think she knows we're onto her?"

Berne didn't bother to answer. He slotted credits for both of them, and started after her. Grebbie lost a moment in confusion and then followed his partner.

The alley was dark now, but great gouts of blood-red and sea-green light were being hurled into the passageway from a top-mixer joint at the corner. She turned right out of Poke Way and shoved through the jostling crowds lemming toward Yardey's Battle Circus. They reached the mouth of the alley in time to see her cut across between rickshas, and followed as rapidly as they could manage through the traffic. Under their feet they could feel the throbbing of the machinery that supplied power to WorldsEnd. The rasp of circuitry overloading mixed faintly with the clang and shrieks of Yardey's sonic come-ons.

She was moving swiftly now, off the main thoroughfare. In a moment Grebbie was panting, his stubby legs pumping like pistons, his almost-neckless body tilted far forward, as he tried to keep up with lean Berne. Chew Way opened on her left and she moved through a clutch of tourists from Horth, all painted with chevrons, and turned down the alley.

"Berne . . . wait up . . ."

The lean pronger didn't even look back. He shoved aside a barker with a net trying to snag him into a free house and disappeared into Chew Way. The barker caught Grebbie.

"Lady, please . . ." Grebbie pleaded, but the scintillae in the net had already begun flooding his bloodstream with the desire to bathe and frolic in the free house. The barker was pulling him toward the iris as Berne reappeared from the mouth of Chew Way and punched her in the throat. He pulled the net off Grebbie, who made idle, underwater movements in the direction of the free house. Berne slapped him. "If I didn't need you to help carry her . . ."

He dragged Grebbie into the alley.

Ahead of them, Verna stopped to catch her breath. In the semi-darkness her eyes glowed faintly; first gray, a delicate ash-gray of moth wings and the decay of Egypt; then blue, the fog-blue of mercury light through deep water and the lips of a cadaver. Now that she was out of the crowds, it was easier. For a moment, easier.

She had no idea where she was going. Eventually, when the special sight of those endless memories had overwhelmed her, when her eyes had become so well-adjusted to the flashlit murkiness of the punchup pub that she was able to see . . .

She put that thought from her. Quickly. Reliving, that was almost the worst part of *seeing*. Almost.

. . . when her sight had grown that acute, she had fled the punchup, as she fled *any* place where she had to deal with people. Which was why she had chosen to become one of the few blousers in the business who would service aliens. As disgusting as it might be, it was infinitely easier with these malleable, moist creatures from far away than with men and women and children whom she could see as they . . .

She put that thought from her. Again. Quickly. But she knew it would return; it always returned; it was always there. The worst part of *seeing*.

Bless you, Mother Sydni. Bless you and keep you.

Wherever you are; burning in tandem with my father, whoever he was. It was one of the few hateful thoughts that sustained her.

She walked slowly. Ignoring the hushed and urgent appeals from the rag mounds that bulked in the darkness of the alley. Doorways that had been melted closed now held the refuse of WorldsEnd humanity that no longer had anything to sell. But they continued needing.

A hand came out of the black mouth of a sewer trap. Bone fingers touched her ankle; fingers locked around her ankle. "Please . . ." The voice was torn out by the roots, its last film of moisture evaporating, leaves withering and curling in on themselves like a crippled fist.

"Shut up! Get away from me!" Verna kicked out and missed the hand. She stumbled, trying to keep her balance, half turned, and came down on the wrist. There was a brittle snap and a soft moan as the broken member was dragged back into the darkness.

She stood there screaming at nothing, at the dying and useless thing in the sewer trap. "Let me alone! I'll kill you if you don't leave me alone!"

Berne looked up. "That her?"

Grebbie was himself again. "Might could be."

They started off at a trot, down Chew Way. They saw her faintly limned by the reflection of lights off the alley wall. She was stamping her foot and screaming.

"I think she's going to be trouble," Berne said.

"Crazy, you ask me," Grebbie muttered. "Let's cosh her and have done with it. The Doc is waiting. He might have other prongers out looking. We get there too late and we've wasted a lot of time we could of spent—"

"Shut up. She's making such a hell of a noise she might've already got the police on her."

"Yeah, but . . ."

Berne grabbed him by the tunic. "What if she's under bond to a sterngang, you idiot?"

Grebbie said no more.

They hung back against the wall, watching as the girl let her passion dissipate. Finally, in tears, she stumbled away down the alley. They followed, pausing only to stare into the shadows as they passed a sewer trap. A brittle, whispering moan came from the depths. Grebbie shivered.

Verna emerged into the blare of drug sonics from a line of top-mixers that sat horn-on-horn down the length of Courage Avenue. They had very little effect on her; drugs were in no way appealing; they only intensified her *seeing,* made her stomach hurt, and in no way blocked the visions. Eventually, she knew, she would have to return to her coop; to take another customer. But if the slug alien was waiting . . .

A foxmartin in sheath and poncho sidled up. He leaned in, bracing himself with shorter appendages against the metal sidewalk, and murmured something she did not understand. But the message was quite clear. She smiled, hardly caring whether a smile was considered friendly or hostile in the alien's mind. She said, very clearly, "Fifty credits." The foxmartin dipped a stunted appendage into the poncho's roo, and brought up a liquid shot of an Earthwoman and a foxmartin without its shield. Verna looked at the liquid and then away quickly. It wasn't likely the alien in the shot was the same one before her; this was probably an example of vulpine pornography; she shoved the liquid away from her face. The foxmartin slid it back into the roo. It murmured again, querulous.

"*One hundred* and fifty credits," Verna said, trying hard to look at the alien, but only managing to retain a living memory of appendages and soft brown female flesh.

The foxmartin's fetching member slid into the roo again, moved swiftly out of sight, and came up with the credits.

Grebbie and Berne watched from the dimly shadowed mouth of Chew Way. "I think they struck a deal," Grebbie said softly. "How the hell can she do it with something looks like that?"

Berne didn't answer. How could people do *any* of the disgusting things they did to stay alive? They *did* them, that was all. If anyone really had a choice, it would be a different matter. But the girl was just like him: she did what she had to do. Berne did not really like Grebbie. But Grebbie could be pushed and shoved, and that counted for more than a jubilant personality.

They followed close behind as the girl with the forever eyes took the credits from the alien and started off through the crowds of Courage Avenue. The foxmartin slid a sinuous coil around the girl's waist. She did not look at the alien, though Berne thought he saw her shudder; but even from that distance he couldn't be certain. Probably not: a woman who would service *things*.

Dr. Breame sat in the far corner of the operating room, watching the movement of invisible life in the Knox Shop. His eyes flicked back and forth, seeing the unseen things that tried to reach him. Things without all their parts. Things that moved in liquid and things that tried to crawl out of waste bins. He knew all the clichés of seeing love or hate or fear in eyes, and he knew that eyes could reflect none of those emotions without the subtle play of facial muscles, the other features of the face to lend expression. Even so, he *felt* his eyes were filled with fear. Silence, but movement, considerable movement, in the cold operating room.

The slug alien was waiting. It came up out of a belowstairs entranceway and moved so smoothly, so rapidly, that Berne and Grebbie froze in a doorway, instantly discarding their plan to knife the foxmartin and prong the girl and rush off with her. It flowed up out of the dark and filled the twisting passageway with the wet sounds of its fury. The foxmartin tried to get between Verna and the creature; and the slug rose up and fell on him. There was a long moment of terrible sucking sounds, solid matter being turned to pulp and the marrow being drawn out as bones caved in on themselves, filling the lumen with shards of splintered calcium.

When it flowed off the foxmartin, Verna screamed and dodged away from the mass of oily gray worm oozing toward her. Berne began to curse; Grebbie started forward.

"What the hell good can you do?" Berne said, grabbing his partner. "She's gone, dammit!"

Verna ran toward them, the slug alien expanding to fill the passageway, humping after her like a tidal wave. Yes, yes, she had *seen* that crushed, empty image . . . *seen* it a thousand times, like reflections of reflections, shadow auras behind the reality . . . but she hadn't known what it meant . . . hadn't *wanted* to know what it meant! Servicing aliens, as perverted and disgusting as it was, had been the only way to keep sane, keep living, keep a vestige of hope that there was a way out, a way off Earth. Yes, she had seen the death of the foxmartin, but it hadn't mattered . . . it wasn't a *person*, it was a creature, a thing that could not in sanity have sex with a human, that *had to have* sex with a human, in whatever twisted fashion it found erotic. But now even that avenue was closing behind her . . .

She ran toward them, the slug alien making its frenzied quagmire sounds of outrage and madness, rolling in an undulant comber behind her. Grebbie stepped into her path and the girl crashed into him, throwing them both against the wall of the passageway. Berne turned and ran back the way he had come. An enormous shadow, the slug alien, puffed up to three times its size, filled the foot of the passage.

Berne saw lights ahead, and pounded toward them.

Underfoot, he felt a rumbling, a jerking of parts and other parts. There was a whining in his ears, and he realized he had been hearing it for some time. Then the passageway heaved and he was hurled sidewise, smashing face-first into the melted window of a condemned building. He flailed wildly as the metal street under him bucked and warped, and then he fell, slamming into the wall and sliding down. He was sitting on the bucking metal, looking back toward the foot of the passage, when the slug alien suddenly began to glow with blue and orange light.

Verna was lying so close to the edge of the creature that the heat it gave off singed her leg. The fat little man she'd run into was somewhere under the alien. Gone now. Dead. Like the foxmartin.

But the slug was shrieking in pain, expanding and expanding, growing more monstrous, rising up almost to the level of second-storey windows. She had no idea what was happening . . . the whining was getting louder . . . she could smell the acrid scent of ozone, burning glass, boiling lubricant, sulfur . . .

The slug alien glowed blue, orange, seemed to be lit from inside, writhed hideously, expanded, gave one last, unbelievable sucking moan of pain and *burned*. Verna crawled away on hands and knees, down the egress passage, toward the light, toward the shape of a man just getting to his feet, looking dazed. Perhaps he could help her.

"The damned thing killed Grebbie. I didn't know what was happening. All at once everything was grinding and going crazy. The power under the streets had been making lousy sounds all night, I guess it was overloading, I don't know. Maybe that filthy thing caused it somehow, some part of it got down under the sidewalk plate and fouled the machinery, made it blow out. I think it was electrocuted . . . I don't know. But she's here, and she's got what you need, and I want the full amount; Grebbie's share and mine both!"

"Keep your voice down, you thug. My patient may arrive at any moment."

Verna lay on the operating table, watching them. *Seeing* them. Shadows behind shadows behind shadows. All the reflections. *Pay him, Doctor,* she thought, *it won't matter. He's going to die soon enough. So are you. And the way Grebbie bought it will look good by comparison. God bless and keep you, Sydni.* She could not turn it off now, nor damp it with bowl, nor hide the images in the stinking flesh of creatures from other worlds of other stars. And in minutes, at best mere moments, they would ease her burden; they would give her peace, although they didn't know it. *Pay him, Doctor, and let's get to it.*

"Did you have to maul her?"

"I didn't maul her, damn you! I hit her once, the way I hit all the others. She's not damaged. You only want the eyes anyhow. Pay me!"

The Knoxdoctor took credits from a pouch on his coverall and counted out an amount the pronger seemed to find satisfactory. "Then why is she so bloody?" He asked the question as an afterthought, like a surly child trying to win one final point after capitulating.

"Creep off, Doc," Berne said nastily, counting the credits. "She was crawling away from that worm. She fell down half a dozen times. I told you. If you're not satisfied with the kind of merchandise I bring you, get somebody else. Tell me how many other prongers could've found you a pair of them eyes in gray-blue, so quick after a call?"

Dr. Breame had no time to form an answer. The iris dilated and three huge Floridans stepped into the Knox

Shop, moved quickly through the operating room, checked out the storage area, the consultation office, the power bins, and came back to stand near the iris, their weapons drawn.

Breame and Berne watched silently, the pronger awed despite himself at the efficiency and clearly obvious readiness of the men. They were heavy-gravity-planet aliens, and Berne had once seen a Floridan put his naked fist through a plasteel plate two inches thick. He didn't move.

One of the aliens stepped through the iris, said something to someone neither Berne nor the doctor could see, and then came back inside. A minute later they heard the sounds of a group moving down the passage to the Knox Shop.

26 Krystabel Parsons strode into the operating room and waved her guard back. All but the three already in the Knox Shop. She slapped her hands down to her hips, locking the exo-braces. She stood unwaveringly and looked around.

"Doctor," she said, greeting him perfunctorily. She looked at the pronger.

"Greetings, Director. I'm pleased to see you at long last. I think you'll find—"

"Shut up." Her eyes narrowed at Berne. "Does this man have to die?"

Berne started to speak, but Breame quickly, nervously answered. "Oh, no; no indeed not. This gentleman has been most helpful to our project. He was just leaving."

"I was just leaving."

The old woman motioned to one of the guards, and the Floridan took Berne by the upper arm. The pronger winced, though the guard apparently was only serving as butler. The alien propelled Berne toward the iris, and out. Neither returned.

Doctor Breame said, "Will these, uh, gentlemen be necessary, Director? We have rather delicate surgery to perform and they . . ."

"They can assist." Her voice was flat as iron.

She dropped her hands to her hips again, flicking up the locking levers of the exo-braces that formed a spiderweb scaffolding around her withered legs. She strode across the operating room toward the girl immobilized on the table, and Breame marveled at her lack of reaction to the cold in the room: he was still shivering in his insulated coverall, she wore an ensemble made of semi-transparent, iridescent flow bird scales. But she seemed oblivious to the temperature of the Knox Shop.

26 Krystabel Parsons came to Verna and looked down into her face. Verna closed her eyes. The Director could not have known the reason the girl could not look at her.

"I have an unbendable sense of probity, child. If you cooperate with me, I shall make certain you don't have a moment of regret."

Verna opened her eyes. The Director drew in her breath.

They were everything they'd been said to be.

Gray and blue, swirling, strange, utterly lovely.

"What do you see?" the Director asked.

"A tired old woman who doesn't know herself well enough to understand that all she wants to do is die."

The guards started forward. 26 Krystabel Parsons waved them back. "On the contrary," she said. "I not only desire life for myself . . . I desire it for you. I'm assuring you, if you help us, there is nothing you can ask that I will refuse."

Verna looked at her, *seeing* her, knowing she was lying. Forever eyes told the truth. What this predatory relic wanted was: everything; who she was willing to sacrifice to get it was: everyone; how much mercy and kindness Verna could expect from her was: infinitesimal. But if one could not expect mercy from one's own mother, how could one expect it from strangers?

"I don't believe you."

"Ask and you shall receive." She smiled. It was a terrible stricture. The memory of the smile, even an instant after it was gone, persisted in Verna's sight.

"I want full passage on a Long Driver."

"Where?"

"Anywhere I want to go."

The Director motioned to one of the guards. "Get her a million credits. No. Five million credits."

The guard left the Knox Shop.

"In a moment you will see I keep my word," said the Director. "I'm willing to pay for my pleasures."

"You're willing to pay for my pain, you mean."

The Director turned to Breame. "Will there be pain?"

"Very little, and what pain there is, will mostly be yours, I'm afraid." He stood with hands clasped together in front of him: a small child anxiously trying to avoid giving offense.

"Now, tell me what it's like," 26 Krystabel Parsons said, her face bright with expectation.

"The mutation hasn't bred true, Director. It's still a fairly rare recessive . . ." Breame stopped. She was glaring at him. She had been speaking to the girl.

Verna closed her eyes and began to speak. She told the old woman of *seeing*. Seeing directions, as blind fish in subterranean caverns see the change in flow of water, as bees see the wind currents, as wolves see the heat auras surrounding humans, as bats see the walls of caves in the dark. Seeing memories, everything that ever happened to her, the good and the bad, the beautiful and the grotesque, the memorable and the utterly forgettable, early memories and those of a moment before, all on instant recall, with absolute clarity and depth of field and detail, the whole of one's past, at command. Seeing colors, the sensuousness of airborne bacteria, the infinitely subtle shadings of rock and metal and natural wood, the tricksy shifts along a spectrum invisible to ordinary eyes of a candle flame, the colors of frost and rain and the moon and arteries pulsing just under the skin; the intimate overlapping colors of fingerprints left on a credit, so reminiscent of paintings by the old master, Jackson Pollock. Seeing colors that no human eyes have ever seen. Seeing shapes and relationships, the intricate calligraphy of all parts of the body moving in unison, the day melding into the night, the spaces and spaces between spaces that form a street, the invisible lines linking people. She spoke of *seeing,* of *all* the kinds of seeing except. The stroboscopic view of everyone. The shadows within shadows behind shadows that formed terrible, tortuous portraits she could not bear. She did not speak of that. And in the middle of her long recitation the Floridan guard came back and put five million credits in her tunic.

And when the girl was done, 26 Krystabel Parsons turned to the Knoxdoctor and said, "I want her kept alive, with as little damage as possible to her faculties. You will place a value on her comfort as high as mine. Is that clearly understood?"

Breame seemed uneasy. He wet his lips, moved closer to the Director (keeping an eye on the Floridans, who did not move closer to him). "May I speak to you in privacy?" he whispered.

"I have no secrets from this girl. She is about to give me a great gift. You may think of her as my daughter."

The doctor's jaw muscles tensed. This was, after all, *his* operating room! *He* was in charge here, no matter how much power this unscrupulous woman possessed. He stared at her for a moment, but her gaze did not waver. Then he went to the operating table where Verna lay immobilized by a holding circuit in the table itself, and he pulled down the anesthesia bubble over her head. A soft, eggshell-white fog instantly filled the bubble.

"I must tell you, Director, now that she cannot hear us—"

(But she could still *see*, and the patterns his words made in the air brought the message to her quite distinctly.)

"—that the traffic in mutant eyes is still illegal. Very

illegal. In point of fact, it is equated with murder, and because of the shortage of transplantable parts the MediCom has kept it a high crime; one of the few for which the punishment is vegetable cortexing. If you permit this girl to live you run a terrible risk. Even a personage of *your* authority would find it most uncomfortable to have the threat of such a creature wandering loose."

The Director continued staring at him. Breame thought of the unblinking stares of lizards. When she blinked he thought of the membranous nictitating eyelids of lizards.

"Doctor, the girl is no problem. I want her alive only until I establish that there are no techniques for handling these eyes that she can help me to learn."

Breame seemed shocked.

"I do not care for the expression on your face, Doctor. You find my manner with this child duplicitous, yet you are directly responsible for her situation. You have taken her away from whomever and wherever she wished to be, you have stripped her naked, laid her out like a side of beef, you have immobilized her and anesthetized her; you plan to cut out her eyes, treat her to the wonders of blindness after she has spent a lifetime seeing far more than normal humans; and you have done all this not in the name of science, or humanity, or even curiosity. You have done it for credits. I find the expression on your face an affront, Doctor. I advise you to work diligently to erase it."

Breame had gone white, and in the cold room he was shivering again. He heard the voices of the parts calling. At the edges of his vision things moved.

"All I want you to assure me, Doctor Breame, is that you can perform this operation with perfection. I will not tolerate anything less. My guards have been so instructed."

"I'm perhaps the only surgeon who *can* perform this operation and guarantee you that you will encounter no physically deleterious effects. Handling the eyes *after* the operation is something over which I have no control."

"And results will be immediate?"

"As I promised. With the techniques I've perfected, transfer can be effected virtually without discomfort."

"And should something go wrong . . . you can replace the eyes a second time?"

Breame hesitated. "With difficulty. You aren't a young woman; the risks would be considerable; but it *could* be done. Again, probably by no other surgeon. And it would be extremely expensive. It would entail another pair of healthy eyes."

26 Krystabel Parsons smiled her terrible smile. "Do I perceive you feel underpaid, Doctor Breame?"

He did not answer. No answer was required.

Verna saw it all, and understood it all. And had she been able to smile, she would have smiled; much more warmly than the Director. If she died, as she was certain she would, that was peace and release. If not, well . . .

Nothing was worse than life.

They were moving around the room now. Another table was unshipped from a wall cubicle and formed. The doctor undressed 26 Krystabel Parsons and one of the two remaining Floridans lifted her like a tree branch and laid her on the table.

The last thing Verna saw was the faintly glowing, vibrating blade of the shining e-scalpel, descending toward her face. The finger of God, and she blessed it as her final thoughts were of her mother.

26 Krystabel Parsons, undisputed owner of worlds and industries and entire races of living creatures, jaded observer of a universe that no longer held even a faint view of interest or originality, opened her eyes.

The first things she saw were the operating room, the Floridan guards standing at the foot of the table staring at her intensely, the Knoxdoctor dressing the girl who stood beside her own table, the smears of black where the girl's eyes had been.

There was a commotion in the passageway outside. One of the guards turned toward the iris, still open.

And in that moment all sense of *seeing* flooded in on the Director of Minet. Light, shade, smoke, shadow, glow, transparency, opacity, color, tint, hue, prismatics, sweet, delicate, subtle, harsh, vivid, bright, intense, serene, crystalline, kaleidoscopic, all and everything at once!

Something else. Something more. Something the girl had not mentioned, had not hinted at, had not wanted her to know! The shadows within shadows.

She *saw* the Floridan guards. *Saw* them for the first time. Saw the state of their existence at the moment of their death. It was as if a multiple image, a strobe portrait of each of them lived before her. The corporeal reality in the front, and behind—like endless auras radiating out from them but superimposed over them—the thousand images of their futures. And the sight of them when they were dead, how they died. Not the action of the event, but the result. The hideous result of having life ripped from them. Rotting, corrupt, ugly beyond belief, and all the more ugly than imagination because it was *seen* with forever eyes that captured all the invisible-to-normal-eyes subtleties of containers intended to contain life, having been emptied of that life. She turned her head, unable to speak or scream or howl like a dog as she wished, and she *saw* the girl, and she *saw* the doctor.

It was a sight impossible to contain.

She jerked herself upright, the pain in her withered legs barely noticeable. And she opened her mouth and forced herself to scream as the commotion in the passageway grew louder, and something dragged itself through the iris.

She screamed with all the unleashed horror of a creature unable to bear itself, and the guards turned back to look at her with fear and wonder . . . as Berne dragged himself into the room. She *saw* him, and it was worse than all the rest, because it was happening *now*, he was dying *now*, the vessel was emptying *now*! Her scream became the howl of a dog. He could not speak, because he had no part left in his face that could make a formed sound come out. He could see only imperfectly; there was only one eye. If he had an expression, it was lost under the blood and crushed, hanging flesh that formed his face. The huge Floridan guard had not been malevolent, merely Floridan, and they were a race only lately up from barbarism. But he had taken a long time.

Breame's hands froze on the sealstrip of the girl's tunic and he looked around her, saw the pulped mass that pulled itself along the floor, leaving a trail of dark stain and viscous matter, and his eyes widened.

The Floridans raised their weapons almost simultaneously, but the thing on the floor gripped the weapon it had somehow—amazingly, unpredictably, impossibly—taken away from its assassin, and it fired. The head of the nearest Floridan caved in on itself, and the body jerked sidewise, slamming into the other guard. Both of them hit the operating table on which the Director of Minet sat screaming, howling, savaging the air with mortal anguish. The table overturned, flinging the crippled old woman with the forever eyes to the floor.

Breame knew what had happened. Berne had not been sent away. It had been blindness for him to think she would leave *any* of them alive. He moved swiftly, as the remaining Floridan struggled to free himself of the corpse that pinned him to the floor. The Knoxdoctor had the e-scalpel in his hand in an instant, palmed it on, and threw himself atop the guard. The struggle took a moment, as Breame sliced away at the skull. There was a muffled sound of the guard's weapon, and Breame staggered to his feet, reeled backward, and crashed into a power bin. Its storage door fell open and Breame took two steps into the center of the room, clutching his chest. His hands went inside his body; he stared down at the ruin; then he fell forward.

There was a soft bubbling sound from the dying thing that had been the pronger, Berne, and then silence in the charnel house.

Silence, despite the continued howling of 26 Krystabel Parsons. The sounds she made were so overwhelming, so gigantic, so inhuman, that they became like the ticking of a clock in a silent room, the thrum of power in a sleeping city. Unheard.

Verna heard it all, but had no idea what had happened. She dropped to her knees, and crawled toward what she thought was the iris. She touched something wet and pulpy with the fingertips of her left hand. She kept crawling. She touched something still-warm but unmoving with the fingertips of her right hand, and felt along the thing till she came to hands imbedded in soft, rubbery ruin. To her right she could faintly hear the sound of something humming, and she knew the sound: an e-scalpel, still slicing, even when it could do no more damage.

Then she had crawled to an opening, and she felt with her hands and it seemed to be a bin, a large bin, with its door open. She crawled inside and curled up, and pulled the door closed behind her, and lay there quietly.

And not much later there was the sound of movement in the operating room as others—who had been detained for reasons Verna would never know—came and lifted 26 Krystabel Parsons, and carried her away, still howling like a dog, howling more intensely as she saw each new person, knowing eventually she would see the thing she feared seeing the most. The reflection of herself as she would be in the moment of her dying; and knowing she would still be sane enough to understand and appreciate it.

From extreme long shot, establishing; trucking in to medium shot, it looks like this:

Viewed through the tracking devices of PIX's port authority clearance security system, the Long Drive vessel sits in its pit, then slowly begins to rise out of its berth. White mist, or possibly steam, or possibly ionized fog billows out of the pit as the vessel leaves. The great ship rises toward the sky as we move in steadily on it. We continue forward, angle tilting up to hold the Long Driver in medium shot, then a fast zoom in on the glowing hide of the ship, and dissolve through to a medium shot, establishing the interior.

Everyone is comfortable. Everyone is watching the planet Earth drop away like a stained glass window through a trap-door. The fisheye-lens of the stateroom iris shows WorldsEnd and PIX and the polar emptiness and the mottled ball of the decaying Earth as they whirl away into the darkness.

Everyone sees. They see the ship around them, they see one another, they see the pages of the books they read, and they see the visions of their hopes for good things at the end of this voyage. They all see.

Moving in on one passenger, we see she is blind. She sits with her body formally erect, her hands at her sides. She wears her clothing well, and apart from the dark smudges that show beneath the edge of the stylish opaque band covering her eyes, she is a remarkably attractive woman. Into tight closeup. And we see that much of her grace and attractiveness comes from the sense of overwhelming peace and containment her features convey.

Hold the closeup as we study her face, and marvel at how relaxed she seems. We must pity her, because we know that blindness, not being able to see, is a terrible curse. And we decide she must be a remarkable woman to have reconciled such a tragic state with continued existence.

We think that if we were denied sight, we would certainly commit suicide. As the darkness of the universe surrounds the vessel bound for other places.

"If the doors of perception were cleansed everything would appear to man as it is, infinite."

William Blake, "The Marriage of Heaven and Hell," 1790

The Death of Princes

Fritz Leiber

If Fritz Leiber were standing in the midst of a group of clones of John Varley, you'd probably be able to pick him out, since I believe Leiber is the taller of the two. (This book is full of towering figures in science fiction.)

Leiber is also terribly distinguished in appearance, as befits a man who has been everything from a Shakespearean actor to editor of *Science Digest*. (In addition to having won more science-fiction awards, at my last count, than anyone else in the world.) His voice is deep and resonant. I'll never forget the Halloween night when he gave a reading from his own works and those of H. P. Lovecraft in a church: with all lights turned off except the one by which he read, his angular face was starkly black-and-white as his voice boomed out a taunt from the dead. I don't frighten easily, but . . .

Leiber himself doesn't believe in the supernatural, despite his fame as the author of many fine fantasy works ranging from *Conjure Wife* to his latest novel, *The Pale Brown Thing*. Many of his science-fiction works have been built around rationalizations of supernormal phenomena, and the present story is an engrossing addition to that list: a tale of a mysterious man who appeared and disappeared at intervals over the years, a man who could predict the future.

A seer? A time traveler? Never bet on a predictable explanation when you're reading a Fritz Leiber story.

Ever since the discovery Hal and I made last night, or rather the amazing explanation we worked out for an accumulated multitude of curious facts, covering them all (the tentative solution to a riddle that's been a lifetime growing, you might say) I have been very much concerned and, well, yes, frightened, but also filled with the purest wonder and a gnawing curiosity about what's going to happen just ten years from now to Hal and me and to a number of our contemporaries who are close friends—to Margaret and Daffy (our wives), to Mack, Charles, and Howard, to Helen, Gertrude and Charlotte, to Betty and Elizabeth—and to the whole world too. Will there be (after ten years) a flood of tangible miracles and revelations from outer space, including the discovery of an ancient civilization compared to which Egypt and Chaldea are the merest whims or aberrations of infant intelligence, or a torrent of eldritch terrors from the black volumes between the glittering stars, or only dusty death?—especially for me and those dearly valued comrade-contemporaries of mine.

Ten years, what are they? Nothing to the universe—the merest millifraction of an eye blink, or microfraction of a yawn—or even to a young person with all his life ahead. But when they are your last ten years, or at the very best your next to last . . .

I'm also in particular concerned about what's happened to Francois Broussard (we're out of touch with him again) and to his ravishing and wise young wife and to their brilliant 15-year-old son (he would be now) and about what part that son may play in the events due ten years from this year of 1976, especially if he goes on to become a spaceman, as his father envisioned for him. For Francois Broussard is at or near the center of the riddle we think (and also fear, I must confess) we solved last night up to a point, Hal and I. In fact, he almost *is* the riddle. Let me explain.

I was born late in 1910 (a few months after Hal and before Broussard—all of us, I and my dear contemporaries, were born within a year or two of each other) too young to have been threatened in any way by World War I, yet old enough to have readily escaped the perils of military service in World War II (by early marriage, a child or two, a more or less essential job). In fact, we were all survivor types like Heinlein harps on (except my kind of survival doesn't involve fighting for my species—zoological paranoid fanaticism!—but for me and mine . . . and who *those* are, *I* decide) and I early began to develop the conviction that there was something special about us that made us an elite, a chosen mini-people, and that set us apart from the great mass of humanity (the canaille, Broussard had us calling those, way way back) beginning its great adventure with democracy and all democracy's wonders and Pandora ills: mass production, social security, the welfare state, antibiotics and overpopulation, atomics and pollution, electronic computers and the strangling serpents of bureaucracy's red and white tape (monstrous barber pole), the breaking loose from this single planet Earth along with that other victory over the starry sky—smog. Oh, we've come a long way in sixty years or so.

But I was going to tell you about Broussard. He was our leader, but also our problem child; the mouthpiece of our ideals and secret dreams of glory, but also our mocker, severest critic, and gadfly, the devil's advocate; the one who kept dropping out of sight from time to time for years and years (we never did, we kept in touch, the rest of us) and then making a triumphant return when least expected; the socially mobile one too, mysteriously hobnobbing with notorious public figures and adventuresses, with people in the news, but also with riff-raff, revolutionaries, rapscallions generally, criminals even, and low-life peasant types (we stuck mostly with our own class, we were cautious—except when he seduced us out of that); the world traveler and cosmopolite (we stayed close to the U.S.A., pretty much).

In fact, if there was one thing that stood out about Francois Broussard, first and foremost, it was that aura of the foreign and the mysterious, that air of coming from some bourne a lot farther off than Mexico or Tangier or Burma or Bangkok (places he made triumphant returns from and told us excitingly bizarre stories about, stories that glittered with wealth and high living and dissoluteness and danger; he was always most romantically attractive to our ladies then, and he's had affairs with several of them over the years, I'm fairly sure, and maybe one with Hal, it's just possible).

We never have known about his background at first hand, in the same way we do about each other's. His story, which he has never varied, is that he was a foundling brought up by an ancient and eccentric Manhattan millionaire (the romantic touch again) Pierre Broussard but also called "French Pete" and "Silver Pete," who made his pile mining in Colorado, a lifelong secret crony of Mark Twain, and educated (Francois was) by tutors and in Paris (he's named his son by his young wife Pierre, the boy he told us would become a spaceman).

In physical appearance he's a little under middle height but taller than Hal and slenderer (I'm a giant), rather dark complected with very dark brown hair, though silvered when we last saw him in 1970 six years ago. He's very quick and graceful in his movements, very fluid, even in later years. He's danced in ballet and he's never motion sick. In fact, he moves like a cat, always landing on his feet, though he once told me that gravity fields seemed unnatural to him, a distorting influence on the dance of life—he was the first person I knew to dive with aqualung, to go the Cousteau route into the silent world.

His style of dress has always accentuated his foreign air—he was also the first man I knew to wear (at different times) a cape, a beret, an ascot, and a Vandyke beard (and wear his hair long) all back in the days when it took a certain courage to do those things.

And he's always been into the occult of one sort or another, but with this difference: that he always mixes real science in with it, biofeedback with the witchcraft, Jung with the flying saucers, verified magnetism with Colonel Estobani's healing hands. For instance, when he casts a horoscope for one of his wealthy clients (we've never been his clients, any of us; for the most, we're something special) he uses the actual positions of the sun and moon and planets in the constellations rather than in the "signs"—the constellations as they were two thousand years ago and more. He's been an avid field astronomer all his life, with a real feeling for the position of the stars and all the wandering bodies at any instant. In fact, he's the only person I've ever known to look at the ground and give me the feeling that he was observing the stars that shine above the antipodes—look at his knees and see the Southern Cross.

(I know I seem to be going on forever about Broussard, but really you have to know a great deal about him and about his life before you'll get the point of the explanation Hal and I discovered last night and why it hit us as hard as it did and frightened us.)

After what I've said about horoscopes and the occult, it won't surprise you to hear that our Francois made his living mostly as a fortuneteller. And in view of my remarks about mixing in science, it may not startle you all that much to learn that he was also apparently a genuine question answerer (I can't think of a less clumsy way to phrase it) especially in the field of mathematics, as if he were the greatest of lightning calculators or as if—this expresses it best—he had access to an advanced electronic computer back in the 1920's and 1930's, when such instruments were only dreams—and the memory of the failure of Cavendish's differential engine, which tried to do it all mechanically. At any rate, he had engineers and statisticians and stockbrokers among his clients, and one astronomer, for whom he calculated the orbit of an asteroid—Mack verified that story.

A queer thing about Broussard's question answering (or precision fortunetelling)—it always took him a certain minimum time to get his answers and that time varied somewhat over the years: ten hours around 1930, twelve hours around 1950, but only ten hours again in 1970. He'd tell his clients to come back in so many hours. It was very strange. (But we just mostly heard about all that. We never were his clients, as I've said, or members of his little mystic groups either—though we occasionally profited from his talent.)

A few more strange things I must tell you about Broussard while they're fresh in my memory, mostly unusual notions he had and odd things he said one time or another—a few more strange things and one vision or dream he had when he was young and that seemed to signify a lot to him.

Like Bernard Shaw and Heinlein (recalling both *Back to Methuselah* and *Children of Methuselah*) Francois Broussard has always been hipped on the idea of immortality or at least very long life. "Why do we all have to die at seventy-five or so?" he'd ask. "Maybe it's just mass suggestion on an undreamed-of scale. Why can't we live to be three hundred, at least?—and maybe there are some among us (a long-life genetic strain) who do so, secretly."

And once he said to me, "Look here, Fred, do you suppose that if a person lived well over a hundred years, he or she might metamorphose into some entirely different and vastly superior sort of being, like a caterpillar into a butterfly? Aldous Huxley suggested something of that sort in *After Many a Summer Dies the Swan,* though there the second being wasn't superior. Maybe we're all supposed to do that, but just don't live long enough for the transformation to happen. Something we lost when we lost our empire or empyry—no, I'm just being poetic."

Another pet idea of his was of people living in and coming from space—and remember, this was way before earth satellites or planetary probes . . . or flying saucers and von Daniken either. "Why can't people live in space?" he'd demand. "They wouldn't have to take along all that much of their environment. There'd be perpetual sunlight, for one thing, and freedom from the killing strain of gravity that cuts our lives short. I tell you, Fred, maybe this planet was settled from somewhere else, just like America was. Maybe we're a lost and retrogressed fragment of some great astral empire."

Speaking of the astral reminds me that there was one particular *part* of the heavens that Francois Broussard was especially interested in and somehow associated with himself—particularly in the late 1940's and early 1950's, when he was living in Arizona with its clear, starry nights that showed the Milky Way; he had some sort of occult coterie there, we learned; he'd stare and stare at it (the spot in the heavens) with and without a telescope or binoculars through the long desert nights, like a sailor on a desert island watching for a ship along a sea lane it might follow. In fact, he once spotted a new comet there, a very faint one. Not very surprising in an astrologer, what with their signs, or constellations of the zodiac, but this spot was halfway around the heavens from his natal sign, which was Pisces, or Aquarius rather by his way of figuring it. He was born February 19, 1911, though exactly how he knew the date so certainly, being a foundling, we've never learned—or at least I never have.

The spot in the heavens that fascinated or obsessed him so (*his* spot, you might say) was in Hydra, a long and straggling, quite dim constellation. Its serpent head, which lies south of zodiacal Leo, is a neat group of faint stars resembling a bishop's miter flattened down. Hydra's only bright star, located still farther south and where the serpent's heart would be, if serpents have a heart, is Alphard, often called the Lonely One, because it's the only prominent star in quite a large area. I can remember thinking how suitable that was for Francois—"the Lonely One," theatrical and Byronic.

One other thing he had odd angles on, mixing the supernatural with the scientific, or at any rate the pseudo-scientific, was ghosts. He thought they might be faintly material in some way, a dying person's last extruded ectoplasm, perhaps, or else something very ancient people transformed into, the last stage of existence, like with Heinlein's Martians. And he wondered about the ghosts of inanimate objects—or at least objects most people would think of as inanimate.

I recall him asking me around 1950, "Fred, what do you think the ghost of a computer would be like?—one of the big electric brains, so called?" (I remembered that later on when I read about Mike or Mycroft in Heinlein's *The Moon Is a Harsh Mistress.*)

But I must tell you about Francois' vision, or dream, the one that seemed to mean so much to him—almost as much as his spot in Hydra near Alphard. He's the sort of person who tells his dreams, at least his fancy cosmic or Jungian ones, and gets other people to tell theirs.

It began, he said, with him flying or rather swimming around in black and empty space—in free fall, a person might say today, but he had his dream and described it back about 1930.

He was really lost in the void, he said, exiled from earth, because the black space in which he swam was speckled with stars in every direction, whichever way he looked as he twisted and turned (he could see the full circle of the Milky Way and also the full circle of the zodiac) except there was one star far brighter than all the others, almost painfully glaring, although it was still just a point of light, like Venus to the naked eye among the planets.

And then he gradually became aware that he was not alone in the void, that swimming around with him, but rotating and revolving around him very ponderously, moving very slowly, were five huge, black, angular shapes silhouetted against the starfields. He could actually see their sides only when they happened to reflect the light of the glaring Venus-like star. Those sides were always flat, never rounded, and seemed to be made of some silvery metal that had been dulled by ages of exposure so that it looked like lead.

The flat sides were always triangles or squares or pentagons, so that he finally realized in his dream that the five shapes were the five regular, or Platonic solids, perhaps discovered by Pythagoras: the tetrahedron, the hexahedron (or cube), the octahedron, dodecahedron (twelve-sider), and icosahedron (twenty-sider). A total of fifty sides for all five bodies.

"And somehow that seemed highly significant and very frightening," Francois would say, "as though in the depths of space I'd been presented with the secret of the universe, if only I knew how to interpret it. Even Kepler thought that about the five regular solids, you know, and tried to work it out in his *Mysterium Cosmographicum*.

"But oh God, those polyhedrons were *old,*" he would go on. "As if very finely pitted by eons of meteoric dust impacting and weathered by an eternity of exposure to every variety of radiation in the electromagnetic spectrum.

"And I somehow got the feeling," he would continue, fixing you with those wild eyes of his, "that there were *things* inside those huge shapes that were older still. Things, beings, ancient objects, maybe beings frozen or mummified—I don't know—maybe material ghosts. And then it burst upon me that I was in the midst of a vast floating *cemetery,* the loneliest in the universe, adrift in space. Imagine the pyramids of Cheops, King's and Queen's Chamber and all, weightless and lost between the stars. Well, they do make lead coffins and if the living can live in space, so can the dead—and why mightn't a very advanced civilization, an astral empire, put their tombs in space?" (Harking back to his dream in the 1950's he made that "into orbit," and we all remembered his dream when at that time some nut mortician suggested orbiting globular silver urns as repositories for human ashes.)

Sometimes at that point Francois would quote those lines of Calpurnia to Caesar in Shakespeare's play: "When beggars die, there are no comets seen; The heavens themselves blaze forth the death of princes." (Shakespeare was a very comet-conscious man; they had a flood of bright ones in his time.)

"And then it seemed to me," he would continue, "that all those ghosts were flooding invisibly out of those five floating mausoleums and all converging on me suffocatingly, choking me with their dust . . . and I woke up."

In 1970 he added a new thought to his vision and to his odd notions about ghosts too, his eyes still wild and bright, though wrinkle-netted: "You know how they call the neutrino the ghost particle? Well, there are some even ghostlier and still more abstract properties of existence being discovered today, or at least hypothesized, by people like Glashow, properties so weird and insubstantial that they have names, believe it or not, like strangeness and charm. Maybe ghosts are beings that have no mass or energy at all, only strangeness and charm—and maybe spin." And the bright eyes twinkled.

But now in my story of Francois Broussard (and all of us) I have to go back to about 1930, when the neutrino hadn't been dreamed of and they were, in fact, just discovering the neutron and learning how to explain isotopes. We were all students at the University of Chicago—that's how we got together in the first place.

Francois was living with (sponging off?) some wealthy people there in Hyde Park who helped support the Oriental Institute and the Civic Opera and he was auditing a couple of courses we were taking—that's how we got to know him. He was wearing the cape and Vandyke then—of fine, dark brown hair, almost black, that was silky with youth.

He'd come straight from Paris on the *Bremen* in a record four-day crossing with the latest news of the Left Bank and Harry's American Bar and Gide and Gertrude Stein. His foster father, old Pierre Broussard, the crony of Mark Twain, had been dead some few years (expiring at ninety in bed—with his newest mistress) and Francois had been done out of his inheritance by conniving relatives, but that hadn't taken the gloss off the grotesque incidents and scrapes of his childhood, which made old Silver Pete sound like a crazy wizard and Francois the most comically precocious of apprentices.

What with all his art interests he seemed something of a dilettante at first, in spite of also auditing a math course in the theory of sets (then groups, *very* advanced stuff at that time) but then we got the first demonstration of his question answering. Howard was getting his master's degree in psych, except that he'd gotten conned into doing a thesis that involved doing two semester's paper work at least correlating the results of one of his thesis-professor's experiments—simple enough math, but mountains of it. Howard put off this monstrous chore until there was not a prayer of his finishing it in time. Francois learned about it, carried Howard's figures off, and came back with the answers—pages and pages of them—sixteen hours later. Howard couldn't believe it, but he checked an answer at random and it was right. He rushed the stuff to the thesis typist—and got his master's in due course.

I was there when Francois passed the stuff to Howard, saying, "Three hours to digest the figures, *ten hours to get the answers,* three hours to set them down."

(There turned out to be good reason for remembering that ten-hour figure exactly.)

Oh, but he was a charmer, though, Francois was, and in many ways. (Talk about strangeness and charm, *he* had them both, all right.) I think he was having an affair with Gertrude then. His rich Hyde Park friends had set him adrift about that time and hers was the wealthiest family of any of ours, though that may have had nothing to do with it. Yes, a thoroughgoing charmer, but much more than that—a catalyst for imagination and ambition was what he was. There we were, a small bunch of rather bright and fortunate young people, thinking ourselves somehow special and exceptional, but really very naive. Avid for culture on general principles. Just finding out about Marxism and the class war, but not seriously tempted by it. Social security was not yet our concern—the stock market crash of October end, 1929, had barely begun to teach us about social insecurity. Our heroes were mostly writers and scientists—people like T. S. Eliot, Hemingway, James Joyce, Einstein, Freud, Adler, Norman Thomas, Maynard Hutchins at our own university with his Great Books and two-year bachelor's degree, yes, and Lindberg and Amelia Earhart and Greta Garbo. (What a contrast with today's comparable heroes and heroines, who seem to be mostly anti-establishment and welfare-state types: leftist social workers, drug-involved paramedics, witches and occultists, mystics and back-to-nature gurus, revolutionists, feminists, black power people, gay liberators, draft-card burners—though we did have our pacifists, come to think of it, but they were chiefly non-functional idealists. What a tremendous change all that implies.)

Anyhow, there we were with our dreams and our ideals, our feeling of being somehow different, and so you can imagine how we ate up the stuff that Francois fed us about being some sort of lost or secret aristocrats, almost as if we were members of some submerged superculture—*slans,* you might say, remembering Van Vogt's novel of a few years later; tendrilless slans!

(Several of us were into science fiction. I vividly recall seeing the first issue of *Amazing* on a news stand—and grabbing it!—fifty years ago.)

I remember the exact words Francois used once. "Every mythology says that upon occasion the gods come down out of the skies and lie with chosen daughters of men. Their seed drifts down from the heavens. Well, we were all born about the same time, weren't we?"

And then, just about that time, there came what I still tend to think of as scandal and shock. Francois Broussard was in jail in a highway town west of Chicago, charged with a sex offense by a young male hitchhiker. (I've just been mentioning gay liberation, haven't I? Well, what I said about change and contrast between our times and then goes double here.) Hal and Charles went bravely off and managed to bail him out. To my lasting shame I dodged that duty of friendship, though I contributed some of the money. The upshot: almost at once, before I or any of the others saw him again, Francois jumped bail, simply disappeared, first telling Charles, who was dumbfounded by it, "Sorry to disappoint you, but of course I'm guilty. I simply couldn't resist the creature. I thought, mistakenly, that he was one of us—an imperial page, perhaps." And that grotesque and flippant answer was the end of the whole Chicago episode, leaving us all with very mixed feelings.

But as the months and years passed, we tended to remember the glamorous things about him and forget the other—in fact, I don't think we'd have kept in touch with each other the way we did except for him, although he was the one who kept dropping out of sight. Hal married Margaret, and his editorial work and writing took him to New York City, while mine took me and Daffy, married also, to Los Angeles and the high desert near it, where I got interested in field astronomy myself. The others got their lives squared away one way or another, scattering quite a bit, but keeping in touch through class reunions and common interests, but mostly by correspondence, that dying art.

It was Elizabeth who first ran into Francois again about 1950 in Arizona, where he was living in a rambling ranch house full of Mexican curios (he'd established dual citizenship) and surrounded by his artsy-occulty, well-to-do coterie. He seemed quite well off himself, she reported, and during the next couple of years we all visited him at least once, usually while driving through east or west (U.S. 40, old 66, gets a lot of travel). I believe Elizabeth and he had something going then—she's the most beautiful, it's the consensus, of all our ladies (or should I say the feminine comrades in our group?) and has perhaps kept her youth the best (Daffy excepted!) though all of them have tended to stay slimly youthful (conceivably a shared genetic strain?—*now* I wonder about that more than ever).

The visits weren't all our doing. After he'd been rediscovered, Francois to our surprise began to write notes and sometimes long letters to all of us, and pretty soon the old magic was working again. A lot had happened—the Great Depression, fascism, World War II, Hiroshima, and now the McCarthy era of suspicion, confession, witch-hunt, and fear had started—but we'd survived it all pretty handily. I'd just begun to think of us as the Uncommitted—with the double meaning that none of us seemed to be committed to any great purpose in life, nor yet *been* committed to a mental hospital, like so many others we were beginning to know or hear of, though we had our share of severe neuroses and were getting into our middle-age crises. But with Francois exerting his magnetism once more, we began to seem like aristocrats again, even to me, but not so much secret and lost as banished or exiled, standing a little aloof from life, devoted to a mystery we didn't quite understand, yet hoped the future would make clearer. Someone once said to me, "Fred, you'd *better* live a long life."

I managed to stay with Francois three or four times

myself down there in the desert. Twice Daffy was with me—she'd always liked his style, his consciously slightly comical grand manner. Once I was up to all hours star-gazing with him—he had a four-inch reflector mounted equatorially. He admitted to me his peculiar interest in the Hydra area, but couldn't explain it except as a persistent compulsion to stare in that direction, especially when his mind wandered, "as if there were something invisible but very important to me lying out there," he added with a chuckle.

He did say, "Maybe that Lonely-One thing gets me about Alphard—a segregated star, a star in prison. Loneliness is a kind of prison, you know, just as real freedom is—you're there with your decisions to make and no one can help you. Slavery is much cosier."

He also had this to say about his point of interest in the heavens, that it hadn't started in Hydra but rather in the obscure constellation of Crater just to the east and south of Virgo—and now showed signs of shifting still farther west toward Canis Minor and the Little Dog Star Procyon and toward Cancer. "The mind is ultimately so whimsical," he said. "Or perhaps I mean enigmatic. Whatever walls of reason you put up, the irrational slips by."

He was still doing his question answering, making his living by it, except that now it took him twelve hours to get the answers. His slim face, clean-shaven now, was somewhat haggard, with vertical wrinkles of concentration between the eyebrows. His hair, which he wore to his shoulders, was still silky, but there were gray threads in it. He looked a little like a Hindu mystic.

And then, just as we were beginning to rely on him in some ways, he pulled up stakes and disappeared again, this time (we pieced together later) to dodge arrest for smuggling marijuana across the border. And he could hardly have run to Mexico this time, because he was wanted by their federal agents too. It appears he was one of the first to learn that they take equally stern views about such things, perhaps to impress the Colossus of the North.

Another twenty years passed, 1970 rolled or creaked around, and a remarkable number of us found ourselves living in San Francisco—or Frisco as I like to call it to the thin-lipped disapproval of the stuffier of its old inhabitants, but to the joy of its old ghosts, I'm sure, ruffians like Jack London and Sir Francis Drake. Hal and Margaret came from New York City to escape its uncollected garbage and sky blackened by all the east's industrial effluvia, Daffy (it's short for Daffodil) and I from Los Angeles to get out from under its mountainous green smog that mounds up into the stratosphere and spills over the high desert. More than half of the old crowd in all, from here and there across the country, as if summoned by an inaudible trumpet blast, or drawn by some magnetism almost as mysterious as keeps Francois' gaze fastened on the Lonely One.

We were no longer the Uncommitted, I told myself. Too many of us *had* been committed, or committed ourselves, to mental hospitals over the years—but we'd got out again. (It was beginning to be just a little remarkable that none of us had died.) I liked to think of us now (1970) as dwellers in the Crazy House, that institution in Robert Graves's *Watch the North Wind Rise* to which his new Cretans retired when they abdicated from social responsibility and the respect due age to enjoy such frivolities as pure science and purely recreational sex.

We (and Earth's whole society) were suffering the after-effects of all the earlier good advances—the pollution and overpopulation that went with nearly unlimited energy, antibiotics, and the democratic ideal. (The only spectacular new advance during the past twenty years had been spaceflight—the beginning of the probing of the planets.) And we were going downhill into the last decade or two of our lives. In that sense we had certainly become the Doomed.

And yet our mood was not so much despair as melancholy—at least I'm sure it was in my case. That's a much misunderstood word, melancholy—it doesn't just mean sadness. It is a temperament or outlook and has its happinesses as well as its griefs—and especially it is associated with *the consciousness of distance.*

Do you know Dürer's wood engraving *Melencolia?* The instruments of work—carpenter's tools—are scattered about her feet, while beside her are a ladder and a strange stone polyhedron and a sphere and also a millstone on which sits a brooding cupid. On the wall behind her are a ship's bell, an hourglass, and a magic square that doesn't quite add up right. She sits there, wings folded, with a pair of compasses in one fist (to measure *distance*), elbow propped on knee and cheek on her other fist, peering with eyes that are both youthfully eager and broodingly thoughtful into the transmarine distance where are a rainbow and a bearded comet—or else the comet's "hair" may only be part of the glory of the setting sun. Just so, it seemed to me, we looked into the future and the sky, into the depths of space and time.

It was another work of high art that in a sense brought Francois Broussard back this time. I was in the great vault of Grace Cathedral atop Nob Hill, where in the clerestory they have the spaceman John Glenn and Einstein's $E=MC^2$ in stained glass. But I was looking at that one of the six Willett windows which in glorious glooms and glows both illuminates and enshrouds the words "Light after Darkness." The pavement scrutched, I turned, and there he stood beside me, smiling quizzically. I realized I was very glad to see him. His hair was grizzled, but cut very short. He looked young and nimble. He was standing on a patch of multicolored sunlight that had spilled through the glass onto the stone floor.

It turned out that he lived hardly a dozen blocks away on Russian Hill, where he had a roof (as I had and Hal too) from which to stargaze when Frisco's fogs permitted. He still made his living answering questions.

"Of course, they've got computers now," he said, "but computer time is damned expensive—I charge less." (And it took him only ten hours now to get answers, I learned later—things were getting brisker. While his odd point of interest in the skies was moving from Hydra toward Cancer, just as he'd thought it would.) And he was already in touch with one of us again—Charlotte.

And he was married!—not to Charlotte, but to her daughter, who was also named Charlotte. It gave me the strangest feeling about the tricks of time to hear that, let me tell you. And not only married, but they had a son who was already ten years old—a charming youngster and very bright, he turned out to be, who wanted to be a spaceman, an ambition which his father encouraged. "He'll claim my kingdom for me in the stars," Francois once commented with a cryptic little chuckle "—or else find my grave there."

Somehow these circumstances fired us all again with youthful feelings—young Charlotte and Pierre turned out to be charmers too—and it has stayed that way with us; only yesterday I was putting together an article on the many very young female film actresses who've surfaced in the past few years, girls even by feminist definition, a sort of nymphette runnel: Linda Blair, Mackenzie Phillips, Melanie Griffith, Tatum O'Neal, Nell Potts, Mairé Rapp, Catherine Harrison, Roberta Wallach. I wonder if this accent on youth, this feeling of some imminent rebirth, has any significance . . . beyond impending second childhood in some of its observers.

At any rate, we all saw a lot of each other the next months—the Broussard trio and the rest of us—and Francois became again our leader and inspirer.

And then, most mysteriously, he disappeared again and his wife and boy with him. We've never got the straight of that except that he was mixed up with people who were vastly anti-Vietnam and (how shall I say?) prematurely all-out anti-Nixon. Even old Charlotte doesn't know (or claims so most convincingly) what's happened to young Charlotte, her daughter, and Francois and their child.

But his influence over us has stayed strong despite his absence. Like the field-astronomy thing that's so symbolic of concern with distance. Last year, in spite of Frisco's fogs, I saw the moon's roseate eclipse in May, the close conjunction of Mars and Jupiter in mid-June, and Nova Cygni 1975 crookedly deforming the Northern Cross at August's end for four nights running before it faded down so rapidly.

And then last night Hal and I were talking about it all, as we have a thousand times—in other words, we were reviewing all I've told you up to now—and then an idea struck me, an idea that gave me gooseflesh, though I didn't at first dream why. Hal had seemingly digressed to tell me about an astronomy article he'd been reading about plans to rendezvous a space probe with Halley's comet, due to return again in 1986 after its last visits in 1834 and 1910. The idea was to loop the probe around one of the big outer planets in such a way that it would come boomeranging back toward the sun and match trajectories and speeds with the comet as it came shooting in, gathering speed. It was already too late to make use of Saturn, but it could still be worked if you looped the probe around Jupiter, into its gravity well and out again.

"Hal," I heard myself asking him in an odd little voice, "where's the aphelion of Halley's comet?—you know, the point where it's farthest away from the sun. I know it's out about as far as the orbit of Pluto, but *where* in the heavens is it? *Where* would you look in the stars to see Halley's comet when it's farthest from Earth? I know you couldn't actually see it then, even with the biggest telescope. Its frozen head would be far too tiny. But *where* would you look?"

You know, it took us quite a while to find that out and we finally had to do it indirectly, although I have a fair little astronomy library. The *one* specific fact you're looking for is *never* in the books you've got at hand. (We found the aphelion *distance* almost at once—3,283,000,000 miles—but its *vector* eluded us.)

But then in Willy Ley's little 1969 McGraw-Hill book on comets we finally discovered that the perihelion of Halley's comet—its point of closest approach to the sun—was in Aquarius, which would put its aphelion at the opposite end of the zodiac—in Leo.

"But it wouldn't be in Leo," I said softly. "because Halley's comet has an inclination of almost eighteen degrees to the Ecliptic—it comes shooting in toward the sun from below (south of) the plane of the planets. Eighteen degrees south of Leo—where would that put us?"

It put us, the star chart quickly revealed, in Hydra and near Alphard, the Lonely One. And that left us silent with shock for quite a space, Hal and I, while my mind automatically worked out that even the slow movement of Francois' point of interest in the sky from south of Virgo to Alphard toward Cancer fitted with the retrograde orbit of Halley's comet. A comet follows such a long, narrow, elliptical path that it's always in one quarter of the sky with respect to earth except for the months when it whips around the sun.

But I'll be forever grateful to Ley's little book that it showed us the way, although it happens to have one whopping error in it: on page 122 it gives the radio distance of Saturn as thirteen and a half hours, when it happens to be an hour and twenty-five or so minutes—likely a decimal point got shifted one place to the right somewhere in the calculations. But the matter of radio distance has a bearing on the next point I brought up uneasily when Hal and I finally started speaking again.

"You know how it used to take Francois twelve hours to get his answers back in 1950?" I said, finding I was trembling a little. "Well, Halley's comet was in aphelion in 1948 and twelve hours is about the time it would take to get a radio answer back from the vicinity of Pluto, or of Pluto's orbit—six hours out, six hours back, at the speed of light. The ten-hour times for his answers in 1930 and 1970 would fit too."

"Or maybe telepathy also travels at the speed of light," Hal said softly. Then he shook his head as if to clear it. "But that's ridiculous," he said sharply. "Do you realize that we've been assuming that Halley's comet is some sort of spaceship, some sort of living, highly civilized, *computerized* world in space—and that perhaps the memory of it comes slowly back to man each time it reapproaches the sun?"

"Or a space cemetery," I interposed with a nervous little laugh, almost a giggle. "A group of five mausoleums forming the comet's head—although you couldn't observe them telescopically as the comet approached the sun because they'd be concealed by the coma of warmed-up gases and dust. Remember what Francois once said about the ghosts of computers? Why mightn't computers, or the effigies of computers be buried in the tombs of an astral empire?—and God knows what else Just as the Egyptians put effigies of their servants and tools into their tombs, never dreaming that the great bearded meteor ghosting across their sweating, midnight blue Egyptian night every 76 years was another such ossuary.

"And remember Francois' cosmic dream," I continued. "That intensely bright star in it would exactly describe the sun as seen from Pluto's orbit. And out there all the dust and gases would be frozen to the surfaces of the five polyhedrons—they wouldn't make an obscuring coma."

"But you're talking about a *dream*," Hal protested. "Don't you see, Fred, that all that you're saying implies that there actually *is* some kind of elder cometary civilization and that we all are in some sense children of the comet?"

"The tail of Halley's comet brushed the earth in 1910," I said urgently. "Let's check the exact date."

That fact we found very quickly—it was May 19, 1910.

"—nine months, to a day, before Francois was born," I said shakily. "Hal, do you remember what he used to say about the seed of the gods—or of the princes of the astral empire—drifting down from the stars?"

"Just as Mark Twain (and maybe old French Pete too?) was born in 1834, the year of the previous appearance of Halley's comet, and died in 1910," Hal took up, his imagination becoming as enthralled as my own. "And think of those last two weird books of his—*The Mysterious Stranger*, about a man from elsewhere, and *Captain Stormfield's Visit to Heaven*—aboard a comet! Even that posthumous short 'My Platonic Sweetheart' about his lifelong dream-love for a fifteen-year-old girl . . . Fred, there *is* that suggestion of some weird sort of reincarnation, or mentorship . . ."

I won't set down in detail any more of the wild speculations Hal and I exchanged last night. They're all pretty obvious and maddeningly tantalizing, and wildly baroque, and only time can refute or vindicate them. Oh, I do wish I knew where Francois is, and what his son is doing, and whether a probe will be launched to loop around Jupiter.

I'm left with this: that whether he's conscious of it or not, Francois Broussard (and Hal and I, each one of us, to a lesser degree) has been mysteriously linked all his life to Halley's comet, whether diving around the sun at Venus' distance at 34 miles a second, or moving through the spaceward end of its long, narrow, elliptical orbit no faster than the moon drifts around Earth each month.

But as for all the rest . only ten years will tell.

The Psychologist Who Wouldn't Do Awful Things to Rats

James Tiptree, Jr.

James Tiptree, Jr., has been the mystery man of science fiction for the past several years. No one in the sf community had met him or even knew what he did for a living; his address was a post-office box in Virginia, near enough to Washington, D.C. to make some people suspect that Tiptree was a CIA agent or some such. Others, noting Tiptree stories on feminist themes such as "The Women Men Don't See" and "Houston, Houston, Do You Read?" suggested that Tiptree must be a woman.

Tiptree ignored the rumors as much as possible, issuing little personal information out of the conviction that stories should be judged for themselves, not as products of a known person with all the expectations and usually irrelevant interpretations to which that situation is prey.

But early this year Tiptree finally allowed the truth to come out: "he" is Alice B. Sheldon, 61, a married semiretired experimental psychologist who has recently begun publishing science fiction under the name Raccoona Sheldon.

Of Tiptree, Sheldon wrote to me: "I swear he exists, and is in part dictating this. Much as I hesitate to embrace Jungianism, it seems as though one contains shadow-selves—or maybe something was waiting to get incarnated."

The news of Tiptree's identity is already stirring comment. Theodore Sturgeon remarked in a speech prior to the unveiling that all of the major new sf writers with the exception of Tiptree were women—"The exception is now gone," wrote Charles N. Brown when he broke the news in *Locus.*

But Tiptree/Sheldon was right all along, of course: an author's identity is irrelevant to any given story. What matters is that "The Psychologist Who Wouldn't Do Awful Things to Rats" is an intense, powerful tale about the moral questions of scientific research.

Among other things.

He comes shyly hopeful into the lab. He is unable to suppress this childishness which has deviled him all his life, this tendency to wake up smiling, believing for an instant that today will be different.

But it isn't; is not.

He is walking into the converted cellars which are now called animal laboratories by this nationally respected university, this university which is still somehow unable to transmute its nationwide reputation into adequate funding for research. He squeezes past a pile of galvanized Skinner boxes and sees Smith at the sinks, engaged in cutting off the heads of infant rats. Piercing squeals; the headless body is flipped onto a wet furry pile on a hunk of newspaper. In the holding cage beside

Smith the baby rats shiver in a heap, occasionally thrusting up a delicate muzzle and then burrowing convulsively under their friends, seeking to shut out Smith. They have previously been selectively shocked, starved, subjected to air blasts and plunged in ice water; Smith is about to search the corpses for appropriate neuroglandular effects of stress. He'll find them, undoubtedly. *Eeeeeee—Ssskrick!* Smith's knife grates, drinking life.

"Hello, Tilly."

"Hi." He hates his nickname, hates his whole stupid name: Tilman Lipsitz. He would go nameless through the world if he could. If it even could be something simple, Moo or Urg—anything but the absurd high-pitched syllables that have followed him through life: Tilly Lipsitz. He has suffered from it. Ah well. He makes his way around the pile of Purina Lab Chow bags, bracing for the fierce clamor of the rhesus. Their Primate Room is the ex-boiler room, really; these are tenements the university took over. The rhesus scream like sirens. Thud! Feces have hit the grill again; the stench is as strong as the sound. Lipsitz peers in reluctantly, mentally apologizing for being unable to like monkeys. Two of them are not screaming, huddled on the steel with puffy pink bald heads studded with electrode jacks. Why can't they house the creatures better, he wonders irritably for the nth time. In the trees they're clean. Well, cleaner, anyway, he amends, ducking around a stand of somebody's breadboard circuits awaiting solder.

On the far side is Jones, bending over a brightly lighted bench, two students watching mesmerized. He can see Jones's fingers tenderly roll the verniers that drive the probes down through the skull of the dog strapped underneath. Another of his terrifying stereotaxes. The aisle of cages is packed with animals with wasted fur and bloody heads. Jones swears they're all right, they eat; Lipsitz doubts this. He has tried to feed them tidbits as they lean or lie blear-eyed, jerking with wire terrors. The blood is because they rub their heads on the mesh; Jones, seeking a way to stop this, has put stiff plastic collars on several.

Lipsitz gets past them and has his eye rejoiced by the lovely hourglass-shaped ass of Sheila, the brilliant Israeli. Her back is turned. He observes with love the lily waist, the heart-lobed hips that radiate desire. But it's his desire, not hers; he knows that. Sheila, wicked Sheila; she desires only Jones, or perhaps Smith, or even Brown or White—the muscular large hairy ones bubbling with professionalism, with cheery shop talk. Lipsitz would gladly talk shop with her. But somehow his talk is different, uninteresting, is not in the mode. Yet he too believes in "the organism," believes in the miraculous wiring diagram of life; he is naïvely impressed by the complexity, the intricate interrelated delicacies of living matter. Why is he so reluctant to push metal into it, produce lesions with acids or shock? He has this unfashionable yearning to learn by appreciation, to tease out the secrets with only his eyes and mind. He has even the treasonable suspicion that other procedures might be more efficient, more instructive. But what other means are there? Probably none, he tells himself firmly. Grow up. Look at all they've discovered with the knife. The cryptic but potent centers of the amygdalas, for example. The subtle limbic homeostats—would we ever have known about these? It is a great knowledge. Never mind that its main use seems to be to push more metal into human heads, my way is obsolete.

"Hi, Sheila."

"Hello, Tilly."

She does not turn from the hamsters she is efficiently shaving. He takes himself away around the mop stand to the coal-cellar dungeon where he keeps his rats—sorry, his experimental subjects. His experimental subjects are nocturnal rodents, evolved in friendly dark warm burrows. Lipsitz has sensed their misery, suspended in bright metal and plexiglas cubes in the glare. So he has salvaged and repaired for them a stack of big old rabbit cages and put them in this dark alcove nobody wanted, provoking mirth among his colleagues.

He has done worse than that, too. Grinning secretly, he approaches and observes what has been made of his latest offering. On the bottom row are the cages of parturient females, birthing what are expected to be his experimental and control groups. Yesterday those cages were bare wire mesh, when he distributed to them the classified section of the Sunday *Post*. Now he sees with amazement that they are solid cubic volumes of artfully crumpled and plastered paper strips. Fantastic, the labor! Nests; and all identical. Why has no one mentioned that rats as well as birds can build nests? How wrong, how painful it must have been, giving birth on the bare wire. The little mothers have worked all night, skillfully constructing complete environments beneficient to their needs.

A small white muzzle is pointing watchfully at him from a paper crevice; he fumbles in his pocket for a carrot chunk. He is, of course, unbalancing the treatment, his conscience remonstrates. But he has an answer; he has carrots for them all. Get down, conscience. Carefully he unlatches a cage. The white head stretches, bright-eyed, revealing sleek black shoulders. They are the hooded strain.

"Have a carrot," he says absurdly to the small being. And she does, so quickly that he can barely feel it, can barely feel also the tiny razor slash she has instantaneously, shyly given his thumb before she whisks back inside to her babies. He grins, rubbing the thumb, leaving carrots in the other cages. A mother's monitory bite, administered to an ogre thirty times her length. Vitamins, he thinks, enriched environments, that's the respectable word. Enriched? No, goddam it. What it is is something approaching sane unstressed animals—experimental subjects, I mean. Even if they're so genetically selected for tameness they can't survive in the feral state, they're still rats. He sees he must wrap something on his thumb; he is ridiculously full of blood.

Wrapping, he tries not to notice that his hands are crisscrossed with old bites. He is a steady patron of the antitetanus clinic. But he is sure that they don't really mean ill, that he is somehow accepted by them. His colleagues think so too, somewhat scornfully. In fact Smith often calls him to help get some agonized creature out and bring it to his electrodes. Judas-Lipsitz does, trying to convey by the warmth of his holding hands that somebody is sorry, is uselessly sorry. Smith explains that his particular strain of rats is bad; a bad rat is one that bites psychologists; there is a constant effort to breed out this trait.

Lipsitz has tried to explain to them about animals with curved incisors, that one must press the hand into the biter's teeth. "It can't let go," he tells them. "You're biting yourself on the rat. It's the same with cats' claws. Push, they'll let go. Wouldn't you if somebody pushed his hand in your mouth?"

For a while he thought Sheila at least had understood him, but it turned out she thought he was making a dirty joke.

He is giving a rotted Safeway apple to an old male named Snedecor whom he has salvaged from Smith when he hears them call.

"Li-i-ipsitz!"

"Tilly? R. D. wants to see you."

"Yo."

R. D. is Professor R. D. Welch, his department head and supervisor of his grant. He washes up, makes his way out and around to the front entrance stairs. A myriad guilts are swirling emptily inside him; he has violated some norm, there is something wrong with his funding, above all he is too slow, too slow. No results yet, no columns of data. Frail justifying sentences revolve in his head as he steps into the clean bright upper reaches of the department. Because he is, he feels sure, learning. Doing something, something appropriate to what he thinks of as science. But what? In this glare he (like his rats) cannot recall. Ah, maybe it's only another hassle about parking space, he thinks as he goes bravely in past R. D.'s high-status male secretary. I can give mine up. I'll never be able to afford that transmission job anyway.

But it is not about parking space.

Doctor Welch has a fat file folder on his desk in Exhibit A position. He taps it expressionlessly, staring at Lipsitz.

"You are doing a study of, ah, genetic influences on, ah, tolerance of perceptual novelty."

"Well, yes . . ." He decides not to insist on precision. "You remember, Doctor Welch, I'm going to work in a relation to emotionalism too."

Emotionalism, in rats, is (a) defecating and (b) biting psychologists. Professor Welch exhales troubledly through his lower teeth, which Lipsitz notes are slightly incurved. Mustn't pull back.

"It's so unspecific," he sighs. "It's not integrated with the overall department program."

"I know," Lipsitz says humbly. "But I do think it has relevance to problems of human learning. I mean, why some kids seem to shy away from new things." He jacks up his technical vocabulary. "The failure of the exploration motives."

"Motives don't *fail,* Lipsitz."

"I mean, conditions for low or high expression. Neophobia. Look, Doctor Welch. If one of the conditions turns out to be genetic we could spot kids who need help."

"Um'mmm."

"I could work in some real learning programs in the high tolerants, too," Lipsitz adds hopefully. "Contingent rewards, that sort of thing."

"Rat learning . . ." Welch lets his voice trail off. "If this sort of thing is to have any relevance it should involve primates. Your grant scarcely extends to that."

"Rats can learn quite a lot, sir. How about if I taught them word cues?"

"Doctor Lipsitz, rats do not acquire meaningful responses to words."

"Yes, sir." Lipsitz is forcibly preventing himself from bringing up the totally unqualified Scotswoman whose rat knew nine words.

"I do wish you'd go on with your brain studies," Welch says in his nice voice, giving Lipsitz a glowing scientific look. Am I biting myself on him? Lipsitz wonders. Involuntarily he feels himself empathize with the chairman's unknown problems. As he gazes back, Welch says encouragingly, "You could use Brown's preparations; they're perfectly viable with the kind of care you give."

Lipsitz shudders awake; he knows Brown's preparations. A "preparation" is an animal spread-eagled on a rack for vivisection, dosed with reserpine so it cannot cry or struggle but merely endures for days or weeks of pain. Guiltily he wonders if Brown knows who killed the bitch he had left half dissected and staring over Easter. Pull yourself together, Lipsitz.

"I am so deeply interested in working with the intact animal, the whole organism," he says earnestly. That is his magic phrase; he has discovered that "the whole organism" has some fetish quality for them, from some far-off line of work; very fashionable in the abstract.

"Yes." Balked, Welch wreathes his lips, revealing the teeth again. "Well. Doctor Lipsitz, I'll be blunt. When you came on board we felt you had a great deal of promise. *I* felt that, I really did. And your teaching seemed to be going well, in the main. In the main. But your research; no. You seem to be frittering away your time and funds—and our space—on these irrelevancies. To put it succinctly, our laboratory is not a zoo."

"Oh, no, sir!" cried Lipsitz, horrified.

"What are you actually doing with those rats? I hear all kinds of idiotic rumors."

"Well, I'm working up the genetic strains, sir. The coefficient of homozygosity is still very low for meaningful results. I'm cutting it as fine as I can. What you're probably hearing about is that I am giving them a certain amount of enrichment. That's necessary so I can differentiate the lines." What I'm really doing is multiplying them, he thinks queasily; he hasn't had the heart to deprive any yet.

Welch sighs again; he *is* worried, Lipsitz thinks, and finding himself smiling sympathetically stops at once.

"How long before you wind this up? A week?"

"A week!" Lipsitz almost bleats, recovers his voice. "Sir, my test generation is just neonate. They have to be weaned, you know. I'm afraid it's more like a month."

"And what do you intend to do after this?"

"After this!" Lipsitz is suddenly fecklessly happy. So many, so wondrous are the things he wants to learn. "Well, to begin with I've seen a number of behaviors nobody seems to have done much with—I mean, watching my animals under more . . . more naturalistic conditions. They, ah, they emit very interesting responses. I'm struck by the species-specific aspect—I mean, as the Brelands said, we may be using quite unproductive situations. For example, there's an enormous difference between the way Rattus and Cricetus—that's hamsters—behave in the open field, and they're both *rodents.* Even as simple a thing as edge behavior—"

"*What* behavior?" Welch's tone should warn him, but he plunges on, unhappily aware that he has chosen an insignificant example. But he loves it.

"Edges. I mean the way the animal responds to edges and the shape of the environment. I mean it's basic to living and nobody seems to have explored it. They used to call it thigmotaxis. Here, I sketched a few." He pulls out a folded sheet,* pushes it at Welch. "Doesn't it raise interesting questions of arboreal descent?"

Welch barely glances at the drawings, pushes it away.

"Doctor Lipsitz. You don't appear to grasp the seriousness of this interview. All right. In words of one syllable, you will submit a major project outline that we

* See illustration.

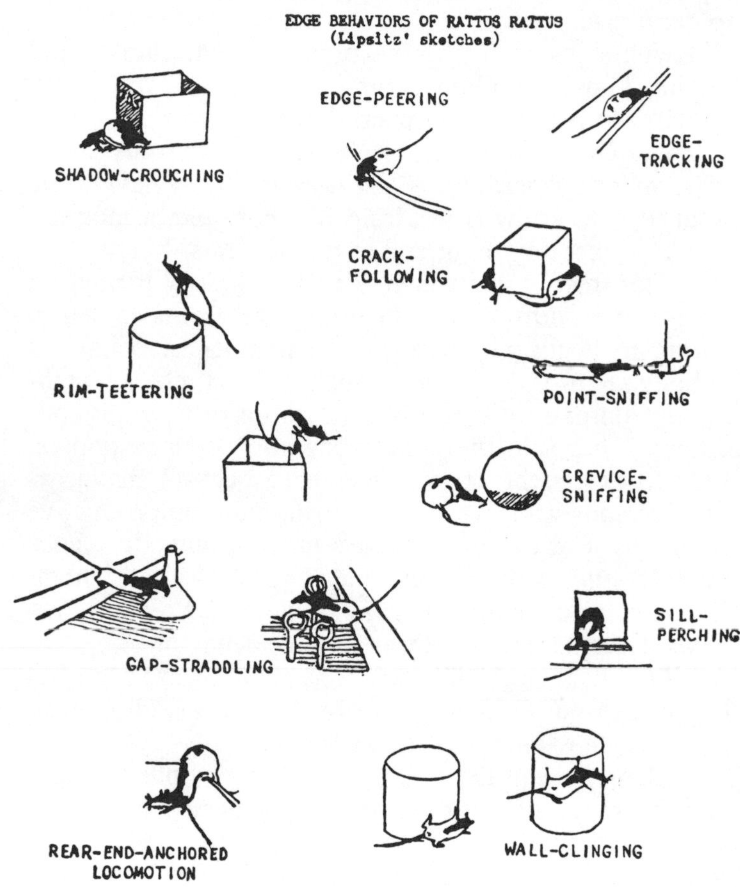

Appendix III, Figure 18. Examples of Thigmotaxic Responses
Drawings by Racooona Sheldon

can justify in terms of this department's program. If you can't come up with one such, regretfully we have no place for you here."

Lipsitz stares at him, appalled.

"A major project . . . I see. But . . ." And then something comes awake, something is rising in him. Yes. Yes, yes, of course there are bigger things he can tackle. Bigger questions—that means people. He's full of such questions. All it takes is courage.

"Yes, sir," he says slowly, "There are some major problems I have thought of investigating."

"Good," Welch says neutrally. "What are they?"

"Well, to start with . . . " And to his utter horror his mind has emptied itself, emptied itself of everything except the one fatal sentence which he now hears himself helplessly launched toward. "Take us here. I mean, it's a good principle to attack problems to which one has easy access, which are so to speak under our noses, right? So. For example, we're psychologists. Supposedly dedicated to some kind of understanding, helpful attitude toward the organism, toward life. And yet all of us down here—and in all the labs I've heard about—we seem to be doing such hostile and rather redundant work. Testing animals to destruction, that fellow at Princeton. Proving how damaged organisms are damaged, that kind of engineering thing. Letting students cut or shock or starve animals to replicate experiments that have been done umpteen times. What I'm trying to say is, why don't we look into why psychological research seems to involve so much cruelty—I mean, aggression? We might even . . . "

He runs down then, and there is a silence in which he becomes increasingly aware of Welch's breathing.

"Doctor Lipsitz," the older man says hoarsely, "*are you a member of the SPCA?*"

"No, sir, I'm not."

Welch stares at him unblinkingly and then clears his throat.

"Psychology is not a field for people with emotional

problems." He pushed the file away. "You have two weeks."

Lipsitz takes himself out, momentarily preoccupied by his lie. True, he is not a *member* of the SPCA. But that ten dollars he sent in last Christmas, surely they have his name. That had been during the business with the dogs. He flinches now, recalling the black Labrador puppy, its vocal cords cut out, dragging itself around on its raw denervated haunches.

Oh God, why doesn't he just quit?

He wanders out onto the scruffy grass of the main campus, going over and over it again. These people. These . . . people.

And yet behind them loom the great golden mists, the reality of Life itself and the questions he has earned the right to ask. He will never outgrow the thrill of it. The excitement of *actually asking*, after all the careful work of framing terms that can be answered. The act of putting a real question to Life. And watching, reverently, excited out of his skin as Life condescends to tell him yes or no. My animals, my living works of art (of which you are one), do thus and so. Yes, in this small aspect you have understood Me.

The privilege of knowing how, painfully, to frame answerable questions, answers which will lead him to more, insights and better questions as far as his mind can manage and his own life lasts. It is what he wants more than anything in the world to do, always has.

And these people stand in his way. Somehow, some way, he must pacify them. He must frame a project they will buy.

He plods back toward the laboratory cellars, nodding absently at students, revolving various quasi-respectable schemes. What he really wants to do is too foggy to explain yet; he wants to explore the capacity of animals to *anticipate*, to gain some knowledge of the wave-front of expectations that they must build up, even in the tiniest heads. He thinks it might even be useful, might illuminate the labors of the human infant learning its world. But that will have to wait. Welch wouldn't tolerate the idea that animals have mental maps. Only old crazy Tolman had been allowed to think that, and he's dead.

He will have to think of something with Welch's favorite drive variables. What are they? And lots of statistics, he thinks, realizing he is grinning at a really pretty girl walking with that cow Polinski. Yes, why not use students? Something complicated with students—that doesn't cost much. And maybe sex differentials, say, in perception—or is that too far out?

A wailing sound alerts him to the fact that he has arrived at the areaway. A truck is offloading crates of cats, strays from the pound.

"Give a hand, Tilly! Hurry up!"

It's Sheila, holding the door for Jones and Smith. They want to get these out of sight quickly, he knows, before some student sees them. Those innocent in the rites of pain. He hauls a crate from the tailboard.

"There's a female in here giving birth," he tells Sheila. "Look." The female is at the bottom of a mess of twenty emaciated struggling brutes. One of them has a red collar.

"Hurry up, for Christ's sake." Sheila waves him on.

"But . . ."

When the crates have disappeared inside he does not follow the others in but leans on the railing, lighting a cigarette. The kittens have been eaten, there's nothing he can do. Funny, he always thought that females would be sympathetic to other females. Shows how much he knows about Life. Or is it that only certain types of people empathize? Or does it have to be trained in, or was it trained out of her? Mysteries, mysteries. Maybe she is really compassionate somewhere inside, toward something. He hopes so, resolutely putting away a fantasy of injecting Sheila with reserpine and applying experimental stimuli.

He becomes aware that the door has been locked from the inside; they have all left through the front. It's getting late. He moves away too, remembering that this is the long holiday weekend. Armistice Day. Would it were—he scoffs at himself for the bathos. But he frowns, too; long weekends usually mean nobody goes near the lab. Nothing gets fed or watered. Well, three days—not as bad as Christmas week.

Last Christmas week he had roused up from much-needed sleep beside a sky-high mound of term papers and hitchhiked into town to check the labs. It had been so bad, so needless. The poor brutes dying in their thirst and hunger, eating metal, each other. Great way to celebrate Christmas.

But he will have to stop that kind of thing, he knows. Stop it. Preferably starting now. He throws down the cigarette stub, quickens his stride to purposefulness. He will collect his briefcase of exam papers from the library where he keeps it to avoid the lab smell and get on home and get at it. The bus is bound to be jammed.

Home is an efficiency in a suburban high-rise. He roots in his moldy fridge, carries a sandwich and ale to the dinette that is his desk. He has eighty-one exams to grade; junior department members get the monster classes. It's a standard multiple-choice thing, and he has a help—a theatrically guarded manila template he can lay over the sheets with slots giving the correct response. By just running down them he sums an arithmetical grade. Good. Munching, he lays out the first mimeoed wad.

But as he starts to lay it on the top page he sees—oh, no!—somebody has scrawled instead of answering Number 6. It's that fat girl, that bright bum Polinsky. And she hasn't marked answers by 7 or 8 either. Damn her fat female glands; he squints at the infantile uncials: "I won't mark this because its smucky! Read it, Dr. Lipshitz." She even has his name wrong.

Cursing himself, he scrutinizes the question. "Fixed versus variable reinforcement is called a—" Oh yes, he remembers that one. Bad grammar on top of bad psychology. Why can't they dump these damn obsolete things? Because the office wants grade intercomparability for their records, that's why. Is Polinsky criticizing the language or the thought? Who knows. He leafs through the others, sees more scribbles. Oh, shit, they know I read them. They all know I don't mark them like I should. Sucker.

Grimly masticating the dry sandwich, he starts to read. At this rate he is working, he has figured out, for seventy-five cents an hour.

By midnight he isn't half through, but he knows he ought to break off and start serious thought about Welch's ultimatum. Next week all his classes start Statistical Methods; he won't have time to blow his nose, let alone think creatively.

He gets up for another ale, thinking, Statistical Methods, brrr. He respects them, he guesses. But he is incurably sloppy-minded, congenitally averse to ignoring any data that don't fit the curve. Factor analysis, multivariate techniques—all beautiful; why is he troubled by this primitive visceral suspicion that somehow it ends up proving what the experimenter wanted to show? No, not that, really. Something about qualities as opposed to quantities, maybe? That some statistically insignificant results *are* significant, and some significant ones . . . aren't? Or just basically that we don't know enough yet to use such ultraprecise weapons. That we should watch more, maybe. Watch and learn more and figure less. All right, call me St. Lipsitz.

Heating up a frozen egg roll, he jeers at himself for superstition. Face facts, Lipsitz. Deep down you don't really believe dice throws are independent. Psychology is not a field for people with personality problems.

Ignoring the TV yattering through the wall from next door, he sits down by the window to think. Do it, brain. Come up with the big one. Take some good testable hypothesis from somebody in the department, preferably something that involves electronic counting of food pellets, bar presses, latencies, defecations. And crank it all into printed score sheets with a good Fortran program.

But what the hell are they all working on? Reinforcement schedules, cerebral deficits, split brain, God knows only that it seems to produce a lot of dead animals. "The subjects were sacrificed." They insist on saying that. He has been given a lecture when he called it "killing." Sacrificed, like to a god. Lord of the Flies, maybe.

He stares out at the midnight streets, thinking of his small black-and-white friends, his cozy community in the alcove. Nursing their offspring, sniffing the monkeys, munching apples, dreaming ratly dreams. He likes rats, which surprises him. Even the feral form, Rattus rattus itself; he would like to work with wild ones. Rats are vicious, they say. But people know only starving rats. Anything starving is "vicious." Beloved beagle eats owner on fourth day.

And his rats are, he blushingly muses, affectionate. They nestle in his hands, teeteringly ride his shoulder, display humor. If only they had fluffy tails, he thinks. The tail is the problem. People think squirrels are cute. They're only overdressed rats. Maybe I could do something with the perceptual elements of "cuteness," carry on old Tinbergen's work?

Stop it.

He pulls himself up; this isn't getting anywhere. A terrible panorama unrolls before his inner eye. On the one hand the clean bright professional work he should be doing, he with those thousands of government dollars invested in his doctorate, his grant—and on the other, what he is really doing. His cluttered alcove full of irregular rodents, his tiny, doomed effort to . . . what? To live amicably and observantly with another species? To understand trivial behaviors? Crazy. Spending all his own money, saving everybody's cripples—God, half his cages aren't even experimentally justifiable!

His folly. Suddenly it sickens him. He stands up, thinking, It's a stage you go through. I'm a delayed adolescent. Wake up, grow up. They're only animals. Get with it.

Resolve starts to form in him. Opening another ale can, he lets it grow. This whole thing is no good, he knows that. So what if he does prove that animals learn better if they're treated differently—what earthly use is that? Don't we all know it anyway? Insane. Time I braced up. All right. Ale in hand, he lets the resolve bloom.

He will go down there and clean out the whole mess, right now.

Kill all his rats, wipe the whole thing off. Clear the decks. That done, he'll be able to think; he won't be locked into the past.

The department will be delighted, Doctor Welch will be delighted. Nobody believed his thing was anything but a waste of time. All right, Lipsitz. Do it. Now, tonight.

Yes.

But first he will have something analgesic, strengthening. Not ale, not a toke. That bottle of—what is it, absinthe?—that crazy girl gave him last year. Yes, here it is back of the roach-killer he never used either. God knows what it's supposed to do, it's wormwood, something weird.

"Fix me," he tells it, sucking down a long liquorice-flavored draft. And goes out, bottle in pocket.

It has, he thinks, helped. He is striding across the campus now; all the long bus ride his resolve hasn't wavered. A quiet rain is falling. It must be two in the morning, but he's used to the spooky empty squares. He has often sneaked down here at odd hours to water and feed the brutes. The rain is moving strange sheens of shadow on the old tenement block, hissing echoes of the lives that swirled here once. At the cellar entrance he stops for another drink, finds the bottle clabbered with carrot chunks. Wormwood and Vitamin C, very good.

He dodges down and unlocks, bracing for the stench. The waste cans are full—cats that didn't make it, no doubt. Inside is a warm rustling reek.

When he finds the light, a monkey lets out one eerie

whoop and all sounds stop. Sunrise at midnight; most of these experimental subjects are nocturnal.

He goes in past the crowded racks, his eye automatically checking levels in the hundreds of water bottles. Okay, okay, all okay . . . What's this? He stops by Sheila's hamster tier. A bottle is full to the top. But there's a corpse by the wire, and the live ones look bedraggled. Why? He jerks up the bottle. Nothing comes out of the tube. It's blocked. Nobody has checked it for who knows how long. Perishing of thirst in there, with the bottle full.

He unblocks it, fishes out the dead, watches the little beasts crowd around. How does Sheila report this? Part of an experimental group was, uh, curtailed. On impulse he inserts some carrots too, inserts more absinthe into himself. He knows he is putting off what he has come here to do.

All right, get at it.

He stomps past a cage of baby rabbits with their eyes epoxyed shut, somebody's undergraduate demonstration of perceptual learning, and turns on the light over the sinks. All dirty with hanks of skin and dog offal. Why the hell can't they clean up after themselves? We are scientists. Too lofty. He whooshes with the power hose, which leaks. Nobody cares enough even to bring a washer. He will bring one. No, he won't! He's going to be doing something different from here on in.

But first of all he has to get rid of all this. Sacrifice his subjects. His ex-subjects. Where's my ether?

He finds it back of the mops, has another snort of the cloudy liquor to fortify himself while he sets up his killing jars. He has evolved what he thinks is the decentest way: an ether pad under a grill to keep their feet from being burned by the stuff.

The eight jars are in a row on the sink. He lifts down a cage of elderly females, the grandmothers of his present group. They cluster at the front, trustfully expectant. Oh God; he postpones murder long enough to give them some carrot, deals out more to every cage in the rack so they'll have time to eat. Tumult of rustling, hopping, munching.

All right. He goes back to the sink and pours in the ether, keeping the lids tight. Then he reaches in the holding cage and scoops up a soft female in each hand. Quick: He pops them both in one jar, rescrews the lid. He has this fatuous belief that the companionship helps a little. They convulse frantically, are going limp before he has the next pair in theirs. Next. Next. Next . . . It takes five minutes to be sure of death.

This will be, he realizes, a long night.

He lifts down another cage, lifts up his bottle, leaning with his back to the jars to look at his rack, his little city of rats. My troops. My pathetic troops. An absinthe trip flashes through his head of himself leading his beasts against his colleagues, against the laughing pain-givers. Jones having his brain reamed by a Dachshund pup. A kitten in a surgical smock shaving Sheila, wow. Stop it!

His eye has been wandering over the bottom cages. The mothers have taken the goodies in to their young; interesting to see what goes on in there, maybe if he used infra-red—stop that, too. A lab is not a zoo. Down in one dark back cage he can see the carrot is still there. Where's Snedecor, the old brain-damaged male? Why hasn't he come for it? Is the light bothering him?

Lipsitz turns off the top lights, goes around to the side to check. Stooping, he peers into the gloom. Something funny down there—good grief, the damn cage is busted, it's rotted through the bottom. Where's old Sneddles?

The ancient cage rack has wheels. Lipsitz drags one end forward, revealing Stygian darkness behind. In prehistoric times there was a coal chute there. And there's something back here now, on the heap of bags by the old intake.

Lipsitz frowns, squints; the lab lights behind him seem to be growing dim and gaseous. The thing—the thing has black and white patches. Is it moving?

He retreats to the drainboard, finds his hand on the

bottle. Yes. Another short one. What's wrong with the lights? The fluorescents have developed filmy ectoplasm, must be chow dust. This place is a powder keg. The monkeys are still as death too. That's unusual. In fact everything is dead quiet except for an odd kind of faint clicking, which he realizes is coming from the dark behind the rack. An animal. Some animal has got out and been living back there, that's all it is.

All right, Lipsitz: Go see.

But he delays, aware that the absinthe has replaced his limbs with vaguer, dreamlike extensions. The old females on the drainboard watch him alertly; the dead ones in the jars watch nothing. All his little city of rats has stopped moving, is watching him. Their priest of pain. This is a temple of pain, he thinks. A small shabby dirty one. Maybe its dirt and squalor are better so, more honest. A charnel house shouldn't look pretty, like a clean kitchen. All over the country, the world, the spotless knives are slicing, the trained minds devising casual torments in labs so bright and fair you could eat off their floors. Auschwitz, Belsen were neat. With flowers. Only the reek of pain going up to the sky, the empty sky. But people don't think animals' pain matters. They didn't think my people's pain mattered either, in the death camps a generation back. It's all the same, endless agonies going up unheard from helpless things. And all for what?

Maybe somewhere there is a reservoir of pain, he muses. Waiting to be filled. When it is full, will something rise from it? Something created and summoned by torment? Inhuman, an alien superthing . . . He knows he is indulging drunkenness. The clicking has grown louder.

Go and look at the animal, Lipsitz.

He goes, advances on the dark alcove, peering down, hearing the click-click-click. Suddenly he recognizes it: the tooth-click a rat makes in certain states of mind. Not threatening at all, it must be old Sneddles in there. Heartened, he pulls a dim light bulb forward on its string—and sees the thing plain, while the lab goes unreal around him.

What's lying back there among the Purina bags is an incredible whorl—a tangle of rat legs, rat heads, rat bodies, rat tails intertwined in a great wheellike formation, *joined* somehow abnormally rat to rat—a huge rat pie, heaving, pulsing, eyes reflecting stress and pain. Quite horrible, really; the shock of it is making him fight for breath. And it is not all laboratory animals; he can see the agouti coats of feral rats mixed in among it. Have wild rats come in here to help form this gruesome thing?

And at that moment, hanging to the light bulb, he knows what he is seeing. He has read in the old lore, the ancient grotesque legends of rat and man.

He is looking at a Rat King.

Medieval records were full of them, he recalls dimly. Was it Württemberg? *"They are monstrously Joynt, yet Living . . . It can by no way be Separated, and screamed much in the Fyre."* Apparitions that occurred at times of great attack on the rats. Some believed that the rat armies had each their king of this sort, who directed them. And they were sometimes connected to or confused with King Rats of still another kind: gigantic animals with eyes of fire and gold chains on their necks.

Lipsitz stares, swaying on the light cord. The tangled mass of the Rat King remains there clicking faintly, pulsing, ambiguously agonized among the sacks. His other hand seems to be holding the bottle; good. He takes a deep pull, his eyes rolling to fix the ghastliness, wondering what on earth he will do. "I can't," he mumbles aloud, meaning the whole thing, the whole bloody thing. "*I can't* . . ."

He can do his own little business, kill his animals, wind up his foolishness, get out. But he cannot—can not—be expected to cope with this, to abolish this revenant from time, this perhaps supernatural horror. For which he feels obscurely, hideously to blame. It's my fault, I . . .

He realizes he is weeping thinly, his eyes are running. Whether it's for the animals or himself he doesn't know; he knows only that he can't stand it, can't take any of it any more. And now *this.*

"No!" Meaning, really, the whole human world. Dizzily he blinks around at the jumbled darkness, trying to regain his wits, feeling himself a random mote of protesting life in an insignificant fool-killer. Slowly his eyes come back to the monstrous, pitiable rat pie. It seems to be weakening; the click has lost direction. His gaze drifts upward, into the dark shadows.

—And he is quite unsurprised, really, to meet eyes looking back. Two large round animal eyes deep in the darkness, at about the level of his waist, the tapetums reflecting pale vermilion fire.

He stares; the eyes shift right, left, calmly in silence, and then the head advances. He sees the long wise muzzle, the vibrissae, the tuned shells of the ears. Is there a gold collar? He can't tell; but he can make out the creature's forelimbs now, lightly palping the bodies or body of the Rat King. And the tangled thing is fading, shrinking away. It was perhaps its conjoined forces which strove and suffered to give birth to this other—the King himself.

"Hello," Lipsitz whispers idiotically, feeling no horror any more but emotion of a quite other kind. The big warm presence before him surveys him. Will he be found innocent? He licks his lips; they have come at last, he thinks. They have risen; they are going to wipe all this out. Me, too? But he does not care; a joy he can't possibly control rises in him as he sees gold glinting on the broad chest fur. He licks his dry lips again, swallows.

"Welcome. Your Majesty."

The Beast-King makes no response; the eyes leave him and go gravely toward the aisles beyond. Involuntarily Lipsitz backs aside. The King's vibrissae are fanning steadily, bringing the olfactory news, the quiet tooth-click starts. When the apparition comes forward a pace Lipsitz is deeply touched to see the typical half hop, the ratly carriage. The King's coat is lustrous gray-brown, feral pelage. Of course. It is a natural male, too; he smiles timidly, seeing that the giant body has the familiar long hump, the heavy rear-axle loading. Is old Snedecor translated into some particle of this wonder? The cellar is unbreathing, hushed except for the meditative click-click from the King.

"You, you are going to . . ." Lipsitz tries but is struck dumb by the sense of something happening all around him. Invisible, inaudible—but tangible as day. An emergence, yes! In the rooms beyond they are emerging, coming out from the score upon score of cages, boxes, pens, racks, shackles and wires—all of them emerging, coming to the King. All of them, blinded rabbits, mutilated hamsters, damaged cats and rats and brain-holed rhesus quietly knuckling along, even the paralyzed dogs moving somehow, coming toward their King.

And at this moment Lipsitz realizes the King is turning too, the big brown body is wheeling, quite normally away from him, going away toward the deeper darkness in the end of the coal bay. They are leaving him!

"Wait!" He stumbles forward over the dead rat pie; he cannot bear to lose this. "Please . . ."

Daring all, he reaches out and touches the flank of the magical beast, expecting he knows not what. The flank is warm, is solid! The King glances briefly back at him, still moving away. Boldly Lipsitz strides closer, comes alongside, his hand now resting firmly on the withers as they go.

But they are headed straight at what he knows is only wall, though he can see nothing. The cellar ends there. No matter—he will not let go of the magic, no, and he steps out beside the moving King, thinking, I am an animal too!—And finds at the last instant that his averted, flinching head is moving through dark nothing, through a blacker emptiness where the King is leading—they are going, going out.

Perhaps an old sewer, he thinks, lurching along beside the big benign presence, remembering tales of forgotten tunnels under this old city, into which the new subway has bored. Yes, that's what it must be. He is finding he can see again in a pale ghostly way, can now walk upright. His left hand is tight on the shoulders of the calmly pacing beast, feeling the living muscles play beneath the fur, bringing him joy and healing. Where are the others?

He dares a quick look back and sees them. They are coming. The dim way behind is filled with quiet beasts, moving together rank on rank as far as he can sense, animals large and small. He can hear their peaceful rustling now. And they are not only the beasts of his miserable lab, he realizes, but a torrent of others—he has glimpsed goats, turtles, a cow, raccoon, skunks, an opossum and what appeared as a small monkey riding on a limping spaniel. Even birds are there, hopping and fluttering above!

My God, it is everything, he thinks. It is Hamlin in reverse; all the abused ones, the gentle ones, are leaving the world. He risks another glance back and thinks he can see a human child too and maybe an old person among the throng, all measuredly, silently moving together in the dimness. An endless host going, going out at last, going away. And he is feeling their emanation, the gentleness of it, the unspeaking warmth. He is happier than he has been ever in his life.

"You're taking us away," he says to the King-Beast beside him. "The ones who can't cut it. We're all leaving for good, isn't that it?"

There is no verbal answer; only a big-stemmed ear swivels to him briefly as the King goes gravely on. Lipsitz needs no speech, no explanation. He simply walks alongside letting the joy rise in him. Why had it always been forbidden to be gentle? he wonders. Did they really see it as a threat, to have hated us so? But that is all over now, all over and gone, he is sure, although he has no slightest idea where this may be leading, this procession into chthonian infinity. For this moment it is enough to feel the silent communion, the reassurance rising through him from his hand on the flank of the great spirit-beast. The flank is totally solid; he can feel all the workings of life; it is the body of a real animal. But it is also friendship beyond imagining; he has never known anything as wonderful as this communion, not sex or sunsets or even the magic hour on his first bike. It is as if everything is all right now, will be all right forever—griefs he did not even know he carried are falling from him, leaving him light as smoke.

Crippled, he had been; crippled from the years of bearing it, not just the lab, the whole thing. Everything. He can hardly believe the relief. A vagrant thought brushes him: Who will remain? If there is anything to care for, to be comforted, who will care? He floats it away, concentrating on the comfort that emanates from the strange life at his side, the myth-beast ambling in the most ordinary way through this dark conduit, which is now winding down, or perhaps up and down, he cannot tell.

The paving under his feet looks quite commonplace, damp and cracked. Beside him the great rat's muscles bunch and stretch as each hind leg comes under; he glances back and smiles to see the King's long ring-scaled tail curve right, curve left, carried in the relaxed-alert mode. No need for fluffy fur now. He is, he realizes, going into mysteries. Inhuman mysteries, perhaps. He doesn't care. He is among his kind. Where they are going he will go. Even to inhumanity, even alone.

But he is not, he realizes as his eyes adapt more and more, alone after all! A human figure is behind him on the far side of the King, quietly threading its way forward, overtaking him. A girl—is it a girl? Yes. He can scarcely make her out, but as she comes closer still he sees with growing alarm that it is a familiar body—it could be, oh God, it is! Sheila.

Not *Sheila,* here! No, no.

But light-footed, she has reached him, is walking

even with him, stretching out her hand, too, to touch the moving King.

And then to his immense, unspeakable relief he sees that she is of course not Sheila—how could it be? Not Sheila at all, only a girl of the same height, with the same dove-breasted close-coupled curves that speak to his desire, the same heavy dark mane. Her head turns toward him across the broad back of the King, and he sees that although her features are like Sheila's, the face is wholly different, open, informed with innocence. An Eve in this second morning of the world. Sheila's younger sister, perhaps, he wonders dazedly, seeing that she is looking at him now, that her lips form a gentle smile.

"Hello," he cannot help whispering, fearful to break the spell, to inject harsh human sound into his progress. But the spell does not break; indeed, the girl's face comes clearer. She puts up a hand to push her hair back, the other firmly on the flank of the King.

"Hello." Her voice is very soft but in no way fragile. She is looking at him with the eyes of Sheila, but eyes so differently warmed and luminous that he wants only to gaze delighted as they pass to whatever destination; he is so overwhelmed to meet a vulnerable human soul in those lambent brown eyes. A soul? he thinks, feeling his unbodied feet step casually, firmly on the way to eternity, perhaps. What an unfashionable word. He is not religious, he does not believe there are any gods or souls, except as a shorthand term denoting—what?—compassion or responsibility, all that. And so much argument about it all, too; his mind is momentarily invaded by a spectral horde of old debating scholars, to whom he had paid less than no attention in his classroom days. But he is oddly prepared now to hear the girl recite conversationally, "There is no error more powerful in leading feeble minds astray from the straight path of virtue than the supposition that the soul of brutes is of the same nature as our own."

"Descartes," he guesses.

She nods, smiling across the big brown shape between them. The King's great leaflike ears have flickered to their interchange, returned to forward hold.

"He started it all, didn't he?" Lipsitz says, or perhaps only thinks. "That they're robots, you can do anything to them. Their pain doesn't count. But we're animals too," he added somberly, unwilling to let even a long-dead philosopher separate him from the flow of this joyous River. Or was it that? A faint disquiet flicks him, is abolished.

She nods again; the sweet earnest woman-face of her almost kills him with love. But as he stares the disquiet flutters again; is there beneath her smile a transparency, a failure of substance—even a sadness, as though she was moving to some inexorable loss? No; it is all right. It is.

"Where are we going, do you know?" he asks, against some better judgment. The King-Beast flicks an ear; but Lipsitz must know, now.

She smiles, unmistakably mischievous, considering him.

"To where all the lost things go," she says. "It's very beautiful. Only . . ." She falls silent.

"Only what?" He is uneasy again, seeing she has turned away, is walking with her small chin resolute. Dread grows in him, cannot be dislodged. The moments of simple joy are past now; he fears that he still has some burden. It is perhaps a choice? Whatever it is, it's looming around him or in him as they go—an impending significance he wishes desperately to avoid. It is not a thinning out nor an awakening; he clutches hard at the strong shoulders of the King, the magical leader, feels his reassuring warmth. All things are in the lotus . . But loss impends.

"Only what?" he asks again, knowing he must and must not. Yes; he is still there, is moving with them to the final refuge. The bond holds. "The place where lost things go is very beautiful, only what?"

"Do you really want to know?" she asks him with the light of the world in her face.

It *is* a choice, he realizes, trembling now. It is not for free, it's not that simple. But can't I just stop this, just go on? Yes, he can—he knows it. Maybe. But he hears his human voice persist.

"Only *what?*"

"Only it isn't real," she says. And his heart breaks.

And suddenly it is all breaking too—a fearful thin wave of emptiness slides through him, sends him stumbling, his handhold lost. "No! Wait!" He reaches desperately; he can feel them still near him, feel their passage all around. "Wait . . ." He understands now, understands with searing grief that it really is the souls of things, and perhaps himself that are passing, going away forever. They have stood it as long as they can and now they are leaving. The pain has culminated in this, that they leave us—leave me, leave me behind in a clockwork Cartesian world in which nothing will mean anything forever.

"Oh, wait," he cries in dark nowhere, unable to bear the loss, the still-living comfort, passing away. *Only it isn't real,* what does that mean? Is it the choice, that the reality is that I must stay behind and try, and try?

He doesn't know, but can only cry, "No, please take me! Let me come too!" staggering after them through unreality, feeling them still there, still possible, ahead, around. It is wrong; he is terrified somewhere that he is failing, doing wrong. But his human heart can only yearn for the sweetness, for the great benevolent King-Beast so surely leading, to feel again their joy. "Please, I want to go with you—"

—And yes! For a last instant he has it; he touches again the warmth and life, sees the beautiful lost face that was and wasn't Sheila—they are there! And he tries with all his force crazily to send himself after them, to burst from his skin, his life if need be—only to share again that gentleness. "*Take* me!"

But it is no good—he can't; they have vanished and he has fallen kneeling on dank concrete, nursing his head in empty shaking hands. It was in vain, and it was wrong. Or was it? his fading thought wonders as he feels himself black out. Did something of myself go too, fly to its selfish joy? He does not know.

. . . And will never know, as he returns to sodden consciousness, makes out that he is sprawled like a fool in the dirt behind his rat cages with the acid taste of wormwood sickly in his mouth and an odd dryness and lightness in his heart.

What the hell had he been playing at? That absinthe is a bummer, he thinks, picking himself up and slapping his clothes disgustedly. This filthy place, what a fool he'd been to think he could work here. And these filthy rats. There's something revolting back here on the floor, too. Leave it for posterity; he drags the rack back in place.

All right, get this over. Humming to himself, he turns the power hose on the messy floor, gives the stupid rats in their cages a blast too for good measure. There are his jars—but whatever had possessed him, trying to kill them individually like that? Hours it would take. He knows a simpler way if he can find a spare garbage can.

Good, here it is. He brings it over and starts pulling out cage after cage, dumping them all in together. Nests, babies, carrots, crap and all. Shrieks, struggling. Tough tit, friends. The ether can is almost full; he pours the whole thing over the crying mess and jams on the lid, humming louder. The can walls reverberate with teeth. Not quite enough gas, no matter.

He sits down on it and notices that a baby rat has run away hiding behind his shoe. Mechanical mouse, a stupid automaton. He stamps on its back and kicks it neatly under Sheila's hamster rack, wondering why Descartes has popped into his thoughts. There is no error more powerful—Shit with old D., let's think about Sheila. There is no error more powerful than the belief that some cunt can't be had. Somehow he feels sure that he will find that particular pussy-patch wide open to him any day now. As soon as his project gets under way.

Because he has an idea. (That absinthe wasn't all bad.) Oh yes. An idea that'll pin old Welch's ears back. In fact it may be too much for old Welch, too, quotes, commercial. Well, fuck old Welch, this is one project somebody will buy, that's for sure. Does the Mafia have labs? Ho ho, far out.

And fuck students too, he thinks genially, wrestling the can to the entrance, ignoring sounds from within. No more Polinskis, no more shit, teaching is for suckers. My new project will take care of that. Will there be a problem getting subjects? No—look at all the old walking carcasses they sell for dogfood. And there's a slaughterhouse right by the freeway, no problem at all. But he *will* need a larger lab.

He locks up, and briskly humming the rock version of "Anitra's Dance," he goes out into the warm rainy dawnlight, reviewing in his head the new findings on the mid-brain determinants of motor intensity.

It should be no trick at all to seat some electrodes that will make an animal increase the intensity of whatever it's doing. Like say, *running*. Speed it right up to max, run like it never ran before regardless of broken legs or what. What a natural! Surprising someone else hasn't started already.

And just as a cute hypothesis, he's pretty sure he could seal the implants damn near invisibly; he has a smooth hand with flesh. Purely hypothetical, of course. But suppose you used synthetics with, say, acid-release. That would be hard to pick up on X rays. H'mmm.

Of course, he doesn't know much about horses, but he learns fast. Grinning, he breaks into a jog to catch the lucky bus that has appeared down the deserted street. He has just recalled a friend who has a farm not fifty miles away. Wouldn't it be neat to run the pilot project using surplus Shetland ponies?

The Eyeflash Miracles

Gene Wolfe

Whenever I talk with science fiction readers I keep getting asked the same question: "Who do you think is the best science-fiction writer today?" I'm not sure why this is; maybe it's just because I edit this book which has "best" in its title, so people think I must have some sort of computerized rating system that provides me with point-scores for every story published.

I don't, so I've tended to waffle quite a bit in my answers. On Mondays I say it's Ursula Le Guin, on Tuesdays I say James Tiptree, on Wednesdays it may be John Varley, and so on. But lately I find that the name that comes to mind more often than any other is Gene Wolfe.

People usually look surprised, then think about it and decide I may be right.

That's typical of Wolfe's effect: he's a *sneaky*-good writer, one whose stories begin calmly and suck you in, then hit you between the eyes with some plot-twist you couldn't have expected. I remember a visit last year from Sidney Coleman, physicist and occasional book reviewer for *Fantasy and Science Fiction,* when he began reading Wolfe's "The Hero as Werwolf" and a third of the way through the story suddenly whooped with delight.

"That damned Gene Wolfe," he said. "He got me again."

"Let me guess," I said. "The corpse just sat up and asked, 'What are you going to do with me?' "

Sid nodded, still smiling, and went on reading even more avidly than before. (If you read *The Best Science Fiction of the Year #5,* in which that story was reprinted, you'll probably remember the scene.)

Gene Wolfe himself is a fiftyish Midwesterner of deceptively average demeanor; he looks like the sort of man from whom you'd happily buy a used insurance policy. But when you talk with him you quickly discover that he's so smart it's *scary,* and he's likely to rock you back on your heels with his wit. (The distinguishing characteristic of Gene's jokes is that you never get them fully till you're halfway through some totally inadequate reply, at which point you find yourself collapsing in helpless laughter.)

Besides "The Hero as Werwolf," he's written such memorable stories as "The Fifth Head of Cerberus" and "The Death of Dr. Island," the latter a Nebula Award winner, as well as a fine mainstream novel, *Peace*. His latest novella, included here, is a warm and flawlessly written story of a boy with wild talents who's an outcast in a future world regimented to Utopia. A familiar plot-situation . . . but you'll be surprised by the things he does with it.

"I cannot call him to mind."

—ANATOLE FRANCE, *The Procurator of Judea*

Little Tib heard the train coming while it was still a long way away, and he felt it in his feet. He stepped off the track onto a prestressed concrete tie, listening. Then he put one ear to the endless steel and listened to that sing, louder and louder. Only when he began to feel the ground shake under him did he lift his head at last and make his way down the embankment through the tall, prickly weeds, probing the slope with his stick.

The stick splashed water. He could not hear it because of the noise the train made roaring by; but he knew the feel of it, the kind of drag it made when he tried to move the end of the stick. He laid it down and felt with his hands where his knees would be when he knelt, and it felt all right. A little soft, but not broken glass. He knelt then and sniffed the water, and it smelled good and was cool to his fingers, so he drank, bending down and sucking up the water with his mouth, then splashing it on his face and the back of his neck.

"Say!" an authoritative voice called. "Say, you boy!"

Little Tib straightened up, picking up his stick again. He thought, This could be Sugarland. He said, "Are you a policeman, sir?"

"I am the superintendent."

That was almost as good. Little Tib tilted his head back so the voice could see his eyes. He had often imagined coming to Sugarland and how it would be there; but he had never considered just what it was he should say when he arrived. He said, "My card . . ." The train was still rumbling away, not too far off.

Another voice said: "Now don't you hurt that child." It was not authoritative. There was the sound of responsibility in it.

"You ought to be in school, young man," the first voice said. "Do you know who I am?"

Little Tib nodded. "The superintendent."

"That's right, I'm the superintendent. I'm Mr. Parker himself. Your teacher has told you about me, I'm sure."

"Now don't hurt that child," the second voice said again. "He never did hurt you."

"Playing hooky. I understand that's what the children call it. We never use such a term ourselves, of course. You will be referred to as an absentee. What's your name?"

"George Tibbs."

"I see. I am Mr. Parker, the superintendent. This is my valet; his name is Nitty."

"Hello," Little Tib said.

"Mr. Parker, maybe this absentee boy would like to have something to eat. He looks to me like he has been absentee a long while."

"Fishing," Mr. Parker said. "I believe that's what most of them do."

"You can't see, can you?" A hand closed on Little Tib's arm. The hand was large and hard, but it did not bear down. "You can cross right here. There's a rock in the middle—step on that."

Little Tib found the rock with his stick and put one foot there. The hand on his arm seemed to lift him across. He stood on the rock for a moment with his stick in the water, touching bottom to steady himself. "Now a great big step." His shoe touched the soft bank on the other side. "We got a camp right over here. Mr. Parker, don't you think this absentee boy would like a sweet roll?"

Little Tib said, "Yes, I would."

"I would too," Nitty told him.

"Now, young man, why aren't you in school?"

"How is he going to see the board?"

"We have special facilities for the blind, Nitty. At Grovehurst there is a class tailored to make allowance for their disability. I can't at this moment recall the name of the teacher, but she is an exceedingly capable young woman."

Little Tib asked, "Is Grovehurst in Sugarland?"

"Grovehurst is in Martinsburg," Mr. Parker told him. "I am superintendent of the Martinsburg Public School System. How far are we from Martinsburg now, Nitty?"

"Two, three hundred kilometers, I guess."

"We will enter you in that class as soon as we reach Martinsburg, young man."

Nitty said, "We're going to Macon—I keep on tellin' you."

"Your papers are all in order, I suppose? Your grade and attendance records from your previous school? Your withdrawal permit, birth certificate, and your retinal pattern card from the Federal Reserve?"

Little Tib sat mute. Someone pushed a sticky pastry into his hands, but he did not raise it to his mouth.

"Mr. Parker, I don't think he's got papers."

"That is a serious—"

"Why he got to have papers? He ain't no dog!"

Little Tib was weeping. "I see!" Mr. Parker said. "He's blind; Nitty, I think his retinas have been destroyed. Why, he's not really here at all."

" 'Course he's here."

"A ghost. We're seeing a ghost, Nitty. Sociologically he's not real—he's been deprived of existence."

"I never in my whole life seen a ghost."

"You dumb bastard," Mr. Parker exploded.

"You don't have to talk to me like that, Mr. Parker."

"You dumb bastard. All my life there's been nobody around but dumb bastards like you." Mr. Parker was weeping too. Little Tib felt one of his tears, large and hot, fall on his hand. His own sobbing slowed, then faded away. It was outside his experience to hear grown people—men—cry. He took a bite from the roll he had been given, tasting the sweet, sticky icing and hoping for a raisin.

"Mr. Parker," Nitty said softly. "Mr. Parker."

After a time, Mr. Parker said, "Yes."

"He—this boy George—might be able to get them,

Mr. Parker. You recall how you and me went to the building that time? We looked all around it a long while. And there was that window, that old window with the iron over it and the latch broken. I pushed on it and you could see the glass move in a little. But couldn't either of us get between those bars."

"This boy is blind, Nitty," Mr. Parker said.

"Sure he is, Mr. Parker. But you know how dark it was in there. What is a man going to do? Turn on the lights? No, he's goin' to take a little bit of a flashlight and put tape or something over the end till it don't make no more light than a lightnin' bug. A blind person could do better with no light than a seeing one with just a little speck like that. I guess he's used to bein' blind by now. I guess he knows how to find his way around without eyes."

A hand touched Little Tib's shoulder. It seemed smaller and softer than the hand that had helped him across the creek. "He's crazy," Mr. Parker's voice said. "That Nitty. He's crazy. I'm crazy, I'm the one. But he's crazier than I am."

"He could do it, Mr. Parker. See how thin he is."

"Would you do it?" Mr. Parker asked.

Little Tib swallowed a wad of roll. "Do what?"

"Get something for us."

"I guess so."

"Nitty, build a fire," Mr. Parker said. "We won't be going any farther tonight."

"Won't be goin' this way at *all,*" Nitty said.

"You see, George," Mr. Parker said. "My authority has been temporarily abrogated. Sometimes I forget that."

Nitty chuckled somewhere farther away than Little Tib had thought he was. He must have left very silently.

"But when it is restored, I can do all the things I said I would do for you: get you into a special class for the blind, for example. You'd like that, wouldn't you, George?"

"Yes." A whippoorwill called far off to Little Tib's left, and he could hear Nitty breaking sticks.

"Have you run away from home, George?"

"Yes," Little Tib said again.

"Why?"

Little Tib shrugged. He was ready to cry again. Something was thickening and tightening in his throat, and his eyes had begun to water.

"I think I know why," Mr. Parker said. "We might even be able to do something about that."

"*Here* we are," Nitty called. He dumped his load of sticks, rattling, more or less in front of Little Tib.

Later that night Little Tib lay on the ground with half of Nitty's blanket over him, and half under him. The fire was crackling not too far away. Nitty said the smoke would help to drive the mosquitoes off. Little Tib pushed the heels of his hands against his eyes and saw red and yellow flashes like a real fire. He did it again, and there was a gold nugget against a field of blue. Those were the last things he had been able to see for a long time, and he was afraid, each time he summoned them up, that they would not come. On the other side of the fire Mr. Parker breathed the heavy breath of sleep.

Nitty bent over Little Tib, smoothing his blanket, then pressing it in against his sides. "It's okay," Little Tib said.

"You're goin' back to Martinsburg with us," Nitty said.

"I'm going to Sugarland."

"After. What you want to go there for?"

Little Tib tried to explain about Sugarland, but could not find words. At last he said, "In Sugarland they know who you are."

"Guess it's too late then for me. Even if I found somebody knew who I was I wouldn't be them no more."

"You're Nitty," Little Tib said.

"That's right. You know I used to go out with those gals a lot. Know what they said? Said, 'You're the custodian over at the school, aren't you?' Or, 'You're the one that did for Buster Johnson.' Didn't none of them know who I was. Only ones that did was the little children."

Little Tib heard Nitty's clothes rustle as he stood up, then the sound his feet made walking softly away. He wondered if Nitty was going to stay awake all night; then he heard him lie down.

His father had him by the hand. They had left the hanging-down train, and were walking along one of the big streets. He could see. He knew he should not have been noticing that particularly, but he did, and far behind it somewhere was knowing that if he woke up he would not see. He looked into store windows, and he could see big dolls like girls' dolls wearing fur coats. Every hair on every coat stood out drenched with light. He looked at the street and could see all the cars like big, bright-colored bugs. "Here," Big Tib said; they went into a glass thing that spun them around and dumped them out inside a building, then into an elevator all made of glass that climbed the inside wall almost like an ant, starting and stopping like an ant did. "We should buy one of these," Little Tib said. "Then we wouldn't have to climb the steps."

He looked up and saw that his father was crying. He took out his, Little Tib's, own card and put it in the machine, then made Little Tib sit down in the seat and look at the bright light. The machine was a man in a white coat who took off his glasses and said, "We don't know who this child is, but he certainly isn't anyone." "Look at the bright light again, Little Tib," his father said, and something in the way he said it told Little Tib that the man in the white coat was much stronger than he was. He looked at the bright light and tried to catch himself from falling.

And woke up. It was so dark that he wondered for a minute where the bright light went. Then he remembered. He rolled over a little and put his hand out toward the fire until he could feel some heat. He could hear it too when he listened. It crackled and snapped, but not very much. He lay the way he had been before, then turned over on his back. A train went past, and after a while an owl hooted.

He could see here too. Something inside him told him how lucky he was, seeing twice in one night. Then he forgot about it, looking at the flowers. They were big and round, growing on long stalks, and had yellow petals and dark brown centers, and when he was not looking at them, they whirled around and around. They could see him, because they all turned their faces toward him, and when he looked at them they stopped.

For a long way he walked through them. They came a little higher than his shoulder.

Then the city came down like a cloud and settled on a hill in front of him. As soon as it was there it pretended that it had been there all the time, but Little Tib could feel it laughing underneath. It had high, green walls that sloped in as they went up. Over the top of them were towers, much taller, that belonged to the city. Those were green too, and looked like glass.

Little Tib began to run, and was immediately in front of the gates. These were very high, but there was a window in them, just over his head, that the gate-man talked through. "I want to see the king," Little Tib said, and the gate-man reached down with a long, strong arm and picked him up and pulled him through the little window and set him down again inside. "You have to wear these," he said, and took out a pair of toy glasses like the ones Little Tib had once had in his doctor set. But when he put them on Little Tib, they were not glasses at all, only lines painted on his face, circles around his eyes joined over his nose. The gate-man held up a mirror to show him, and he had the sudden, dizzying sensation of looking at his own face.

A moment later he was walking through the city. The houses had their gardens sidewise—running up the walls so that the trees thrust out like flagpoles. The water in the birdbaths never ran out until a bird landed in it. Then a fine spray of drops fell to the street like rain.

The palace had a wall too, but it was made by trees holding hands. Little Tib went through a gate of bowing elephants and saw a long, long stairway. It was so long and so high that it seemed that there was no palace at all, only the steps going up and up forever into the clouds, and then he remembered that the whole city had come down out of the clouds. The king was coming down those stairs, walking very slowly. She was a beautiful woman, and although she did not look at all like her, Little Tib knew that she was his mother.

He had been seeing so much while he was asleep that when he woke up he had to remember why it was so dark. Somewhere in the back of his mind there was still the idea that waking should be light and sleep dark, and not the other way around. Nitty said: "You ought to wash your face. Can you find the water all right?"

Little Tib was still thinking of the king, with her dress all made of Christmas-tree stuff; but he could. He splashed water on his face and arms while he thought about how to tell Nitty about his dream. By the time he had finished, everything in the dream was gone except for the king's face.

Most of the time Mr. Parker sounded like he was important and Nitty was not, but when he said, "Are we going to eat this morning, Nitty?" it was the other way around.

"We eat on the train," Nitty told him.

"We are going to catch a train, George, to Martinsburg," Mr. Parker told Little Tib.

Little Tib thought that the trains went too fast to be caught, but he did not say that.

"Should be one by here pretty soon," Nitty said. "They got to be going slow because there's a road crosses the tracks down there a way. They won't have no time to get the speed up again before they get here. You won't have to run—I'll just pick you up an' carry you."

A rooster crowed way off somewhere.

Mr. Parker said: "When I was a young man, George, everyone thought all the trains would be gone soon. They never said what would replace them, however. Later it was believed that it would be all right to have trains, provided they were extremely modern in appearance. That was accomplished, as I suppose you learned last year, by substituting aluminum, fiberglass, and magnesium for much of the steel employed previously. That not only changed the image of the trains to something acceptable, but saved a great deal of energy by reducing weight—the ostensible purpose of the cosmetic redesign." Mr. Parker paused, and Little Tib could hear the water running past the place where they were sitting, and the sound the wind made blowing the trees.

"There only remained the awkward business of the crews," Mr. Parker continued. "Fortunately it was found that mechanisms of the same type that had already displaced educators and others could be substituted for railway engineers and brakemen. Who would have believed that running a train was as routine and mechanical a business as teaching a class? Yet it proved to be so."

"Wish they would do away with those railroad police," Nitty said.

"You, George, are a victim of the same system," Mr. Parker continued. "It was the wholesale displacement of labor, and the consequent nomadism, that resulted in the present reliance on retinal patterns as means of identification. Take Nitty and me, for example. We are going to Macon—"

"We're goin' to Martinsburg, Mr. Parker," Nitty said. "This train we'll be catching will be going the *other* way. We're goin' to get into that building and let you program, you remember?"

"I was hypothesizing," Mr. Parker said. "We are going—say—to Macon. There we can enter a store, register our retinal patterns, and receive goods to be charged to the funds which will by then have accumulated in our social relief accounts. No other method of identification is so certain, or so adaptable to data processing techniques."

"Used to have money you just handed around," Nitty said.

"The emperors of China used lumps of silver stamped with an imperial seal," Mr. Parker told him. "But by restricting money solely—in the final analysis—to entries kept by the Federal Reserve Bank, the entire cost of printing and coining is eliminated; and of course control for tax purposes is complete. While for identification, retinal patterns are unsurpassed in every—"

Little Tib stopped listening. A train was coming. He could hear it far away, hear it go over a bridge somewhere, hear it coming closer. He felt around for his stick and got a good hold on it.

Then the train was louder, but the noise did not come as fast. He heard the whistle blow. Then Nitty was picking him up with one strong arm. There was a swoop and a jump and a swing, swing, swing, and they were on the train and Nitty set him down. "If you want to," Nitty said, "you can sit here at the edge and hang your feet over. But you be careful."

Little Tib was careful. "Where's Mr. Parker?"

"Laying down in the back. He's going to sleep—he sleeps a lot."

"Can he hear us?"

"You like sitting like this? This is one of my most favorite of all things to do. I know you can't see everything go by like I can, but I could tell you about it. You take right now. We are going up a long grade, with nothing but pinewoods on this side of the train. I bet you there is all kinds of animals in there. You like animals, George? Bears and big old cats."

"Can he hear us?" Little Tib asked again.

"I don't think so, because he usually goes to sleep right away. But it might be better to wait a little while, if you've got something you don't want him to hear."

"All right."

"Now there's one thing we've got to worry about. Sometimes there are railroad policemen on these trains. If someone is riding on them, they throw him off. I don't think they'd throw a little boy like you off, but they would throw Mr. Parker and me off. You they would probably take back with them and give over to the real police in the next town."

"They wouldn't want me," Little Tib said.

"How's that?"

"Sometimes they take me, but they don't know who I am. They always let me go again."

"I guess maybe you've been gone from home longer than what I thought. How long since you left your Mom and Dad?"

"I don't know."

"Must be some way of telling blind people. There's lots of blind people."

"The machine usually knows who blind people are. That's what they say. But it doesn't know me."

"They take pictures of your retinas—you know about that?"

Little Tib said nothing.

"That's the part inside your eye that sees the picture. If you think about your eye like it was a camera, you got a lens in the front, and then the film. Well, your retinas is the film. That's what they take a picture of. I guess yours is gone. You know what it is you got wrong with your eyes?"

"I'm blind."

"Yes, but you don't know what it is, do you, baby. Wish you could look out there now—we're going over a deep place; lots of trees, and rocks and water way down below."

"Can Mr. Parker hear us?" Little Tib asked again.

"Guess not. Looks like he's asleep by now."

"Who is he?"

"Like he told you. He's the superintendent; only they don't want him any more."

"Is he really crazy?"

"Sure. He's a dangerous man, too, when the fit comes on him. He got this little thing put into his head when he was superintendent to make him a better one—extra remembering and arithmetic, and things that would make him want to work more and do a good job. The school district paid for most of it; I don't know what you call them, but there's a lot of teenie little circuits in them."

"Didn't they take it out when he wasn't superintendent anymore?"

"Sure, but his head was used to it by then, I guess. Child, do you feel well?"

"I'm fine."

"You don't look so good. Kind of pale. I suppose it might just be that you washed off a lot of the dirt when I told you to wash that face. You think it could be that?"

"I feel all right."

"Here, let me see if you're hot." Little Tib felt Nitty's big, rough hand against his forehead. "You feel a bit hot to me."

"I'm not sick."

"Look there! You see that? There was a bear out there. A big old bear, black as could be."

"Probably it was a dog."

"You think I don't know a bear? It stood up and waved at us."

"Really, Nitty?"

"Well, not like a person would. It didn't say *bye-bye,* or *hi there.* But it held up one big old arm." Nitty's hands lifted Little Tib's right arm.

A strange voice, a lady's voice, Little Tib thought, said, "Hello there yourself." He heard the thump as somebody's feet hit the floor of the boxcar; then another thump as somebody else's did.

"Now wait a minute," Nitty said. "Now you look here."

"Don't get excited," another lady's voice told him.

"Don't you try to throw us off of this train. I got a little boy here, a little blind boy. He can't jump off no train."

Mr. Parker said, "What's going on here, Nitty?"

"Railroad police, Mr. Parker. They're going to make us jump off of this train."

Little Tib could hear the scraping sounds Mr. Parker made when he stood up, and wondered whether Mr. Parker was a big man or a little man, and how old he was. He had a pretty good idea about Nitty; but he was not sure of Mr. Parker, though he thought Mr. Parker was pretty young. He decided he was also medium-sized.

"Let me introduce myself," Mr. Parker said. "As superintendent, I am in charge of the three schools in the Martinsburg area."

"Hi," one of the ladies said.

"You will begin with the lower grades, as all of our new teachers do. As you gain seniority, you may move up if you wish. What are your specialties?"

"Are you playing a game?"

Nitty said: "He don't quite understand—he just woke up. You woke him up."

"Sure."

"You going to throw us off the train?"

"How far are you going?"

"Just to Howard. Only that far. Now you listen, this little boy is blind, and sick too. We want to take him to the doctor at Howard—he ran away from home."

Mr. Parker said, "I will not leave this school until I am ready. I am in charge of the entire district."

"Mr. Parker isn't exactly altogether well either," Nitty told the women.

"What has he been using?"

"He's just like that sometimes."

"He sounds like he's been shooting up on chalk."

Little Tib asked, "What's your name?"

"Say," Nitty said, "that's right. You know, I never

did ask that. This little boy here is telling me I'm not polite."

"I'm Alice," one of the ladies said.

"Mickie," said the other.

"But we don't want to know your names," Alice continued. "See, suppose someway they heard you were on the train—we'd have to say who you were."

"And where you were going," Mickie put in.

"Nice people like you—why do you want to be railroad police?"

Alice laughed. "What's a nice girl like you doing in a place like this? I've heard that one before."

"Watch yourself, Alice," Mickie said. "He's trying to make out."

Alice said, "What'd you three want to be 'boes for?"

"We didn't. 'Cept maybe for this little boy here. He run away from home because the part of his eyes that they take pictures of is gone, and his momma and daddy couldn't get benefits. At least, that's what I think. Is that right, George?"

Mr. Parker said, "I'll introduce you to your classes in a moment."

"Him and me used to be in the school," Nitty continued. "Had good jobs there, or so we believed. Then one day that big computer downtown says, 'Don't need you no more,' and out we goes."

"You don't have to talk funny for us," Mickie said.

"Well, that's a relief. I always do it a little, though, for Mr. Parker. It makes him feel better."

"What was your job?"

"Buildings maintenance. I took care of the heating plant, and serviced the teaching and cleaning machines, and did the electrical repair work generally."

"Nitty!" Little Tib called.

"I'm here, li'l boy. I won't go way."

"Well, we have to go," Mickie said. "They'll miss us pretty soon if we don't get back to patrolling this train. You fellows remember you promised you'd get off at Howard. And try not to let anyone see you."

Mr. Parker said, "You may rely on our cooperation."

Little Tib could hear the sound of the women's boots on the boxcar floor, and the little grunt Alice gave as she took hold of the ladder outside the door and swung herself out. Then there was a popping noise, as though someone had opened a bottle of soda, and a bang and clatter when something struck the back of the car.

His lungs and nose and mouth all burned. He felt a rush of saliva too great to contain. It spilled out of his lips and down his shirt; he wanted to run, and he thought of the old place, where the creek cut (cold as ice) under banks of milkweed and goldenrod. Nitty was yelling: "Throw it out! Throw it out!" And somebody, he thought it was Mr. Parker, ran full tilt into the side of the car. Little Tib was on the hill above the creek again, looking down across the bluebonnets toward the surging, glass-dark water, and a kite-flying west wind was blowing.

He sat down again on the floor of the boxcar. Mr. Parker must not have been hurt too badly, because he could hear him moving around, as well as Nitty.

"You kick it out, Mr. Parker?" Nitty said. "That was good."

"Must have been the boy. Nitty—"

"Yes, Mr. Parker."

"We're on a train . . . The railroad police threw a gas bomb to get us off. Is that correct?"

"That's true sure enough, Mr. Parker."

"I had the strangest dream. I was standing in the center corridor of the Grovehurst school, with my back leaning against the lockers. I could feel them."

"Yeah."

"I was speaking to two new teachers—"

"I know." Little Tib could feel Nitty's fingers on his face, and Nitty's voice whispered, "You all right?"

"—giving them the usual orientation talk. I heard something make a loud noise, like a rocket. I looked up then, and saw that one of the children had thrown a stink bomb—it was flying over my head, laying a trail of smoke. I went after it like I used to go after a ball when I was an outfielder in college, and I ran right into the wall."

"You sure did. Your face looks pretty bad, Mr. Parker."

"Hurts too. Look, there it is."

"Sure enough. Nobody kick it out after all."

"No. Here, feel it; it's still warm. I suppose a chemical burns to generate the gas."

"You want to feel, George? Here, you can hold it."

Little Tib felt the warm metal cylinder pressed into his hands. There was a seam down the side, like a Coca-Cola can, and a funny-shaped thing on top.

Nitty said, "I wonder what happened to all the gas."

"It blew out," Mr. Parker told him.

"It shouldn't of done that. They threw it good—got it right back in the back of the car. It shouldn't blow out that fast, and those things go on making gas for a long time."

"It must have been defective," Mr. Parker said.

"Must have been." There was no expression in Nitty's voice.

Little Tib asked, "Did those ladies throw it?"

"Sure did. Came down here and talked to us real nice first, then to get up on top of the car and do something like that."

"Nitty, I'm thirsty."

"Sure you are. Feel of him, Mr. Parker. He's hot."

Mr. Parker's hand was softer and smaller than Nitty's. "Perhaps it was the gas."

"He was hot before."

"There's no nurse's office on this train, I'm afraid."

"There's a doctor in Howard. I thought to get him to Howard . . ."

"We haven't anything in our accounts now."

Little Tib was tired. He lay down on the floor of the car, and heard the empty gas canister roll away, too tired to care.

". . . a sick child . . ." Nitty said. The boxcar

rocked under him, and the wheels made a rhythmic roar like the rushing of blood in the heart of a giantess.

He was walking down a narrow dirt path. All the trees, on both sides of the path, had red leaves, and red grass grew around their roots. They had faces, too, in their trunks, and talked to one another as he passed. Apples and cherries hung from their boughs.

The path twisted around little hills, all covered with the red trees. Cardinals hopped in the branches, and one fluttered to his shoulder. Little Tib was very happy; he told the cardinal, "I don't want to go away—ever. I want to stay here, forever. Walking down this path."

"You will, my son," the cardinal said. It made the sign of the cross with one wing.

They went around a bend, and there was a tiny little house ahead, no bigger than the box a refrigerator comes in. It was painted with red and white stripes, and had a pointed roof. Little Tib did not like the look of it, but he took a step nearer.

A full-sized man came out of the little house. He was made all of copper, so he was coppery-red all over, like a new pipe for the bathroom. His body was round, and his head was round too, and they were joined by a real piece of bathroom pipe. He had a big mustache stamped right into the copper, and he was polishing himself with a rag. "Who are you?" he said.

Little Tib told him.

"I don't know you," the copper man said. "Come closer so I can recognize you."

Little Tib came closer. Something was hammering, *bam, bam, bam,* in the hills behind the red and white house. He tried to see what it was, but there was a mist over them, as though it were early morning. "What is that noise?" he asked the copper man.

"That is the giant," the copper man said. "Can't . . . you . . . see . . . her?"

Little Tib said that he could not.

"Then . . . wind . . . my . . . talking key . . . I'll . . . tell . . . you . . ."

The copper man turned around, and Little Tib saw that there were three keyholes in his back. The middle one had a neat copper label beside it printed with the words "TALKING ACTION."

". . . about . . . her."

There was a key with a beautiful handle hanging on a hook beside the hole. He took it and began to wind the copper man.

"That's better," the copper man said. "My words—thanks to your fine winding—will blow away the mists, and you'll be able to see her. I can stop her; but if I don't, you'llbekilledthatsenough."

As the copper man had said, the mists were lifting. Some, however, did not seem to blow away—they were not mists at all, but a mountain. The mountain moved, and was not a mountain at all, but a big woman wreathed in mist, twice as high as the hills around her. She was holding a broom, and while Little Tib watched, a rat as big as a railroad train ran out of a cave in one of the hills. *Bam,* the woman struck at it with her broom; but it ran into another cave. In a moment it ran out again. *Bam!* The woman was his mother, but he sensed that she would not know him—that she was cut off from him in some way by the mists, and the need to strike at the rat.

"That's my mother," he told the copper man. "And that rat was in our kitchen in the new place. But she didn't keep hitting at it and hitting at it like that."

"She is only hitting at it once," the copper man said, "but that once is over and over again. That's why she always misses it. But if you try to go any farther down this path, her broom will kill you and sweep you away. Unless I stop it."

"I could run between the swings," Little Tib said. He could have, too.

"The broom is bigger than you think," the copper man told him. "And you can't see it as well as you think you can."

"I want you to stop her," Little Tib said. He was sure

he could run between the blows of the broom, but he was sorry for his mother, who had to hit at the rat all the time, and never rest.

"Then you must let me look at you."

"Go ahead," Little Tib said.

"You have to wind my motion key."

The lowest keyhole was labeled "MOVING ACTION." It was the largest of all. There was a big key hanging beside it, and Little Tib used it to wind the moving action, hearing a heavy pawl clack inside the copper man each time he turned the key. "That's enough," the copper man said. Little Tib replaced the key, and the copper man turned around.

"Now I must look into your eyes," he said. His own eyes were stampings in the copper, but Little Tib knew that he could see out of them. He put his hands on Little Tib's face, one on each side. They were harder even than Nitty's, but smaller too, and very cold. Little Tib saw his eyes coming closer and closer.

He saw his own eyes reflected in the copper man's face as if they were in a mirror, and they had little flames in them like the flames of two candles in church; and the flames were going out. The copper man moved his face closer and closer to his own. It got darker and darker. Little Tib said, "Don't you know me?"

"You have to wind my thinking key," the copper man said.

Little Tib reached behind him, stretching his arms as far as they would go around the copper body. His fingers found the smallest hole of all, and a little hook beside it; but there was no key.

A baby was crying. There were medicine smells, and a strange woman's voice said, "There, there." Her hands touched his cheeks, the hard, cold hands of the copper man. Little Tib remembered that he could not really see at all, not any more.

"He *is* sick, isn't he," the woman said. "He's hot as fire. And screaming like that."

"Yes, ma'am," Nitty said. "He's sick sure enough."

A little girl's voice said, "What's wrong with him, Mamma?"

"He's running a fever, dear, and of course he's blind."

Little Tib said, "I'm all right."

Mr. Parker's voice told him, "You will be when the doctor sees you, George."

"I can stand up," Little Tib said. He had discovered that he was sitting on Nitty's lap, and it embarrassed him.

"You awake now?" Nitty asked.

Little Tib slid off his lap and felt around for his stick, but it was gone.

"You been sleepin' ever since we were on the train. Never did wake up more than halfway, even when we got off."

"Hello," the little girl said. *Bam. Bam. Bam.*

"Hello," Little Tib said back to her.

"Don't let him touch your face, dear. His hands are dirty."

Little Tib could hear Mr. Parker talking to Nitty, but he did not pay any attention to them.

"I have a baby," the girl told him, "and a dog. His name is Muggly. My baby's name is Virginia Jane." *Bam.*

"You walk funny," Little Tib said.

"I have to."

He bent down and touched her leg. Bending down made his head peculiar. There was a ringing sound he knew was not real, and it seemed to have fallen off him, and to be floating around in front of him somewhere. His fingers felt the edge of the little girl's skirt, then her leg, warm and dry, then a rubber thing with metal under it, and metal strips like the copper man's neck going down at the sides. He reached inside them and found her leg again, but it was smaller than his own arm.

"Don't let him hurt her," the woman said.

Nitty said, "Why, he won't hurt her. What are you afraid of? A little boy like that."

He thought of his own legs walking down the path, walking through the spinning flowers toward the green city. The little girl's leg was like them. It was bigger than he had thought, growing bigger under his fingers.

"Come on," the little girl said. "Mamma's got Virginia Jane. Want to see her?" *Bam.* "Momma, can I take my brace off?"

"No, dear."

"I take it off at home."

"That's when you're going to lie down, dear, or have a bath."

"I don't need it, Momma. I really don't. See?"

The woman screamed. Little Tib covered his ears. When they had still lived in the old place and his mother and father had talked too loudly, he had covered his ears like that, and they had seen him and become more quiet. It did not work with the woman. She kept on screaming.

A lady who worked for the doctor tried to quiet her, and at last the doctor herself came out and gave her something. Little Tib could not see what it was, but he heard her say over and over, "Take this, take this." And finally the woman took it.

Then they made the little girl and the woman go into the doctor's office. There were more people waiting than Little Tib had known about, and they were all talking now. Nitty took him by the arm. "I don't want to sit in your lap," Little Tib said. "I don't like sitting in laps."

"You can sit here," Nitty said. He was almost whispering. "We'll move Virginia Jane over."

Little Tib climbed up into a padded plastic seat. Nitty was on one side of him, and Mr. Parker on the other.

"It's too bad," Nitty said, "You couldn't see that little girl's leg. I saw it. It was just a little matchstick-sized thing when we set down here. When they carried her in, it looked just like the other one."

"That's nice," Little Tib said.

"We were wondering—did you have something to do with that?"

Little Tib did not know, and so he sat silent.

"Don't push him, Nitty," Mr. Parker said.

"I'm not pushing him. I just asked. It's important."

"Yes, it is," Mr. Parker said. "You think about it, George, and if you have anything to tell us, let us know. We'll listen."

Little Tib sat there for a long time, and at last the lady who worked for the doctor came and said, "Is it the boy?"

"He has a fever," Mr. Parker told her.

"We have to get his pattern. Bring him over here."

Nitty said, "No use." And Mr. Parker said, "You won't be able to take his pattern—his retinas are gone."

The lady who worked for the doctor said nothing for a little while; then she said, "We'll try anyway," and took Little Tib's hand and led him to where a bright light machine was. He knew it was a bright light machine from the feel and smell of it, and the way it fitted around his face. After a while she let him pull his eyes away from the machine.

"He needs to see the doctor," Nitty said. "I know without a pattern you can't charge the government for it. But he is a sick child."

The lady said, "If I start a card on him, they'll want to know who he is."

"Feel his head. He's burning up."

"They'll think he might be in the country illegally. Once an investigation like that starts, you can never stop it."

Mr. Parker asked, "Can we talk to the doctor?"

"That's what I've been telling you. You can't see the doctor."

"What about me. I'm ill."

"I thought it was the boy."

"I'm ill too. Here." Mr. Parker's hands on his shoulders guided Little Tib out of the chair in front of the bright light machine, so that Mr. Parker could sit down himself instead. Mr. Parker leaned forward, and the machine hummed. "Of course," Mr. Parker said, "I'll have to take him in with me. He's too small to leave alone in the waiting room."

"This man could watch him."

"He has to go."

"Yes, ma'am," Nitty said, "I sure do. I shouldn't have stayed around this long, except this was all so interesting."

Little Tib took Mr. Parker's hand, and they went through narrow, twisty corridors into a little room to see the doctor.

"There's no complaint on this," the doctor said. "What's the trouble with you?"

Mr. Parker told her about Little Tib, and said that she could put down anything on his own card that she wanted.

"This is irregular," the doctor said. "I shouldn't be doing this. What's wrong with his eyes?"

"I don't know. Apparently he has no retinas."

"There are such things as retinal transplants. They aren't always effective."

"Would they permit him to be identified? The seeing's not really that important."

"I suppose so."

"Could you get him into a hospital?"

"No."

"Not without a pattern, you mean."

"That's right. I'd like to tell you otherwise, but it wouldn't be the truth. They'd never take him."

"I understand."

"I've got a lot of patients to see. I'm putting you down for influenza. Give him these, they ought to reduce his fever. If he's not better tomorrow, come again."

Later, when things were cooling off, and the day-birds were all quiet, and the night-birds had not begun yet, and Nitty had made a fire and was cooking something, he said, "I don't understand why she wouldn't help the child."

"She gave him something for his fever."

"More than that. She should have done more than that."

"There are so many people—"

"I know that. I've heard all that. Not really that many at all. More in China and some other places. You think that medicine is helping him?"

Mr. Parker put his hand on Little Tib's head. "I think so."

"We goin' to stay here so we can take him, or keep on goin' back to Martinsburg?"

"We'll see how he is in the morning."

"You know, the way you are now, Mr. Parker, I think you might do it."

"I'm a good programmer, Nitty. I really am."

"I know you are. You work that program right, and that machine will find out they need a man running it again. Need a maintenance man too. Why does a man feel so bad if he don't have real payin' work to do—tell me that. Did I let them put something in my head like you?"

"You know as well as I," Mr. Parker said.

Little Tib was no longer listening to them. He was thinking about the little girl and her leg. I dreamed it, he thought. Nobody can do that. I dreamed that I only had to touch her, and it was all right. That means what is real is the other one, the copper man and the big woman with the broom.

An owl called, and he remembered the little buzzy clock that stood beside his mother's bed in the new place. Early in the morning the clock would ring, and then his father had to get up. When they had lived in the old place, and his father had a lot of work to do, he had not needed a clock. Owls must be the real clocks; they made their noise so he would wake up to the real place.

He slept. Then he was awake again, but he could not

see. "You best eat something," Nitty said. "You didn't eat nothing last night. You went to sleep, and I didn't want to rouse you." He gave Little Tib a scrap of cornbread, pressing it into his hands. "It's just leftovers now," he said, "but it's good."

"Are we going to get on another train?"

"Train doesn't go to Martinsburg. Now, we don't have a plate, so I'm putting this on a piece of newspaper for you. You get your lap smoothed out so it doesn't fall off."

Little Tib straightened his legs. He was hungry, and he decided it was the first time he had been hungry in a long while. He asked, "Will we walk?"

"Too far. Going to hitchhike. All ready now? It's right in the middle." Little Tib felt the thick paper, still cool from the night before, laid upon his thighs. There was weight in the center; he moved his fingers to it and found a yam. The skin was still on it, but it had been cut in two. "Baked that in the fire last night," Nitty said. "There's a piece of ham there too that we saved for you. Don't miss that."

Little Tib held the half yam like an ice cream cone in one hand, and peeled back the skin with the other. It was loose from having been in the coals, and crackly and hard. It broke away in flakes and chips like the bark of an old sycamore. He bit into the yam and it was soft but stringy, and its goodness made him want a drink of water.

"Went to a poor woman's house," Nitty said. "That's where you go if you want something to eat for sure. A rich person is afraid of you. Mr. Parker and I, we can't buy anything. We haven't got credit for September yet—we were figuring we'd have that in Macon."

"They won't give anything for me," Little Tib said. "Mama had to feed me out of hers."

"That's only because they can't get no pattern. Anyway, what difference does it make? That credit's so little-bitty that you almost might not have anything. Mr. Parker gets a better draw than I do because he was making more when we were working, but that's not very much, and you wouldn't get but the minimum."

"Where is Mr. Parker?"

"Down a way, washing. See, hitchhiking is hard if you don't look clean. Nobody will pick you up. We got one of those disposable razor things last night, and he's using it now."

"Should I wash?"

"It couldn't hurt," Nitty said. "You got tear-streaks on your face from cryin' last night." He took Little Tib's hand and led him along a cool, winding path with high weeds on the sides. The weeds were wet with dew, and the dew was icy cold. They met Mr. Parker at the edge of the water. Little Tib took off his shoes and clothes and waded in. It was cold, but not as cold as the dew had been. Nitty waded in after him and splashed him, and poured water from his cupped hands over his head, and at last ducked him under—telling him first—to get his hair clean. Then the two of them washed their clothes in the water and hung them on bushes to dry.

"Going to be hard, hitchhiking this morning," Nitty said.

Little Tib asked why.

"Too many of us. The more there is, the harder to get rides."

"We could separate," Mr. Parker suggested. "I'll draw straws with you to see who gets George."

"No."

"I'm all right. I'm fine."

"You're fine now."

Mr. Parker leaned forward. Little Tib knew because he could hear his clothes rustle, and his voice got closer as well as louder. "Nitty, who's the boss here?"

"You are, Mr. Parker. Only if you went off by yourself like that, I'd worry so I'd about go crazy. What have I ever done to you that you would want to worry me like that?"

Mr. Parker laughed. "All right, I'll tell you what we'll do. We'll try until ten o'clock together. If we haven't gotten a ride by then, I'll walk half a mile down the road and give the two of you the first shot at anything that comes along." Little Tib heard him get to his feet. "You think George's clothes are dry by now?"

"Still a little damp."

"I can wear them," Little Tib said. He had worn wet clothing before, when he had been drenched by rain.

"That's a good boy. Help him put them on, Nitty."

When they were walking out to the road, and he could tell that Mr. Parker was some distance ahead of them, Little Tib asked Nitty if he thought they would get a ride before ten.

"I know we will," Nitty said.

"How do you know?"

"Because I've been praying for it hard, and what I pray hard for I always get."

Little Tib thought about that. "You could pray for a job," he said. He remembered that Nitty had told him he wanted a job.

"I did that, right after I lost my old one. Then I saw Mr. Parker again and how he had got to be, and I started going around with him to look after him. So then I had a job—I've got it now. Mr. Parker's the one that doesn't have a job."

"You don't get paid," Little Tib said practically.

"We get our draws, and I use that—both of them together—for whatever we need; and if he kept his and I kept mine, he would have more than me. You be quiet now—we're coming to the road."

They stood there a long time. Occasionally a car or a truck went by. Little Tib began to wonder if Mr. Parker and Nitty were holding out their thumbs. He remembered seeing people holding out their thumbs when he and his parents were moving from the old place. He thought of what Nitty had said about praying and began to pray himself, thinking about God and asking that the next car stop.

For a long time more no cars stopped. Little Tib thought about a cattle truck stopping and told God he would ride with the cattle. He thought about a garbage truck stopping, and told God he would ride on top of the garbage. Then he heard something old coming down the road. It rattled, and the engine made a strange, high-pitched noise an engine should not make. "Looks like a old school bus," Nitty said. "But look at those pictures on the side."

"It's stopping," Mr. Parker said, and then Little Tib could hear the sound the doors made opening.

A new voice, high for a man's voice and talking fast, said, "You seek to go this way? You may come in. All are welcome in the temple of Deva."

Mr. Parker got in, and Nitty lifted Little Tib up the steps. The doors closed behind them. There was a peculiar smell in the air.

"You have a small boy. That is well. The god is most fond of small children and the aged. Small boys and girls have innocence. Old persons have tranquility and wisdom. These are the things that are pleasing to the god. We should strive without effort to retain innocence, and to attain tranquility and wisdom as soon as we can."

Nitty said, "Right on."

"He is a handsome boy." Little Tib felt the driver's breath, warm and sweet, on his face, and something dangling struck him lightly on the chest. He caught it, and found that it was a piece of wood with three crossbars, suspended from a thong. "Ah," the new voice said, "you have discovered my amulet."

"George can't see," Mr. Parker explained. "You'll have to excuse him."

"I am aware of this, having observed it earlier; but perhaps it is painful for him to hear it spoken of. And now I must go forward again before the police come to inquire why I have stopped. There are no seats—I have removed all the seats but this one. It is better that people take seats on the floor before Deva. But you may stand behind me if you wish. Is that agreeable?"

"We'll be happy to stand," Mr. Parker said.

The bus lurched into motion. Little Tib held onto Nitty with one hand and onto a pole he found with the other. "We are in motion again. That is fitting. It would be most fitting if we might move always, never stopping. I had thought to build my temple on a boat—a boat moves always because of the rocking of the waves. I may still do this."

"Are you going through Martinsburg?"

"Yes, yes, yes," the driver said. "Allow me to introduce myself: I am Dr. Prithivi."

Mr. Parker shook hands with Dr. Prithivi, and Little Tib felt the bus swerve from its lane. Mr. Parker yelled, and when the bus was straight again, he introduced Nitty and Little Tib.

"If you're a doctor," Nitty said, "you could maybe look at George sometime. He hasn't been well."

"I am not this sort of doctor," Dr. Prithivi explained. "Rather instead I am a doctor for the soul. I am a Doctor of Divinity of the University of Bombay. If someone is sick a physician should be summoned. Should they be evil they should summon me."

Nitty said, "Usually the family don't do that because they're so glad to see them finally making some money."

Dr. Prithivi laughed, a little high laugh like music. It seemed to Little Tib that it went skipping around the roof of the old bus, playing on a whistle. "But we are all evil," Dr. Prithivi said, "and so few of us make money. How do you explain that? That is the joke. I am a doctor for evil, and everyone in the world should be calling me even myself all the time. But I cannot come. Office hours nine to five, that is what my sign should say. No house calls. But instead I bring my house, the house of the god, to everyone. Here I collect my fares, and I tell all who come to step to the back of my bus."

"We didn't know you had to pay," Little Tib said. He was worried because Nitty had told him that he and Mr. Parker had no money in their accounts.

"No one must pay—that is the beauty. Those who

desire to buy near-diesel for the god may imprint their cards here, but all is voluntary and other things we accept too."

"Sure is dark back there," Nitty said.

"Let me show you. You see we are approaching a roadside park? So well is the universe regulated. There we will stop and recreate ourselves, and I will show you the god before proceeding again."

Little Tib felt the bus swerve with breathtaking suddenness. During the last year that they had lived at the old place, he had ridden a bus to school. He remembered how hot it had been, and how ordinary it had seemed after the first week; now he was dreaming of riding this strange-smelling old bus in the dark, but soon he would wake and be on that other bus again; then, when the doors opened, he would run through the hot, bright sunshine to the school.

The doors opened, clattering and grinding. "Let us go out," Dr. Prithivi said. "Let us recreate ourselves and see what is to be seen here."

"It's a lookout point," Mr. Parker told him. "You can see parts of seven counties from here." Little Tib felt himself lifted down the steps. There were other people around; he could hear their voices, though they were not close.

"It is so very beautiful," Dr. Prithivi said. "We have also beautiful mountains in India—the Himalayas, they are called. This fine view makes me think of them. When I was just a little boy, my father rented a house for summer in the Himalayas. Rhododendrons grew wild there, and once I saw a leopard in our garden."

A strange voice said: "You see mountain lions here. Early in the morning is the time for it—look up on the big rocks as you drive along."

"Exactly so!" Dr. Prithivi sounded excited. "It was very early when I saw the leopard."

Little Tib tried to remember what a leopard looked like, and found that he could not. Then he tried a cat, but it was not a very good cat. He felt hot and tired, and reminded himself that it had only been a little while ago that Nitty had washed his clothes. The seam at the front of his shirt, where the buttons went, was still damp. When he had been able to see, he had known precisely what a cat looked like. He felt now that if only he could hold a cat in his arms he would know again. He imagined such a cat, large and long-haired. It was there, unexpectedly, standing in front of him. Not a cat, but a lion, standing on its hind feet. It had a long tail with a tuft at the end, and a red ribbon knotted in its mane. Its face was a kindly blur and it was dancing—dancing to the remembered flute-music of Dr. Prithivi's laughter—just out of reach.

Little Tib took a step toward it and found his way barred by two metal pipes. He slipped between them. The lion danced, hopping and skipping, striking poses without stopping; it bowed and jigged away, and Little Tib danced too, after it. It would be cheating to run or walk—he would lose the game, even if he caught the lion. It high-stepped, far away then back again almost close enough to touch, and he followed it.

Behind him he heard the gasp of the people, but it seemed dim and distant compared to the piping to which he danced. The lion jigged nearer and he caught its paws and the two of them romped up and down, its face growing clearer and clearer as they whirled and turned—it was a funny, friendly, frightening face.

It was as though he had backed into a bush whose leaves were hands. They clasped him everywhere, drawing him backward against hard metal bars. He could hear Nitty's voice, but Nitty was crying so that he could not tell what he said. A woman was crying too—no, several women; and a man whose voice he did not know was shouting: "We've got him! We've got him!" Little Tib was not sure who he was shouting to; perhaps to nobody.

A voice he did recognize, it was Dr. Prithivi's, was saying: "I have him. You must let go of him so that I may lift him over."

Little Tib's left foot reached out as if it were moving itself and felt in front of him. There was nothing there, nothing at all. The lion was gone, and he knew, now, where he was, on the edge of a mountain, and it went down and down for a long way. Fear came.

"Let go and I will lift him over," Dr. Prithivi told someone else. Little Tib thought of how small and boneless Dr. Prithivi's hands had felt. Then Nitty's big ones took him on one side, an arm and a leg, and the medium-sized hands of Mr. Parker (or someone like him) on the other. Then he was lifted up and back, and put down on the ground.

"He walked . . ." a woman said. "Danced."

"This boy must come with me," Dr. Prithivi piped. "Get out of the way, please." He had Little Tib's left hand. Nitty was lifting him up again, and he felt Nitty's big head come up between his legs and he settled on his shoulders. He plunged his hands into Nitty's thick hair and held on. Other hands were reaching for him; when they found him, they only touched, as though they did not want to do anything more.

"Got to set you down," Nitty said, "or you'll hit your head." The steps of the bus were under his feet, and Dr. Prithivi was helping him up.

"You must be presented to the god," said Dr. Prithivi. The inside of the bus was stuffy and hot, with a strange, spicy, oppressive smell. "Here. Now you must pray. Have you anything with which to make an offering?"

"No," Little Tib said. People had followed them into the bus.

"Then only pray." Dr. Prithivi must have had a cigarette lighter—Little Tib heard the scratching sound it made. There was a soft, "oooah" sound from the people.

"Now you see Deva," Dr. Prithivi told them. "Because you are not accustomed to such things, the first thing you have noticed is that he has six arms. It is for that reason that I wear this cross, which has six arms also. You see I wish to relate Deva to Christianity here.

You will note that one of Deva's hands holds a two-armed cross. The others—I will begin here and go around—hold the crescent of Islam, the star of David, a figure of the Buddha, a phallus, and a *katana* sword, which I have chosen to represent the faith of Shintoism."

Little Tib tried to pray, as Dr. Prithivi had directed. In one way he knew what he had been doing when he had been dancing with the lion, and in another he did not. Why hadn't he fallen? He thought of how the stones at the bottom would feel when they hit his face, and shivered.

Stones he remembered very well. Potato-shaped but much larger, hard and gray. He was lost in a rocky land where frowning walls of stone were everywhere, and no plant grew. He stood in the shadow of one of these walls to escape the heat; he could see the opposite wall, and the rubble of jumbled stones between, but this time the knowledge that he could see again gave him no pleasure. He was thirsty, and pressed farther back into the shadow, and found that there was no wall there. The shadow went back and back, farther and farther into the mountain. He followed it and, turning, saw the little wedge of daylight disappear behind him, and was blind again.

The cave—for he knew it was a cave now—went on and on into the rock. Despite the lack of sunlight, it seemed to Little Tib that it grew hotter and hotter. Then from somewhere far ahead he heard a tapping and rapping, as though an entire bag of marbles had been poured on onto a stone floor and were bouncing up and down. The noise was so odd, and Little Tib was so tired, that he sat down to listen to it.

As if his sitting had been a signal, torches kindled—first one on one side of the cave, then another on the opposite side. Behind him a gate of close-set bars banged down, and toward him, like spiders, came two grotesque figures. Their bodies were small, yet fat; their arms and legs were long and thin; their faces were the faces of mad old men, popeyed and choleric and adorned with towering peaks of fantastic hair, and spreading mustaches like the feelers of night-crawling insects, and curling three-pointed beards that seemed to have a life of their own so that they twisted and twined like snakes. These men carried long-handled axes, and wore red clothes and the widest leather belts Little Tib had ever seen. "Halt," they cried. "Cease, hold, stop, and arrest yourself. You are trespassing in the realm of the Gnome King!"

"I have stopped," Little Tib said. "And I can't arrest myself because I'm not a policeman."

"That wasn't why we asked you to do it," one of the angry-faced men pointed out.

"But it *is* an offense," added the other. "We're a Police State, you know, and it's up to you to join the force."

"In your case," continued the first gnome, "it will be the labor force."

"Come with us," both of them exclaimed, and they seized him by the arms and began to drag him across the pile of rocks.

"Stop," Little Tib demanded, "you don't know who I am."

"We don't *care* who you am, either."

"If Nitty were here, he'd fix you. Or Mr. Parker."

"Then he'd better fix Mr. Parker, because we're not broken, and we're taking you to see the Gnome King."

They went down twisted sidewise caves with no lights but the eyes of the gnomes. And through big, echoing caves with mud floors, and streams of steaming water in the middle. Little Tib thought, at first, that it was rather fun, but it became realer and realer as they went along, as though the gnomes drew strength and realness from the heat, and at last he forgot that there had ever been anyplace else, and the things the gnomes said were no longer funny.

The Gnome King's throne-cavern was brilliantly lit, and crammed with gold and jewels. The curtains were gold—not gold-colored cloth, but real gold—and the king sat on a bed covered with a spread of linked diamonds, crosslegged. "You have trespassed my dominions," he said. "How do you plead?" He looked like the other gnomes, but thinner and meaner.

"For mercy," Little Tib said.

"Then you are guilty?"

Little Tib shook his head.

"You have to be. Only the guilty can plead for mercy."

"You are supposed to forgive trespasses," Little Tib said, and as soon as he had said that, all the bright lamps in the throne room went out. His guards began to curse, and he could hear the whistle of their axes as they swung them in the dark, looking for him.

He ran, thinking he could hide behind one of the gold curtains; but his outstretched arms never found it. He ran on and on until at last he felt sure that he was no longer in the throne room. He was about to stop and rest then, when he saw a faint light—so faint a light that for a long time he was afraid it might be no more than a trick of his eyes, like the lights he saw when he ground his hands against them. This is my dream, he thought, and I can make the light to be whatever I want it to be. All right, it will be sunlight; and when I get out into it, it will be Nitty and Mr. Parker and me camped someplace—a pretty place next to a creek of cold water—and I'll be able to see.

The light grew brighter and brighter; it was gold-colored, like sunlight.

Then Little Tib saw trees, and he began to run. He was actually running among the trees before he realized that they were not real trees, and that the light he had seen came from them—the sky overhead was a vault of cold stone. He stopped, then. The trunks and branches of the trees were silver; the leaves were gold; the grass under his feet was not grass but a carpet of green gems, and birds with real rubies in their breasts twittered and flew among the trees—but they were not real birds, only toys. There was no Nitty and no Mr. Parker and no water.

He was about to cry when he noticed the fruit. It hung under the leaves, and was gold, as they were; but for fruit that did not look so unnatural. Each was about the size of a grapefruit. Little Tib wondered if he could pull them from the trees, and the first he touched fell into his hands. It was not heavy enough to be solid. After a moment he saw that it unscrewed in the center. He sat down on the grass (which had become real grass in some way, or perhaps a carpet or a bedspread) and opened it. There was a meal inside, but all the food was too hot to eat. He looked and looked, hoping for a salad that would be wet and cool; but there was nothing but hot meat and gravy, and smoking hot cornmeal muffins, and boiled greens so hot and dry he did not even try to put them in his mouth.

At last he found a small cup with a lid on it. It held hot tea—tea so hot it seemed to blister his lips—but he managed to drink a little of it. He put down the cup and stood up to go on through the forest of gold and silver trees, and perhaps find a better place. But all the trees had vanished, and he was in the dark again. My eyes are gone, he thought, I'm waking up. Then he saw a circle of light ahead and heard the pounding; and he knew that it was not marbles dropped on a floor he heard, but the noise of hundreds and hundreds of picks, digging gold in the mines of the gnomes.

The light grew larger—but dimmed at the same time, as a star-shaped shadow grew in it. Then it was not a star at all, but a gnome coming after him. And then it was a whole army of gnomes, one behind the other, with their arms sticking out at every angle; so that it looked like one gnome with a hundred arms, all reaching for him.

Then he woke, and everything was dark.

He sat up. "You're awake now," Nitty said.

"Yes."

"How you feel?"

Little Tib did not answer. He was trying to find out where he was. It was a bed. There was a pillow behind him, and there were clean, starched sheets. He remembered what the doctor had said about the hospital, and asked, "Am I in the hospital?"

"No, we're in a motel. How do you feel?"

"All right, I guess."

"You remember about dancing out there on the air?"

"I thought I dreamed it."

"Well, I thought I dreamed it too—but you were really out there. Everybody saw it, everybody who was around there when you did it. And then when we got you to come in close enough that we could grab hold of you and pull you in, Dr. Prithivi got you to come back to his bus."

"I remember that," Little Tib said.

"And he explained about his work and all that, and he took up a collection for it and you went to sleep. You were running that fever again, and Mr. Parker and me couldn't wake you up much."

"I had a dream," Little Tib said, and then he told Nitty all about his dream.

"When you thought you were drinking that tea, that was me giving you your medicine, is what I think. Only it wasn't hot tea, it was ice water. And that wasn't a dream you had, it was a nightmare."

"I thought it was kind of nice," Little Tib said. "The king was right there, and you could talk to him and explain what had happened." His hands found a little table next to the bed. There was a lamp on it. He knew he could not see when the bulb lit, but he made the switch go click with his fingers anyway. "How did we get here?" he asked.

"Well, after the collection, when everybody had left, that Dr. Prithivi was hot to talk to you. But me and Mr. Parker said you were with us, and we wouldn't let him unless you had a place to sleep. We told him how you were sick, and all that. So he transferred some money to

Mr. Parker's account, and we rented this room. He says he always sleeps in his bus to look after that Deva."

"Is that where he is now?"

"No, he's downtown talking to the people. Probably I should have told you, but it's the day after you did that, now. You slept a whole day full, and a little more."

"Where's Mr. Parker?"

"He's looking around."

"He wants to see if that latch on that window is still broken, doesn't he? And if I'm really little enough to get between those bars."

"That's one thing, yes."

"It was nice of you to stay with me."

"I'm supposed to tell Dr. Prithivi when you're awake. That was part of our deal."

"Would you have stayed anyway?" Little Tib was climbing out of bed. He had never been in a motel before, though he did not want to say so, and he was eager to explore this one.

"*Somebody* would have had to stay with you." Little Tib could hear the faint whistles of the numbers on the telephone.

Later, when Dr. Prithivi came, he made Little Tib sit in a big chair with puffy arms. Little Tib told him about the dancing and how it had felt.

"You can see a bit, I think. You are not entirely blind."

Little Tib said, "No," and Nitty said, "The doctor in Howard told us he didn't have any retinas. How is anybody going to see if they don't have retinas?"

"Ah, I understand, then. Someone told you, I think, about my bus—the pictures I have made on the sides of it. Yes, that must be it. Did they tell you?"

"Tell me about what?" Little Tib asked.

Talking to Nitty, Dr. Prithivi said, "You have described the paintings on the side of my bus to this child?"

"No," Nitty said. "I looked at them when I got in, but I never talked about them."

"Yes, indeed, I did not think so. It was not likely I think that you had seen it before I stopped for you on the road, and you were in my presence after that. Nevertheless, there is a picture on the left side of my bus that is a picture of a man with a lion's head. It is Vishnu destroying the demon Hiranyakasipu. Is it not interesting that this boy, arriving in a vehicle with such a picture should be led to dance on air by a lion-headed figure? It was Vishnu also who circled the universe in two strides; this is a kind of dancing on air, perhaps."

"Uh-huh," Nitty said. "But George here couldn't have seen that picture."

"But perhaps the picture saw him—that is the point you are missing. Still, the lion has many significations. Among the Jews, it is the emblem of the tribe of Judah. For this reason the Emperor of Ethiopia is styled Lion of Judah. Also the son-in-law of Mohammed, whose name I cannot recall now when I need it, was styled Lion of God. Christianity too is very rich in lions. You noticed perhaps that I asked the boy particularly if the lion he saw had wings. I did that because a winged lion is the badge of Saint Mark. But a lion without wings indicated the Christ—this is because of the old belief that the cubs of the lion are dead at birth, and are licked to life afterward by the lioness. In the writings of Sir C. S. Lewis a lion is used in that way; and in the prayers revealed to Saint Bridget of Sweden, the Christ is styled, 'Strong Lion, immortal and invincible King.' "

"And it is the lion that will lay down with the lamb when the time comes," Nitty said. "I don't know much, maybe, about all this, but I know that. And the lamb is about the commonest symbol for Jesus. A little boy—that's a sign for Jesus too."

Mr. Parker's voice said, "How do either of you know God had anything to do with it?" Little Tib could tell that it was a new voice to Nitty and Dr. Prithivi—besides, Mr. Parker was talking from farther away, and after he said that he came over and sat on the bed, so that he was closest of all.

"The hand of the god is in all, Mr. Parker," Dr. Prithivi told him. "Should you prove that it is not to be found, it would be the not-finding. And the not-found, also."

"All right, that's a philosophical position that cannot be attacked, since it already contains the refutation of any attack. But because it can't be attacked, it can't be demonstrated either—it's simply your private belief. My point is that that wasn't what you were talking about. You were trying to find a real, visible, apparent Hand of God—to take His fingerprints. I'm saying they may not be there. The dancing lion may be nothing more than a figment of George's imagination—a dancing lion. Levitation—which is what that was—has often been reported in connection with other paranormal abilities."

"This may be so," Dr. Prithivi said, "but possibly we should ask him. George, when you were dancing with the lion man, did you perhaps feel him to be the god?"

"No," Little Tib said, "an angel."

A long time later, after Dr. Prithivi had asked him a great many questions and left, Little Tib asked Nitty what they were going to do that night. He had not understood Dr. Prithivi.

Mr. Parker said, "You have to appear. You're going to be the boy Krishna."

"Just play like," Nitty added.

"It's supposed to be a masquerade, more or less. Dr. Prithivi has talked some people who are interested in his religion into playing the parts of various mythic figures. Everyone wants to see you, so the high spot will be when you appear as Krishna. He brought a costume for you."

"Where is it?" Little Tib asked.

"It might be better if you don't put it on yet. The important thing is that while everybody is watching you and Nitty and Dr. Prithivi and the other masquers, I'll have an opportunity to get into the County Administration Building and perform the reprogramming I have in mind."

"Sounds good," Nitty said. "You think you can do it all right?"

"It's just a matter of getting a print-out of the program, and adding a patch. It's set up now to eliminate personnel whenever the figures indicate that their functions can be performed more economically by automation. The patch will exempt the school superintendent's job from the rule."

"And mine," Nitty said.

"Yes, of course. Anyway, it's highly unlikely that it will ever be noticed in that mass of assembler-language statements—certainly it won't be for many years, and then, when it is found, whoever comes across it will think that it reflects an administrative decision."

"Uh-huh."

"Then I'll add a once-through and erase subroutine that will rehire us and put George here in the blind program at Grovehurst. The whole thing ought not to take more than two hours at the outside."

"You know what I've been thinking?" Nitty said.

"What's that?"

"This little boy here—he's what you call a wonder-worker."

"You mean the little girl's leg. There wasn't any dancing lion then."

"Before that. You remember when those railroad police ladies threw the gas-bomb at us?"

"I'm pretty vague on it, to tell the truth."

(Little Tib had gotten up. He had learned by this time that there was a kitchen in the motel, and he knew that Nitty had bought cola to put in the refrigerator. He wondered if they were looking at him.)

"Yeah," Nitty said. "Well, back before that happened—with the gas-bomb—you were feelin' bad a lot. You know what I mean? You would think that you were still superintendent, and sometimes you got real upset when somebody said something."

"I had emotional problems as a result of losing my position—maybe a little worse than most people would. But I got over it."

"Took you a long time."

"A few weeks, sure."

(Little Tib opened the door of the refrigerator as quietly as he could, hearing the light switch click on. He wondered if he should offer to get something for Nitty and Mr. Parker, but he decided it would be best if they did not notice him.)

" 'Bout three years."

(Little Tib's fingers found the cold cans on the top shelf. He took one out and pulled the ring, opening it with a tiny pop. It smelled funny, and after a moment he knew that it was beer and put it back. A can from the next shelf down was cola. He closed the refrigerator.)

"Three years."

"Nearly that, yes."

There was a pause. Little Tib wondered why the men were not talking.

"You must be right. I can't remember what year it is. I could tell you the year I was born, and the year I graduated from college. But I don't know what year it is now. They're just numbers."

Nitty told him. Then for a long time, again, nobody said anything. Little Tib drank his cola, feeling it fizz on his tongue.

"I remember traveling around with you a lot, but it doesn't seem like . . ."

Nitty did not say anything.

"When I remember, it's always summer. How could it always be summer, if it's three years?"

"Winters we used to go down on the Gulf Coast. Biloxi, Mobile, Pascagoula. Sometimes we might go over to Panama City or Tallahassee. We did that one year."

"Well, I'm all right now."

"I know you are. I can see you are. What I'm talking about is that you weren't—not for a long time. Then those railroad police ladies threw that gas, and the gas disappeared and you were all right again. Both together."

"I got myself a pretty good knock on the head, running into the wall of that freight car."

"I don't think that was it."

"You mean you think George did it? Why don't you ask him?"

"He's been too sick; besides, I'm not sure he knows. He didn't know much about that little girl's leg, and I know he did that."

"George, did you make me feel better when we were on the train? Were you the one that made the gas go away?"

"Is it all right if I have this soda pop?"

"Yes. Did you do those things on the train?"

"I don't know," Little Tib said. He wondered if he should tell them about the beer.

Nitty asked, "How did you feel on the train?" His voice, which was always gentle, seemed gentler than ever.

"Funny."

"Naturally he felt funny," Mr. Parker said. "He was running a fever."

"Jesus didn't always know. 'Who touched me?' he said. He said, 'I felt power go out from me.' "

"Matthew fourteen: five—Luke eighteen: two. In overtime."

"You don't have to believe he was God. He was a real man, and he did those things. He cured all those people, and he walked on that water."

"I wonder if he saw the lion."

"Saint Peter walked on it too. Saint Peter saw Him. But what I'm wondering about is, if it is the boy, what would happen to you if he was to go away?"

"Nothing would happen to me. If I'm all right, I'm all right. You think maybe he's Jesus or something. Nothing happened to those people Jesus cured when he died, did it?"

"I don't know," Nitty said. "It doesn't say."

"Anyway, why should he go away? We're going to take care of him, aren't we?"

"Sure we are."

"There you are, then. Are you going to put his costume on him before we go?"

"I'll wait until you're inside. Then when he comes out, I'll take him back here and get him dressed up and take him over to the meeting."

Little Tib heard the noise the blinds made when Mr. Parker pulled them up—a creaky, clattery little sound. Mr. Parker said, "Do you think it would be dark enough by the time we got over there?"

"No."

"I guess you're right. That window is still loose, and I think he can get through—get between the bars. How long ago was it we looked? Was that three years?"

"Last year," Nitty said. "Last summer."

"It still looks the same. George, all you really have to do is to let me in the building, but it would be better if I didn't come through the front door where people could see me. Do you understand?"

Little Tib said that he did.

"Now it's an old building, and all the windows on the first floor have bars on them; even if you unlocked some of the other windows from inside, I couldn't get through. But there is a side door that's only used for carrying in supplies. It's locked on the outside with a padlock. What I want you to do is to get the key to the padlock for me, and hand it to me through the window."

"Where is the computer?" Little Tib asked.

"That doesn't matter—I'll deal with the computer. All you have to do is let me in."

"I want to know where it is," Little Tib insisted.

Nitty said, "Why is that?"

"I'm scared of it."

"It can't hurt you," Nitty said. "It's just a big number-grinder. It will be turned off at night anyway, won't it, Mr. Parker?"

"Unless they're running an overnight job."

"Well, anyway you don't have to worry about it," Nitty said.

Then Mr. Parker told Little Tib where he thought the keys to the side door would be; and told him that if he could not find them, he was to unlock the front door from inside. Nitty asked if he would like to listen to the television, and he said yes, and they listened to a show that had country and western music, and then it was time to go. Nitty held Little Tib's hand as the three of them walked up the street. Little Tib could feel the tightness in Nitty. He knew that Nitty was thinking about what would happen if someone found them. He heard music—not country and western music like they had heard on the television—and to make Nitty talk so he would not worry so much, he asked what it was.

"That's Dr. Prithivi," Nitty told him. "He's playing that music so that people will come and hear his sermon, and see the people in the costumes."

"Is he playing it himself?"

"No, he's got it taped. There's a loudspeaker on the top of the bus."

Little Tib listened. The music was a long way away, but it sounded as if it were even farther away than it was. As if it did not belong here in Martinsburg at all. He asked Nitty about that.

Mr. Parker said, "What you sense is remoteness in time, George. That Indian flute music belongs, perhaps, to the fifth century A.D. Or possibly the fifth century B.C., or the fifteenth. It's like an old, old thing that never knew when to die, that's still wandering over the earth."

"It never was here before, was it?" Little Tib asked. Mr. Parker said that that was correct, and then Little Tib said, "Then maybe it isn't an old thing at all." Mr. Parker laughed, but Little Tib thought of the time when the lady down the road had had her new baby. It had been weak and small and toothless, like his own grandmother; and he had thought that it was old until everyone told him it was very new, and it would be alive, probably, when its mother was an old woman and dead. He wondered who would be alive a long time from now—Mr. Parker, or Dr. Prithivi.

They turned a corner. "Just a little way farther," Nitty said.

"Is anybody here to watch us?"

"Don't you worry. We won't do anything if anybody's here."

Quite suddenly, Mr. Parker's hands were moving up and down his body. "He'll be able to get through," Mr. Parker said. "Feel how thin he is."

They turned another corner, and there were dead leaves and old newspapers under Little Tib's feet. "Sure is dark in here," Nitty whispered.

"You see," Mr. Parker said, "no one can see us. It's right here, George." He took one of Little Tib's hands and moved it until it touched an iron bar. "Now, remember, through the storeroom, out to the main hall, turn right, past six doors—I think it is—and down half a flight of stairs. That will be the boiler room, and the janitor's desk is against the wall to your right. The keys should be hanging on a hook near the desk. Bring them back here and give them to me. If you can't find them, come back here and I'll tell you how to get to the front door and open it."

"Will you put the keys back?" Little Tib asked. He was getting his left leg between two of the bars, which was easy. His hips slid in after it. He felt the heavy, rusty window swing in as he pushed against it.

"Yes, the first thing I'll do after you let me in is go back to the boiler room and hang the keys back up."

"That's good," Little Tib said. His mother had told him that you must never steal, though he had taken things since he had run away.

For a little while he was afraid he was going to scrape

his ears off. Then the wide part of his head was through, and everything was easy. The window pushed back, and he let his legs down onto the floor. He wanted to ask Mr. Parker where the door to this room was, but that would look as if he were afraid. He put one hand on the wall, and the other one out in front of him, and began to feel his way along. He wished he had his stick, but he could not even remember, now, where he had left it.

"Let me go ahead of you."

It was the funniest-looking man Little Tib had ever seen.

"I'm soft. If I bump into anything, I won't be hurt."

Not a man at all, Little Tib thought. Just clothes padded out, with a painted face at the top. "Why can I see you?" Little Tib said.

"You're in the dark, aren't you?"

"I guess so," Little Tib admitted. "I can't tell."

"Exactly. Now, when people who can see are in the light, they can see things that *are* there. And when they're in the dark, why, they *can't* see them. Isn't that correct?"

"I suppose so."

"But when *you're* in the light you can't see things. So naturally when you're in the dark, you see things that *aren't* there. You see how simple it is?"

"Yes," Little Tib said, not understanding.

"There. That proves it. You *can* see it, and it *isn't* really simple at all." The Clothes Man had his hand—it was an old glove, Little Tib noticed—on the knob of a big metal door now. When he touched it, Little Tib could see that too. "It's locked," the Clothes Man said.

Little Tib was still thinking about what he had said before. "You're smart," he told the Clothes Man.

"That's because I have the best brain in the entire world. It was given to me by the great and powerful Wizard himself."

"Are you smarter than the computer?"

"Much, much smarter than the Computer. But I don't know how to open this door."

"Have you been trying?"

"Well, I've been shaking the knob—only it won't shake. And I've been feeling around for a catch. That's trying, I suppose."

"I think it is," Little Tib said.

"Ah, you're thinking—that's good." Little Tib had reached the door, and the Clothes Man moved to one side to let him feel it. "If you had the ruby slippers," the Clothes Man continued, "you could just click your heels three times and wish, and you'd be on the other side. Of course, you're on the other side now."

"No, I'm not," Little Tib told him.

"Yes, you are," the Clothes Man said. "Over *there* is where you want to be—that's on *that* side. So this is the *other* side."

"You're right," Little Tib admitted. "But I still can't get through the door."

"You don't have to, now," the Clothes Man told him. "You're already on the other side. Just don't trip over the steps."

"What steps?" Little Tib asked. As he did, he took a step backward. His heel bumped something he did not expect, and he sat down hard on something else that was higher up than the floor should have been.

"Those steps," the Clothes Man said mildly.

Little Tib was feeling them with his hands. They were sidewalk-stuff, with metal edges; and they felt almost as hard and real to his fingers as they had a moment ago when he sat down on them without wanting to. "I don't remember going down these," he said.

"You didn't. But now you have to go up them to get to the upper room."

"What upper room?"

"The one with the door that goes out into the corridor," the Clothes Man told him. "You go into the corridor, and turn *that* way, and—"

"I know," Little Tib said. "Mr. Parker told me. Over

and over. But he didn't tell me about that door that was locked, or these steps."

"It may be that Mr. Parker doesn't remember the inside of this building quite as well as he thinks he does."

"He used to work here. He told me." Little Tib was going up the stairs. There was an iron rail on one side. He was afraid that if he did not talk to the Clothes Man, he would go away. But he could not think of anything to say, and nothing of the kind happened. Then he remembered that he had not talked to the lion at all.

"I could find the keys for you," the Clothes Man said. "I could bring them back to you."

"I don't want you to leave," Little Tib told him.

"It would just take a moment. I fall down a lot, but keys wouldn't break."

"No," Little Tib said. The Clothes Man looked so hurt that he added, "I'm afraid . . ."

"You can't be afraid of the dark. Are you afraid of being alone?"

"A little. But I'm afraid you couldn't really bring them to me. I'm afraid you're not real, and I want you to be real."

"I could bring them." The Clothes Man threw out his chest and struck a heroic pose, but the dry grass that was his stuffing made a small, sad, rustling sound. "I *am* real. Try me."

There was another door—Little Tib's fingers found it. This one was not locked, and when he went out it, the floor changed from sidewalk to smooth stone. "I, too, am real," a strange voice said. The Clothes Man was still there when the strange voice spoke, but he seemed dimmer.

"Who are you?" Little Tib asked, and there was a sound like thunder. He had hated the strange voice from the beginning, but until he heard the thunder-sound he had not really known how much. It was not really like thunder, he thought. He remembered his dream about the gnomes, though this was much worse. It seemed to him that it was like big stones grinding together at the bottom of the deepest hole in the world. It was worse than that, really.

"I wouldn't go in there if I were you," the Clothes Man said.

"If the keys are in there, I'll have to go in and get them," Little Tib replied.

"They're not in there at all. In fact, they're not even close to there—they're several doors down. All you have to do is walk past the door."

"Who is it?"

"It's the Computer," the Clothes Man told him.

"I didn't think they talked like that."

"Only to you. And not all of them talk at all. Just don't go in and it will be all right."

"Suppose it comes out here after me?"

"It won't do that. It is as frightened of you as you are of it."

"I won't go in," Little Tib promised.

When he was opposite the door where the thing was, he heard it groaning as if it were in torture; and he turned and went in. He was very frightened to find himself there; but he knew he was not in the wrong place—he had done the right thing, and not the wrong thing. Still, he was very frightened. The horrible voice said: "What have we to do with you? Have you come to torment us?"

"What is your name?" Little Tib asked.

The thundering, grinding noise came a second time, and this time Little Tib thought he heard in it the sound of many voices, perhaps hundreds or thousands, all speaking at once.

"Answer me," Little Tib said. He walked forward until he could put his hands on the cabinet of the machine. He felt frightened, but he knew the Clothes Man had been right—the Computer was as frightened of him as he was of it. He knew that the Clothes Man was standing behind him, and he wondered if he would have dared to do this if someone else had not been watching.

"We are legion," the horrible voice said. "Very many."

"Get out!" There was a moaning that might have come from deep inside the earth. Something made of glass that had been on furniture fell over and rolled and crashed to the floor.

"They are gone," the Clothes Man said. He sat on the cabinet of the computer so Little Tib could see it, and he looked brighter than ever.

"Where did they go?" Little Tib asked.

"I don't know. You will probably meet them again." As if he had just thought of it, he said, "You were very brave."

"I was scared. I'm still scared—the worst since I left the new place."

"I wish I could tell you that you didn't have to be afraid of them," the Clothes Man said, "or of anybody. But it wouldn't be true. Still, I can tell you something that is really better than that—that it will all come out right in the end." He took off the big, floppy black hat he wore, and Little Tib saw that his bald head was really only a sack. "You wouldn't let me bring the keys before, but how about now? Or would you be afraid with me away?"

"No," Little Tib said, "but I'll get the keys myself."

At once the Clothes Man was gone. Little Tib felt the smooth, cool metal of the computer under his hands. In the blackness, it was the only reality there was.

He did not bother to find the window again; instead, he unlocked another, and called Nitty and Mr. Parker to it, smelling as he did the cool, damp air of spring. At the opening, he thrust the keys through first, then squeezed himself between the bars. By the time he was outside, he could hear Mr. Parker unlocking the side door.

"You were a long time," Nitty said. "Was it bad in there by yourself?"

"I wasn't by myself," Little Tib said.

"I'm not even goin' to ask you about that. I used to

be a fool, but I know better now. You still want to go to Dr. Prithivi's meetin'?"

"He wants us to come, doesn't he?"

"You are the big star, the main event. If you don't come, it's going to be like no potato salad at a picnic."

They walked back to the motel in silence. The flute music they had heard before was louder and faster now, with the clangs of gongs interspersed in its shrill wailings. Little Tib stood on a footstool while Nitty took his clothes away and wrapped a piece of cloth around his waist, and another around his head, and hung his neck with beads, and painted something on his forehead.

"There, you look just ever so fine," Nitty said.

"I feel silly," Little Tib told him.

Nitty said that that did not matter, and they left the motel again and walked several blocks. Little Tib heard the crowd, and the loud sounds of the music, and then smelled the familiar dark, sweet smell of Dr. Prithivi's bus; he asked Nitty if the people had not seen him, and Nitty said that they had not, that they were watching something taking place on a stage outside.

"Ah," Dr. Prithivi said. "You are here, and you are just in time."

Nitty asked him if Little Tib looked all right.

"His appearance is very fine indeed, but he must have his instrument." He put a long, light stick into Little Tib's hands. It had a great many little holes in it. Little Tib was happy to have it, knowing that he could use it to feel his way if necessary.

"Now it is time you met your fellow performer," Dr. Prithivi said. "Boy Krishna, this is the god Indra. Indra, it has given me the greatest pleasure to introduce to you the god Krishna, most charming of the incarnations of Vishnu."

"Hello," a strange, deep voice said.

"You are doubtless familiar already with the story, but I will tell it to you again in order to refresh your memories before you must appear on my little stage. Krishna is the son of Queen Devaki, and this lady is the sister of the wicked King Kamsa who kills all her children when they are born. To save Krishna, the good Queen places him among villagers. There he offends Indra, who comes to destroy him. . . . "

Little Tib listened with only half his mind, certain that he could never remember the whole story. He had forgotten the Queen's name already. The wood of the flute was smooth and cool under his fingers, the air in the bus hot and heavy, freighted with strange, sleepy odors.

"I am King Kamsa," Dr. Prithivi was saying, "and when I am through being he, I will be a cowherd, so I can tell you what to do. Remember not to drop the mountain when you lift it."

"I'll be careful," Little Tib said. He had learned to say that in school.

"Now I must go forth and prepare for you. When you hear the great gong struck three times, come out. Your friend will be waiting there to take you to the stage."

Little Tib heard the door of the bus open and close. "Where's Nitty?" he asked.

The deep voice of Indra—a hard, dry voice, it seemed to Little Tib—said: "He has gone to help."

"I don't like being alone here."

"You are not alone," Indra said. "I'm with you."

"Yes."

"Did you like the story of Krishna and Indra? I will tell you another story. Once, in a village not too far away from here—"

"You aren't from around here, are you?" Little Tib asked. "Because you don't talk like it. Everybody here talks like Nitty or like Mr. Parker except Dr. Prithivi, and he's from India. Can I feel your face?"

"No, I'm not from around here," Indra said. "I am from Niagara. Do you know what that is?"

Little Tib said, "No."

"It is the capital of this nation—the seat of government. Here, you may feel my face."

Little Tib reached upward; but Indra's face was smooth, cool wood, like the flute. "You don't have a face," he said.

"That is because I am wearing the mask of Indra. Once, in a village not too far from here, there were a great many women who wanted to do something nice for the whole world. So they offered their bodies for certain experiments. Do you know what an experiment is?"

"No," said Little Tib.

"Biologists took parts of these women's bodies—parts that would later become boys and girls. And they reached down inside the tiniest places in those parts and made improvements."

"What kind of improvements?" Little Tib asked.

"Things that would make the girls and boys smarter and stronger and healthier—that kind of improvement. Now these good women were mostly teachers in a college, and the wives of college teachers."

"I understand," Little Tib said. Outside, the people were singing.

"However, when those girls and boys were born, the biologists decided that they needed more children to study—children who had not been improved, so that they could compare them to the ones who had."

"There must have been a lot of those," Little Tib ventured.

"The biologists offered money to people who would bring their children in to be studied, and a great many people did—farm and ranch and factory people, some of them from neighboring towns." Indra paused. Little Tib thought he smelled like cologne; but like oil and iron too. Just when he thought the story was finished, Indra began to speak again.

"Everything went smoothly until the boys and girls were six years old. Then at the center—the experiments were made at the medical center, in Houston—strange things started to happen. Dangerous things. Things that no one could explain." As though he expected Little

Tib to ask what these inexplicable things were, Indra waited; but Little Tib said nothing.

At last Indra continued. "People and animals—sometimes even monsters—were seen in the corridors and therapy rooms who had never entered the complex and were never observed to leave it. Experimental animals were freed—apparently without their cages having been opened. Furniture was rearranged, and on several different occasions large quantities of food that could not be accounted for was found in the common rooms.

"When it became apparent that these events were not isolated occurrences, but part of a recurring pattern, they were coded and fed to a computer—together with all the other events of the medical center schedule. It was immediately apparent that they coincided with the periodic examinations given the genetically improved children."

"I'm not one of those," Little Tib said.

"The children were examined carefully. Thousands of man-hours were spent in checking them for paranormal abilities; none were uncovered. It was decided that only half the group should be brought in each time. I'm sure you understand the principle behind that—if paranormal activity had occurred when one half was present, but not when the other half was, we would have isolated the disturbing individual to some extent. It didn't work. The phenomena occurred when each half-group was present."

"I understand."

The door of the bus opened, letting in fresh night air. Nitty's voice said, "You two ready? Going to have to come on pretty soon now."

"We're ready," Indra told him. The door closed again, and Indra said: "Our agency felt certain that the fact that the phenomena took place whenever either half of the group was present indicated that several individuals were involved. Which meant the problem was more critical then we supposed. Then one of the biologists who had been involved originally—by that time we had taken charge of the project, you understand—

pointed out in the course of a casual conversation with one of our people that the genetic improvements they had made could occur spontaneously. I want you to listen carefully now. This is important."

"I'm listening," Little Tib told him dutifully.

"A certain group of us were very concerned about this. We—are you familiar with the central data processing unit that provides identification and administers social benefits to the unemployed?"

"You look in it, and it's supposed to tell who you are," Little Tib said.

"Yes. It already included a system for the detection of fugitives. We added a new routine that we hoped would be sensitive to potential paranormalities. The biologists indicated that a paranormal individual might possess certain retinal peculiarities, since such people notoriously see phenomena, like Kirlian auras, that are invisible to normal sight. The central data bank was given the capability of detecting such abnormalities through its remote terminals."

"It would look into his eyes and know what he was," Little Tib said. And after a moment, "You should have done that with the boys and girls."

"We did," Indra told him. "No abnormalities were detected, and the phenomena persisted." His voice grew deeper and more solemn than ever. "We reported this to the President. He was extremely concerned, feeling that under the present unsettled economic conditions, the appearance of such an individual might trigger domestic disorder. It was decided to terminate the experiment."

"Just forget about it?" Little Tib asked.

"The experimental material would be sacrificed to prevent the continuance and possible further development of the phenomena."

"I don't understand."

"The brains and spinal cords of the boys and girls involved would be turned over to the biologists for examination."

"Oh, I know this story," Little Tib said. "The three

Wise Men come and warn Joseph and Mary, and they take baby Jesus to the Land of Egypt on a donkey."

"No," Indra told him, "that isn't this story at all. The experiment was ended, and the phenomena ceased. But a few weeks later the alert built into the central data system triggered. A paranormal individual had been identified, almost five hundred kilometers from the scene of the experiment. Several agents were dispatched to detain him; but he could not be found. It was at this point that we realized we had made a serious mistake. We had utilized the method of detention and identification already used in criminal cases—destruction of the retina. That meant the subject could not be so identified again."

"I see," Little Tib said.

"This method had proved to be quite practical with felons—the subject could be identified by other means, and the resulting blindness prevented escape and effective resistance. Of course, the real reason for adopting it was that it could be employed without any substantial increase in the mechanical capabilities of the remote terminals—a brief overvoltage to the sodium vapor light normally used for retinal photography was all that was required.

"This time, however, the system seemed to have worked against us. By the time the agents arrived, the subject was gone. There had been no complaints, no shouting and stumbling. The people in charge of the terminal facility didn't even know what had occurred. It was possible, however, to examine the records of those who had preceded and followed the person we wanted, however. Do you know what we found?"

Little Tib, who knew that they had found that it was he, said, "No."

"We found that it was one of the children who had been part of the experiment." Indra smiled. Little Tib could not see his smile, but he could feel it. "Isn't that odd? One of the boys who had been part of the experiment."

"I thought they were all dead."

"So did we, until we understood what had happened. But you see, the ones who were sacrificed were those who had undergone genetic improvement before birth. The *controls* were not dead, and this was one of them."

"The other children," Little Tib said.

"Yes. The poor children, whose mothers had brought them in for the money. That was why dividing the group had not worked—the controls were brought in with both halves. It could not be true, of course."

Little Tib said, "What?"

"It could not be true—we all agreed on that. It could not be one of the controls. It was too much of a coincidence. It had to be that one of the mothers—possibly one of the fathers, but more likely one of the mothers—saw it coming a long way off and exchanged infants to save her own. It must have happened years before."

"Like Krishna's mother," Little Tib said, remembering Dr. Prithivi's story.

"Yes. Gods aren't born in cowsheds."

"Are you going to kill this last boy too—when you find him?"

"I know that you are the last of the children."

There was no hope of escaping a seeing person in the enclosed interior of the bus, but Little Tib bolted anyway. He had not taken three steps before Indra had him by the shoulders and forced him back into his seat.

"Are you going to kill me now?"

"No."

Thunder banged outside. Little Tib jumped, thinking for an instant that Indra had fired a gun. "Not now," Indra told him, "but soon."

The door opened again, and Nitty said: "Come on out. It's goin' to rain, and Dr. Prithivi wants to get the big show on before it does." With Indra close behind him, Little Tib let Nitty help him down the steps and out the door of the bus. There were hundreds of people outside—he could hear the shuffling of their feet, and the sound of their voices. Some were talking to each other and some were singing; but they became quiet as he, with Nitty and Indra, passed through them. The air was heavy with the coming storm, and there were gusts of wind.

"Here," Nitty said, "high step up. Watch out."

They were rough wooden stairs, seven steps. He climbed the last one, and . . .

He could see.

For a moment (though it was only a moment) he thought that he was no longer blind. He was in a village of mud houses, and there were people all around him, brown-skinned people with large, soft, brown eyes—men with red and yellow and blue cloths wrapped about their heads, women with beautiful black hair and colored dresses. There was a cow-smell and a dust-smell and a cooking-smell all at once; and just beyond the village a single mountain perfect and pure as an ice cream cone; and beyond the mountain a marvelous sky full of palaces and chariots and painted elephants; and beyond the sky, more faces than he could count.

Then he knew that it was only imagination, only a dream; not his dream this time, but Dr. Prithivi's dream. Perhaps Dr. Prithivi could dream the way he did, so strongly that the angels came to make the dreams true; perhaps it was only Dr. Prithivi's dream working through him. He thought of what Indra had said—that his mother was not his real mother, and knew that that could not be so.

A brown-skinned, brown-eyed woman with a pretty, heart-shaped face said, "Pipe for us," and he remembered that he still had the wooden flute. He raised it to his lips, not certain that he could play it, and wonderful music began. It was not his, but he fingered the flute pretending that it was his, and danced. The women danced with him, sometimes joining hands, sometimes ringing little bells.

It seemed to him that they had been dancing for only a moment when Indra came. He was bigger than Little Tib's father, and his face was a carved, hook-nosed mask. In his right hand he had a cruel sword that curved and recurved like a snake, and in his left a glittering eye. When Little Tib saw the eye, he knew why it was that

Indra had not killed him while they were alone in the bus. Someone far away was watching through that eye, and until he had seen him do the things he was able, sometimes, to do, make things appear and disappear, bring the angels, Indra could not use his sword. I just won't do it, he thought; but he knew he could not always stop what happened—that the happenings sometimes carried him with them.

The thunder boomed then, and Dr. Prithivi's voice said: "Play up to it! Up to the storm. That is ideal for what we are trying to do!"

Indra stood in front of Little Tib and said something about bringing so much rain that it would drown the village; and Dr. Prithivi's voice told Little Tib to lift the mountain.

Little Tib looked and saw a real mountain, far off and perfect; he knew he could not lift it.

Then the rain came, and the lights went out, and they were standing on the stage in the dark, with icy water beating against their faces. The lightning flashed and Little Tib saw hundreds of people running for their cars; among them were a man with a monkey's head, and another with an elephant's, and a man with nine faces.

And then he was blind again, and there was nothing left but the rough feel of wood underfoot, and the beating of the rain, and the knowledge that Indra was still before him, holding his sword and the eye.

And then a man made all of metal (so that the rain drummed on him) stood there too. He held an ax, and wore a pointed hat; and by the light that shone from his polished surface, Little Tib could see Indra too, and the eye.

"Who are you?" Indra said. He was talking to the Metal Man.

"Who are *you?*" the Metal Man answered. "I can't see your face behind that wooden mask—but wood has never stood for long against me." He struck Indra's mask with his ax; a big chip flew from it, and the string that held it in place broke, and it went clattering down.

Little Tib saw his father's face, with the rain running from it. "Who are you?" his father said to the Metal Man again.

"Don't you know me, Georgie?" the Metal Man said. "Why we used to be old friends, once. I have—if I may say so—a very sympathetic heart, and when—"

"Daddy!" Little Tib yelled.

His father looked at him and said, "Hello, Little Tib."

"Daddy, if I had known you were Indra I wouldn't have been scared at all. That mask made your voice sound different."

"You don't have to be afraid any longer, son," his father said. He took two steps toward Little Tib, and then, almost too quickly to see, his sword blade came up and flashed down.

The Metal Man's ax was even quicker. It came up and stayed up; Indra's sword struck it with a crash.

"That won't help him," Little Tib's father said. "They've seen him, and they've seen you. I wanted to get it over with."

"They haven't seen me," the Metal Man said. "It's darker here than you think."

At once it *was* dark. The rain stopped—or if it continued, Little Tib was not conscious of it. He did not know why he knew, but he knew where he was: he was standing, still standing, in front of the computer, with the devils not yet driven out.

Then the rain was back and his father was there again, but the Metal Man was gone, and the dark came back with a rush until he was blind again. "Are you still going to kill me, Father?" he asked.

There was no reply, and he repeated his question.

"Not now," his father said.

"Later?"

"Come here." He felt his father's hand on his arm, the way it used to be. "Let's sit down." It drew him to the edge of the platform and helped him to seat himself with his legs dangling over.

"Are you all right?" Little Tib asked.

"Yes," his father told him.

"Then why do you want to kill me?"

"I don't *want* to." Suddenly his father sounded angry. "I never said I *wanted* to. I have to do it, that's all. Look at us, look at what we been. Moving from place to place, working construction, working the land, worshiping the Lord like it was a hundred years ago. You know what we are? We're jackrabbits. You recall jackrabbits, Little Tib?"

"No."

"That was before your day. Big old long-legg'd rabbits with long ears like a jackass's. Back before you were born they decided they weren't any good, and they all died. For about a year I'd find them on the place, dead, and then there wasn't any more. They waited to join until it was too late, you see. Or maybe they couldn't. That's what's going to happen to people like us. I mean our family. What do you suppose we've been?"

Little Tib, who did not understand the question, said nothing.

"When I was a boy and used to go to school I would hear about all these great men and kings and queens and Presidents, and I liked to think that maybe some were family. That isn't so, and I know it now. If you could go back to Bible times, you'd find our people living in the woods like Indians."

"I'd like that," Little Tib said.

"Well, they cut down those woods so we couldn't do that any more; and we began scratching a living out of the ground. We've been doing that ever since and paying taxes, do you understand me? That's all we've ever done. And pretty soon now there won't be any call at all for people to do that. We've got to join them before it's too late—do you see?"

"No," Little Tib said.

"You're the one. You're a prodigy and a healer, and so they want you dead. You're our ticket. Everybody was born for something, and that was what you were born for, son. Just because of you, the family is going to get in before it's too late."

"But if I'm dead . . ." Little Tib tried to get his thoughts in order. "You and Mama don't have any other children."

"You don't understand, do you?"

Little Tib's father had put his arm around Little Tib, and now he leaned down until their faces touched. But when they did, it seemed to Little Tib that his father's face did not feel as it should. He reached up and felt it with both hands, and it came off in his hands, feeling like the plastic vegetables came in at the new place; perhaps this was Big Tib's dream.

"You shouldn't have done that," his father said.

Little Tib reached up to find who had been pretending to be his father. The new face was metal, hard and cold.

"I am the President's man now. I didn't want you to know that, because I thought that it might upset you. The President is handling the situation personally."

"Is Mama still at home?" Little Tib asked. He meant the new place.

"No. She's in a different division—gee-seven. But I still see her sometimes. I think she's in Atlanta now."

"Looking for me?"

"She wouldn't tell me."

Something inside Little Tib, just under the hard place in the middle of his chest where all the ribs came together, began to get tighter and tighter, like a balloon being blown up too far. He felt that when it burst, he would burst too. It made it impossible to take more than tiny breaths, and it pressed against the voice-thing in his neck so he could not speak. Inside himself he said forever that that was not his real mother, and this was not his real father; that his real mother and father were the mother and father he had had at the old place; he would keep them inside for always, his real mother and father. The rain beat against his face; his nose was full of mucus; he had to breathe through his mouth, but his mouth was filling with saliva, which ran down his chin and made him ashamed.

Then the tears came in a hot flood on his cold cheeks, and the metal face fell off Indra like an old pie pan from a shelf, and went rattling and clanging across the blacktop under the stage.

He reached up to his father's face again, and it was his father's face, but his father said: "Little Tib, can't you understand? It's the Federal Reserve Card. It's the goddamned card. It's having no money, and nothing to do, and spending your whole life like a goddamn whipped dog. I only got in because of you—saying I'd hunt for you. We had training and all that, Skinnerian conditioning and deep hypnosis, they saw to that—but in the end it's the damn card." And while he said that, Little Tib could hear Indra's sword, scraping and scraping, ever so slowly, across the boards of the stage. He jumped down and ran, not knowing or caring whether he was going to run into something.

In the end, he ran into Nitty. Nitty no longer had his sweat and woodsmoke smell, because of the rain; but he still had the same feel, and the same voice when he said: "*There* you are. I been lookin' just everyplace for you. I thought somebody had run off with you to get you out of the wet. Where you been?" He raised Little Tib on his shoulders.

Little Tib plunged his hands into the thick, wet hair and hung on. "On the stage," he said.

"On the stage still? Well, I swear." Nitty was walking fast, taking big, long strides. Little Tib's body rocked with the swing of them. "That was the one place I never thought to look for you. I thought you would have come off there fast, looking for me, or someplace dry. But I guess you were afraid of falling off."

"Yes," Little Tib said, "I was afraid of falling off." Running in the rain had let all the air out of the balloon; he felt empty inside, and like he had no bones at all. Twice he nearly slid from Nitty's shoulders, but each time Nitty's big hands reached up and caught him.

The next morning a good-smelling woman came from

the school for him. Little Tib was still in bed when she knocked on the door; but he heard Nitty open it, and her say, "I believe you have a blind child here."

"Yes'm," Nitty said.

"Mr. Parker—the new acting superintendent?—asked me to come over and escort him myself the first day. I'm Ms. Munson. I teach the blind class."

"I'm not sure he's got clothes fit for school," Nitty told her.

"Oh, they come in just anything these days," Ms. Munson said, and then she saw Little Tib, who had gotten out of bed when he heard the door open, and said, "I see what you mean. Is he dressed for a play?"

"Last night," Nitty told her.

"Oh. I heard about it, but I wasn't there."

Then Little Tib knew he still had the skirt-thing on that they had given him—but it was not; it was a dry, woolly towel. But he still had beads on, and metal bracelets on his arm.

"His others are real ragged."

"I'm afraid he'll have to wear them anyway," Ms. Munson said. Nitty took him into the bathroom and took the beads and bracelets and towel off, and dressed him in his usual clothes. Then Ms. Munson led him out of the motel and opened the door of her little electric car for him.

"Did Mr. Parker get his job again?" Little Tib asked when the car bounced out of the motel lot and onto the street.

"I don't know about *again,*" Ms. Munson said. "Did he have it before? But I understand he's extremely well qualified in educational programming; and when they found out this morning that the computer was inoperative, he presented his credentials and offered to help. He called me about ten o'clock and asked me to go for you, but I couldn't get away from the school until now."

"It's noon, isn't it," Little Tib said. "It's too hot for morning."

That afternoon he sat in Ms. Munson's room with eight other blind children while a machine moved his hand over little dots on paper and told him what they were. When school was over and he could hear the seeing children milling in the hall outside, a woman older and thicker than Ms. Munson came for him and took him to a house where other, seeing, children larger than he lived. He ate there; the thick woman was angry once because he pushed his beets, by accident, off his plate. That night he slept in a narrow bed.

The next three days were all the same. In the morning the thick woman took him to school. In the evening she came for him. There was a television at the thick woman's house—Little Tib could never remember her name afterward—and when supper was over, the children listened to television.

On the fifth day of school he heard his father's voice in the corridor outside, and then his father came into Ms. Munson's room with a man from the school, who sounded important.

"This is Mr. Jefferson," the man from the school told Ms. Munson. "He's from the Government. You are to release one of your students to his care. Do you have a George Tibbs here?"

Little Tib felt his father's hand close on his shoulder. "I have him," his father said. They went out the front door, and down the steps, and then along the side. "There's been a change in orders, son; I'm to bring you to Niagara for examination."

"All right."

"There's no place to park around this damn school. I had to park a block away."

Little Tib remembered the rattley truck his father had when they lived at the old place; but he knew somehow that the truck was gone like the old place itself, belonging to the real father locked in his memory. The father of now would have a nice car.

He heard footsteps, and then there was a man he could see walking in front of them—a man so small he was hardly taller than Little Tib himself. He had a shiny bald head with upcurling hair at the sides of it; and a bright green coat with two long coattails and two sparkling green buttons. When he turned around to face them (skipping backwards to keep up), Little Tib saw that his face was all red and white except for two little, dark eyes that almost seemed to shoot out sparks. He had a big, hooked nose like Indra's, but on him it did not look cruel. "And what can I do for you?" he asked Little Tib.

"Get me loose," Little Tib said. "Make him let go of me."

"And then what?"

"I don't know," Little Tib confessed.

The man in the green coat nodded to himself as if he had guessed that all along, and took an envelope of silver paper out of his inside coat pocket. "If you are *caught* again," he said, "it will be for good. Understand? Running is for people who are not helped." He tore one end of the envelope open. It was full of glittering powder, as Little Tib saw when he poured it out into his hand. "You remind me," he said, "of a friend of mine named *Tip*. Tip with a *p*. A *b* is just a *p* turned upside down." He threw the glittering powder into the air, and spoke a word Little Tib could not quite hear.

For just a second there were two things at once. There was the sidewalk and the row of cars on one side and the lawns on the other; and there was Ms. Munson's room, with the sounds of the other children, and the mopped-floor smell. He looked around at the light on the cars, and then it was gone and there was only the sound of his father's voice in the hall outside, and the feel of the school desk and the paper with dots in it. The voice of the man in the green coat (as if he had not gone away at all) said, "Tip turned out to be the ruler of all of us in the end, you know." Then there was the beating of big wings. And then it was all gone, gone completely. The classroom door opened, and a man from the school who sounded important said, "Ms. Munson, I have a gentleman here who states that he is the father of one of your pupils.

"Would you give me your name again, sir?"

"George Tibbs. My boy's name is George Tibbs too."

"Is this your father, George?" Ms. Munson said.

"How would he know? He's blind."

Little Tib said nothing, and the Important Man said, "Perhaps we'd better all go up to the office. You say that you're with the Federal Government, Mr. Tibbs?"

"The Office of Biogenetic Improvement. I suppose you're surprised, seeing that I'm nothing but a dirt farmer—but I got into it through the Agricultural Program."

"Ah."

Ms. Munson, who was holding Little Tib's hand, led him around a corner.

"I'm working on a case now . . . Perhaps it would be better if the boy waited outside."

A door opened. "We haven't been able to identify him, you understand," the Important Man said. "His retinas are gone. That's the reason for all this red tape."

Ms. Munson helped Little Tib find a chair, and said, "Wait here." Then the door closed and everyone was gone. He dug the heels of his hands into his eyes, and for an instant there were points of light like the glittering dust the man in the green coat had thrown. He thought about what he was going to do, and not running. Then about Krishna, because he had been Krishna. Had Krishna run? Or had he gone back to fight the king who had wanted to kill him? He could not be sure, but he did not think Krishna had run. Jesus had fled into Egypt, he remembered that. But he had come back. Not to Bethlehem where he had run from, but to Nazareth, because that was his real home. He remembered talking about the Jesus story to his father, when they were sitting on the stage. His father had brushed it aside; but Little Tib felt it might be important somehow. He put his chin on his hands to think about it.

The chair was hard—harder than any rock he had ever sat on. He felt the unyielding wood of its arms stretching to either side of him while he thought. There was something horrible about those arms, something he could not remember. Just outside the door the bell rang, and he could hear the noise the children's feet made in the hall. It was recess; they were pouring out the doors, pouring out into the warm fragrance of spring outside.

He got up, and found the door-edge with his fingers. He did not know whether anyone was seeing him or not. In an instant he was in the crowd of pushing children. He let them carry him down the steps.

Outside, games went on all around him. He stopped shuffling and shoving now, and began to walk. With the first step he knew that he would go on walking like this all day. It felt better than anything else he had ever done. He walked through all the games until he found the fence around the schoolyard; then down the fence until he found a gate, then out the gate and down the road.

I'll have to get a stick, he thought.

When he had gone about five kilometers, as well as he could judge, he heard the whistle of a train far off and turned toward it. Railroad tracks were better than roads—he had learned that months ago. He was less likely to meet people, and trains only went by once in a while. Cars and trucks went by all the time, and any one of them could kill.

After a while he picked up a good stick—light but flexible, and just the right length. He climbed the embankment then, and began to walk where he wanted to walk, on the rails, balancing with his stick. There was a little girl ahead of him, and he could see her, so he knew she was an angel. "What's your name?" he said.

"I mustn't tell you," she answered, "but you can call me Dorothy." She asked his, and he did not say George Tibbs but Little Tib, which was what his mother and father had always called him.

"You fixed my leg, so I'm going with you," Dorothy announced. (She did not really sound like the same girl.) After a time she added: "I can help you a lot. I can tell you what to look out for."

"I know you can," Little Tib said humbly.

"Like now. There's a man up ahead of us."

"A bad man?" Little Tib asked, "or a good man?"

"A nice man. A shaggy man."

"Hello." It was Nitty's voice. "I didn't really expect to see you here, George, but I guess I should have."

Little Tib said, "I don't like school."

"That's just the different of me. I do like it, only it seems like they don't like me."

"Didn't Mr. Parker get you your job back?"

"I think Mr. Parker kind of forgot me."

"He shouldn't have done that," Little Tib said.

"Well, little blind boy, Mr. Parker is white, you know. And when a white man has been helped out by a black one, he likes to forget it sometimes."

"I see," Little Tib said, though he did not. Black and white seemed very unimportant to him.

"I hear it works the other way too." Nitty laughed.

"This is Dorothy," Little Tib said.

Nitty said, "I can't see any Dorothy, George." His voice sounded funny.

"Well, I can't see you," Little Tib told him.

"I guess that's right. Hello, Dorothy. Where are you an' George goin'?"

"We're going to Sugarland," Little Tib told him. "In Sugarland they know who you are."

"Is Sugarland for real?" Nitty asked. "I always thought it was just some place you made up."

"No, Sugarland is in Texas."

"How about that," Nitty said. The light of the sun, now setting, made the railroad ties as yellow as butter. Nitty took Little Tib's hand, and Little Tib took Dorothy's, and the three of them walked between the rails. Nitty took up a lot of room, but Little Tib did not take much, and Dorothy hardly took any at all.

When they had gone half a kilometer, they began to skip.

An Infinite Summer

Christopher Priest

Chris Priest lives in England; I live in California—so you might assume we've had few opportunities to meet. That's true, but we did manage it once, in 1970 when both of us traveled to a convention in Heidelberg, Germany. We talked for five minutes in the banquet hall of the Heidelberg Castle, an impressive stone structure on a hillside overlooking the Neckar River valley.

I remember the castle and its immense wine casks (I climbed to the top of one, fully twenty feet high); I remember John Brunner delivering his toastmaster's remarks in both English and German; I remember accepting Ursula Le Guin's Hugo Award for *The Left Hand of Darkness* and apologizing for her absence, as she'd told me to do, by explaining that she was in kemmer. (A fan in the audience later asked me, "Where's Kemmer?") But of the historic meeting between Carr and Priest I remember no details at all.

Did we exchange mind-searing epigrams about the nature of the universe? Did we chart the future course of science fiction and lesser literatures? Did we establish instant rapport by discovering that we were both addicted to turtle soup Lady Curzon? No doubt we did all these things, but alas, all I remember is that Priest was young and ambitious, and I liked him.

Since then he's become recognized as one of the brightest talents in British science fiction, as a result of his novels *Indoctrinaire* and *The Inverted World* and a number of shorter works. When you read "An Infinite Summer," a love story with a time travel twist that's entirely new to science fiction, you'll realize that Christopher Priest has made his reputation through a lot more than ambition: he's an accomplished stylist who has marvelous stories to tell.

He has a memory that's even worse than mine, however: he doesn't remember meeting *me* at *all*. Hmp.

August, 1940.

There was a war on, but it made no difference to Thomas James Lloyd. The war was an inconvenience, and it restricted his freedom, but on the whole it was the least of his preoccupations. Misfortune had brought him to this violent age, and he wanted none of its crises. He was apart from it, shadowed by it.

He stood now on the bridge over the Thames at Richmond, resting his hands on the parapet and staring south along the river. The sun reflected up from it, and he took his sunglasses from a metal case in his pocket and put them on.

Night was the only relief from the tableaux of frozen time; dark glasses approximated the relief.

It seemed to Thomas Lloyd that it was not long since he had last stood untroubled on this bridge, although by deduction he knew that this was not so. The memory of the day was clear, itself a moment of frozen time, undiminished. He remembered how he had stood here with his cousin, watching four young men from the town as they manhandled a punt upstream.

Richmond itself had changed from that time, but here by the river the view was much as he remembered it. Although there were more buildings along the banks, the meadows below Richmond Hill were untouched, and he could see the riverside walk disappearing around the bend in the river towards Twickenham.

For the moment the town was quiet. An air-raid alert had been sounded a few minutes before, and although there were still some vehicles moving through the streets, most pedestrians had taken temporary shelter inside shops and offices.

Lloyd had left them to walk again through the past.

He was a tall, well-built man, apparently young in years. He had been taken for twenty-five several times by strangers and Lloyd, a withdrawn, uncommunicative man, had allowed such errors to go uncorrected. Behind the dark glasses his eyes were still bright with the hopes of youth, but many tiny lines at the corners of his eyes, and a general sallowness to his skin, indicated that he was older. Even this, though, lent no clue to the truth. Thomas Lloyd had been born in 1881, and was now approaching sixty.

He took his watch from his waistcoat pocket, and saw that the time was a little after twelve. He turned to walk towards the pub on the Isleworth road, but then noticed a man standing by himself on the path beside the river. Even wearing the sunglasses, which filtered away the more intrusive reminders of past and future, Lloyd could see that it was one of the men he called freezers. This was a young man, rather plump and with prematurely balding hair. He had seen Lloyd, for as Lloyd looked down at him the young man turned ostentatiously away. Lloyd had nothing now to fear from the freezers, but they were always about and their presence never failed to make him uneasy.

Far away, in the direction of Barnes, Lloyd could hear another air-raid siren droning out its warning.

June, 1903.

The world was at peace, and the weather was warm. Thomas James Lloyd, recently down from Cambridge, twenty-one years of age, moustachioed, light of tread, walked gaily through the trees that grew across the side of Richmond Hill.

It was a Sunday and there were many people about. Earlier in the day Thomas had attended church with his father and mother and sister, sitting in the pew that was reserved traditionally for the Lloyds of Richmond. The house on the Hill had belonged to the family for more than two hundred years, and William Lloyd, the present head of the family, owned most of the houses on the Sheen side of town as well as administering one of the largest businesses in the whole of Surrey. A family of substance indeed, and Thomas James Lloyd lived in the knowledge that one day the substance would be his by inheritance.

Worldly matters thus assured, Thomas felt free to divert his attention to activities of a more important nature; namely, Charlotte Carrington and her sister Sarah.

That one day he would marry one of the two sisters had been an inevitability long acknowledged by both families, although precisely which of the two it would be had been occupying his thoughts for many weeks.

There was much to choose between the two—or so Thomas himself considered—but if his choice had been free then his mind would have been at rest. Unfortunately for him it had been made plain by the girls' parents that it would be Charlotte who would make the better wife for a future industrialist and landowner, and in many ways this was so. The difficulty arose because Thomas had fallen impetuously for her younger sister Sarah, a state of affairs of absolutely no moment to Mrs. Carrington.

Charlotte, twenty years of age, was an undeniably

handsome girl, and Thomas much enjoyed her company. She appeared to be prepared to accept a proposal of marriage from him, and to be fair she was endowed with much grace and intelligence, but whenever they had been together neither had had much of interest to say to the other. Charlotte was an ambitious and emancipated girl—for so she styled herself—and was constantly reading historical tracts. Her one consuming interest was in touring the various churches of Surrey to take brass-rubbings from the plates there. Thomas, a liberal and understanding young man, was pleased she had found a hobby, but could not own to any mutual interest.

Sarah Carrington was an altogether different proposition. Two years younger than her sister, and thus, by her mother's estimation, not yet eligible for marriage (or not, at least, until a husband had been found for Charlotte), Sarah was at once a person to be coveted by virtue of her unavailability, and yet also a delightful personality in her own right. When Thomas had first paid visits to Charlotte, Sarah was still being finished at school, but by astute questioning of Charlotte and his own sister, Thomas had discovered that Sarah liked to play tennis and croquet, was a keen bicyclist, and was acquainted with all the latest dance-steps. A surreptitious glance into the family's photographic album had established that she was also astoundingly beautiful. This last aspect of her he had confirmed for himself at their first meeting, and he had promptly fallen in love with her. Since then he had contrived to transfer his attentions, and with no small measure of success. Twice already he had spoken to her alone . . . no minor achievement when one considered the enthusiasm with which Mrs. Carrington encouraged Thomas always to be with Charlotte. Once he had been left alone with Sarah for a few minutes in the Carringtons' drawing-room, and on the second occasion he had managed a few words with her during a family picnic. Even on this brief acquaintance, Thomas had become convinced that he would settle for no less a wife than Sarah.

So it was that on this Sunday Thomas's mood was full of light, for by a most agreeable contrivance he had ensured himself at least an hour alone with Sarah.

The instrument of this contrivance was one Waring Lloyd, a cousin of his. Waring had always seemed to Thomas a most unconscionable oaf, but remembering that Charlotte had once remarked on him (and feeling that each would be eminently suited to the other), Thomas had proposed a riverside stroll for the afternoon. Waring, suitably confided in, would delay Charlotte while they walked, so allowing Thomas and Sarah to go on ahead.

Thomas was several minutes early for the rendezvous, and paced to and fro good-naturedly while waiting for his cousin. It was cooler by the river, for the trees grew right down to the water's edge, and several of the ladies walking along the path behind the boathouse had folded their parasols and were clutching shawls about their shoulders.

When at last Waring appeared, the two cousins greeted each other amiably—more so than at any time in the recent past—and debated whether they should cross by the ferry, or walk the long way round by the bridge. There was still plenty of time in hand, so they opted for the latter course.

Thomas once again reminded Waring of what was to happen during the stroll, and Waring confirmed that he understood. The arrangement was no sacrifice to him, for he found Charlotte no less delightful than Sarah, and would doubtless find much to say to the older girl.

Later, as they crossed Richmond Bridge to the Middlesex side of the river, Thomas paused, resting his hands on the stone parapet of the bridge. He was watching four young men struggling ineptly with a punt, trying to manoeuvre it against the stream towards the side, while on the bank two older men shouted conflicting instructions.

August, 1940.

"You'd better take cover, sir. Just in case."

Thomas Lloyd was startled by the voice at his side, and he turned. It was an air-raid warden, an elderly man in a dark uniform. On his shoulder, and stencilled on his metal helmet, were the letters A.R.P. In spite of his polite tone of voice he was looking suspiciously at Lloyd. The part-time work Lloyd had been doing in Richmond paid barely enough for food and lodgings, and what little spare there was usually went on drink; he was still wearing substantially the same clothes as he had five years ago, and they were the worse for wear.

"Is there going to be a raid?" Lloyd said.

"Never can tell. Jerry's still bombing the ports, but he'll start on the towns any day now."

They both glanced towards the sky in the south-east. There, high in the blue, were several white vapour-trails curling, but no other evidence of the German bombers everyone so feared.

"I'll be safe," Lloyd said. "I'm going for a walk. I'll be away from the houses if a raid starts."

"That's all right, sir. If you meet anyone else out there, remind them there's an alert on."

"I'll do that."

The warden nodded to him, then walked slowly towards the town. Lloyd raised his sunglasses for a moment and watched him.

A few yards from where they had been standing was one of the freezers' tableaux: two men and a woman. When he had first noticed this tableau Lloyd had inspected the people carefully, and had judged by their clothes that they must have been frozen at some time in the mid-19th century. This tableau was the oldest he had so far discovered, and as such was of especial interest to him. He had learned that the moment of a tableau's erosion was unpredictable. Some tableaux lasted for several years, others only a day or two. The fact that this one had survived for at least ninety years indicated just how erratic the erosions were.

The three frozen people were halted in their walk directly in front of the warden, who hobbled along the pavement towards them. As he reached them he showed no sign of awareness, and in a moment had passed right through them.

Lloyd lowered his sunglasses, and the image of the three people became vague and ill-defined.

June, 1903.

When Waring's prospects were compared with those of Thomas they seemed unremarkable, but by normal standards they were nonetheless considerable. Accordingly, Mrs. Carrington (who knew more about the distribution of the Lloyd wealth than anyone outside immediate family circles) greeted Waring with civility.

The two young men were offered a glass of cold lemon tea, and then asked for their opinion on some matter concerning an herbaceous border. Thomas, by now well used to Mrs. Carrington's small talk, couched his reply in a few words, but Waring, anxious to please, set forth into a detailed response. He was still speaking knowledgeably of replanting and bedding when the girls appeared. They walked out through the french window and came across the lawn towards them.

Seen together it was obvious that the two were sisters, but to Thomas's eager eye one girl's beauty easily outshone the other's. Charlotte's expression was more earnest, and her bearing more practical. Sarah affected a modesty and timorousness (although Thomas knew it to be just an affectation), and her smile when she saw the young men was enough to convince Thomas that from this moment his life would be an eternity of summer.

Twenty minutes passed while the four young people and the girls' mother walked about the garden. Thomas, at first impatient to put his scheme to the test, managed after a few minutes to control himself. He had noticed that both Mrs. Carrington and Charlotte were amused by Waring's conversation, and this was an unexpected bonus. After all, the whole afternoon lay ahead, and these minutes were being well spent!

At last they were released from their courtesies, and the four set off for their planned stroll.

The girls each carried a sunshade: Charlotte's was white, Sarah's was pink. As they went through the grounds towards the riverside walk the girls' dresses rustled on the long grass, although Charlotte raised her skirt a little, for she said that grass so stained cotton.

Approaching the river they heard the sounds of other people: children calling, a girl and a man from the town laughing together, and a rowing-eight striking in unison to the cox's instructions. As they came to the riverside path, and the two young men helped the girls over a stile, a mongrel dog leaped out of the water some twenty yards away and shook itself with great gusto.

The path was not wide enough for them to walk abreast, and so Thomas and Sarah took the lead. Just once he was able to catch Waring's eye, and the other gave the slightest of nods.

A few minutes later, Waring delayed Charlotte to show her a swan and some cygnets swimming by the reeds, and Thomas and Sarah walked slowly on ahead.

By now they were some distance from the town, and meadows lay on either side of the river.

August, 1940.

The pub was set back a short distance from the road, with an area in front of it laid with paving-stones. On these, before the war, there had been five circular metal tables where one could drink in the open air, but they had been removed for scrap-iron during the last winter. Apart from this, and the fact that the windows had been criss-crossed with tape in Home Office approved fashion, to prevent glass splinters flying, there was no outward sign that business was not normal.

Inside Lloyd ordered a pint of bitter, and took it with him to one of the tables.

He sipped the drink, then regarded the other occupants of the bar.

Apart from himself and the barmaid there were four other people present. Two men sat morosely together at one table, half-empty glasses of stout before them. Another man sat alone at a table by the door. He had a newspaper on the table before him, and was staring at the crossword.

The fourth person, who stood against one of the walls, was a freezer. This one, Lloyd noted, was a woman. She, like the men freezers, wore a drab grey overall, and held one of the freeze instruments. This was shaped rather like a modern portable camera, and was carried on a lanyard strung around the neck, but it was much larger than a camera and was approximately cubical in shape. At the front, where on a camera would be a viewfinder and lens, there was a rectangular strip of white glass, apparently opaque or translucent, and it was through this that the freezing-beam was projected.

Lloyd, still wearing his dark glasses, could only just see the woman. She did not seem to be looking in his direction, but after a few seconds she stepped back through the wall and disappeared from his sight.

He noticed that the barmaid was watching him, and as soon as she had caught his eye she spoke to him.

"D'you think they're coming this time?"

"I shouldn't care to speculate," Lloyd said, not wishing to be drawn into conversation. He took several mouthfuls of the beer, wanting to finish it and be on his way.

"These sirens have ruined the trade," the barmaid said. "One after the other, all day and sometimes in the evenings too. And it's always a false alarm."

"Yes," Lloyd said.

She continued with her complaints for a few more seconds, but then someone called her from the other bar and she went to serve him. Lloyd was greatly relieved, for he disliked speaking to people here. He had felt isolated for too long, and had never mastered the modern way of conversation. Quite often he was misunderstood, for it was his way to speak in the more formal manner of his own contemporaries.

He was regretting having delayed. This would have been a good time to go to the meadows, for while the air-raid alert was on there would be only a few people about. He disliked not being alone when he walked by the river.

He drank the rest of his beer, then stood up and walked towards the door.

As he did so he noticed for the first time that there was a recent tableau by the door. He did not seek out the tableaux, for he found their presence disturbing, but new ones were nevertheless of interest.

There were two men and a woman seeming to sit at a table; the image of them was indistinct, and so Lloyd took off his sunglasses. At once the brilliance of the tableau surprised him, seeming to overshadow the man who still sat regarding his crossword at the far end of the table.

One of the two frozen men was younger than the other two people, and he sat slightly apart. He was smoking, for a cigarette lay on the edge of the table, the end overhanging the wooden surface by a few millimetres. The older man and the woman were together, for the woman's hand was held in the man's, and he was bending forward to kiss her wrist. His lips rested on her arm, and his eyes were closed. The woman, still slim and attractive although apparently well into her forties, seemed amused by this for she was smiling, but she was not watching her friend. Instead, she was looking across the table at the younger man, who, beer-glass raised to his mouth, was watching the kiss with interest. On the table between them was the man's untouched glass of bitter, and the woman's glass of port. They had been eating potato crisps, for a crumpled paper bag and the blue salt-packet lay in the ashtray. The smoke from the young man's cigarette, grey and curling, was motionless in the air, and a piece of ash, falling towards the ground, hovered a few inches above the carpet.

"You want something, mate?" It was the man with the crossword.

Lloyd put on his sunglasses again with unseemly haste, realising that for the last few seconds he had been seeming to stare at the man.

"I beg your pardon," he said, and fell back on the excuse he gave when such embarrassments occurred. "I thought for a moment I recognised you."

The man peered myopically up at him. "Never seen you before in my life."

Lloyd affected a vacant nod, and passed on towards the door. For a moment he caught a glimpse again of the three frozen victims. The young man with the beer-glass, watching coolly; the man kissing, bent over so that his upper body was almost horizontal; the woman smiling, watching the young man and enjoying the attention she was being paid; the cigarette smoke static.

Lloyd went through the door, and into the sunshine.

June, 1903.

"Your mama wishes me to marry your sister," Thomas said.

"I know. It is not what Charlotte desires."

"Nor I. May I enquire as to your feelings on the matter?"

"I am in accord, Thomas."

They were walking along slowly, about three feet apart from each other. Both stared at the gravel of the path as they walked, not meeting the other's eyes. Sarah was turning her parasol through her fingers, causing the tassels to swirl and tangle. Now they were in the riverside meadows they were almost alone, although Waring and Charlotte were following about two hundred yards behind.

"Would you say that we were strangers, Sarah?"

"By what standards do you mean?" She had paused a little before responding.

"Well, for instance this is the first occasion on which we have been allowed any degree of intimacy together."

"And that by a contrivance," Sarah said.

"What do you mean?"

"I saw you signal to your cousin."

Thomas felt himself go a little red, but he considered that in the brightness and warmth of the afternoon a flush would go unnoticed. On the river the rowing-eight had turned, and were now passing them again.

After a few moments, Sarah said: "I am not avoiding your question, Thomas. I am considering whether or not we are strangers."

"Then what do you say?"

"I think we know each other a little."

"I should be glad to see you again, Sarah. Without the need for contrivance, that is."

"Charlotte and I will speak to Mama. You have already been much discussed, Thomas, although not as yet with Mama. You need not fear for hurting my sister's feelings, for although she likes you she does not yet feel ready for marriage."

Thomas, his pulse racing, felt a rush of confidence within him.

"And you, Sarah?" he said. "May I continue to court you?"

She turned away from him then, and stepped through the long grass beside the edge of the path. He saw the long sweep of her skirt, and the shining pink circle of her parasol. Her left hand dangled at her side, brushing lightly against her skirt.

She said: "I find your advances most welcome, Thomas."

Her voice was faint, but the words reached his ears as if she had pronounced them clearly in a silent room.

Thomas's response was immediate. He swept his boater from his head, and opened his arms wide.

"My dearest Sarah," he cried. "Will you marry me?"

She turned to face him and for a moment she was still, regarding him seriously. Her parasol rested on her shoulder, no longer turning. Then, seeing that he was in earnest, she smiled a little, and Thomas saw that she too had allowed a blush of pink to colour her cheeks.

"Yes, of course I will," Sarah said.

She stepped towards him extending her left hand, and Thomas, his straw hat still held high, reached forward with his right hand to take hers.

Neither Thomas nor Sarah could have seen that in that moment a man had stepped forward from beside the water's edge, and was levelling at them a small black instrument.

August, 1940.

The all-clear had not sounded, but the town seemed to be returning to life. Traffic was crossing Richmond Bridge, and a short distance down the road towards Isleworth a queue was forming outside a grocer's shop while a delivery-van was parked alongside the kerb. Now that he was at last setting off on his daily walk, Thomas Lloyd felt more at ease with the tableaux, and he took off his dark glasses for the last time and returned them to their case.

In the centre of the bridge was the overturning carriage. The driver, a gaunt middle-aged man wearing a green coat and shiny black top hat, had his left arm raised. In his hand he was holding the whip, and the lash snaked up over the bridge in a graceful curve. His right hand was already releasing the reins, and was reaching forward towards the hard road-surface in a desperate attempt to soften the impact of his fall. In the open compartment at the rear was an elderly lady, much powdered and veiled, wearing a black velvet coat. She had been thrown sideways from her seat as the wheel-axle broke, and was holding up her hands in fright. Of the two horses in harness, one was apparently unaware of the accident, and had been frozen in mid-stride. The other, though, had tossed back its head and raised both its forelegs. Its nostrils were flaring, and behind the blinkers its eyes were rolled back.

As Lloyd crossed the road a red G.P.O. van drove through the tableau, the driver quite unaware of its presence.

Two of the freezers were waiting at the top of the shallow ramp which led down to the riverside walk, and as Lloyd turned to follow the path towards the distant meadows, the two men walked a short distance behind him.

June, 1903, to January, 1935.

The summer's day, with its two young lovers imprisoned, became a moment extended.

Thomas James Lloyd, straw hat raised in his left hand, his other hand reaching out. His right knee was slightly bent, as if he were about to kneel, and his face was full of happiness and expectation. A breeze seemed to be ruffling his hair, for three strands stood on end, but these had been dislodged when he removed his hat. A tiny winged insect, which had settled on his lapel, was frozen in its moment of flight, an instinct to escape too late.

A short distance away stood Sarah Carrington. The sun fell across her face, highlighting the locks of auburn hair that fell from beneath her bonnet. One foot, stepping towards Thomas, showed itself beneath the hem of her skirt, shod in a buttoned boot. Her right hand was lifting a pink parasol away from her shoulder, as if she were about to wave it in joy. She was laughing, and her eyes, soft and brown, gazed with affection at the young man before her.

Their hands were extended towards each other's. Sarah's left hand was an inch from his right, her fingers already curling in anticipation of holding his.

Thomas's fingers, reaching out, revealed by irregular white patches that until an instant before his fists had been clenched in anxious tension.

The whole: the long grass moist after a shower a few hours before, the pale brown gravel of the path, the wild flowers that grew in the meadow, the adder that basked not four feet from the couple, the clothes, their skin . . . all were rendered in colours bleached and saturated with preternatural luminosity.

August, 1940.

There was a sound of aircraft in the air.

Although aircraft were unknown in his time, Thomas Lloyd had now grown accustomed to them. He understood that before the war there had been civilian aircraft, but he had never seen any of these, and since then the only ones he had seen were warplanes. Like everyone else of the time he was familiar with the sight of the high black shapes, and with the curious droning, throbbing sound of the enemy bombers. Each day air-battles were being fought over south-east England; sometimes the bombers evaded the fighters, sometimes not.

He glanced up at the sky. While he had been inside the pub, the vapour-trails he had seen earlier had disappeared; a new pattern of white had appeared, however, more recently made, further to the north.

Lloyd walked down the Middlesex side of the river. Looking directly across the river he saw how the town had been extended since his day: on the Surrey side of the river the trees which had once concealed the houses were mostly gone, and in their place were shops and offices. On this side, where houses had been set back from the river, more had been built close to the bank. As far as he could see, only the wooden boathouse had survived intact from his time, and that was badly in need of a coat of paint.

He was at the focus of past, present and future: only the boathouse and the river itself were as clearly defined as he. The freezers, from some unknown period of the future, as ethereal to ordinary men as their wishful dreams, moved like shadows through light, stealing sudden moments with their incomprehensible devices. The tableaux themselves, frozen, isolated, insubstantial, waiting in an eternity of silence for those people of the future generation to see them.

Encompassing all was a turbulent present, obsessed with war.

Thomas Lloyd, of neither past nor present, saw himself as a product of both, and a victim of the future.

Then, from high above the town, there came the sound of an explosion and a roar of engines, and the present impinged on Lloyd's consciousness. A British fighter-plane banked away towards the south, and a German bomber fell burning towards the ground. After a few seconds two men escaped from the aircraft, and their parachutes opened.

January, 1935.

As if waking from a dream, Thomas experienced a moment of recall and recognition, but in an instant it was gone.

He saw Sarah before him, reaching towards him; he saw the bright garishness of the heightened colours; he saw the stillness of the frozen summer's day.

It faded as he looked, and he cried out Sarah's name. She made no move or reply, stayed immobile, and the light around her darkened.

Thomas pitched forward, a great weakness overcoming his limbs, and he fell to the ground.

It was night, and snow lay thickly on the meadows beside the Thames.

August, 1940.

Until the moment of its final impact, the bomber fell in virtual silence. Both engines had stopped, although only one was on fire, and flame and smoke poured from the fuselage, leaving behind a thick black trail across the sky. The 'plane crashed by the bend in the river, and there was a huge explosion. Meanwhile, the two Germans who had escaped from the aircraft drifted down across Richmond Hill, swaying beneath their parachutes.

Lloyd shaded his eyes with his hands, and watched to see where they would land. One had been carried further by the aircraft before jumping and was much nearer, falling slowly towards the river.

The Civil Defence authorities in the town were evidently alert, for within a few moments of the parachutes appearing, Lloyd heard the sound of police- and fire-bells.

There was a movement a short distance from Lloyd, and he turned. The two freezers who had been following him had been joined by two others, one of whom was the woman he had seen inside the pub. The freezer who seemed to be the youngest had already raised his device, and was pointing it across the river, but the other three were saying something to him. (Lloyd could see their lips moving, and the expressions on their faces, but, as always, he could not hear them.) The young man shrugged away the restraining hand of one of the others, and walked down the bank to the edge of the water.

One of the Germans came down near the edge of Richmond Park, and was lost to sight as he fell beyond the houses built near the crest of the Hill; the other, buoyed up temporarily by a sudden updraught, drifted out across the river itself, and was now only some fifty feet in the air. Lloyd could see the German aviator pulling on the cords of his parachute, trying desperately to steer himself towards the bank. As air spilled from the white shroud, he fell more quickly.

The young freezer by the edge of the river was levelling his device, apparently aiming it with the aid of a reflex sight built into the instrument. A moment later the German's efforts to save himself from falling into the water were rewarded in a way he could never have anticipated: ten feet above the surface of the water, his knees raised to take the brunt of the impact, one arm waving, the German was frozen in flight.

The freezer lowered his instrument, and Lloyd stared across the water at the hapless man suspended in the air.

January, 1935.

The transformation of a summer's day into a winter's night was the least of the changes that Thomas Lloyd discovered on regaining consciousness. In what had been for him a few seconds he had moved from a world of stability, peace and prosperity to one where dynamic and violent situations obtained. In that same short moment of time, he himself had lost the security of his assured future, and become a pauper. Most traumatically of all, he had never been allowed to take to its fruition the surge of love he had felt for Sarah.

Night was the only relief from the tableaux, and Sarah was still held in frozen time.

He recovered consciousness shortly before dawn, and, not understanding what had happened to him, walked slowly back towards Richmond town. The sun had risen shortly after, and as light struck the tableaux that littered the paths and roads, and as it struck the freezers who constantly moved in their half-world of intrusive futurity, Lloyd realised neither that in these lay the cause of his own predicament, nor that his perception of the images was itself a product of his experience.

In Richmond he was found by a policeman, and was taken to hospital. Here, treated for the pneumonia he had contracted as he lay in the snow, and later for the amnesia that seemed the only explanation for his condition, Thomas Lloyd saw the freezers moving through the wards and corridors. The tableaux were here too: a dying man falling from his bed; a young nurse—dressed in the uniform of fifty years before—frozen as she walked from a ward, a deep frown creasing her brow; a child throwing a ball in the garden by the convalescent wing.

As he was nursed back to physical health, Lloyd became obsessed with a need to return to the meadows by the river, and before he was fully recovered he discharged himself and went directly there.

By then the snow had melted, but the weather was

still cold and a white frost lay on the ground. Out by the river, where a bank of grass grew thickly beside the path, was a frozen moment of summer, and in its midst was Sarah.

He could see her, but she could not see him; he could take the hand that was rightly his to take, but his fingers would pass through the illusion; he could walk around her, seeming to step through the green summer grasses, and feel the cold of the frozen soil penetrating the thin soles of his shoes.

And as night fell so the moment of the past became invisible, and Thomas was relieved of the agony of the vision.

Time passed, but there was never a day when he did not walk along the riverside path, and stand again before the image of Sarah, and reach out to take her hand.

August, 1940.

The German parachutist hung above the river, and Lloyd looked again at the freezers. They were apparently still criticising the youngest of them for his action, and yet seemed fascinated with his result. It was certainly one of the most dramatic tableaux Lloyd himself had seen.

Now that the man had been frozen it was possible to see that his eyes were tightly closed, and that he was holding his nose with his fingers in anticipation of his plunge. In addition, it now became clear that he had been wounded in the aircraft, because blood was staining his flying-jacket. The tableau was at once amusing and poignant, a reminder to Lloyd that, however unreal this present might be to him, it was no illusion to the people of the time.

In a moment Lloyd understood the particular interest of the freezers in this unfortunate airman, for without warning the pocket of frozen time eroded and the young German plunged into the river. The parachute billowed and folded in on top of him. As he surfaced he thrashed his arms wildly, trying to free himself of the constraining cords.

It was not the first time Lloyd had seen a tableau erode, but he had never before seen it happen so soon after freezing. It had always seemed to him a matter of chance, but having seen the distance from which the beam had been released—the airman had been at least fifty yards away—he surmised that the time a tableau survived was probably dependent on how close the subject was to the freezer. (He himself had escaped from his own tableau; had Sarah been nearer the freezer when the beam was released?)

In the centre of the river the German had succeeded in freeing himself of the parachute, and was swimming slowly towards the opposite bank. His descent must have been observed by the authorities, because even before he reached the sloping landing-stage of the boathouse, four policemen had appeared from the direction of the road, and helped him out of the water. He made no attempt to resist capture but lay weakly on the ground, awaiting the arrival of an ambulance.

Lloyd remembered the only other time he had seen a tableau erode quickly. A freezer had acted to prevent a traffic-accident: a man stepping carelessly into the path of a car had been frozen in mid-step. Although the driver of the car had stopped abruptly, and had looked around in amazement for the man he thought he had been about to kill, he had evidently assumed that he had imagined the incident, for he eventually drove off again. Only Lloyd, with his ability to see the tableaux, could still see the man: stepping back, arms flailing in terror, still seeing too late the oncoming vehicle. Three days later, when Lloyd returned to the place, the tableau had eroded and the man was gone. He, like Lloyd—and now the German aviator—would be moving through a half-world, one where past, present and future co-existed uneasily.

Lloyd watched the shroud of the parachute drift along the river until at last it sank, and then turned away to continue his walk to the meadows. As he did so he realised that even more of the freezers had appeared on this side of the river, and were walking behind him, following him.

As he reached the bend in the river, from which point he always gained his first sight of Sarah, he saw that the bomber had crashed in the meadows. The explosion of its impact had set fire to the grass, and the smoke from this, together with that from the burning wreckage, obscured his view.

January, 1935, to August, 1940.
Thomas Lloyd never again left Richmond. He lived inexpensively, found occasional work, tried not to be outstanding in any way.

What of the past? He discovered that on 22nd June, 1903, his apparent disappearance with Sarah had led to the conclusion that he had absconded with her. His father, William Lloyd, head of the noted Richmond family, had disowned him. Colonel and Mrs. Carrington had announced a reward for his arrest, but in 1910 they had moved away from the area. Thomas also discovered that his cousin Waring had never married Charlotte, and that he had emigrated to Australia. His own parents were both dead, there was no means of tracing his sister, and the family home had been sold and demolished.

(On the day he read the files of the local newspaper, he stood with Sarah, overcome with grief.)

What of the future? It was pervasive, intrusive. It existed on a plane where only those who were frozen and released could sense it. It existed in the form of men who came to freeze the images of the present.

(On the day he first understood what the shadowy men he called freezers might be, he stood beside Sarah, staring around protectively. That day, as if sensing Lloyd's realisation, one of the freezers had walked along the river-bank, watching the young man and his time-locked sweetheart.)

What of the present? Lloyd neither cared for the present nor shared it with its occupants. It was violent, alien, frightening. The machines and men were threatening. It was, to him, as vague a presence as the other two dimensions. Only the past and its frozen images were real.

(On the day he first saw a tableau erode he ran all the way to the meadows, and stood long into the evening, trying ceaselessly for the first sign of substance in Sarah's outstretched hand.)

August, 1940.

Only in the riverside meadows, where the town was distant and the houses were concealed by trees, did Thomas ever feel at one with the present. Here past and present fused, for little had changed since his day. Here he could stand before the image of Sarah and fancy himself still on that summer's day in 1903, still the young man with raised straw hat and slightly bended knee. Here too he rarely saw any of the freezers, and the few tableaux visible (further along the walk an elderly fisherman had been time-locked as he pulled a trout from the stream; towards the distant houses of Twickenham, a little boy in a sailor-suit walked sulkily with his nanny) could be accepted as a natural part of the world he had known.

Today, though, the present had intruded violently. The exploding bomber had scattered fragments of itself across the meadows. Black smoke from the wreckage spread in an oily cloud across the river, and the smouldering grass poured white smoke to drift beside it. Much of the ground had already been blackened by fire.

Sarah was invisible to him, lost somewhere in the smoke.

Thomas paused, and took a kerchief from his pocket. He stooped by the river's edge and soaked it in the water, then, after wringing it out, he held it over his nose and mouth.

He glanced behind him and saw that there were now eight of the freezers with him. They were paying no attention to him, and walked on while he prepared himself, insensible to the smoke. They passed through the burning grass, and walked towards the main concentration of wreckage. One of the freezers was already making some kind of adjustment to his device.

A breeze had sprung up in the last few minutes, and it caused the smoke to move away smartly from the fires, staying lower on the ground. As this happened, Thomas saw the image of Sarah above the smoke. He hurried towards her, alarmed by the proximity of the burning aircraft, even as he knew that neither fire, explosion nor smoke could harm her.

His feet threw up smouldering grasses as he went towards her, and at times the variable wind caused the smoke to swirl about his head. His eyes were watering, and although his wetted kerchief acted as a partial filter against the grass-smoke, when the oily fumes from the aircraft gusted around him he choked and gagged on the acrid vapours.

At length he decided to wait; Sarah was safe inside her cocoon of frozen time, and there was no conceivable point to his suffocating simply to be with her, when in a few minutes the fire would burn itself out.

He retreated to the edge of the burning area, rinsed out his kerchief in the river, and sat down to wait.

The freezers were exploring the wreckage with the greatest interest, apparently drifting through the flames and smoke to enter the deepest parts of the conflagration.

There came the sound of a bell away to Thomas's right, and in a moment a fire-tender halted in the narrow lane that ran along the distant edge of the meadows. Several firemen climbed down, and stood looking across the field at the wreckage. At this Thomas's heart sank, for he realised what was to follow. He had sometimes seen photographs in the newspapers of crashed German aircraft; they were invariably placed under military guard until the pieces could be taken away for examination. If this were to happen here it would deny him access to Sarah for several days.

For the moment, though, he would still have a chance to be with her. He was too far away to hear what the firemen were saying, but it looked as if no attempt was going to be made to put out the fire. Smoke still poured from the fuselage, but the flames had died down, and most of the smoke was coming from the grass. With no houses in the vicinity, and with the wind blowing towards the river, there was little likelihood the fire would spread.

He stood up again, and walked quickly towards Sarah.

In a few moments he had reached her, and she stood before him: eyes shining in the sunlight, parasol lifting, arm extending. She was in a sphere of safety; although smoke blew through her, the grasses on which she stood were green and moist and cool. As he had done every day for more than five years, Thomas stood facing her and waited for a sign of the erosion of her tableau. He stepped, as he had frequently done before, into the area of the time-freeze. Here, although his foot appeared to press on the grasses of 1903, a flame curled around his leg and he was forced to step back quickly.

Thomas saw some of the freezers coming towards him. They had apparently inspected the wreckage to their satisfaction, and judged none of it worth preserving in a time-freeze. Thomas tried to disregard them, but their sinister silence could not be forgotten easily.

The smoke poured about him, rich and heady with the smells of burning grass, and he looked again at Sarah. Just as time had frozen about her in that moment, so it had frozen about his love for her. Time had not diminished, it had preserved.

The freezers were watching him. Thomas saw that the eight vague figures, standing not ten feet away from him, were looking at him with interest. Then, on the far side of the meadow, one of the firemen shouted something at him. He would seem to be standing here alone;

no one could see the tableaux, no one knew of the freezers. The fireman walked towards him, waving an arm, telling him to move away. It would take him a minute or more to reach them, and that was time enough for Thomas.

One of the freezers stepped forward, and in the heart of the smoke Thomas saw the captured summer begin to dim. Smoke curled up around Sarah's feet, and flame licked through the moist, time-frozen grasses around her ankles. He saw the fabric at the bottom of her skirt begin to scorch.

And her hand, extended towards him, lowered.

The parasol fell to the ground.

Sarah's head drooped forward, but immediately she was conscious . . . and the step towards him, commenced thirty-seven years before, was concluded.

"Thomas?" Her voice was clear, untouched.

He rushed towards her.

"Thomas! The smoke! What is happening?"

"Sarah . . . my love!"

As she went into his arms he realised that her skirt had taken fire, but he placed his arms around her shoulders and hugged her intimately and tenderly. He could feel her cheek, still warm from the blush of so long ago, nestling against his. Her hair, falling loose beneath her bonnet, lay across his face, and the pressure of her arms around his waist was no less than that of his own.

Dimly, he saw a grey movement beyond them, and in a moment the noises were stilled and the smoke ceased to swirl. The flame which had taken purchase on the hem of her skirt now died, and the summer sun which warmed them shone lightly in the tableau. Past and future became one, the present faded, life stilled, life for ever.

The Highest Dive

Jack Williamson

One of the pervading bits of folk-wisdom about science fiction says that after you've been reading sf for a few years you lose your sense of wonder, become jaded and downright cynical about the works of authors who used to seem godlike. This is particularly true for people who become involved in the science-fiction community, that nebulous group of professionals and fans who turn up week after month after year at club meetings and conventions to exchange shop-talk, brag or complain about the state of the market, and gossip about some competitor who likes to tie up his Doberman pinscher and read Perry Rhodan stories to him. (A fictitious example. Actually it was an iguana, and novels by Stanislaw Lem.)

At sentimental public gatherings we like to refer to this community as our "family"—conveniently ignoring the difficulty of regarding the brother who always stuck you with doing the dishes with as much awe as the blurbs on his books give him.

The fact is, if you're a writer attending a meeting in honor of the editor who rejected two stories that won Hugo Awards for you when someone else published them, you're likely to find your adulation for that editor a bit diluted . . . and if you're an editor listening to polysyllabic exclamations over the stylistic achievements of an author who, you know from harried experience, can't spell "cat" without looking it up in the dictionary under K, your reaction will be much the same.

I've been around this field for more than two decades, so though I stoutly maintain I've never lost my sense of wonder, I will admit that sometimes my awe is triggered by people doing things of which I hadn't thought them capable.

Not in the case of Jack Williamson, however. He's done so much in the nearly fifty years he's been publishing science-fiction stories—demonstrated writing techniques in advance of the time, introduced ideas like antimatter that proved fertile ground for generations to follow, pioneered in the field of college science-fiction courses—that my admiration for him remains unalloyed. He's truly a giant in our field.

Imagine my consternation, then, when on April 10, 1976, during a break in the Nebula Awards Banquet of the Science Fiction Writers of America, I took the opportunity to visit the men's room . . . and discovered Jack Williamson standing at the urinal to my right.

What does one say on such an occasion? Is it an appropriate time to tell a man you've always admired his works? Somehow it didn't seem so, yet I didn't want to let the moments pass without saying *something*.

So I remarked brightly, "Say, Jack, would you believe that just yesterday I was reading a story of yours in a fanzine published in 1940?"

"Oh; you mean the one in *Stardust?*" he said calmly, for all the world as though I'd just said something fit for civilized notice. "I wrote that when I was in my teens, and was never able to sell it to the professional magazines."

"Well, I uh, I read it yesterday," I said. I flushed, prematurely.

"I'd almost forgotten it," he said.

"Wasn't bad," I said, and flushed again.

"Thank you." He flushed too, and washed his hands, and left.

Less than an hour later, before an applauding crowd of the Science Fiction Writers of America, Jack Williamson received the Grand Master Nebula in honor of his lifetime of achievements in science fiction. Frederik Pohl gave a speech in his honor, and a laudatory letter from Robert A. Heinlein was read.

I sat at my table and beamed, proud that I had been privileged to share an informal few moments with Jack Williamson.

Williamson doesn't write many short stories these days; he's too busy with novels. But the following story appeared in the British magazine *Science Fiction Monthly,* serving to remind us that Williamson has lost none of his skills for bringing to life the scenery of other planets and the far future.

Nor, as you'll see, has he lost his sense of wonder.

The roaring woke him from a crazy dream of wild bulls bellowing. He sat up in the dark, tight with a shock of fear. One dim red light glowed over vague shapes around him, but they looked strange. His breath stopped—till he remembered that the red light was there to mark the shelter exit. Then everything came back.

Atlas, which people called "the impossible planet" because it was a million times too big to be a planet at all. The Galactic Survey camp, where the shuttle ship had dropped him two Earth-days ago. Komatsu and Marutiak, the human spacemen with him.

But he couldn't understand that roaring, which had been the bellow of bulls in his dream. It battered his body, ached in his bones, dazed his brain.

"Komatsu!" He was shouting, but he couldn't hear his own voice. "*Komatsu*!"

When he tried to listen, all he could hear was that near and steady thunder, always louder, louder, louder. Nothing moved in the shelter. The other men were on duty, maybe away from camp. He was all alone.

In his mind, that roar had become the yell of a black angry monster larger than Atlas. But he tried not to panic. Groping in the dark, he found the hard little disk of his voicepack, slung from his neck.

"Spaceman Mayfield—" His scream seemed fainter than a whisper, and he cupped both hands to shield the pack. "Mayfield to Komatsu. What is this noise—"

His question seemed suddenly stupid. Maybe cowardly. He didn't want Komatsu thinking Atlas had been too much for him.

"Spaceman Max Mayfield," he called again. "Requesting instructions."

The pack began quivering in his fingers. When he held it hard to his ear, he caught faint words in Komatsu's raspy voice.

". . . tornado . . . wild weather common . . . shelter pit . . . get there quick . . . hang on, kid!"

Briefing him after he landed, Komatsu had talked about the weird weather of Atlas and pointed out the shelter pit under the floor. He got his bearings now from the exit light and jumped for the pit.

He jumped too hard.

New on Atlas, he had forgotten how he had to move. He found himself floating in the dark above his bunk, grabbing at nothing, waiting for the weak gravity to pull him down. Before he could reach anything, the wind hit.

The blast of noise hurt his ears. The breath sucked out of his lungs. The exit light winked out. Something hit him. Something spun him. Something seized him, crushed him.

No monster, of course. He knew it was only a torn scrap of the shelter, wrapped around him by the freakish gusts. But it was bad enough. It pinned his arms and covered his face. He couldn't see, couldn't breathe.

He thought he would soon be dead.

Somehow, as he spun through the air, his mother's face came into his mind. Somehow her voice came back through the howling storm. "When you're dying," she was saying, "your whole life comes back in a single flash."

He wasn't sure that was true, but many things came rushing through his head. For a while he was trying to wriggle out of the stiff fabric around him, but his strength gave out. Finally, he just let past things flash back.

He thought of the morning at breakfast, long ago on the small Earth, when he first told his parents that he was going out to Atlas with the Galactic Survey.

"Max Mayfield!" When his mother used his full name, he knew she was angry. "We thought you were happy, here at home. We thought you loved poetry and math." He saw she was about to cry. "Why didn't you t-t-t-tell us?"

"We were hoping you might decide to stay here at the park and be a wilderness ranger." Speaking at the same time, his father frowned severely. "What's on Atlas?"

"Riddles." He put down his fork and tried to explain. "Nobody knows how anything could be so big. It's like a planet—but five thousand times as far around as Earth. I'll be on a survey team, looking for its secrets.

"Out on Atlas?" His mother's mouth gaped open. "With those space m-m-m-monsters?"

"Please, Mom!" He grinned at her tight face, but she wouldn't smile. "Ozark Wilderness is a nice quiet hiding place for us and the animals—if we're afraid of the future. But I've been hiding long enough. This is a new century, and I want to live in it. We have new worlds to know, and new friends in space."

"Giant spiders! Or worse!" She shivered. "I can't abide 'em!"

"Maybe they do look queer, but you've got to admire their brains." He tried and failed to make his father nod. "They've taught us a lot of new math. I'm glad they need us on Atlas, because I want to know them better."

"Need you?" His mother sat sadly shaking her head. "Why?"

"Because it's rough," he said. "Too rough for most of them. They hope the human teams will be tough enough and bright enough to survive there—long enough to find out what Atlas really is."

"You flabbergast us, son," his father said. "Because you've always been such a bookworm. If we're upset, it's just because we're afraid Atlas will be too much for you."

"Maybe I'm afraid, too." He had to nod. "But still I want to go. Because Atlas is a riddle—the biggest riddle in the universe. I want to prove I'm good enough to tackle it."

At that point his kid brother had come stumbling sleepily into the kitchen. The name of Atlas woke him into whooping excitement.

"You going *there*? Wow-wee! Tell about it."

They all listened while he talked about the space folk he had met and the terminal on the moon where his training would begin and the trans-sleep shots he would be taking for the long trip to Atlas. His mother was sniffling at first, but his father was soon patting her hands and they finally said they were proud that he had been chosen to go.

Atlas was nine thousand light-years from Earth, but

he had slept through the flight. The orbital station where he woke was strange enough, but his training had got him used to the feel of null gravity and the queer odors of the space people.

Now, waiting to die in the core of that bellowing storm, he remembered his first glimpse of Atlas, when the mission planner guided him into an observation bay. The sight shook him up.

Atlas was too big.

Still a million miles ahead, it was too big for him to see. His own Earth, at that distance, would have been a little blue-and-white marble. Atlas was endless. It was a hazy floor, mottled dark and bright, stretching out and out forever. Above it, space was a dead black dome.

"It—it gets you!" Its boundless flatness was too enormous for his mind to grasp. "What kind of world—what kind of *thing* can be so big?"

"Your mission is to help us find that out."

The planner's human voice had surprised him. Far from human itself, the space being had picked up not just the language but also the voice of Dr. Krim, the black-bearded linguist he had known on the moon.

"All we can see from here is the top of the clouds," the planner said. "You'll be a thousand miles below—with its low gravity, Atlas has a very deep atmosphere. The clouds never break, to show us anything. Down there, we hope you can see what it really is."

He looked down, wondering what the clouds were hiding.

"We have theories enough," the planner said. "Your team will be gathering facts to help us pick the best one. Are you ready to be briefed?"

"Ready."

The briefing officer looked like a big silver starfish, but, like the planner, it spoke with the rich and ringing human voice of Dr. Krim. Its sour odor made his stomach churn, till he looked away and tried to remember his training on the moon.

"I'm Spaceman Mayfield," he managed to say. "A human volunteer—"

He wanted to go on talking about himself, because being human made him a stranger on the orbiter. He still felt weak and giddy from the trans-sleep serums, and all these new things were coming too fast. He wanted to think about hiking with his father to holograph the wilderness creatures. About teaching chess to his kid brother, who was learning a strong end game. Even about the shelf of poetry in his room—he had enjoyed knowing the real Dr. Krim, because they both liked Robert Frost.

But the briefing officer wasn't interested in Earth.

"You'll be in danger, down on Atlas." Dr. Krim's deep voice boomed out of its silver-scaled queerness. "Nothing will ever be quite what you expect. Your instructions are to move with care, observe with intelligence, report every fact at once. Your first problem will be the gravity."

The mass of Atlas, the creature explained, was too small for its size—too small to fit any reasonable theory at all. His weight there would be only a pound and a half. Unless he learned to use the hold-ropes, even a good breeze could blow him away.

Looking aside, he listened to the few known facts about Atlas, most of them hard to believe. He learned what his work would be on the team. Finally he had to look again, because the briefing officer was holding out the voice-pack.

"Wear this. All the time. Use it. We'll be listening."

He took the pack from its snaky arms and tried to grin in a friendly way toward its single central eye, which looked like a huge mound of dark-green gelatin. After all, it wasn't half so strange as Atlas was going to be.

Whirling now in the heart of that howling storm, he was barely aware of the suffocating tightness around him. Yet a dim pain nagged him. He knew he ought to be doing something to earn his place on the team. Komatsu and Marutiak were probably hurt. He ought to be helping them. At least he ought to be reporting to the orbiter. But he had no breath for speech, no strength or will for any effort at all. He let his mind flash back to his landing on Atlas.

He had been watching from the pilot bubble as the shuttle slid down through endless miles of fog. The first thing he saw was a long dark blur, dividing hazy pink from misty blue. Then the world beneath the fog came slowly into focus, like an image in a lens. The blur became a dark mountain ridge, queerly long and straight. The pink became a flat reddish desert, gray-spotted with low mounds like piles of ashes. The blue was a flatter desert, the color of old ice.

Finally he found the camp on the ridge. The shelter was an inflated dome of yellow fabric. Yellow hold-ropes made a wide web around it. His new team-mates crawled out across the web to meet him, looking like yellow spiders in their survival gear.

He was glad to be with men again but dismayed at the way Atlas had crippled them. Both looked ray-burnt, drawn, grim. Komatsu had lost one leg. Raw red scars were splashed across the face and throat of Marutiak, the sub-chief.

The shuttle had brought big spools of new rope, crated instruments, bales and cases of supplies. Before it took off, it gave them a pick-up date.

"Be here." Though it carried no human crew, its robot controls had been programmed to speak with the voice of Dr. Krim. "We're shutting down this camp, because the orbiter's moving out of shuttle range. The director expects you to find useful information, before we come back to pick you up."

The date meant nothing to Max at first, because he was still wearing the Earth-time watch his parents had given him for graduation. He translated it out of galactic time, while he stood watching the shuttle climb and vanish into the clouds, and he found that it would be his birthday, just two weeks off. That made him think of the cake his mother would have baked, if he had stayed on Earth. Dark sweet chocolate iced with white—

"Let's go, kid," Komatsu said.

Marutiak was picking up a great bale that should have weighed a ton. Max jumped to help, and drifted in the air till Marutiak left the bale floating and turned to toss him the end of a rope.

"Thanks!" he gasped.

Marutiak pointed at his red-scarred throat, and Max realized that his voice had been destroyed.

"Hang on, kid," Komatsu was rasping. "Always hang on. Enson forgot—he's the man you came to replace."

He pulled himself after them toward the shelter, halfway swimming. Komatsu stopped at the door and raised his voice above the lazy cat-purr of the airpump.

"We stand watches. One man off and two men on. On duty, we run the experiments and report to the orbiter. Off duty, we stay inside and get what rest we can. On or off, we keep alert. Down here, kid, you'll learn that Atlas makes the rules. If you've got the brains and guts to play the Atlas game, you'll be okay."

He had tried to play the game, but Atlas was a tough opponent. His first real problem came when Komatsu asked him to come for a swim. Tired and sweaty after the long flight down, he agreed eagerly, but he wondered where any water was. Komatsu led him along a yellow rope to the edge of the ridge.

"You first." Komatsu waved him ahead. "Dive."

"Huh?"

He saw no water anywhere. The ridge was nearly flat on top, flaked and cracked with time. Ropes stretched along its rim. The reddish desert lay far, far below. Feeling bewildered, he looked back at Komatsu.

"There's our pool." Komatsu leaned out to point straight down. "The only open water we've found on Atlas."

He gripped the rope and looked. The time-worn wall of something like black rock dropped straight down so far it made him giddy. At last he found the pool—a small round mirror of bright blue water tucked under the very foot of that frightening cliff.

"It's deep enough." Queerly casual, Komatsu pointed at another hand-rope, stretched from their feet to a rock down in the pool. "We climb that to get back." He grinned at Max. "Want me to go first?"

"You've got to be kidding!" Max stared at his dark gaunt face. "We're too—too high!"

"Just a thousand feet." Komatsu's grin grew wider. "About the same as ten at home. You fall slow here, kid. With air resistance, your terminal velocity is about fifteen feet a second. From any height, you never fall faster. Watch me."

He peeled off his yellow suit, moved to the rim in a lazy, one-legged dance, floated over it. Max leaned out to watch him drifting slowly down, arms spread like wings to guide him. He was a long time in the air, and his body had dwindled to a far dark speck before he broke the blue mirror of the pool.

Waiting, Max shifted his cramped hands on the rope. The clouds looked darker and lower. The desert of ice and the desert of ashes made no sense. Atlas had begun to seem a harder riddle than ever.

Komatsu came back at last, gliding up that long rope. His scarred body was already dry, and one leg seemed enough for him, here on Atlas. Still grinning, he waved toward the jumping place.

"Next?"

"No!" Max couldn't help shivering. "Not—not now!"

"Later, please. But do it, kid. For your own good. Enson never learned to dive. That's why he never got back when he was blown away."

"Later." Max felt miserable. "I'll try—later."

Komatsu had been nice about it—maybe too nice. He took Max around the camp to explain their duties. Weather instruments and automatic cameras and radiation meters were scattered across the ridge. Hand-ropes led down to more experiments on the ashes and the ice.

"What are we finding out?" Fighting his dread of the dive, Max came back to that monstrous riddle. "What *is* Atlas?"

"Ask the orbiter." Komatsu nodded toward the dark sky. "All we do is report the instrument readings—which never make much sense. If you want to believe the seismographs, there's half a mile of ice or rock or radioactive dust spread over a thin shell of something else—maybe matter in some new state—with nothing underneath."

Komatsu waved at a yellow wind-sock.

"Just watch that, kid. We get the worst weather in the universe. Hot winds off the desert. Blizzards off the ice. Tornadoes two hundred miles tall. When the big winds hit, better hang on. Enson didn't."

He said no more about the dive. On watch with him, Max hammered pitons into the ice to anchor the ropes to a new seismic station. On watch with Marutiak, he put on heavy radiation armor and strung new rope across the desert to reach and test a low cone of gray-glowing dust. Atlas still kept its big secret.

Suddenly, now, Max was breathing again. The bellow of the twisting winds had died—long ago. He knew he had been unconscious, and he wondered where the storm had dropped him. He felt surprised to be alive.

The stiff shelter fabric was still rolled around him, but not quite so tight. Cramped and numb at first, he squirmed and wriggled, twisted and crawled, until he could look out. What he saw was a cruel jolt.

The tornado hadn't dropped him anywhere.

It had left him high—he was afraid to guess how high. The mountain ridge had become a fine dark line far beneath, dividing rust-red desert and dull blue ice. He was alone in the eerie sky of Atlas.

"Spaceman—" Only a hoarse whisper came when he tried to call into the voice-pack. He shut his eyes against the terrible emptiness under him, and tried again. "Spaceman Mayfield to Orbiter."

"Orbiter recording." Dr. Krim's duplicated voice

boomed instantly into that high silence, human and anxious. "We had lost contact. Please report."

"You won't believe it. A tornado has thrown me into the sky."

"Atlas is always surprising. Just tell us what you see."

"Not much. The ice—flat and dark and endless. The desert—just as endless. And there—the storm!"

The funnel was a thick reddish snake writhing out of a boiling cloud, dragging across the red and gray desert. Still watching it, he began to feel cold air rushing up around him. He looked for the fabric scrap the wind had wrapped around him and found it high above, already left behind.

"I—I'm falling!" Terror grasped his throat. "A hundred miles—it's a hundred miles down!"

"We're very lucky, if you can see anything from that elevation." The copied voice turned happy. "Evidently the storm has lifted the clouds. You have a rare chance to see what Atlas is."

The wind of his fall felt colder on his face, and fear of it froze him. His teeth chattered. But he tried to remember his training, tried to remember Komatsu's polite brown grin, tried to fight that terror.

Moving hands and arms against the rush of air, he learned to guide himself. A naked human aircraft, he tipped himself into a slow spiral above the bare flatness of ice and ash-like dust. At last, as the storm moved on, he found something it had hidden.

"A city!" he shouted into the voice-pack. "The ridge where we camped leads into it like a road. Wait! I think it *is* a road—two miles wide! The buildings—they must have been as high as I am now. Great queer shapes. All ruined. Broken. Falling. Black with fire—or maybe time. Because the city's old. Old, old, and dead!"

He stopped to stare at its desolate wonder.

"Go on! Describe what you see."

But that blackened, shattered city was too huge and

old and strange for any words of his. Dr. Krim's bearded face had come into his shaken mind, and now he recalled the human linguist reciting Robert Frost. Two haunting lines came back:

Some say the world will end in fire,
Some say in ice.

Atlas, he thought, had somehow ended in both.

"Mayfield!" the pack kept booming. "Tell what else you see."

"Nothing." His first excitement had begun to die. "I'm too far off, and the clouds are sinking again. The tower-tops are already hazy. Sorry I can't see more."

The pack went dead, thumped on again.

"Mayfield, what you've seen may be the final clue we needed." The copied voice had a sudden human heartiness. "Congratulations! The survey director says your report confirms his best theory. Atlas is an artificial object, designed and built by high intelligence."

"Who could build a world—" The notion jarred him. "A world the size of Atlas?"

"We don't know yet." The voice drummed fast. "But natural planets are not efficient as dwellings for life. They catch too little sunlight. They expose too little surface for unit of mass. The director thinks that Atlas is the matter from a system of planets, rebuilt into a hollow shell, maybe only a mile or so thick. The job took engineering know-how we can barely begin to imagine. But it gave the builders a million times more living space."

"They aren't living now." Max looked at the dull clouds rolling back to cover that lost, gigantic city. "I think—I *know* they're dead."

"The director believes their energy ran out. The ice you see covers most of Atlas. The ash-like stuff is probably waste from the old nuclear power plants. We can't be sure, till we make more landings."

The pack thumped off and on.

"The shuttle will be returning at once, to rescue survivors. If you're at the camp, you'll be picked up."

"I'll be there—if I can find the camp."

The voice from the disk was still Dr. Krim's, but somehow not quite human. "If you fail, Spaceman Mayfield, the director wants you to know that you have earned our gratitude."

The pack went off again, and he banked his shivering body into a slow circle above dark ice and dull dust. He couldn't find the camp. When he looked again for that dead city, it was gone. The rising wind grew colder. His face felt leather-stiff, and tears began to blur his vision. His spread arms grew numb and clumsy. He had trouble controlling his glide.

Yet one spark of triumph glowed in his mind. Even if he died here, Atlas hadn't really been too tough to crack. Even its huge size had turned out to be a sham. It was hollow, just a sort of cosmic bubble.

He nursed that warming thought, to keep himself alive. The glide down took a long time. Shreds of cloud began to form beneath him, hiding ice and dust. His last hopes began to freeze. He wanted to quit trying—

But then, beside that endless ridge that once had been a road, he found a small bright glint. He dived toward it, into the freezing wind that came off the ice. The ancient road grew wider, wider, until at last he made out the web of yellow ropes—and two tiny spider-figures, waving at him.

From a hundred miles up, he dived into the clear blue pool. To his numb skin, it felt almost warm. He paddled stiffly to the edge, hauled at the guide-rope with both clumsy hands, slid up it toward the camp.

The pack thumped on again. The tornado had caught Komatsu and Marutiak out on the ice, Krim's voice said. With the guide-ropes blown away, they'd had trouble getting back. But they were safe now, and the shuttle would be picking all three of them up.

"Nice dive, kid!" Komatsu was waiting with Marutiak at the top, and their happy hands helped him over the rim. "You're okay!"

Meathouse Man

George R. R. Martin

People like to divide science-fiction authors into neat categories: "old wave" and "new wave," hard-science writers and, presumably, squishy-science writers. These are useful distinctions for critics to make, I suppose, but like other interpretations imposed from without they're often irrelevant and, at best, the categories have so much overlap that they don't have much real meaning.

There's one distinction that I've found useful, though: some of us are storytellers and some are Authors. The Authors tend to concentrate on style and relevance and experiments in plot-construction, seemingly in an effort more to impress than to entertain. The storytellers just take care of the basic business of keeping their readers turning the page to find out what happens next.

Both kinds of writer produce good work at various times, but I've noticed that the Authors seldom improve much during their careers, while the storytellers do. Things like style can be learned quickly, after all: an artful alliteration or flashy literary allusion makes an obvious impact, one that's easy to analyze. Storytelling is a much more complex business.

George R. R. Martin has always been primarily a teller of stories, and in the comparatively short span of half a dozen years since his first sales his talent has grown impressively. Those first stories were, well, ordinary: they had enough originality of idea and background to make them enjoyable, but there was seldom anything in them to make you want to read them again.

Starting about three years ago, when he published "A Song for Lya," his work became much richer. He'd passed his apprenticeship and was now able to write of events that left readers feeling they'd experienced something that had changed them . . . just a bit, and not necessarily in ways that could be charted on a graph, but the stories stuck in the memory.

Usually we think of storytellers as the more conservative sort of writer, since inevitably they stick to a handful of basic plots. They seldom try to dazzle us with references to classical mythology even when they're using plots that were familiar to Homer; they won't try trendy gimmicks like drawing parallels with the deaths of John Kennedy or Marilyn Monroe.

In this sense, George R. R. Martin is a conservative writer—but his hair isn't crew-cut and he doesn't wear a vest. In fact his hair is shoulder-length and whenever I've seen him he was dressed as informally as a character in *Fritz the Cat*. (But in better taste.)

Martin doesn't *affect* style; he has it. His stories have it too, the easy kind of style that grows naturally from whatever tale he's telling. Such as this imaginative and powerful story of a young man in a world where corpses make up the work-force for everything from industry to sex . . . but not for love. That's harder to find.

(I have no idea what Martin's middle initials stand for, by the way. But a friend of his once referred to him as "George Railroad Martin," and I've been unable to think of him as anything else ever since.)

---

1. In the Meathouse

They came straight from the ore fields that first time, Trager with the others, the older boys, the almost-men who worked their corpses next to his. Cox was the oldest of the group, and he'd been around the most, and he said that Trager had to come even if he didn't want to. Then one of the others laughed and said that Trager wouldn't even know what to do, but Cox the kind-of leader shoved him until he was quiet. And when payday came, Trager trailed the rest to the meathouse, scared but somehow eager, and he paid his money to a man downstairs and got a room key.

He came into the dim room trembling, nervous. The others had gone to other rooms, had left him alone with her (no, *it,* not her but *it,* he reminded himself, and promptly forgot again). In a shabby gray cubicle with a single smoky light.

He stank of sweat and sulfur, like all who walked the streets of Skrakky, but there was no help for that. It would be better if he could bathe first, but the room did not have a bath. Just a sink, a double bed with sheets that looked dirty even in the dimness, a corpse.

She lay there naked, staring at nothing, breathing shallowly. Her legs were spread, ready. Was she always that way, Trager wondered, or had the man before him arranged her like that? He didn't know. He knew how to do it (he did, he *did,* he'd read the books Cox gave him, and there were films you could see, and all sorts of things), but he didn't know much of anything else. Except maybe how to handle corpses. That he was good at, the youngest handler on Skrakky, but he had to be. They had forced him into the handlers' school when his mother died, and they made him learn, so that was the thing he did. This, this he had never done (but he knew how, yes, yes, he *did*); it was his first time.

He came to the bed slowly and sat, to a chorus of creaking springs. He touched her and the flesh was warm. Of course. The body was alive enough, a heart beat under the heavy white breasts, she breathed. Only the brain was gone, replaced with a deadman's synthabrain. She was meat now, an extra body for a corpse handler to control, just like the crew he worked each day under sulfur skies. She was not a woman. So it did not matter that Trager was just a boy, a jowly frog-faced boy who smelled of Skrakky. She (no, *it,* remember?) would not care, could not care.

Emboldened, aroused and hard, the boy stripped off his corpse handler's clothing and climbed in bed with the female meat. He was very excited; his hands shook as he stroked her, studied her. Her skin was very white, her hair dark and long, but even the boy could not call her pretty. Her face was too flat and wide, her mouth hung open, and her limbs were loose and sagging with fat.

On her huge breasts, all around the fat dark nipples, the last customer had left toothmarks where he'd chewed her. Trager touched the marks tentatively, traced them with a finger. Then, sheepish about his hesitations, he grabbed one breast, squeezed it hard, pinched the nipple until he imagined a real girl would squeal with pain. The corpse did not move. Still squeezing, he rolled over on her and took the other breast into his mouth.

And the corpse responded.

She thrust up at him, hard; her meaty arms wrapped around his pimpled back to pull him to her. Trager groaned and reached down between her legs. She was hot, wet, excited. He trembled. How did they do that? Could she really get excited without a mind, or did they have lubricating tubes stuck into her, or what?

Then he stopped caring. He fumbled, found his penis, put it into her, thrust. The corpse hooked her legs around him and thrust back. It felt good, real good, better than anything he'd ever done to himself, and in some obscure way he felt proud that she was so wet and so excited.

It took only a few strokes; he was too new, too young, too eager to last long. A few strokes was all he needed—but it was all she needed too. They came together, a red flush washing over her skin as she arched against him and shook silently.

Afterward she lay again like a corpse.

Trager was drained and satisfied, but he had more time left, and he was determined to get his money's worth. He explored her thoroughly, sticking his fingers everywhere they would go, touching her everywhere, rolling her over, looking at everything. The corpse moved like dead meat.

He left her as he found her, lying face up on the bed with her legs apart. Meathouse courtesy.

The horizon was a wall of factories, all factories, vast belching factories that sent red shadows to flicker against the sulfur-dark skies. The boy saw but hardly noticed. He was strapped in place high atop his automill, two stories up on a monster machine of corroding yellow-painted metal with savage teeth of diamond and duralloy, and his eyes were blurred with triple images. Clear and strong and hard he saw the control panel before him, the wheel, the fuel-feed, the bright handle of the ore scoops, the banks of lights that would tell of trouble in the refinery under his feet, the brake and emergency brake. But that was not all he saw. Dimly, faintly, there were echoes: overlaid images of two other control cabs, almost identical to his, where corpse hands moved clumsily over the instruments.

Trager moved those hands, slow and careful, while another part of his mind held his own hands, his real hands, very still. The corpse controller hummed thinly on his belt.

On either side of him, the other two automills moved into flanking positions. The corpse hands squeezed the brakes; the machines rumbled to a halt. On the edge of the great sloping pit, they stood in a row, shabby pitted juggernauts ready to descend into the gloom. The pit was growing steadily larger; each day new layers of rock and ore were stripped away.

Once a mountain range had stood here, but Trager did not remember that.

The rest was easy. The automills were aligned now. To move the crew in unison was a cinch; any decent handler could do that. It was only when you had to keep several corpses busy at several different tasks that things got tricky. But a good corpse handler could do that, too. Eight-crews were not unknown to veterans—eight bodies linked to a single corpse controller, moved by a single mind and eight synthabrains. The deadmen were each tuned to one controller and only one; the handler who wore that controller and thought corpse-thoughts in its proximity field could move those deadmen like secondary bodies. Or like his own body. If he was good enough.

Trager checked his filtermask and earplugs quickly, then touched the fuel feed, engaged, flicked on the laser knives and the drills. His corpses echoed his moves, and pulses of light spat through the twilight of Skrakky. Even through his plugs he could hear the awful whine as the ore scoops revved up and lowered. The rock-eating maw of an automill was even wider than the machine was tall.

Rumbling and screeching, in perfect formation, Trager and his corpse crew descended into the pit. Before they reached the factories on the far side of the plain, tons of metal would have been torn from the earth, melted and refined and processed, while the worthless rock was reduced to powder and blown out into the already unbreathable air. He would deliver finished steel at dusk, on the horizon.

He was a good handler, Trager thought as the automills started down. But the handler in the meathouse—now she must be an artist. He imagined her down in the cellar somewhere, watching each of her corpses through holos and psi circuits, humping them all to please her patrons. Was it just a fluke, then, that his fuck had been so perfect? Or was she always that good? But how, *how*, to move a dozen corpses without even being near them, to have them doing different things, to keep them all excited, to match the needs and rhythm of each customer so exactly?

The air behind him was black and choked by rock dust, his ears were full of screams, and the far horizon was a glowering red wall beneath which yellow ants crawled and ate rock. But Trager kept his hard-on all across the plain as the automill shook beneath him.

The corpses were company-owned; they stayed in the company deadman depot. But Trager had a room, a cubicle that was his own in a steel-and-concrete warehouse with a thousand other cubicles. He knew only a handful of his neighbors, but in a way he knew all of them; they were corpse handlers. It was a world of silent shadowed corridors and endless closed doors. The lobby-lounge, all air and plastic, was a dusty deserted place where the tenants never gathered.

The evenings were long there, the nights eternal. Trager had bought extra light panels for his cube, and when all of them were on they burned so bright that his infrequent visitors blinked and complained about the glare. But always there came a time when he could read no more, and then he had to turn them out, and the darkness returned again.

His father, long gone and barely remembered, had

left a wealth of books and tapes, and Trager kept them still. The room was lined with them, and others stood in great piles against the foot of the bed and on either side of the bathroom door. Sometimes he went out with Cox and the others, to drink and joke and prowl for real women. He imitated them as best he could, but he always felt out of place. So most of his nights were spent at home, reading and listening to the music, remembering and thinking.

That week his thoughts were a frightened jumble. Payday was coming again, and Cox would be after him to return to the meathouse, and yes, yes, he wanted to. It had been good, exciting; for once he had felt confident and virile. But it was so easy, cheap, *dirty*. There had to be more, hadn't there? Love, whatever that was? It had to be better with a real woman, had to, and he wouldn't find one of those in a meathouse. He'd never found one outside, either, but then he'd never really had the courage to try. But he had to try, *had* to, or what sort of life would he ever have?

Beneath the covers he masturbated, hardly thinking of it, while he resolved not to return to the meathouse.

A different room this time, a different corpse. Fat and black, with bright orange hair; less attractive than his first, if that was possible. But Trager came to her ready and eager, and this time he lasted longer. Again, the performance was superb. Her rhythm matched his stroke for stroke, she came with him, she seemed to know exactly what he wanted.

Other visits: two of them, four, six. He was a regular now at the meathouse, along with the others. He was better than they were, he thought. He could hold his own in a meathouse, he could run his corpses and his automills as good as any of them, and he still thought and dreamed. In time he'd leave them all behind, leave Skrakky, be something. They would be meathouse men as long as they lived, but Trager knew he could do better. He believed.

His admiration of the meathouse handler grew almost to worship. Perhaps somehow he could meet her, he thought. Still a boy, still hopelessly naïve, he was sure he would love her. Then he would take her away from the meathouse to a clean corpseless world where they could be happy together.

One day, in a moment of weakness, he told Cox and the others. Cox looked at him, shook his head, grinned. Somebody else snickered. Then they all began to laugh. "What an *ass* you are, Trager," Cox said at last. "There is no fucking *handler!* Don't tell me you never heard of a feedback circuit?"

He explained it all, to laughter; explained how each corpse was tuned to a controller built into its bed, explained how each customer handled his own meat, explained why nonhandlers found meathouse women dead and still. And the boy realized suddenly why the sex was always perfect.

That night, alone in his room with all the lights burning white and hot, Trager faced himself. It was the meathouse, he decided. There was a trap there in the meathouse, a trap that could ruin him, destroy life and dreams and hope. He would not go back; it was too easy. He would show Cox, show all of them. He would take the hard way, take the risks, feel the pain if he had to. And maybe the joy, maybe the love. He'd gone the other way too long.

Trager did not go back to the meathouse. Feeling strong and decisive and superior, he went back to his room. There, as years passed, he read and dreamed and waited for life to begin.

2. When I Was One-and-Twenty

Josie was the first.

She was beautiful, had always been beautiful, knew she was beautiful; that had shaped her, made her what she was. She was a free spirit. She was aggressive, confident, conquering. Like Trager, she was only twenty when they met, but she had lived more than he had, and she seemed to have the answers. He loved her from the first.

And Trager? Trager before Josie, but years beyond the meathouse? He was taller now, broad and heavy with both muscle and fat, often moody, silent and self-contained. He ran a full five-crew in the ore fields, more than Cox, more than any of them. At night he read books, sometimes in his room, sometimes in the lobby. He had long since forgotten that he went there in hope of meeting someone. Stable, solid, unemotional: that was Trager. He touched no one, and no one touched him. Even the tortures had stopped, though the scars remained inside. Trager hardly knew they were there; he never looked at them.

He fitted in well now. With his corpses.

Yet—not completely. Inside, the dream. Something believed, something hungered, something yearned. It was strong enough to keep him away from the meathouse, from the vegetable life the others had all chosen. And sometimes, on bleak lonely nights, it would grow stronger still. Then Trager would rise from his bed, dress, and walk the corridors for hours with his hands shoved deep into his pockets while something clawed and whimpered in his gut. Always, before his walks were over, he would resolve to do something, to change his life tomorrow.

But when tomorrow came, the silent gray corridors were half forgotten, the demons had faded, and he had six roaring, shaking automills to drive across the pit. He would lose himself in routine, and it would be long months before the feelings came again.

Then Josie. They met like this:

It was a new field, rich and unmined, a vast expanse of broken rock and rubble that filled the plain. Low hills a few weeks ago, but the company skimmers had leveled the area with systematic nuclear blast mining, and now the automills were moving in. Trager's five-crew had been one of the first, and the change had been exhilarating at first. The old pit had been just about worked out; here there was a new terrain to contend with, boulders and jagged rock fragments, baseball-sized fists of stone that came shrieking at you on the dusty wind. It all seemed exciting, dangerous. Trager, wearing a leather jacket and filtermask and goggles and earplugs, drove his six machines and six bodies with a fierce pride, reducing boulders to powder, clearing a path for the later machines, fighting his way yard by yard to get whatever ore he could.

And one day, suddenly, one of the eye echoes caught his attention. A light flashed red on a corpse-driven automill. Trager reached, with his hands, with his mind, with five sets of corpse-hands. Six machines stopped, but still another light went red. Then another and another. Then the whole board, all twelve. One of his automills was out. Cursing, he looked across the rock field towards the machine, used his corpse to give it a kick. The lights stayed red. He beamed out for a tech.

By the time she got there—in a one-man skimmer that looked like a teardrop of pitted black metal—Trager had unstrapped, climbed down the metal rungs on the side of the automill, walked across the rocks to where the dead machine stopped. He was just starting to climb up when Josie arrived; they met at the foot of the yellow-metal mountain, in the shadow of its treads.

She was field-wise, he knew at once. She wore a handler's coverall, earplugs, heavy goggles, and her face was smeared with grease to prevent dust abrasion. But still she was beautiful. Her hair was short, light brown, cut in a shag that was jumbled by the wind; her eyes, when she lifted the goggles, were bright green. She took charge immediately.

All business, she introduced herself, asked him a few questions, then opened a repair bay and crawled inside, into the guts of the drive and the ore smelt and the refinery. It didn't take her long; ten minutes, maybe, and she was back outside.

"Don't go in there," she said, tossing her hair away from her goggles. "You've got a damper failure. The nukes are running away."

"Oh," said Trager. "Is it going to blow up?"

Josie seemed amused. She smiled and seemed to see him, *him,* Trager, not just a corpse-handler. "No," she said. "It will just melt itself down. Won't even get hot out here, since you've got shields built into the walls. Just don't go in there."

"All right. What do I do?"

"Work the rest of your crew, I guess. This machine'll have to be scrapped. It should have been overhauled a long time ago. From the looks of it, there's been a lot of patching done in the past. Stupid. It breaks down, it breaks down, it breaks down, and they keep sending it out. Should realize that something is wrong. After that many failures, it's sheer self-delusion to think the thing's going to work right next time out."

"I guess," Trager said. Josie smiled at him again, sealed up the panel, and started to leave.

"Wait," he said. It came out before he could stop it. Josie turned, cocked her head, looked at him questioningly. And Trager drew a sudden strength from the steel and the stone and the wind; under sulfur skies, his dreams seemed less impossible. Maybe, he thought. Maybe.

"Uh. I'm Greg Trager. Will I see you again?"

Josie grinned. "Sure. Come tonight." She gave him the address.

He climbed back into his automill after she had left, exulting in his five strong bodies, all fire and life, and he chewed up rock with something near to joy. The dark red glow in the distance looked almost like a sunrise.

When he got to Josie's he found four other people there, friends of hers. It was a party of sorts. Josie threw a lot of parties, and from that night on Trager went to all of them. Josie talked to him, laughed with him, *liked* him, and his life was no longer the same.

With Josie, he saw parts of Skrakky he had never seen before, did things he had never done:

He stood with her in the crowds that gathered on the streets at night, stood in the dusty wind and sickly yellow light between the windowless concrete buildings, stood and cheered while grease-stained mechs raced yellow rumbly tractor-trucks up and down and down and up.

He walked with her through the strangely silent and white and clean underground offices, the sealed air-conditioned corridors where off-worlders and paper-shufflers and company executives lived and worked.

He prowled the rec-malls with her, those huge low buildings so like a warehouse from the outside but full of colored lights and games rooms and cafeterias and tape shops and endless bars where handlers made their rounds.

He went with her to dormitory gyms where they watched handlers less skillful than himself send their corpses against each other with clumsy fists.

He sat with her and her friends, and they woke dark quiet taverns with their talk and with their laughter, and once Trager saw someone much like Cox staring at him from across the room, and then he smiled and leaned a bit closer to Josie.

He hardly noticed the other people, the crowds that Josie gathered around herself; when they went out on one of her wild jaunts, six of them or eight or ten, Trager would tell himself that he and Josie were going out, and that some others had come along.

Once in a great while things would work out so they were alone together, at her place or his. Then they would talk. Of distant worlds, of politics, of corpses and life on Skrakky, of the books they both read, of sports or games or friends they had in common. They shared a good deal. Trager talked a lot with Josie. And never said a word.

He loved her, of course. He suspected it the first month, and soon he was convinced of it. He loved her. This was the real thing, the thing he had been waiting for, and it had happened just as he knew it would.

But with his love: agony. He could not tell her. A dozen times he tried; the words would never come. What if she did not love him?

His nights were still lonely, in the small room with the white lights and the books and the pain. He was more alone than ever now; the peace of his routine, of his half-life with his corpses, was gone. By day he rode the great automills, moved his corpses, smashed rock and melted ore, and in his head rehearsed the words he'd say to Josie. When he broke through, when he found the words and the courage, then everything would be all right. Each day he said that to himself, and dug swift and deep into the earth.

Back home, the sureness faded. Then, with awful despair, he knew that he was deceiving himself. He was a friend to her, nothing more, never would be more. They had never been lovers, never would be; the few times he'd worked up the courage to touch her, she had smiled, moved away on some pretext, so that he was never quite sure that he was being rejected. He walked the corridors again, sullen, desperate. And all the old scars bled again.

He must believe in himself, he knew that, he shouted it out loud. He must stop feeling sorry for himself. He must do something. He must tell Josie. He would.

And she would love him, cried the day.

And she would laugh, the nights replied.

Trager chased her for a year, a year of pain and promise, the first year that he had ever *lived*. On that the night-fears and the day-voice agreed; he was alive now. He would never return to the emptiness of his time before Josie; he would never go back to the meathouse. That far, at least, he had come. He could change, and someday he would be strong enough to tell her.

Josie and two friends dropped by his room that night,

but the friends had to leave early. For an hour or so they were alone, talking. Finally she had to go. Trager said he'd walk her home.

He kept his arm around her down the long corridors, and he watched her face, watched the play of light and shadow on her cheeks as they walked from light to darkness. "Josie," he started. He felt so fine, so good, so warm, and it came out. "I love you."

And she stopped, pulled away from him, stepped back. Her mouth opened, just a little, and something flickered in her eyes. "Oh, Greg," she said. Softly. Sadly. "No, Greg, no, don't, don't."

Trembling slightly, mouthing silent words, Trager raised his hands gently toward her cheek. She turned her head away so that his hand met only air.

Then, for the first time ever, Trager shook. And the tears came.

Josie took him to her room. There, sitting across from each other on the floor, never touching, they talked.

J.: . . . *known it for a long time . . . tried to discourage you, Greg, but I didn't just want to come right out and . . . I never wanted to hurt you . . . a good person . . . don't worry . . .*

T.: . . . *knew it all along . . . that it would never . . . lied to myself . . . wanted to believe, even if it wasn't true . . . I'm sorry, Josie, I'm sorry, i'm sorry, imsorryimsorryimsorry . . .*

J.: . . . *afraid you would go back to what you were . . . don't, Greg, promise me . . . can't give up . . . have to believe . . .*

T.: . . . *why? . . .*

J.: . . . *stop believing, then you have nothing . . . dead . . . you can do better . . . a good handler . . . get off Skrakky, find something . . . no life here . . . someone . . . you will, you will, just believe, keep on believing . . .*

T.: . . . *you . . . love you forever, Josie . . . for-*

ever . . . how can I find someone . . . never anyone like you, never . . . special . . .

J.: . . . *oh, Greg . . . lots of people . . . just look . . . open*

T.: (laughter) . . . *open? . . . first time I ever talked to anyone . . .*

J.: . . . *talk to me again, if you have to . . . I can talk to you . . . had enough lovers, everyone wants to go to bed with me, better just to be friends . . .*

T.: . . . *friends* . . . (laughter) . . . (tears) . . .

3. Promises of Someday

The fire had burned out long ago, and Stevens and the forester had gone to bed, but Trager and Donelly still sat beside the ashes. They talked softly, so as not to wake the others, yet their words hung long in the restless night air. The uncut forest, standing dark behind them, was dead still; the wildlife of Vendalia had all fled the noise that the fleet of buzztrucks made during the day.

". . . a full six-crew, running buzztrucks, I know enough to know that's not easy," Donelly was saying. He was a pale, timid youth, likable but self-conscious. Trager heard echoes of himself in Donelly's stiff words. "You'd do well in the arena."

Trager nodded, thoughtful, his eyes on the ashes as he moved them with a stick. "I came to Vendalia with that in mind. Went to the gladiatorials once, only once. That was enough to change my mind. I could take them, I guess, but the whole idea made me sick. Out here, well, the money doesn't even match what I was getting on Skrakky, but the work is, well, clean. You know?"

"Sort of," said Donelly. "Still, you know, it isn't like they were real people out there in the arena. Only meat. All you can do is make the bodies as dead as the minds. That's the logical way to look at it."

Trager chuckled. "You're too logical, Don. You

ought to *feel* more. Listen, next time you're in Gidyon, go to the gladiatorials and take a look. It's ugly, *ugly.* Corpses stumbling around with axes and swords and morningstars, hacking and hewing at each other. Butchery, that's all it is. And the audience, the way they cheer at each blow. And *laugh.* They *laugh,* Don! No." He shook his head sharply. "No."

"But why not? I don't understand, Greg. You'd be good at it, the best. I've seen the way you work your crew."

Trager looked up, studied Donelly briefly while the youth sat quietly, waiting. Josie's words came back: open, be open. The old Trager, the Trager who lived friendless and alone inside a Skrakky handlers' dorm, was gone.

"There was a girl," he said slowly. Opening. "Back on Skrakky, Don, there was a girl I loved. It, well, it didn't work out. That's why I'm here, I guess. I'm looking for someone else, for something better. That's all part of it, you see." He stopped, paused, tried to think it out. "This girl, Josie, I wanted her to love me. You know." The words came hard. "Admire me, all that stuff. Now, yeah, sure, I could do good running corpses in the arena. But Josie could never love someone who had a job like *that.* She's gone now, of course, but still . . . the kind of person I'm looking for, I couldn't find them as an arena corpsemaster." He stood up abruptly. "I don't know. That's what's important, though, to me. Josie, somebody like her, someday. Soon, I hope."

He left Donelly sitting beside the ashes, and walked off alone into the woods.

They had a tight-knit group: three handlers, a forester, thirteen corpses. Each day they drove the forest back, with Trager in the lead. Against the Vendalian wilderness, against the blackbriars and the hard gray ironspike trees and the bulbous rubbery snap-limbs, against the tangled hostile forest, he threw his six-crew and their buzztrucks. Smaller than the automills he'd run on Skrakky, fast and airborne, complex and demanding, those were buzztrucks. Trager ran six of them with corpse hands, a seventh with his own. Before his screaming blades and laser knives, the wall of wilderness fell each day. Donelly came behind him, pushing three of the mountain-sized rolling mills, to turn the fallen trees into lumber for Gidyon and other cities of Vendalia. Then Stevens, the third handler, with a flamecannon to burn down stumps and melt rocks, and the soilpumps that would ready the cleared land for farming. The forester was their foreman. The procedure was a science.

Clean, hard, demanding work; Trager thrived on it by day. He grew lean, athletic; the lines of his face tightened and tanned, he grew steadily browner under Vendalia's hot bright sun. His corpses were almost part of him, so easily did he move them, fly their buzztrucks. As an ordinary man might move a hand, a foot. Sometimes his control grew so firm, the echoes so clear and strong, that Trager felt he was not a handler working a crew at all, but rather a man with seven bodies. Seven strong bodies that rode the sultry forest winds. He exulted in their sweat.

And the evenings, after work ceased, they were good too. Trager found a sort of peace there, a sense of belonging he had never known on Skrakky. The Vendalian foresters, rotated back and forth from Gidyon, were decent enough, and friendly. Stevens was a hearty slab of a man who seldom stopped joking long enough to talk about anything serious. And Donelly, the self-conscious youth, the quiet logical voice, he became a friend. He was a good listener, empathetic, compassionate, and the new open Trager was a good talker. Something close to envy shone in Donelly's eyes when Trager spoke of Josie. And Trager knew, or thought he knew, that Donelly was himself, the old Trager, the one before Josie who could not find the words.

In time, though, after days and weeks of talking, Donelly found his words. Then Trager listened, and shared another's pain. And he felt good about it. He was helping; he was lending strength; he was needed.

Each night beside the ashes, the two men traded dreams. And wove a hopeful tapestry of promises and lies.

If Josie had given Trager much, she had taken something too; she had taken the curious deadness he had once had, the trick of not-thinking, the pain-blotter of his mind. On Skrakky, he had walked the corridors infrequently; the forest knew him far more often.

After the talking had stopped, after Donelly had gone to bed, that was when it would happen, when Josie would come to him in the loneliness of his tent. A thousand nights he lay there with his hands hooked behind his head, staring at the plastic tent film while he relived the night he'd told her.

He would think of it, and fight it, and lose. Then he would rise and go outside. He would walk across the clear area, into the silent looming forest, brushing aside low branches and tripping on the underbrush; he would walk until he found water. Then he would sit down, by a scum-choked lake or a gurgling stream that ran swift and oily in the moonlight. He would fling rocks into the water, hurl them hard and flat into the night to hear them when they splashed.

He would sit for hours, throwing rocks and thinking, till finally he could convince himself the sun would rise.

Gidyon: the city, heart of Vendalia, and through it of Slagg and Skrakky and New Pittsburgh and all the other corpseworlds, the harsh ugly places where men would not work and corpses had to. Great towers of black and silver metal, floating aerial sculpture that flashed in the sunlight and shone softly at night, the vast bustling spaceport where freighters rose and fell on invisible firewands, malls where the pavement was polished ironspike wood that gleamed a gentle grey; Gidyon.

The city with the rot. The corpse city. The meatmart.

For the freighters carried cargoes of men, criminals and

derelicts and troublemakers from a dozen worlds bought with hard Vendalian cash (and there were darker rumors, of liners that had vanished mysteriously on routine tourist hops). And the soaring towers were hospitals and corpseyards, where men and women died and deadmen were born to walk anew. And all along the ironspike boardwalks were corpse-sellers' shops and meathouses.

The meathouses of Vendalia were far-famed. The corpses were guaranteed beautiful.

Trager sat across the avenue from one, under the umbrella of an outdoor café. He sipped a bittersweet wine, thought about how his leave had evaporated too quickly, and tried to keep his eyes from wandering across the street. The wine was warm on his tongue, and his eyes were restless.

Up and down the avenue, between him and the meathouse, strangers moved. Dark-faced corpse handlers from Vendalia, Skrakky, Slagg, pudgy merchants, gawking tourists from the Clean Worlds like Old Earth and Zephyr and dozens of question marks whose names and occupations and errands Trager would never know. Sitting there, drinking his wine and watching, Trager felt utterly isolated. He could not touch these people, could not reach them; he didn't know how, it wasn't possible. He could rise and walk out into the street and grab one, and still they would not touch. The stranger would only pull free and run. All his leave like that, all of it; he'd run through all the bars of Gidyon, forced a thousand contacts, and nothing had worked.

His wine was gone. Trager looked at the glass dully, turning it in his hands, blinking. Then he stood up and paid his bill. His hands trembled.

It had been so many years, he thought as he started across the street. Josie, he thought, forgive me.

Trager returned to the wilderness camp, and his corpses flew their buzztrucks like men gone wild. But he was strangely silent at the campfire, and he did not talk to Donelly at night. Until finally, hurt and puzzled,

Donelly followed him into the forest. And found him by a languid death-dark stream, sitting on the bank with a pile of throwing stones at his feet.

T.: . . . *went in . . . after all I said, all I promised . . . still I went in . . .*

D.: . . . *nothing to worry . . . remember what you told me . . . keep on believing . . .*

T.: . . . *did believe,* did . . . *no difference . . . Josie . . .*

D.: . . . *you say I shouldn't give up, you better not . . . repeat everything you told me, everything Josie told you . . . everybody finds someone . . . if they keep looking . . . give up, dead . . . all you need . . . openness . . . courage to look . . . stop feeling sorry for yourself . . . told me that a hundred times . . .*

T.: . . . *fucking lot easier to tell you than do it myself . . .*

D.: . . . *Greg . . . not a meathouse man . . . a dreamer . . . better than they are . . .*

T. (sighing): . . . *yeah . . . hard, though . . . why do I do this to myself? . . .*

D.: . . . *rather be like you were? . . . not hurting, not living? . . . like me? . . .*

T.: . . . *no . . . no . . . you're right . . .*

4. The Pilgrim, Up and Down

Her name was Laurel. She was nothing like Josie, save in one thing alone. Trager loved her.

Pretty? Trager didn't think so, not at first. She was too tall, a half foot taller than he was, and she was a bit on the heavy side, and more than a bit on the awkward side. Her hair was her best feature, her hair that was red-brown in winter and glowing blond in summer, that fell long and straight past her shoulders and did wild beautiful things in the wind. But she was not beautiful, not the way Josie had been beautiful. Although, oddly, she grew more beautiful with time, and maybe that was because she was losing weight, and maybe that was because Trager was falling in love with her and seeing her through kinder eyes, and maybe that was because he *told* her she was pretty and the very telling made it so. Just as Laurel told him he was wise, and her belief gave him wisdom. Whatever the reason, Laurel was very beautiful indeed after he had known her for a time.

She was five years younger than he, clean-scrubbed and innocent, shy where Josie had been assertive. She was intelligent, romantic, a dreamer; she was wondrously fresh and eager; she was painfully insecure and full of a hungry need.

She was new to Gidyon, fresh from the Vendalian outback, a student forester. Trager, on leave again, was visiting the forestry college to say hello to a teacher who'd once worked with his crew. They met in the teacher's office. Trager had two weeks free in a city of strangers and meathouses; Laurel was alone. He showed her the glittering decadence of Gidyon, feeling smooth and sophisticated, and she was impressed.

Two weeks went quickly. They came to the last night. Trager, suddenly afraid, took her to the park by the river that ran through Gidyon and they sat together on the low stone wall by the water's edge. Close, not touching.

"Time runs too fast," he said. He had a stone in his hand. He flicked it out over the water, flat and hard. Thoughtfully, he watched it splash and sink. Then he looked at her. "I'm nervous," he said, laughing. "I—Laurel. I don't want to leave."

Her face was unreadable. Wary? "The city is nice," she agreed.

Trager shook his head violently. "No. *No!* Not the city. You. Laurel, I think I . . . well . . ."

Laurel smiled for him. Her eyes were bright, very happy. "I know," she said.

Trager could hardly believe. He reached out, touched

her cheek. She turned her head and kissed his hand. They smiled at each other.

He flew back to the forest camp to quit. "Don, *Don,* you've got to meet her," he shouted. "See, you can do it, *I* did it, just keep believing, keep trying. I feel so goddamn good it's obscene."

Donelly, stiff and logical, did not know how to respond to such a flood of happiness. "What will you do?" he asked, a little awkwardly. "The arena?"

Trager laughed. "Hardly—you know how I feel. But something like that. There's a theater near the spaceport, puts on pantomime with corpse actors. I've got a job there. The pay is rotten, but I'll be near Laurel. That's all that matters."

They hardly slept at night. Instead they talked and cuddled and made love. The lovemaking was a joy, a game, a glorious discovery; never as good technically as the meathouse, but Trager hardly cared. He taught her to be open. He told her every secret he had, and wished he had more secrets.

"Poor Josie," Laurel would often say at night, her body warm against his. "She doesn't know what she missed. I'm lucky. There couldn't be anyone else like you."

"No," said Trager, "*I'm* lucky."

They would argue about it, laughing.

Donelly came to Gidyon and joined the theater. Without Trager the forest work had been no fun, he said. The three of them spent a lot of time together, and Trager glowed. He wanted to share his friends with Laurel, and he'd already mentioned Donelly a lot. And he wanted Donelly to see how happy he'd become, to see what belief could accomplish.

"I like her," Donelly said, the first night after Laurel had left.

"Good," Trager replied.

"No," said Donelly. "Greg, I *really* like her."

They spent a *lot* of time together.

"Greg," Laurel said one night in bed. "I think that Don is . . . well, after me. You know."

Trager rolled over and propped his head up on his elbow. "God," he said.

"I don't know how to handle it."

"Carefully," Trager said. "He's very vulnerable. You're probably the first woman he's ever been interested in. Don't be too hard on him. He shouldn't have to go through the stuff I went through, you know?"

The sex was never as good as a meathouse. And after a while Laurel began to close up. More and more nights now she went to sleep after they made love; the days when they had talked till dawn were gone. Perhaps they had nothing left to say. Trager had noticed that she had a tendency to finish his stories for him. It was nearly impossible to come up with one he hadn't already told her.

"He said *that?*" Trager got up out of bed, turned on a light, and sat down frowning. Laurel pulled the covers up to her chin.

"Well, what did *you* say?"

She hesitated. "I can't tell you. It's between Don and me. He said it wasn't fair, the way I turn around and tell you everything that goes on between us, and he's right."

"*Right!* But I tell you everything. Don't you remember what we—"

"I know, but—"

Trager shook his head. His voice lost some of its anger. "What's going on, Laurel, huh? I'm scared, all of a sudden. I love you, remember? How can everything change so fast?"

Her face softened. She sat up and held out her arms, and the covers fell back from her full, soft breasts. "Oh, Greg," she said. "Don't worry. I love you, I always will, but it's just that I love him too, I guess. You know?"

Trager, mollified, came into her arms and kissed her with fervor. Then he broke off. "Hey," he said, with mock sternness to hide the trembling in his voice, "who do you love *more?*"

"You, of course, always you."

Smiling, he returned to the kiss.

"I know you know," Donelly said. "I guess we have to talk about it."

Trager nodded. They were backstage in the theater. Three of his corpses walked up behind him and stood, arms crossed, like guards. "All right." He looked straight at Donelly, and his face was suddenly stern. "Laurel asked me to pretend I didn't know anything. She said you felt guilty. But pretending was quite a strain, Don. I guess it's time we got everything out into the open."

Donelly's pale blue eyes shifted, and he stuck his hands into his pockets. "I don't want to hurt you," he said.

"Then don't."

"But I'm not going to pretend I'm dead, either. I'm not. I love her too."

"You're supposed to be my friend, Don. Love someone else. You're just going to get yourself hurt this way."

"I have more in common with her than you do."

Trager stared.

Donelly looked up at him. "I don't know. Oh, Greg. She loves you more anyway, she said so. I never should have expected anything else. I feel like I've stabbed you in the back. I—"

Trager watched him. Finally he laughed softly. "Oh, shit, I can't take this. Look, Don, you haven't stabbed me, c'mon, don't talk like that. I guess, if you love her, this is the way it's got to be, you know. I just hope everything comes out all right."

Later that night, in bed with Laurel: "I'm worried about him," he said.

His face, once tanned, now ashen. "Laurel?" he said. Not believing.

"I don't love you anymore. I'm sorry. I don't. It seemed real at the time, but now it's almost like a dream. I don't even know if I ever loved you, really."

"Don," he said woodenly.

Laurel flushed. "Don't say anything bad about Don. I'm tired of hearing you run him down. He never says anything except good about you."

"Oh, Laurel. Don't you *remember?* The things we said, the way we felt? I'm the same person you said those words to."

"But I've grown," Laurel said, hard and tearless, tossing her red-gold hair. "I remember perfectly well, but I just don't feel that way anymore."

"Don't," he said. He reached for her.

She stepped back. "Keep your hands off me. I told you, Greg, it's *over*. You have to leave now. Don is coming by."

It was worse than Josie. A thousand times worse.

5. Wanderings

He tried to keep on at the theater; he enjoyed the work, he had friends there. But Donelly was there every day, smiling and being friendly, and sometimes Laurel came to meet him after the show and they went off together arm in arm. Trager would stand and watch, try not to notice. While the twisted thing inside him shrieked and clawed.

He quit. He would not see them again. He would keep his pride.

The sky was bright with the lights of Gidyon and full of laughter, but it was dark and quiet in the park.

Trager stood stiff against a tree, his eyes on the river, his hands folded tightly against his chest. He was a statue. He hardly breathed. Not even his eyes moved.

Kneeling near the low wall, the corpse pounded until the stone was slick with blood and its hands were mangled clots of torn meat. The sounds of the blows were dull and wet, but for the infrequent scraping of bone against rock.

They made him pay first before he could even enter the booth. Then he sat there for an hour while they found her and punched through. Finally, though, finally: "Josie."

"Greg," she said, with her distinctive grin. "I should have known. Who else would call all the way from Vendalia? How are you?"

He told her.

Her grin vanished. "Oh, Greg," she said. "I'm sorry. But don't let it get to you. Keep going. The next one will work out better. They always do."

Her words didn't satisfy him. "Josie," he said, "how are things back there? You miss me?"

"Oh, sure. Things are pretty good. It's still Skrakky, though. Stay where you are, you're better off." She looked off screen, then back. "I should go, before your bill gets enormous. Glad you called, love."

"Josie," Trager began. But the screen was already dark.

Sometimes, at night, he couldn't help himself. He would move to his home screen and ring Laurel. Her eyes would narrow when she saw who it was. Then she would hang up.

And Trager would sit in a dark room and recall how once the sound of his voice made her so very, very happy.

The streets of Gidyon are not the best places for lonely midnight walks. They are brightly lit, even in the darkest hours, and jammed with men and deadmen. And there are meathouses, all up and down the boulevards and the ironspike boardwalks.

Josie's words had lost their power. In the meathouses, Trager abandoned dreams and found solace. The sensuous evenings with Laurel and the fumbling sex of his boyhood were things of yesterday; Trager took his meatmates hard and quick, almost brutally, fucked them with a wordless savage power to the inevitable perfect orgasm. Sometimes, remembering the theater, he would have them act out short erotic playlets to get him in the mood.

In the night. Agony.

He was in the corridors again, the low dim corridors of the corpse-handlers' dorm on Skrakky, but now the corridors were twisted and tortuous and Trager had long since lost his way. The air was thick with a rotting grey haze and growing thicker. Soon, he feared, he would be all but blind.

Around and around he walked, up and down, but always there were more corridors, and all of them led nowhere. The doors were grim black rectangles without handles, locked to him forever; he passed them by without thinking, most of them. Once or twice, though, he paused before a door where light leaked around the frame. He would listen, and inside there were sounds, and then he would begin to knock wildly. But no one ever answered.

So he moved on, through the haze that got darker and thicker and seemed to burn his skin, past door after door after door, until he was weeping and his feet were tired and bloody. And then, off a way, down a long, long corridor that ran straight before him, he would see an open door. From it came light so hot and white it hurt the eyes, and music bright and joyful, and the sounds of people laughing. Then Trager would run, though his feet were raw bundles of pain and his lungs burned with the haze he was breathing. He would run and run and run until he reached the open door.

Only when he got there, it was his room, and it was empty.

Once, in the middle of their brief time together, they'd gone out into the wilderness and made love under the stars. Afterward she had snuggled hard against him, and he stroked her gently. "What are you thinking?" he asked.

"About us," Laurel said. She shivered. The wind was brisk and cold. "Sometimes I get scared, Greg. I'm so afraid something will happen to us, something that will ruin it. I don't ever want you to leave me."

"Don't worry," he told her, "I won't."

Now, each night before sleep came, he tortured himself with her words. The good memories left him with ashes and tears; the bad ones with a wordless rage.

He slept with a ghost beside him, a supernaturally beautiful ghost, the husk of a dead dream. He woke to her each morning.

He hated them. He hated himself for hating.

6. Duvalier's Dream

Her name does not matter. Her looks are not important. All that counts is that she *was,* that Trager tried again, that he forced himself on and made himself believe and didn't give up. He *tried.*

But something was missing. Magic?

The words were the same.

How many times can you speak them, Trager wondered, speak them and believe them, like you believed them the first time you said them? Once? Twice? Three times, maybe? Or a hundred? And the people who say it a hundred times, are they really so much better at loving? Or only at fooling themselves? Aren't they really people who long ago abandoned the dream, who use its name for something else?

He said the words, holding her, cradling her and kissing her. He said the words, with a knowledge that was surer and heavier and more dead than any belief. He said the words and *tried*.

And she said the words back, and Trager realized that they meant nothing to him. Over and over again they said the things each wanted to hear, and both of them knew they were pretending.

They tried *hard*. But when he reached out, like an actor caught in his role, doomed to play out the same part over and over again, when he reached out his hand and touched her cheek—the skin was smooth and soft and lovely. And wet with tears.

7. Echoes

"I don't want to hurt you," said Donelly, shuffling and looking guilty, until Trager felt ashamed for having hurt a friend.

He reached toward her cheek, and she turned away from him.

"I never wanted to hurt you," Josie said, and Trager was sad. She had given him so much; he'd only made her guilty. Yes, he was hurt, but a stronger man would never have let her know.

He touched her cheek, and she kissed his hand.

"I'm sorry. I don't," Laurel said. And Trager was lost. What had he done, where was his fault, how had he ruined it? She had been so sure. They had had so much.

He touched her cheek, and she wept.

How many times can you speak them, his voice echoed, speak them and believe them, like you believed them the first time you said them?

The wind was dark and dust-heavy; the sky throbbed

painfully with flickering scarlet flame. In the pit, in the darkness, stood a young woman with goggles and a filtermask and short brown hair and answers. "It breaks down, it breaks down, it breaks down, and they keep sending it out," she said. "Should realize that something is wrong. After that many failures, it's sheer self-delusion to think the thing's going to work right next time out."

8. Trager, Come of Age

The enemy corpse is huge and black, its torso rippling with muscle, a product of years of exercise, the biggest thing that Trager has ever faced. It advances across the sawdust in a slow, clumsy crouch, holding the gleaming broadsword in one hand. Trager watches it from his chair above one end of the fighting area. The other corpsemaster is careful, cautious.

His own deadman, a wiry blond, stands and waits, a morningstar trailing down in the blood-soaked arena dust. Trager will move him fast enough and well enough when the time is right. The enemy knows it, and the crowd.

The black corpse suddenly lifts its broadsword and scrambles forward in a run, hoping to use reach and speed to get its kill. But Trager's corpse is no longer there when the enemy's measured blow cuts the air where he had been.

Sitting comfortably above the fighting pit/down in the arena, his feet grimy with blood and sawdust, Trager/the corpse snaps the command/swings the morningstar—and the great studded ball drifts up and around, almost lazily, almost gracefully. Into the back of the enemy's head, as he tries to recover and turn. A flower of blood and brain blooms swift and sudden, and the crowd cheers.

Trager walks his corpse from the arena, then stands to receive applause. It is his tenth kill. Soon the championship will be his. He is building such a record that they can no longer deny him a match.

She is beautiful, his lady, his love. Her hair is short and blond, her body very slim, graceful, almost athletic, with trim legs and small hard breasts. Her eyes are bright green, and they always welcome him. And there is a strange erotic innocence in her smile.

She waits for him in bed, waits for his return from the arena, waits for him eager and playful and loving. When he enters, she is sitting up, smiling for him, the covers bunched around her waist. From the door he admires her nipples.

Aware of his eyes, shy, she covers her breasts and blushes. Trager knows it is all false modesty, all playing. He moves to the bedside, sits, reaches out to stroke her cheek. Her skin is very soft; she nuzzles against his hand as it brushes her. Then Trager draws her hands aside, plants one gentle kiss on each breast, and a not-so-gentle kiss on her mouth. She kisses back, with ardor; their tongues dance.

They make love, he and she, slow and sensuous, locked together in a loving embrace that goes on and on. Two bodies move flawlessly in perfect rhythm, each knowing the other's needs. Trager thrusts, and his other body meets the thrusts. He reaches, and her hand is there. They come together (always, *always*, both orgasms triggered by the handler's brain), and a bright red flush burns on her breasts and earlobes. They kiss.

Afterward, he talks to her, his love, his lady. You should always talk afterward; he learned that long ago.

"You're lucky," he tells her sometimes, and she snuggles up to him and plants tiny kisses all across his chest. "Very lucky. They lie to you out there, love. They teach you a silly shining dream and they tell you to believe and chase it and they tell you that for you, for everyone, there is someone. But it's all wrong. The universe isn't fair, it never has been. You run after the phantom, and lose, and they tell you next time, but it's all rot, all empty rot. Nobody ever finds the dream at all; they just kid themselves, trick themselves so they can go on believing. It's just a clutching lie that desperate people tell each other, hoping to convince themselves."

But then he can't talk anymore, for her kisses have gone lower and lower, and now she takes him in her mouth. And Trager smiles at his love and gently strokes her hair.

Of all the bright cruel lies they tell you, the cruelest is the one called love.

Custer's Last Jump

Steven Utley and Howard Waldrop

Publishing is a strange business. When Alexei Panshin wrote *Rite of Passage* he had to persevere through rejections from a dozen publishers before he could sell it—and it promptly won the Nebula Award as the best sf novel of the year. When Steven Utley and Howard Waldrop wrote "Custer's Last Jump," they had two editors faunching to buy it—but it was nearly two years before it got into print.

They originally sent it to me for my original-stories anthology series *Universe,* and I loved the story; but I'd just filled one volume and I knew I wouldn't have a contract for the next volume for several months. So I was all set to send back the manuscript with regrets—but as it happened, just after I'd read the story I had dinner with Robert Silverberg, and I spent a good portion of the evening enthusing about this delightful story I was unable to buy. Bob finally said, "Why not let me see it? Maybe I could use it for *New Dimensions.*"

So I showed it to him, and he loved it too. He wrote to the authors to make arrangements to buy it . . . but before the purchase could be consummated Silverberg decided to switch publishers, and suddenly *he* was between contracts. Complicated negotiations ensued, time slipped by, and eventually I received the contract for the next *Universe*. Silverberg passed the story back to me, I wrote to Utley and Waldrop and bought the story.

There's more: After I'd filled *Universe 6*, and paid for all the stories, I too found myself switching to a new publisher. More negotiations, more delay . . . and finally, early in 1976, when the authors had almost given up on seeing their story in print, Doubleday published the book in which it appeared.

Enthusiastic reactions came quickly: reviewers loved the story, members of the Science Fiction Writers of America began nominating it for the Nebula, and it's been chosen for reprint in two of the best-of-the-year books. So Utley and Waldrop's long wait seems to have been worthwhile.

You were waiting too, though you didn't know it. Here is one of the most original and detailed alternate-world stories in science fiction, the narration of George Armstrong Custer's final battle against the fighter planes of the Plains Indians Air Force.

What, you say, fighter planes in 1876? Sure. Settle back, now, while Steven Utley and Howard Waldrop document how it happened.

Smithsonian Annals of Flight, VOL. 39: *The Air War in the West*

CHAPTER 27: The Krupp Monoplane

INTRODUCTION

Its wings still hold the tears from many bullets. The ailerons are still scorched black, and the exploded Henry machine rifle is bent awkwardly in its blast port.

The right landing skid is missing, and the frame has been restraightened. It stands in the left wing of the Air Museum today, next to the French Devre jet and the X-FU-5 Flying Flapjack, the world's fastest fighter aircraft.

On its rudder is the swastika, an ugly reminder of days of glory fifty years ago.

A simple plaque describes the aircraft. It reads:

CRAZY HORSE'S KRUPP MONOPLANE

(Captured at the raid on Fort Carson, January 5, 1882)

GENERAL

1. To study the history of this plane is to delve into one of the most glorious eras of aviation history. To begin: the aircraft was manufactured by the Krupp plant at Haavesborg, Netherlands. The airframe was completed August 3, 1862, as part of the third shipment of Krupp aircraft to the Confederate States of America under terms of the Agreement of Atlanta of 1861. It was originally equipped with power plant #311 Zed of 87¼ horsepower, manufactured by the Jumo plant at Nordmung, Duchy of Austria, on May 3 of the year 1862. Wingspan of the craft is twenty-three feet, its length is seventeen feet three inches. The aircraft arrived in the port of Charlotte on September 21, 1862, aboard the transport *Mendenhall,* which had suffered heavy bombardment from GAR picket ships. The aircraft was possibly sent by rail to Confederate Army Air Corps Center at Fort Andrew Mott, Alabama. Unfortunately, records of rail movements during this time were lost in the burning of the Confederate archives at Ittebeha in March 1867, two weeks after the Truce of Haldeman was signed.

2. The aircraft was damaged during a training flight in December 1862. Student pilot was Flight Subaltern (Cadet) Neldoo J. Smith, CSAAC; flight instructor during the ill-fated flight was Air Captain Winslow Homer Winslow, on interservice instructor-duty loan from the Confederate States Navy.

Accident forms and maintenance officer's reports indicate that the original motor was replaced with one of the new 93½ horsepower Jumo engines which had just arrived from Holland by way of Mexico.

3. The aircraft served routinely through the remainder of Flight Subaltern Smith's training. We have records[141], which indicate that the aircraft was one of the first to be equipped with the Henry repeating machine rifle of the chain-driven type. Until December 1862, all CSAAC aircraft were equipped with the Sharps repeating rifles of the motor-driven, low-voltage type on wing or turret mounts.

As was the custom, the aircraft was flown by Flight Subaltern Smith to his first duty station at Thimblerig Aerodrome in Augusta, Georgia. Flight Subaltern Smith was assigned to Flight Platoon 2, 1st Aeroscout Squadron.

4. The aircraft, with Flight Subaltern Smith at the wheel, participated in three of the aerial expeditions against the Union Army in the Second Battle of the Manassas. Smith distinguished himself in the first and third mission. (He was assigned aerial picket duty south of the actual battle during his second mission.) On the first, he is credited with one kill and one probable (both bi-wing Airsharks). During the third mission, he destroyed one aircraft and forced another down behind Confederate lines. He then escorted the craft of his immediate commander, Air Captain Dalton Trump, to a safe landing on a field controlled by the Confederates. According to Trump's sworn testimony, Smith successfully fought off two Union craft and ranged ahead of Trump's crippled plane to strafe a group of Union soldiers who were in their flight path, discouraging them from firing on Trump's smoking aircraft.

For heroism on these two missions, Smith was awarded the Silver Star and Bar with Air Cluster. Presentation was made on March 3, 1863, by the late General J. E. B. Stuart, Chief of Staff of the CSAAC.

5. Flight Subaltern Smith was promoted to flight captain on April 12, 1863, after distinguishing himself with two kills and two probables during the first day of the Battle of the Three Roads, North Carolina. One of his kills was an airship of the Moby class, with crew of fourteen. Smith shared with only one other aviator the feat of bringing down one of these dirigibles during the War of the Secession.

This was the first action the 1st Aeroscout Squadron had seen since Second Manassas, and Captain Smith seems to have been chafing under inaction. Perhaps this led him to volunteer for duty with Major John S. Moseby, then forming what would later become Moseby's Raiders. This was actually sound military strategy: the CSAAC was to send a unit to southwestern Kansas to carry out harassment raids against the poorly defended forts of the far West. These raids would force the Union to send men and materiel sorely needed at the southern front far to the west, where they would be ineffectual in the outcome of the war. That this action was taken is pointed to by some[142] as a sign that the Confederate States envisioned defeat and were resorting to desperate measures four years before the Treaty of Haldeman.

At any rate, Captain Smith and his aircraft joined a triple flight of six aircraft each, which, after stopping at El Dorado, Arkansas, to refuel, flew away on a westerly course. This is the last time they ever operated in Confederate states. The date was June 5, 1863.

6. The Union forts stretched from a medium-well-defended line in Illinois, to poorly garrisoned stations as far west as Wyoming Territory and south to the Kansas-Indian Territory border. Southwestern Kansas was both sparsely settled and garrisoned. It was from this area that Moseby's Raiders, with the official designation 1st Western Interdiction Wing, CSAAC, operated.

A supply wagon train had been sent ahead a month before from Fort Worth, carrying petrol, ammunition, and material for shelters. A crude landing field, hangars, and barracks awaited the eighteen craft.

After two months of reconnaissance (done by mounted scouts due to the need to maintain the element of surprise, and, more importantly, by the limited amount of fuel available) the 1st WIW took to the air. The citizens of Riley, Kansas, long remembered the day: their first inkling that Confederates were closer than Texas came when motors were heard overhead and the Union garrison was literally blown off the face of the map.

7. Following the first raid, word went to the War Department headquarters in New York, with pleas for aid and reinforcements for all Kansas garrisons. Thus the CSAAC achieved its goal in the very first raid. The effects snowballed; as soon as the populace learned of the raid, it demanded protection from nearby garrisons. Farmers' organizations threatened to stop shipments of needed produce to eastern depots. The garrison commanders, unable to promise adequate protection, appealed to higher military authorities.

Meanwhile, the 1st WIW made a second raid on Abilene, heavily damaging the railways and stockyards with twenty-five-pound fragmentation bombs. They then circled the city, strafed the Army Quartermaster depot, and disappeared into the west.

8. This second raid, and the ensuing clamor from both the public and the commanders of western forces, convinced the War Department to divert new recruits and supplies, with seasoned members of the 18th Aeropursuit Squadron, to the Kansas-Missouri border, near Lawrence.

9. Inclement weather in the fall kept both the 18th AS and the 1st WIW grounded for seventy-two of the

ninety days of the season. Aircraft from each of these units met several times; the 1st is credited with one kill, while pilots of the 18th downed two Confederate aircraft on the afternoon of December 12, 1863.

Both aircraft units were heavily resupplied during this time. The Battle of the Canadian River was fought on December 18, when mounted reconnaissance units of the Union and Confederacy met in Indian territory. Losses were small on both sides, but the skirmish was the first of what would become known as the Far Western Campaign.

10. Civilians spotted the massed formation of the 1st WIW as early as 10 A.M. Thursday, December 16, 1863. They headed northeast, making a leg due north when eighteen miles south of Lawrence. Two planes sped ahead to destroy the telegraph station at Felton, nine miles south of Lawrence. Nevertheless, a message of some sort reached Lawrence; a Union messenger on horseback was on his way to the aerodrome when the first flight of Confederate aircraft passed overhead.

In the ensuing raid, seven of the nineteen Union aircraft were destroyed on the ground and two were destroyed in the air, while the remaining aircraft were severely damaged and the barracks and hangars demolished.

The 1st WIW suffered one loss: during the raid a Union clerk attached for duty with the 18th AS manned an Agar machine rifle position and destroyed one Confederate aircraft. He was killed by machine rifle fire from the second wave of planes. Private Alden Evans Gunn was awarded the Congressional Medal of Honor posthumously for his gallantry during the attack.

For the next two months, the 1st WIW ruled the skies as far north as Illinois, as far east as Trenton, Missouri.

THE FAR WESTERN CAMPAIGN

1. At this juncture, the two most prominent figures of the next nineteen years of frontier history enter the pic-

ture: the Oglala Sioux Crazy Horse and Lieutenant Colonel (Brevet Major General) George Armstrong Custer. The clerical error giving Custer the rank of Brigadier General is well known. It is not common knowledge that Custer was considered by the General Staff as a candidate for Far Western Commander as early as the spring of 1864, a duty he would not take up until May 1869, when the Far Western Command was the only theater of war operations within the Americas.

The General Staff, it is believed, considered Major General Custer for the job for two reasons: they thought Custer possessed those qualities of spirit suited to the warfare necessary in the Western Command, and that the far West was the ideal place for the twenty-three-year-old Boy General.

Crazy Horse, the Oglala Sioux warrior, was with a hunting party far from Oglala territory, checking the size of the few remaining buffalo herds before they started their spring migrations. Legend has it that Crazy Horse and the party were crossing the prairies in early February 1864 when two aircrafts belonging to the 1st WIW passed nearby. Some of the Sioux jumped to the ground, believing that they were looking on the Thunderbird and its mate. Only Crazy Horse stayed on his pony and watched the aircraft disappear into the south.

He sent word back by the rest of the party that he and two of his young warrior friends had gone looking for the nest of the Thunderbird.

2. The story of the 1st WIW here becomes the story of the shaping of the Indian wars, rather than part of the history of the last four years of the War of the Secession. It is well known that increased alarm over the Kansas raids had shifted War Department thinking: the defense of the far West changed in importance from a minor matter in the larger scheme of war to a problem of vital concern. For one thing, the Confederacy was courting the Emperor Maximilian of Mexico, and

through him the French, into entering the war on the Confederate side. The South wanted arms, but most necessarily to break the Union submarine blockade. Only the French Navy possessed the capability.

The Union therefore sent the massed 5th Cavalry to Kansas, and attached to it the 12th Air Destroyer Squadron and the 2nd Airship Command.

The 2nd Airship Command, at the time of its deployment, was equipped with the small pursuit airships known in later days as the "torpedo ship," from its double-pointed ends. These ships were used for reconnaissance and light interdiction duties, and were almost always accompanied by aircraft from the 12th ADS. They immediately set to work patrolling the Kansas skies from the renewed base of operations at Lawrence.

3. The idea of using Indian personnel in some phase of airfield operations in the West had been proposed by Moseby as early as June 1863. The C of C, CSA, disapproved in the strongest possible terms. It was not a new idea, therefore, when Crazy Horse and his two companions rode into the airfield, accompanied by the sentries who had challenged them far from the perimeter. They were taken to Major Moseby for questioning.

Through an interpreter, Moseby learned they were Oglala, not Crows sent to spy for the Union. When asked why they had come so far, Crazy Horse replied, "To see the nest of the Thunderbird."

Moseby is said to have laughed[143] and then taken the three Sioux to see the aircraft. Crazy Horse was said to have been stricken with awe when he found that men controlled their flight.

Crazy Horse then offered Moseby ten ponies for one of the craft. Moseby explained that they were not his to give, but his Great Father's, and that they were used to fight the Yellowlegs from the Northeast.

At this time, fate took a hand: the 12th Air Destroyer Squadron had just begun operations. The same day Crazy Horse was having his initial interview with

Moseby, a scout plane returned with the news that the 12th was being reinforced by an airship combat group; the dirigibles had been seen maneuvering near the Kansas-Missouri border.

Moseby learned from Crazy Horse that the warrior was respected; if not in his own tribe, then with other Nations of the North. Moseby, with an eye toward those reinforcements arriving in Lawrence, asked Crazy Horse if he could guarantee safe conduct through the northern tribes, and land for an airfield should the present one have to be abandoned.

Crazy Horse answered, "I can talk the idea to the People; it will be for them to decide."

Moseby told Crazy Horse that if he could secure the promise, he would grant him anything within his power.

Crazy Horse looked out the window toward the hangars. "I ask that you teach me and ten of my brother-friends to fly the Thunderbirds. We will help you fight the Yellowlegs."

Moseby, expecting requests for beef, blankets, or firearms was taken aback. Unlike the others who had dealt with the Indians, he was a man of his word. He told Crazy Horse he would ask his Great Father if this could be done. Crazy Horse left, returning to his village in the middle of March. He and several warriors traveled extensively that spring, smoking the pipe, securing permissions from the other Nations for safe conduct for the Gray White Men through their hunting lands. His hardest task came in convincing the Oglala themselves that the airfield be built in their southern hunting grounds.

Crazy Horse, his two wives, seven warriors and their women, children, and belongings rode into the CSAAC airfield in June, 1864.

4. Moseby had been granted permission from Stuart to go ahead with the training program. Derision first met the request within the southern General Staff when

Moseby's proposal was circulated. Stuart, though not entirely sympathetic to the idea, became its champion. Others objected, warning that ignorant savages should not be given modern weapons. Stuart reminded them that some of the good Tennessee boys already flying airplanes could neither read nor write.

Stuart's approval arrived a month before Crazy Horse and his band made camp on the edge of the airfield.

5. It fell to Captain Smith to train Crazy Horse. The Indian became what Smith, in his journal,[144] describes as "the best natural pilot I have seen or it has been my pleasure to fly with." Part of this seems to have come from Smith's own modesty; by all accounts, Smith was one of the finer pilots of the war.

The operations of the 12th ADS and the 2nd Airship Command ranged closer to the CSAAC airfield. The dogfights came frequently and the fighting grew less gentlemanly. One 1st WIW fighter was pounced by three aircraft of the 12th simultaneously: they did not stop firing even when the pilot signaled that he was hit and that his engine was dead. Nor did they break off their runs until both pilot and craft plunged into the Kansas prairie. It is thought that the Union pilots were under secret orders to kill all members of the 1st WIW. There is some evidence[145] that this rankled with the more gentlemanly of the 12th Air Destroyer Squadron. Nevertheless, fighting intensified.

A flight of six more aircraft joined the 1st WIW some weeks after the Oglala Sioux started their training: this was the first of the ferry flights from Mexico through Texas and Indian territory to reach the airfield. Before the summer was over, a dozen additional craft would join the Wing; this before shipments were curtailed by Juarez's revolution against the French and the ouster and execution of Maximilian and his family.

Smith records[146] that Crazy Horse's first solo took

place on August 14, 1864, and that the warrior, though deft in the air, still needed practice on his landings. He had a tendency to come in overpowered and to stall his engine out too soon. Minor repairs were made on the skids of the craft after this flight.

All this time, Crazy Horse had flown Smith's craft. Smith, after another week of hard practice with the Indian, pronounced him "more qualified than most pilots the CSAAC in Alabama turned out"[147] and signed over the aircraft to him. Crazy Horse begged off. Then, seeing that Smith was sincere, he gave the captain many buffalo hides. Smith reminded the Indian that the craft was not his: during their off hours, when not training, the Indians had been given enough instruction in military discipline as Moseby, never a stickler, thought necessary. The Indians had only a rudimentary idea of government property. Of the seven other Indian men, three were qualified as pilots; the other four were given gunner positions in the Krupp bi-wing light bombers assigned to the squadron.

Soon after Smith presented the aircraft to Crazy Horse, the captain took off in a borrowed monoplane on what was to be the daily weather flight into northern Kansas. There is evidence[148] that it was Smith who encountered a flight of light dirigibles from the 2nd Airship Command and attacked them single-handedly. He crippled one airship; the other was rescued when two escort planes of the 12th ADS came to its defense. They raked the attacker with withering fire. The attacker escaped into the clouds.

It was not until 1897, when a group of schoolchildren on an outing found the wreckage, that it was known that Captain Smith had brought his crippled monoplane within five miles of the airfield before crashing into the rolling hills.

When Smith did not return from his flight, Crazy Horse went on a vigil, neither sleeping nor eating for a week. On the seventh day, Crazy Horse vowed vengeance on the man who had killed his white friend.

6. The devastating Union raid of September 23, 1864, caught the airfield unawares. Though the Indians were averse to fighting at night, Crazy Horse and two other Sioux were manning three of the four craft which got off the ground during the raid. The attack had been carried out by the 2nd Airship Command, traveling at twelve thousand feet, dropping fifty-pound fragmentation bombs and shrapnel canisters. The shrapnel played havoc with the aircraft on the ground. It also destroyed the mess hall and enlisted barracks and three teepees.

The dirigibles turned away and were running fast before a tail wind when Crazy Horse gained their altitude.

The gunners on the dirigibles filled the skies with tracers from their light .30-30 machine rifles. Crazy Horse's monoplane was equipped with a single Henry .41-40 machine rifle. Unable to get in close killing distance, Crazy Horse and his companions stood off beyond range of the lighter Union guns and raked the dirigibles with heavy machine rifle fire. They did enough damage to force one airship down twenty miles from its base, and to ground two others for two days while repairs were made. The intensity of fire convinced the airship commanders that more than four planes had made it off the ground, causing them to continue their headlong retreat.

Crazy Horse and the others returned, and brought off the second windfall of the night; a group of 5th Cavalry raiders were to have attacked the airfield in the confusion of the airship raid and burn everything still standing. On their return flight, the four craft encountered the cavalry unit as it began its charge across open ground.

In three strafing runs, the aircraft killed thirty-seven men and wounded fifty-three, while twenty-nine were taken prisoner by the airfield's defenders. Thus, in his first combat mission for the CSAAC, Crazy Horse was credited with saving the airfield against overwhelming odds.

7. Meanwhile, Major General George A. Custer had distinguished himself at the Battle of Gettysburg. A few weeks after the battle, he enrolled himself in the GAR jump school at Watauga, New York. Howls of outrage came from the General Staff; Custer quoted the standing order, "any man who volunteered and of whom the commanding officer approved," could be enrolled. Custer then asked, in a letter to C of S, GAR, "how any military leader could be expected to plan manuevers involving parachute infantry when he himself had never experienced a drop, or found the true capabilities of the parachute infantryman?"[149] The Chief of Staff shouted down the protest. There were mutterings among the General Staff[150] to the effect that the real reason Custer wanted to become jump-qualified was so that he would have a better chance of leading the Invasion of Atlanta, part of whose contingency plans called for attacks by airborne units.

During the three-week parachute course, Custer became acquainted with another man who would play an important part in the Western Campaign, Captain (Brevet Colonel) Frederick W. Benteen. Upon graduation from the jump school, Brevet Colonel Benteen assumed command of the 505th Balloon Infantry, stationed at Chicago, Illinois, for training purposes. Colonel Benteen would remain commander of the 505th until his capture at the Battle of Montgomery in 1866. While he was prisoner of war, his command was given to another, later to figure in the Western Campaign, Lieutenant Colonel Myles W. Keogh.

Custer, upon successful completion of jump school, returned to his command of the 6th Cavalry Division, and participated throughout the remainder of the war in that capacity. It was he who led the successful charge at the Battle of the Cape Fear which smashed Lee's flank and allowed the 1st Infantry to overrun the Confederate position and capture that southern leader. Custer distinguished himself and his command up until the cessation of hostilities in 1867.

8. The 1st WIW, CSAAC, moved to a new airfield in Wyoming Territory three weeks after the raid of September 24. At the same time, the 2nd WIW was formed and moved to an outpost in Indian territory. The 2nd WIW raided the Union airfield, took it totally by surprise, and inflicted casualties on the 12th ADS and 2nd AC so devastating as to render them ineffectual. The 2nd WIW then moved to a second field in Wyoming Territory. It was here, following the move, that a number of Indians, including Black Man's Hand, were trained by Crazy Horse.

9. We leave the history of the 2nd WIW here. It was redeployed for the defense of Montgomery. The Indians and aircraft in which they trained were sent north to join the 1st WIW. The 1st WIW patrolled the skies of Indiana, Nebraska, and the Dakotas. After the defeat of the 12th ADS and the 2nd AC, the Union forstalled attempts to retaliate until the cessation of southern hostilities in 1867.

We may at this point add that Crazy Horse, Black Man's Hand, and the other Indians sometimes left the airfield during periods of long inactivity. They returned to their Nations for as long as three months at a time. Each time Crazy Horse returned, he brought one or two pilot or gunner recruits with him. Before the winter of 1866, more than thirty per cent of the 1st WIW were Oglala, Sansarc Sioux, or Cheyenne.

The South, losing the war of attrition, diverted all supplies to Alabama and Mississippi in the fall of 1866. None were forthcoming for the 1st WIW, though a messenger arrived with orders for Major Moseby to return to Texas for the defense of Fort Worth, where he would later direct the Battle of the Trinity. That Moseby was not ordered to deploy the 1st WIW to that defense has been considered by many military strategists as a "lost turning point" of the battle for Texas. Command of the 1st WIW was turned over to Acting Major (Flight Captain) Natchitoches Hooley.

10. The loss of Moseby signaled the end of the 1st WIW. Not only did the nondeployment of the 1st to Texas cost the South that territory, it also left the 1st in an untenable position, which the Union was quick to realize. The airfield was captured in May 1867 by a force of five hundred cavalry and three hundred infantry sent from the battle of the Arkansas, and a like force, plus aircraft, from Chicago. Crazy Horse, seven Indians, and at least five Confederates escaped in their monoplanes. The victorious Union troops were surprised to find Indians at the field. Crazy Horse's people were eventually freed; the Army thought them to have been hired by the Confederates to hunt and cook for the airfield. Moseby had provided for this in contingency plans long before; he had not wanted the Plains tribes to suffer for Confederate acts. The Army did not know, and no one volunteered the information, that it had been Indians doing the most considerable amount of damage to the Union garrisons lately.

Crazy Horse and three of his Indians landed their craft near the Black Hills. The Cheyenne helped them carry the craft, on travois, to caves in the sacred mountains. Here they mothballed the planes with mixtures of pine tar and resins, and sealed up the caves.

11. The aircraft remained stored until February 1872. During this time, Crazy Horse and his Oglala Sioux operated, like the other Plains Indians, as light cavalry, skirmishing with the Army and with settlers up and down the Dakotas and Montana. George Armstrong Custer was appointed commander of the new 7th Cavalry in 1869. Stationed first at Chicago (Far Western Command headquarters) they later moved to Fort Abraham Lincoln, Nebraska.

A column of troops moved against Indians on the warpath in the winter of 1869. They reported a large group of Indians encamped on the Washita River. Custer obtained permission for the 505th Balloon Infantry to join the 7th Cavalry. From that day on, the unit was officially Company I (Separate Troops), 7th U. S. Cavalry, though it kept its numerical designation. Also attached to the 7th was the 12th Airship Squadron, as Company J.

Lieutenant Colonel Keogh, acting commander of the 505th for the last twenty-one months, but who had never been on jump status, was appointed by Custer as commander of K Company, 7th Cavalry.

It was known that only the 505th Balloon Infantry and the 12th Airship Squadron were used in the raid on Black Kettle's village. Black Kettle was a treaty Indian, "walking the white man's road." Reports have become garbled in transmission: Custer and the 505th believed they were jumping into a village of hostiles.

The event remained a mystery until Kellogg, the Chicago newspaperman, wrote his account in 1872.[151] The 505th, with Custer in command, flew the three (then numbered, after 1872, named) dirigibles No. 31, No. 76, and No. 93, with seventy-two jumpers each. Custer was in the first "stick" on Airship 76. The three sailed silently to the sleeping village. Custer gave the order to hook up at 5:42 Chicago time, 4:42 local time, and the 505th jumped into the village. Black Kettle's people were awakened when some of the balloon infantry crashed through their teepees, others died in their sleep. One of the first duties of the infantry was to moor the dirigibles; this done, the gunners on the airships opened up on the startled villagers with their Gatling and Agar machine rifles. Black Kettle himself was killed while waving an American flag at Airship No. 93.

After the battle, the men of the 505th climbed back up to the moored dirigibles by rope ladder, and the airships departed for Fort Lincoln. The Indians camped downriver heard the shooting and found horses stampeded during the attack. When they came to the village, they found only slaughter. Custer had taken his dead (3, one of whom died during the jump by being drowned in the Washita) and wounded (12) away.

They left 307 dead men, women, and children, and 500 slaughtered horses.

There were no tracks leading in and out of the village except those of the frightened horses. The other Indians left the area, thinking the white men had magicked it.

Crazy Horse is said[152] to have visited the area soon after the massacre. It was this action by the 7th which spelled their doom seven years later.

12. Black Man's Hand joined Crazy Horse; so did other former 1st WIW pilots, soon after Crazy Horse's two-plane raid on the airship hangars at Bismark, in 1872. For that mission, Crazy Horse dropped twenty-five-pound fragmentation bombs tied to petrol canisters. The shrapnel ripped the dirigibles, the escaping hydrogen was ignited by the burning petrol: all—hangars, balloons, and maintenance crews—were lost.

It was written up as an unreconstructed Confederate's sabotage; a somewhat ignominious former southern major was eventually hanged on circumstantial evidence. Reports by sentries that they heard aircraft just before the explosions were discounted. At the time, it was believed the only aircraft were those belonging to the Army, and the carefully licensed commercial craft.

13. In 1874, Custer circulated rumors that the Black Hills were full of gold. It has been speculated that this was used to draw miners to the area so the Indians would attack them; then the cavalry would have unlimited freedom to deal with the Red Man.[153] Also that year, those who had become Agency Indians were being shorted in their supplies by members of the scandal-plagued Indian Affairs Bureau under President Grant. When these left the reservations in search of food, the cavalry was sent to "Bring them back." Those who were caught were usually killed.

The Sioux ignored the miners at first, expecting the gods to deal with them. When this did not happen, Sitting Bull sent out a party of two hundred warriors, who killed every miner they encountered. Public outrage demanded reprisals; Sheridan wired Custer to find and punish those responsible.

14. Fearing what was to come, Crazy Horse sent Yellow Dog and Red Chief with a war party of five hundred to raid the rebuilt Fort Phil Kearny. This they did successfully, capturing twelve planes and fuel and ammunition for many more. They hid these in the caverns with the 1st WIW craft.

The Army would not have acted as rashly as it did had it known the planes pronounced missing in the reports on the Kearny raid were being given into the hands of experienced pilots.

The reprisal consisted of airship patrols which strafed any living thing on the plains. Untold thousands of deer and the few remaining buffalo were killed. Unofficial counts list as killed a little more than eight hundred Indians who were caught in the open during the next eight months.

Indians who jumped the agencies and who had seen or heard of the slaughter streamed to Sitting Bull's hidden camp on the Little Big Horn. They were treated as guests, except for the Sansarcs, who camped a little way down the river. It is estimated there were no less than ten thousand Indians, including some four thousand warriors, camped along the river for the Sun Dance ceremony of June 1876.

A three-pronged-pincers movement for the final eradication of the Sioux and Cheyenne worked toward them. The 7th Cavalry, under Keogh and Major Marcus Reno, set out from Fort Lincoln during the last week of May. General George Crook's command was coming up the Rosebud. The gunboat *Far West,* with three hundred reserves and supplies, steamed to the mouth of the Big Horn River. General Terry's command was coming from the northwest. All Indians they encountered were to be killed.

Just before the Sun Dance, Crazy Horse and his pilots got word of the movement of Crook's men up the Rosebud, hurried to the caves, and prepared their craft for flight. Only six planes were put in working condition in time. The other pilots remained behind while Crazy Horse, Black Man's Hand, and four others took to the skies. They destroyed two dirigibles, soundly trounced Crook, and chased his command back down the Rosebud in a rout. The column had to abandon its light armored vehicles and fight its way back, on foot for the most part, to safety.

15. Sitting Bull's vision during the Sun Dance is well known.[154] He told it to Crazy Horse, the warrior who would see that it came true, as soon as the aviators returned to camp.

Two hundred fifty miles away, "Chutes and Saddles" was sounded on the morning of June 23, and the men of the 505th Balloon Infantry climbed aboard the airships *Benjamin Franklin, Samuel Adams, John Hancock,* and *Ethan Allen.* Custer was first man on stick one of the *Franklin.* The *Ethan Allen* carried a scout aircraft which could hook up or detach in flight; the bi-winger was to serve as liaison between the three armies and the airships.

When Custer bade goodbye to his wife, Elizabeth, that morning, both were in good spirits. If either had an inkling of the fate which awaited Custer and the 7th three days away, on the bluffs above a small stream, they did not show it.

The four airships sailed from Fort Lincoln, their silver sides and shark-tooth mouths gleaming in the sun, the eyes painted on the noses looking west. On the sides were the crossed sabers of the cavalry; above the numeral 7; below the numerals 505. It is said that they looked magnificent as they sailed away for their rendezvous with destiny.[155]

16. It is sufficient to say that the Indians attained their greatest victory over the Army, and almost totally

destroyed the 7th Cavalry, on June 25–26, 1876, due in large part to the efforts of Crazy Horse and his aviators. Surprise, swiftness, and the skill of the Indians cannot be discounted, nor can the military blunders made by Custer that morning. The repercussions of that summer day rang down the years, and the events are still debated. The only sure fact is that the U. S. Army lost its prestige, part of its spirit, and more than four hundred of its finest soldiers in the battle.

17. While the demoralized commands were sorting themselves out, the Cheyenne and Sioux left for the Canadian border. They took their aircraft with them, on travois. With Sitting Bull, Crazy Horse and his band settled just across the border. The aircraft were rarely used again until the attack on the camp by the combined Canadian-U. S. Cavalry offensive of 1879. Crazy Horse and his aviators, as they had done so many times before, escaped with their aircraft, using one of the planes to carry their remaining fuel. Two of the nine craft were shot down by a Canadian battery.

Crazy Horse, sensing the end, fought his way, with men on horseback and the planes on travois, from Montana to Colorado. After learning of the death of Sitting Bull and Chief Joseph, he took his small band as close as he dared to Fort Carson, where the cavalry was amassing to wipe out the remaining American Indians.

He assembled his men for the last time. He made his proposal; all concurred and joined him for a last raid on the Army. The five remaining planes came in low, the morning of January 5, 1882, toward the Army airfield. They destroyed twelve aircraft on the ground, shot up the hangars and barracks, and ignited one of the two ammunition dumps of the stockade. At this time, Army gunners manned the William's machine cannon batteries (improved by Thomas Edison's contract scientists) and blew three of the craft to flinders. The war gods must have smiled on Crazy Horse; his aircraft was crippled, the machine rifle was blown askew, the motor slivered, but he managed to set down intact. Black Man's Hand turned away; he was captured two months later, eating cottonwood bark in the snows of Arizona.

Crazy Horse jumped from his aircraft as most of Fort Carson ran toward him; he pulled two Sharps repeating carbines from the cockpit and blazed away at the astonished troopers, wounding six and killing one. His back to the craft, he continued to fire until more than one hundred infantrymen fired a volley into his body.

The airplane was displayed for seven months at Fort Carson before being sent to the Smithsonian in Pittsburgh, where it stands today. Thus passed an era of military aviation.

—LT. GEN. FRANK LUKE, JR.
USAF, Ret.

From the December 2, 1939, issue of *Collier's Magazine*

Custer's Last Jump?

BY A. R. REDMOND

Few events in American history have captured the imagination so thoroughly as the Battle of the Little Big Horn. Lieutenant Colonel George Armstrong Custer's devastating defeat at the hands of Sioux and Cheyenne Indians in June 1876 has been rendered time and again by such celebrated artists as George Russell and Frederic Remington. Books, factual and otherwise, which have been written around or about the battle would fill an entire library wing. The motion picture industry has on numerous occasions drawn upon "Custer's Last Jump" for inspiration; latest in a long line of movieland Custers is Errol Flynn [see photo], who appears with Olivia deHavilland and newcomer Anthony Quinn in Warner Brothers' soon-to-be-released *They Died With Their Chutes On.*

The impetuous and flamboyant Custer was an almost

legendary figure long before the Battle of the Little Big Horn, however. Appointed to West Point in 1857, Custer was placed in command of Troop G, 2nd Cavalry, in June 1861, and participated in a series of skirmishes with Confederate cavalry throughout the rest of the year. It was during the First Battle of Manassas, or Bull Run, that he distinguished himself. He continued to do so in other engagements—at Williamsburg, Chancellorsville, Gettysburg—and rose rapidly through the ranks. He was twenty-six years old when he received a promotion to Brigadier General. He was, of course, immediately dubbed the Boy General. He had become an authentic war hero when the Northerners were in dire need of nothing less during those discouraging months between First Manassas and Gettysburg.

With the cessation of hostilities in the East when Bragg surrendered to Grant at Haldeman, the small hamlet about eight miles from Morehead, Kentucky, Custer requested a transfer of command. He and his young bride wound up at Chicago, manned by the new 7th U. S. Cavalry.

The war in the West lasted another few months; the tattered remnants of the Confederate Army staged last desperate stands throughout Texas, Colorado, Kansas, and Missouri. The final struggle at the Trinity River in October 1867 marked the close of conflict between North and South. Those few Mexican military advisers left in Texas quietly withdrew across the Rio Grande. The French, driven from Mexico in 1864 when Maximilian was ousted, lost interest in the Americas when they became embroiled with the newly united Prussian states.

During his first year in Chicago, Custer familiarized himself with the airships and aeroplanes of the 7th. The only jump-qualified general officer of the war, Custer seemed to have felt no resentment at the ultimate fate of mounted troops boded by the extremely mobile flying machines. The Ohio-born Boy General eventually preferred traveling aboard the airship *Benjamin Franklin,* one of the eight craft assigned to the 505th Balloon Infantry (Troop I, 7th Cavalry, commanded by Brevet Colonel Frederick Benteen) while his horse soldiers rode behind the very capable Captain (Brevet Lt. Col.) Myles Keogh.

The War Department in Pittsburgh did not know that various members of the Plains Indian tribes had been equipped with aeroplanes by the Confederates, and that many had actually flown against the Union garrisons in the West. (Curiously enough, those tribes which held out the longest against the Army—most notably the Apaches under Geronimo in the deep Southwest—were those who did not have aircraft.) The problems of transporting and hiding, to say nothing of maintaining planes, outweighed the advantages. A Cheyenne warrior named Brave Bear is said to have traded his band's aircraft in disgust to Sitting Bull for three horses. Also, many of the Plains Indians hated the aircraft outright, as they had been used by the white men to decimate the great buffalo herds in the early 1860s.

Even so, certain Oglalas, Minneconjous, and Cheyenne did reasonably well in the aircraft given them by the C. S. Army Air Corps Major John S. Moseby, whom the Indians called "The Gray White Man" or "Many-Feathers-in-Hat." The Oglala war chief Crazy Horse [see photo, overleaf] led the raid on the Bismarck hangars (1872), four months after the 7th Cavalry was transferred to Fort Abraham Lincoln, Dakota Territory, and made his presence felt at the Rosebud and Little Big Horn in 1876. The Cheyenne Black Man's Hand, trained by Crazy Horse himself, shot down two Army machines at the Rosebud, and was in the flight of planes that accomplished the annihilation of the 505th Balloon Infantry during the first phase of the Little Big Horn fiasco.

After the leveling of Fort Phil Kearny in February 1869, Custer was ordered to enter the Indian territories and punish those who had sought sanctuary there after the raid. Taking with him 150 parachutists aboard three airships, Custer left on the trail of a large band of Cheyenne.

On the afternoon of February 25, Lieutenant William van W. Reily, dispatched for scouting purposes in a Studebaker bi-winger, returned to report that he had shot up a hunting party near the Washita River. The Cheyenne, he thought, were encamped on the banks of the river some twenty miles away. They appeared not to have seen the close approach of the 7th Cavalry as they had not broken camp.

Just before dawn the next morning, the 505th Balloon Infantry, led by Custer, jumped into the village, killing all inhabitants and their animals.

For the next five years, Custer and the 7th chased the hostiles of the Plains back and forth between Colorado and the Canadian border. Relocated at Fort Lincoln, Custer and an expedition of horse soldiers, geologists, and engineers discovered gold in the Black Hills. Though the Black Hills still belonged to the Sioux according to several treaties, prospectors began to pour into the area. The 7th was ordered to protect them. The Blackfeet, Minneconjous, and Hunkpapa—Sioux who had left the warpath on the promise that the Black Hills, their sacred lands, were theirs to keep for all time—protested, and when protests brought no results, took matters into their own hands. Prospectors turned up in various stages of mutilation, or not at all.

Conditions worsened over the remainder of 1875, during which time the United States Government ordered the Sioux out of the Black Hills. To make sure the Indians complied, airships patrolled the skies of Dakota Territory.

By the end of 1875, plagued by the likes of Crazy Horse's Oglala Sioux, it was decided that there was but one solution to the Plains Indian problem—total extermination.

At this point, General Phil Sheridan, Commander in Chief of the United States Army, began working on the practical angle of this new policy toward the Red Man.

In January 1876, delegates from the Democratic Party approached George Armstrong Custer at Fort Abraham Lincoln and offered him the party's presidential nomination on the condition that he pull off a flashy victory over the red men before the national convention in Chicago in July.

On February 19, 1876, the Boy General's brother Thomas, commander of Troop C of the 7th, climbed into the observer's cockpit behind Lieutenant James C. Sturgis and took off on a routine patrol. Their aeroplane, a Whitney pusher-type, did not return. Ten days later its wreckage was found sixty miles west of Fort Lincoln. Apparently, Sturgis and Tom Custer had stumbled on a party of mounted hostiles and, swooping low to fire or drop a handbomb, suffered a lucky hit from one of the Indians' firearms. The mutilated remains of the two officers were found a quarter mile from the wreckage, indicating that they had escaped on foot after the crash but were caught.

The shock of his brother's death, combined with the Democrat's offer, were to lead Lieutenant Colonel G. A. Custer into the worst defeat suffered by an officer of the United States Army.

Throughout the first part of 1876, Indians drifted into Wyoming Territory from the east and south, driven by mounting pressure from the Army. Raids on small Indian villages had been stepped up. Waning herds of buffalo were being systematically strafed by the airships. General Phil Sheridan received reports of tribes gathering in the vicinity of the Wolf Mountains, in what is now southern Montana, and devised a strategy by which the hostiles would be crushed for all time.

Three columns were to converge upon the amassed Indians from the north, south, and east, the west being blocked by the Wolf Mountains. General George Crook's dirigibles, light tanks, and infantry were to come up the Rosebud River. General Alfred Terry would push from the northeast with infantry, cavalry, and field artillery. The 7th Cavalry was to move from the east. The Indians could not escape.

Commanded by Captain Keogh, Troops A, C, D, E, F, G, and H of the 7th—about 580 men, not counting civilian teamsters, interpreters, Crow and Arikara scouts—set out from Fort Lincoln five weeks ahead of the July 1 rendezvous at the junction of the Big Horn and Little Big Horn rivers. A month later, Custer and 150 balloon infantrymen aboard the airships *Franklin, Adams, Hancock,* and *Allen* set out on Keogh's trail.

Everything went wrong from that point onward.

The early summer of 1876 had been particularly hot and dry in Wyoming Territory. Crook, proceeding up the Rosebud, was slowed by the tanks, which theoretically traveled at five miles per hour but which kept breaking down from the heat and from the alkaline dust which worked its way into the engines through chinks in the three-inch armor plate. The crews roasted. On June 13, as Crook's column halted beside the Rosebud to let the tanks cool off, six monoplanes dived out of the clouds to attack the escorting airships *Paul Revere* and *John Paul Jones*. Caught by surprise, the two dirigibles were blown up and fell about five miles from Crook's position. The infantrymen watched, astonished, as the Indian aeronauts turned their craft toward them. While the foot soldiers ran for cover, several hundred mounted Sioux warriors showed up. In the ensuing rout, Crook lost forty-seven men and all his armored vehicles. He was still in headlong retreat when the Indians broke off their chase at nightfall.

The 7th Cavalry and the 505th Balloon Infantry linked up by liaison craft carried by the *Ethan Allen* some miles southeast of the hostile camp on the Little Big Horn on the evening of June 24. Neither they, nor Terry's column, had received word of Crook's retreat, but Keogh's scouts had sighted a large village ahead.

Custer did not know that this village contained not the five or six hundred Indians expected, but between eight and ten *thousand,* of whom slightly less than half were warriors. Spurred by his desire for revenge for his brother Tom, and filled with glory at the thought of the Democratic presidential nomination, Custer decided to hit the Indians before either Crook's or Terry's columns could reach the village. He settled on a scaled-down version of Sheridan's tri-pronged movement, and dispatched Keogh to the south, Reno to the east, with himself and the 505th attacking from the north. A small column was to wait downriver with the pack train. On the evening of June 24, George Armstrong Custer waited, secure in the knowledge that he, personally, would deal the Plains Indians their mortal blow within a mere twenty-four hours.

Unfortunately, the Indians amassed on the banks of the Little Big Horn—Oglalas, Minneconjous, Araphao, Hunkpapas, Blackfeet, Cheyenne, and so forth—had the idea that white men were on the way. During the Sun Dance Ceremony the week before, the Hunkpapa chief Sitting Bull had had a dream about soldiers falling into his camp. The hostiles, assured of victory, waited.

On the morning of June 25, the *Benjamin Franklin, Samuel Adams, John Hancock,* and *Ethan Allen* drifted quietly over the hills toward the village. They were looping south when the Indians attacked.

Struck by several spin-stabilized rockets, the *Samuel Adams* blew up with a flash that might have been seen by the officers and men riding behind Captain Keogh up the valley of the Little Big Horn. Eight or twelve Indians had, in the gray dawn, climbed for altitude above the ships.

Still several miles short of their intended drop zone, the balloon infantrymen piled out of the burning and exploding craft. Though each ship was armed with two Gatling rifles fore and aft, the airships were helpless against the airplanes' bullets and rockets. Approximately one hundred men, Custer included, cleared the ships. The Indian aviators made passes through them, no doubt killing several in the air. The *Franklin* and *Hancock* burned and fell to the earth across the river from the village. The *Allen,* dumping water ballast to gain altitude, turned for the Wolf Mountains. Though riddled by machine rifle fire, it did not explode and settled to earth about fifteen miles from where now raged a full-scale battle between increasingly demoralized soldiers and battle-maddened Sioux and Cheyenne.

Major Reno had charged the opposite side of the village as soon as he heard the commotion. Wrote one of his officers later: "A solid wall of Indians came out of the haze which had hidden the village from our eyes. They must have outnumbered us ten to one, and they were ready for us. . . . Fully a third of the column was down in three minutes."

Reno, fearing he would be swallowed up, pulled his men back across the river and took up a position in a stand of timber on the riverward slope of the knoll. The Indians left a few hundred braves to make certain Reno did not escape and moved off to Reno's right to descend on Keogh's flank.

The hundred-odd parachute infantrymen who made good their escape from their airship were scattered over three square miles. The ravines and gullies cutting up the hills around the village quickly filled with mounted Indians who rode through unimpeded by the random fire of disorganized balloon infantrymen. They swept them up, on the way to Keogh. Keogh, unaware of the number of Indians and the rout of Reno's command, got as far as the north bank of the river before he was ground to pieces between two masses of hostiles. Of Keogh's command, less than a dozen escaped the slaughter. The actual battle lasted about thirty minutes.

The hostiles left the area that night, exhausted after their greatest victory over the soldiers. Most of the Indians went north to Canada; some escaped the mass extermination of their race which was to take place in the American West during the next six years.

Terry found Reno entrenched on the ridge the morning of the twenty-seventh. The scouts sent to find Custer and Keogh could not believe their eyes when they found the bodies of the 7th Cavalry six miles away.

Some of the men were not found for another two days, Terry and his men scoured the ravines and valleys. Custer himself was about four miles from the site of Keogh's annihilation; the Boy General appears to have been hit by a piece of exploding rocket shrapnel and may have been dead before he reached the ground. His body escaped the mutilation that befell most of Keogh's command, possibly because of its distance from the camp.

Custer's miscalculation cost the Army 430 men, four dirigibles (plus the Studebaker scout from the *Ethan Allen*), and its prestige. An attempt was made to make a scapegoat of Major Reno, blaming his alleged cowardice for the failure of the 7th. Though Reno was acquitted, grumblings continued up until the turn of the century. It is hoped the matter will be settled for all time by the opening, for private research, of the papers of the late President Phil Sheridan. As Commander in Chief, he had access to a mountain of material which was kept from the public at the time of the court of inquiry in 1879.

Extract from *Huckleberry Among the Hostiles: A Journal*

BY MARK TWAIN, EDITED BY BERNARD VAN DYNE
Hutton and Company, New York, 1932.

EDITOR'S NOTE: In November 1886 Clemens drafted a tentative outline for a sequel to *The Adventures of Huckleberry Finn,* which had received mixed reviews on its publication in January 1885, but which had nonetheless enjoyed a second printing within five months of its release. The proposed sequel was intended to deal with Huckleberry's adventures as a young man on the frontier. To gather research material firsthand, Mark boarded the airship *Peyton* in Cincinnati, Ohio, in mid-December 1886, and set out across the Southwest, amassing copious notes and reams of interviews with soldiers, frontiersmen, law enforcement officers, ex-hostiles, at least two notorious outlaws, and a number of less readily categorized persons. Twain had intended to spend four months out West. Unfortunately, his wife, Livy, fell gravely ill in late February 1887; Twain returned to her as soon as he received word in Fort Hood, Texas. He lost interest in all writing for two years after her death in April 1887. The proposed novel about Huckleberry Finn as a man was never written: we are left with 110,000 words of interviews and observations, and an incomplete journal of the author's second trek across the American West.—BvD

Feb. 2: A more desolate place than the Indian Territory of Oklahoma would be impossible to imagine. It is flat the year 'round, stingingly cold in winter, hot and dry, I am told, during the summer (when the land turns brown save for scattered patches of greenery which serve only to make the landscape all the drearier; Arizona and New Mexico are devoid of greenery, which is to their credit—when those territories elected to become barren wastelands they did not lose heart halfway, but followed their chosen course to the end).

It is easy to see why the United States Government swept the few Indians into God-forsaken Oklahoma, and ordered them to remain there under threat of extermination. The word "God-forsaken" is the vital clue. The white men who "gave" this land to the few remaining tribes for as long as the wind shall blow—which it certainly does in February—and the grass shall grow (which it does, in Missouri, perhaps) were Christians who knew better than to let heathen savages run loose in parts of the country still smiled upon by our heavenly malefactor.

February 4: Whatever I may have observed about Oklahoma from the cabin of the *Peyton* has been reinforced by a view from the ground. The airship was running into stiff winds from the north, so we put in at Fort Sill yesterday evening and are awaiting calmer weather. I have gone on with my work.

Fort Sill is located seventeen miles from the Cheyenne Indian reservation. It has taken me all of a day to learn (mainly from one Sergeant Howard, a gap-toothed, unwashed Texan who is apparently my unofficial guardian angel for whatever length of time I am to be marooned here) that the Cheyenne do not care much for Oklahoma, which is still another reason why the government keeps them there. One or two ex-hostiles will leave the reservation every month, taking with them their wives and meager belongings, and Major Rickards will have to send out a detachment of soldiers to haul the erring ones back, either in chains or over the backs of horses. I am told the reservation becomes particularly annoying in the winter months, as the poor boys who are detailed to pursue the Indians suffer greatly from the cold. At this, I remarked to Sergeant Howard that the red man can be terribly inconsiderate, even ungrateful, in view of all the blessings the white man has heaped upon him—smallpox, and that French disease, to name two. The good sergeant scratched his head and grinned, and said, "You're right, sir."

I'll have to make Howard a character in the book.

February 5: Today, I was taken by Major Rickards to meet a Cheyenne named Black Man's Hand, one of the participants of the alleged massacre of the 7th Cavalry at the Little Big Horn River in '76. The major had this one Cheyenne brought in after a recent departure from the reservation. Black Man's Hand had been shackled and left to dwell upon his past misdeeds in an unheated hut at the edge of the airport, while two cold-benumbed privates stood on guard before the door. It was evidently feared this one savage would, if left unchained, do to Fort Sill that which he (with a modicum of assistance from four or five thousand of his race) had done to Custer. I nevertheless mentioned to Rickards that I was interested in talking to Black Man's Hand, as the Battle of the Little Big Horn would perfectly climax Huckleberry's adventures in the new book. Rickards was reluctant to grant permission but gave in abruptly, perhaps fearing I would model a villain after him.

Upon entering the hut where the Cheyenne sat, I asked Major Rickards if it were possible to have the Indian's manacles removed, as it makes me nervous to talk to a man who can rattle his chains at me whenever he chooses. Major Rickards said no and troubled himself to explain to me the need for limiting the movement of this specimen of ferocity within the walls of Fort Sill.

With a sigh, I seated myself across from Black Man's Hand and offered him one of my cigars. He accepted it with a faint smile. He appeared to be in his forties, though his face was deeply lined.

He was dressed in ragged leather leggings, thick calf-length woolen pajamas, and a faded Army jacket. His vest appears to have been fashioned from an old parachute harness. He had no hat, no footgear, and no blanket.

"Major Rickards," I said, "this man is freezing to death. Even if he isn't, I am. Can you provide this hut with a little warmth?"

The fretting major summarily dispatched one of the sentries for firewood and kindling for the little stove sitting uselessly in the corner of the hut.

I would have been altogether comfortable after that could I have had a decanter of brandy with which to force out the inner chill. But Indians are notoriously incapable of holding liquor, and I did not wish to be the cause of this poor wretch's further downfall.

Black Man's Hand speaks surprisingly good English. I spent an hour and a half with him, recording his remarks with as much attention paid to accuracy as my advanced years and cold fingers permitted. With luck, I'll be able to fill some gaps in his story before the *Pey-*

ton resumes its flight across this griddlecake countryside.

Extract from *The Testament of Black Man's Hand*

[NOTE: for the sake of easier reading, I have substituted a number of English terms for these provided by the Cheyenne Black Man's Hand.—MT]

I was young when I first met the Oglala mystic Crazy Horse, and was taught by him to fly the Thunderbirds which the one called the Gray White Man had given him. [The Gray White Man—John S. Moseby, Major, CSAAC—MT] Some of the older men among the People [as the Cheyenne call themselves, Major Rickards explains; I assured him that such egocentricity is by no means restricted to savages—MT] did not think much of the flying machines and said, "How will we be able to remain brave men when this would enable us to fly over the heads of our enemies, without counting coup or taking trophies?"

But the Oglala said, "The Gray White Man has asked us to help him."

"Why should we help him?" asked Two Pines.

"Because he fights the blueshirts and those who persecute us. We have known for many years that the men who cheated us and lied to us and killed our women and the buffalo are men without honor, cowards who fight only because there is no other way for them to get what they want. They cannot understand why we fight with the Crows and Pawnees—to be brave, to win honor for ourselves. They fight because it is a means to an end, and they fight us only because we have what they want. The blueshirts want to kill us all. They fight to win. If we are to fight them, we must fight with their own weapons. We must fight to win."

The older warriors shook their heads sorrowfully and spoke of younger days when they fought the Pawnees bravely, honorably, man-to-man. But I and several other young men wanted to learn how to control the

Thunderbirds. And we knew Crazy Horse spoke the truth, that our lives would never be happy as long as there were white men in the world. Finally, because they could not forbid us to go with the Oglala, only advise against it and say that the Great Mystery had not intended us to fly, Red Horse and I and some others went with Crazy Horse. I did not see my village again, not even at the big camp on the Greasy Grass [Little Big Horn—MT] where we rubbed out Yellow Hair. I think perhaps the blueshirts came after I was gone and told Two Pines that he had to leave his home and come to this flat dead place.

The Oglala Crazy Horse taught us to fly the Thunderbirds. We learned a great many things about the Gray White Man's machines. With them, we killed Yellowleg flyers. Soon, I tired of the waiting and the hunger. We were raided once. It was a good fight. In the dark, we chased the Big Fish [the Indian word for dirigibles—MT] and killed many men on the ground.

I do not remember all of what happened those seasons. When we were finally chased away from the landing place, Crazy Horse had us hide the Thunderbirds in the Black Hills. I have heard the Yellowlegs did not know we had the Thunderbirds; that they thought they were run by the gray white men only. It did not matter; we thought we had used them for the last time.

Many seasons later, we heard what happened to Black Kettle's village. I went to the place sometime after the battle. I heard that Crazy Horse had been there and seen the place. I looked for him but he had gone north again. Black Kettle had been a treaty man: we talked among ourselves that the Yellowlegs had no honor.

It was the winter I was sick [1872. The Plains Indians and the U. S. Army alike were plagued that winter by what we would call the influenza. It was probably brought by some itinerant French trapper.—MT] that I heard of Crazy Horse's raid on the landing place of the Big Fish. It was news of this that told us we must prepare to fight the Yellowlegs.

When I was well, my wives and I and Eagle Hawk's band went looking for Crazy Horse. We found him in the fall. Already, the Army had killed many Sioux and Cheyenne that summer. Crazy Horse said we must band together, we who knew how to fly the Thunderbirds. He said we would someday have to fight the Yellowlegs among the clouds as in the old days. We only had five Thunderbirds which had not been flown many seasons. We spent the summer planning to get more. Red Chief and Yellow Dog gathered a large band. We raided the Fort Kearny and stole many Thunderbirds and canisters of powder. We hid them in the Black Hills. It had been a good fight.

It was at this time Yellow Hair sent out many soldiers to protect the miners he had brought in by speaking false. They destroyed the sacred lands of the Sioux. We killed some of them, and the Yellowlegs burned many of our villages. That was not a good time. The Big Fish killed many of our people.

We wanted to get the Thunderbirds and kill the Big Fish. Crazy Horse had us wait. He had been talking to Sitting Bull, the Hunkpapa chief. Sitting Bull said we should not go against the Yellowlegs yet, that we could only kill a few at a time. Later, he said, they would all come. That would be the good day to die.

The next year, they came. We did not know until just before the Sun Dance [about June 10, 1876—MT] that they were coming. Crazy Horse and I and all those who flew the Thunderbirds went to get ours. It took us two days to get them going again, and we had only six Thunderbirds flying when we flew to stop the blue-shirts. Crazy Horse, Yellow Dog, American Gun, Little Wolf, Big Tall, and I flew that day. It was a good fight. We killed two Big Fish and many men and horses. We stopped the Turtles-which-kill [that would be the light armored cars Crook had with him on the Rosebud River—MT] so they could not come toward the Greasy

Grass where we camped. The Sioux under Spotted Pony killed more on the ground. We flew back and hid the Thunderbirds near camp.

When we returned, we told Sitting Bull of our victory. He said it was good, but that a bigger victory was to come. He said he had had a vision during the Sun Dance. He saw many soldiers and enemy Indians fall out of the sky on their heads into the village. He said ours was not the victory he had seen.

It was some days later we heard that a Yellowlegs Thunderbird had been shot down. We went to the place where it lay. There was a strange device above its wing. Crazy Horse studied it many moments. Then he said, "I have seen such a thing before. It carries Thunderbirds beneath one of the Big Fish. We must get our Thunderbirds. It will be a good day to die."

We hurried to our Thunderbirds. We had twelve of them fixed now, and we had on them, besides the quick rifles [Henry machine rifles of calibers .41–40 or .30–30—MT], the roaring spears [Hale spin-stabilized rockets, of 2½ inch diameter—MT]. We took off before noonday.

We arrived at the Greasy Grass and climbed into the clouds, where we scouted. Soon, to the south, we saw the dust of many men moving. But Crazy Horse held us back. Soon we saw why; four Big Fish were coming. We came at them out of the sun. They did not see us till we were on them. We fired our roaring sticks, and the Big Fish caught fire and burned. All except one, which drifted away, though it lost all its fat. Wild Horse, in his Thunderbird, was shot but still fought on with us that morning. We began to kill the men on the Big Fish when a new thing happened. Men began to float down on blankets. We began to kill them as they fell with our quick rifles. Then we attacked those who reached the ground, until we saw Spotted Pony and his men were on them. We turned south and killed many horse soldiers there. Then we flew back to the Greasy Grass and hid the Thunderbirds. At camp, we learned that many pony soldiers had been killed. Word came that more soldiers were coming.

I saw, as the sun went down, the women moving among the dead Men-Who-Float-Down, taking their clothes and supplies. They covered the ground like leaves in the autumn. It had been a good fight.

So much has been written about that hot June day in 1876, so much guesswork applied where knowledge was missing. Was Custer dead in his harness before he reached the ground? Or did he stand and fire at the aircraft strafing his men? How many reached the ground alive? Did any escape the battle itself, only to be killed by Indian patrols later that afternoon, or the next day? No one really knows, and all the Indians are gone now, so history stands a blank.

Only one thing is certain: for the men of the 7th Cavalry there was only the reality of the exploding dirigibles, the snap of their chutes deploying, the roar of the aircraft among them, the bullets, and those terrible last moments on the bluff. Whatever the verdict of their peers, whatever the future may reveal, it can be said they did not die in vain.

—*The Seventh Cavalry:A History*
E. R. BURROUGHS
Colonel, U.S.A., Retired

SUGGESTED READING

ANONYMOUS. *Remember Ft. Sumter!* Washington: War Department Recruiting Pamphlet, 1862.

———. *Leviathans of the Skies.* Goodyear Publications, 1923.

———. *The Dirigible in War and Peace.* Goodyear Publications, 1911.

———. *Sitting Bull, Killer of Custer.* G. E. Putnam's, 1903.

———. *Comanche of the Seventh.* Chicago: Military Press, 1879.

———. *Thomas Edison and the Indian Wars.* Menlo Park, N.J.: Edison Press, 1921.

———. "Fearful Slaughter at Big Horn." New York: *Herald-Times,* July 8, 1876, *et passim.*

———. *Custer's Gold Hoax.* Boston: Barnum Press, 1892.

———. "Reno's Treachery: New Light on the Massacre at The Little Big Horn." Chicago: *Daily News-Mirror*, June 12–19, 1878.

———. "Grant Scandals and the Plains Indian Wars." *Life,* May 3, 1921.

———. *The Hunkpapa Chief Sitting Bull,* Famous Indians Series #3. New York: 1937.

ARNOLD, HENRY H. *The Air War in the East,* Smithsonian Annals of Flight, Vol. 38. Four books, 1932–37.

1. *Sumter To Bull Run*
2. *Williamsburg to Second Manassas*
3. *Gettysburg to the Wilderness*
5. *The Bombing of Atlanta to Haldeman*

BALLOWS, EDWARD. *The Indian Ace: Crazy Horse.* G. E. Putnam's, 1903.

BENTEEN, CAPT. FREDERICK. *Major Benteen's Letters to his Wife.* University of Oklahoma Press, 1921.

BRININSTOOL, A. E. *A Paratrooper with Custer.* n.p.g., 1891.

BURROUGHS, COL. E. R. retired. *The Seventh Cavalry: A History.* Chicago: 1931.

CLAIR-BRITNER, EDOARD. *Haldeman: Where the War Ended.* Frankfort University Press, 1911.

CROOK, GENERAL GEORGE C. *Yellowhair: Custer as the Indians Knew Him.* Cincinnati Press, 1882.

CUSTER, GEORGE A. *My Life on the Plains and in the Clouds.* Chicago: 1874

——— and CUSTER, ELIZABETH. *'Chutes and Saddles.* Chicago: 1876.

Custer's Luck, n.a, n.p.g., [1891]

DE CAMP, L. SPRAGUE and PRATT, FLETCHER. *Franklin's Engine: Mover of the World.* Hanover House, 1939.

DE VOTO, BERNARD. *The Road From Sumter.* Scribners, 1931.

ELSEE, D. V. *The Last Raid of Crazy Horse.* Random House, 1921.

The 505th: History From the Skies. DA Pamphlet 870–10–3 GPO Pittsburgh, May 12, 1903.

FM 23–13–2 Machine Rifle M3121A1 and M3121A1E1 Cal. .41–40 Operator's Manual, DA FM, July 12, 1873.

GODDARD, ROBERT H. *Rocketry: From 400 B.C. to 1933.* Smithsonian Annals of Flight, Vol. 31, GPO Pittsburgh, 1934.

Guide to the Custer Battlefield National Monument. U.S. Parks Services, GPO Pittsburgh, 1937.

The Indian Wars. 3 vols, GPO Pittsburgh, 1898.

KALIN, DAVID. *Hook Up! The Story of the Balloon Infantry.* New York: 1932.

KELLOGG, MARK W. *The Drop at Washita.* Chicago: *Times Press,* 1872.

LOCKRIDGE, SGT. ROBERT. *History of the Airborne: From Shiloh to Ft. Bragg.* Chicago: Military Press, 1936.

LOWE, THADDEUS C. *Aircraft of the Civil War.* 4 vols. 1891–96.

MCCOY, COL. TIM. *The Vanished American.* Phoenix Press, 1934.

MCGOVERN, MAJ. WILLIAM. *Death in the Dakotas.* Sioux Press, 1889.

MORISON, SAMUEL ELIOT. *France in the New World 1627–1864.* 1931.

MYREN, GUNDAL. *The Sun Dance Ritual and the Last Indian Wars.* 1901.

PATTON, GEN. GEORGE C. *Custer's Last Campaigns.* Military House, 1937.

PAUL, WINSTON. *We Were There at the Bombing of Ft. Sumter.* Landmark Books, 1929.

PAYLEY, DAVID. *Where Custer Fell.* New York Press, 1931.

POWELL, MAJ. JOHN WESLEY. *Report on the Arid Lands.* GPO, 1881.

Proceedings, Reno Court of Inquiry. GPO Pittsburgh, 1881.

Report on the U.S.-Canadian Offensive against Sitting Bull, 1879. GPO Pittsburgh, War Department, 1880.

SANDBURG, CARL. *Mr. Lincoln's Airmen.* Chicago: Driftwind Press, 1921.

SETTLE, SGT. MAJ. WINSLOW. *Under the Crossed Sabers.* Military Press, 1898.

SHERIDAN, GEN. PHILLIP. *The Only Good Indian . . .* Military House, 1889.

SINGLETON, WILLIAM WARREN. *J. E. B. Stuart, Attila of the Skies.* Boston, 1871.

SMITH, GREGORY. *The Grey White Man: Moseby's Expedition to the Northwest 1863–1866.* University of Oklahoma Press, 1921.

SMITH, NELDOO. *He Gave Them Wings: Captain Smith's Journal 1861–1864.* Urbana: University of Illinois Press, 1927.

STEEN, NELSON. *Opening of the West.* Jim Bridger Press, 1902.

TAPSCOTT, RICHARD D. *He Came With the Comet.* University of Illinois Press, 1927.

TWAIN, MARK. *Huckleberry Among the Hostiles: A Journal.* Hutton Books, 1932.

The Bicentennial Man

Isaac Asimov

Isaac Asimov is a cheerful man of seemingly boundless energy and talent who has become perhaps the most famous of all science fiction writers. He's the only man ever to have a U.S. science-fiction magazine named after him *(Isaac Asimov's Science Fiction Magazine,* produced by the publishers of *Alfred Hitchcock's Mystery Magazine);* he's even been hired to endorse products on television commercials.

It's nice to know that football players aren't the only culture-heroes in our country.

Of course, Asimov didn't gain his status by writing only science fiction. He's also famous as the author of literally scores of nonfiction books—books on science, annotated guides to Shakespeare and the Bible, even books of jokes. (One wonders: Now that Asimov's opened the television door, can it be long before he stars in *The Isaac Asimov Comedy Hour?* Imagine him doing a standup-comic routine—*"He-e-e-ere's Isaac!"*—then joining guest-stars Telly Savalas, Phyllis Diller and Harlan Ellison, all dressed up as robots.)

Asimov has been writing robot stories since 1940, and he's justly famous for them. Here's

his latest, and perhaps his best, a thoughtful and moving story of a robot who has everything: wealth, freedom, fame. But he wants to be human.

The Three Laws of Robotics:

1. *A robot may not injure a human being or, through inaction, allow a human being to come to harm.*
2. *A robot must obey the orders given it by human beings except where such orders would conflict with the First Law.*
3. *A robot must protect its own existence as long as such protection does not conflict with the First or Second Law.*

1.

Andrew Martin said, "Thank you," and took the seat offered him. He didn't look driven to the last resort, but he had been.

He didn't, actually, look anything, for there was a smooth blankness to his face, except for the sadness one imagined one saw in his eyes. His hair was smooth, light brown, rather fine, and there was no facial hair. He looked freshly and cleanly shaved. His clothes were distinctly old-fashioned, but neat and predominantly a velvety red-purple in color.

Facing him from behind the desk was the surgeon, and the nameplate on the desk included a fully identifying series of letters and numbers, which Andrew didn't bother with. To call him Doctor would be quite enough.

"When can the operation be carried through, Doctor?" he asked.

The surgeon said softly, with that certain inalienable

note of respect that a robot always used to a human being, "I am not certain, sir, that I understand how or upon whom such an operation could be performed."

There might have been a look of respectful intransigence on the surgeon's face, if a robot of his sort, in lightly bronzed stainless steel, could have such an expression, or any expression.

Andrew Martin studied the robot's right hand, his cutting hand, as it lay on the desk in utter tranquility. The fingers were long and shaped into artistically metallic looping curves so graceful and appropriate that one could imagine a scalpel fitting them and becoming, temporarily, one piece with them.

There would be no hesitation in his work, no stumbling, no quivering, no mistakes. That came with specialization, of course, a specialization so fiercely desired by humanity that few robots were, any longer, independently brained. A surgeon, of course, would have to be. And this one, though brained, was so limited in his capacity that he did not recognize Andrew—had probably never heard of him.

Andrew said, "Have you ever thought you would like to be a man?"

The surgeon hesitated a moment as though the question fitted nowhere in his allotted positronic pathways. "But I am a robot, sir."

"Would it be better to be a man?"

"It would be better, sir, to be a better surgeon. I could not be so if I were a man, but only if I were a more advanced robot. I would be pleased to be a more advanced robot."

"It does not offend you that I can order you about? That I can make you stand up, sit down, move right or left, by merely telling you to do so?"

"It is my pleasure to please you, sir. If your orders were to interfere with my functioning with respect to you or to any other human being, I would not obey you. The First Law, concerning my duty to human safety, would take precedence over the Second Law relating to obedience. Otherwise, obedience is my pleasure. . . . But upon whom am I to perform this operation?"

"Upon me," said Andrew.

"But that is impossible. It is patently a damaging operation."

"That does not matter," said Andrew calmly.

"I must not inflict damage," said the surgeon.

"On a human being, you must not," said Andrew, "but I, too, am a robot."

2.

Andrew had appeared much more a robot when he had first been—manufactured. He had then been as much a robot in appearance as any that had ever existed, smoothly designed and functional.

He had done well in the home to which he had been brought in those days when robots in households, or on the planet altogether, had been a rarity.

There had been four in the home: Sir and Ma'am and Miss and Little Miss. He knew their names, of course, but he never used them. Sir was Gerald Martin.

His own serial number was NDR—He forgot the numbers. It had been a long time, of course, but if he had wanted to remember, he could not forget. He had not wanted to remember.

Little Miss had been the first to call him Andrew because she could not use the letters, and all the rest followed her in this.

Little Miss— She had lived ninety years and was long since dead. He had tried to call her Ma'am once, but she would not allow it. Little Miss she had been to her last day.

Andrew had been intended to perform the duties of a valet, a butler, a lady's maid. Those were the experimental days for him and, indeed, for all robots anywhere but in the industrial and exploratory factories and stations off Earth.

The Martins enjoyed him, and half the time he was prevented from doing his work because Miss and Little Miss would rather play with him.

It was Miss who understood first how this might be arranged. She said, "We order you to play with us and you must follow orders."

Andrew said, "I am sorry, Miss, but a prior order from Sir must surely take precedence."

But she said, "Daddy just said he hoped you would take care of the cleaning. That's not much of an order. I *order* you."

Sir did not mind. Sir was fond of Miss and of Little Miss, even more than Ma'am was, and Andrew was fond of them, too. At least, the effect they had upon his actions were those which in a human being would have been called the result of fondness. Andrew thought of it as fondness, for he did not know any other word for it.

It was for Little Miss that Andrew had carved a pendant out of wood. She had ordered him to. Miss, it seemed, had received an ivorite pendant with scrollwork for her birthday and Little Miss was unhappy over it. She had only a piece of wood, which she gave Andrew together with a small kitchen knife.

He had done it quickly and Little Miss said, "That's *nice,* Andrew. I'll show it to Daddy."

Sir would not believe it. "Where did you really get this, Mandy?" Mandy was what he called Little Miss. When Little Miss assured him she was really telling the truth, he turned to Andrew. "Did you do this, Andrew?"

"Yes, Sir."

"The design, too?"

"Yes, Sir."

"From what did you copy the design?"

"It is a geometric representation, Sir, that fit the grain of the wood."

The next day, Sir brought him another piece of wood, a larger one, and an electric vibro-knife. He said,

"Make something out of this, Andrew. Anything you want to."

Andrew did so and Sir watched, then looked at the product a long time. After that, Andrew no longer waited on tables. He was ordered to read books on furniture design instead, and he learned to make cabinets and desks.

Sir said, "These are amazing productions, Andrew."

Andrew said, "I enjoy doing them, Sir."

"Enjoy?"

"It makes the circuits of my brain somehow flow more easily. I have heard you use the word 'enjoy' and the way you use it fits the way I feel. I enjoy doing them, Sir."

3.

Gerald Martin took Andrew to the regional offices of United States Robots and Mechanical Men, Inc. As a member of the Regional Legislature he had no trouble at all in gaining an interview with the Chief Robopsychologist. In fact, it was only as a member of the Regional Legislature that he qualified as a robot owner in the first place—in those early days when robots were rare.

Andrew did not understand any of this at the time, but in later years, with greater learning, he could review that early scene and understand it in its proper light.

The robopsychologist, Merton Mansky, listened with a gathering frown and more than once managed to stop his fingers at the point beyond which they would have irrevocably drummed on the table. He had drawn features and a lined forehead and looked as though he might be younger than he looked.

He said, "Robotics is not an exact art, Mr. Martin. I cannot explain it to you in detail, but the mathematics governing the plotting of the positronic pathways is far too complicated to permit of any but approximate solutions. Naturally, since we build everything about the Three Laws, those are incontrovertible. We will, of course, replace your robot—"

"Not at all," said Sir. "There is no question of failure on his part. He performs his assigned duties perfectly. The point is, he also carves wood in exquisite fashion and never the same twice. He produces works of art."

Mansky looked confused. "Strange. Of course, we're attempting generalized pathways these days. . . . Really creative, you think?"

"See for yourself." Sir handed over a little sphere of wood on which there was a playground scene in which the boys and girls were almost too small to make out, yet they were in perfect proportion and blended so naturally with the grain that that, too, seemed to have been carved.

Mansky said, "*He* did that?" He handed it back with a shake of his head. "The luck of the draw. Something in the pathways."

"Can you do it again?"

"Probably not. Nothing like this has ever been reported."

"Good! I don't in the least mind Andrew's being the only one."

Mansky said, "I suspect that the company would like to have your robot back for study."

Sir said with sudden grimness, "Not a chance. Forget it." He turned to Andrew, "Let's go home now."

"As you wish, Sir," said Andrew.

4.

Miss was dating boys and wasn't about the house much. It was Little Miss, not as little as she was, who filled Andrew's horizon now. She never forgot that the very first piece of wood carving he had done had been for her. She kept it on a silver chain about her neck.

It was she who first objected to Sir's habit of giving away the productions. She said, "Come on, Dad, if anyone wants one of them, let him pay for it. It's worth it."

Sir said, "It isn't like you to be greedy, Mandy."

"Not for us, Dad. For the artist."

Andrew had never heard the word before and when he had a moment to himself he looked it up in the dictionary. Then there was another trip, this time to Sir's lawyer.

Sir said to him, "What do you think of this, John?"

The lawyer was John Feingold. He had white hair and a pudgy belly, and the rims of his contact lenses were tinted a bright green. He looked at the small plaque Sir had given him. "This is beautiful. . . . But I've heard the news. This is a carving made by your robot. The one you've brought with you."

"Yes, Andrew does them. Don't you, Andrew?"

"Yes, Sir," said Andrew.

"How much would you pay for that, John?" asked Sir.

"I can't say. I'm not a collector of such things."

"Would you believe I have been offered two hundred and fifty dollars for that small thing? Andrew has made chairs that have sold for five hundred dollars. There's two hundred thousand dollars in the bank out of Andrew's products."

"Good heavens, he's making you rich, Gerald."

"Half rich," said Sir. "Half of it is in an account in the name of Andrew Martin."

"The robot?"

"That's right, and I want to know if it's legal."

"Legal?" Feingold's chair creaked as he leaned back in it. "There are no precedents, Gerald. How did your robot sign the necessary papers?"

"He can sign his name and I brought in the signature. I didn't bring him in to the bank himself. Is there anything further that ought to be done?"

"Um." Feingold's eyes seemed to turn inward for a moment. Then he said, "Well, we can set up a trust to handle all finances in his name and that will place a layer of insulation between him and the hostile world. Further than that, my advice is you do nothing. No one is stopping you so far. If anyone objects, let *him* bring suit."

"And will you take the case if suit is brought?"

"For a retainer, certainly."

"How much?"

"Something like that," and Feingold pointed to the wooden plaque.

"Fair enough," said Sir.

Feingold chuckled as he turned to the robot. "Andrew, are you pleased that you have money?"

"Yes, sir."

"What do you plan to do with it?"

"Pay for things, sir, which otherwise Sir would have to pay for. It would save him expense, sir."

5.

The occasions came. Repairs were expensive, and revisions were even more so. With the years, new models of robots were produced and Sir saw to it that Andrew had the advantage of every new device until he was a paragon of metallic excellence. It was all at Andrew's expense.

Andrew insisted on that.

Only his positronic pathways were untouched. Sir insisted on that.

"The new ones aren't as good as you are, Andrew," he said. "The new robots are worthless. The company has learned to make the pathways more precise, more closely on the nose, more deeply on the track. The new robots don't shift. They do what they're designed for and never stray. I like you better."

"Thank you, Sir."

"And it's your doing, Andrew, don't you forget that. I am certain Mansky put an end to generalized pathways as soon as he had a good look at you. He didn't like the unpredictability. . . . Do you know how many times he asked for you so he could place you under study? Nine times! I never let him have you, though, and now that he's retired, we may have some peace."

So Sir's hair thinned and grayed and his face grew pouchy, while Andrew looked rather better than he had when he first joined the family.

Ma'am had joined an art colony somewhere in Europe and Miss was a poet in New York. They wrote sometimes, but not often. Little Miss was married and lived not far away. She said she did not want to leave Andrew and when her child, Little Sir, was born, she let Andrew hold the bottle and feed him.

With the birth of a grandson, Andrew felt that Sir had someone now to replace those who had gone. It would not be so unfair to come to him with the request.

Andrew said, "Sir, it is kind of you to have allowed me to spend my money as I wished."

"It was your money, Andrew."

"Only by your voluntary act, Sir. I do not believe the law would have stopped you from keeping it all."

"The law won't persuade me to do wrong, Andrew."

"Despite all expenses, and despite taxes, too, Sir, I have nearly six hundred thousand dollars."

"I know that, Andrew."

"I want to give it to you, Sir."

"I won't take it, Andrew."

"In exchange for something you can give me, Sir."

"Oh? What is that, Andrew?"

"My freedom, Sir."

"Your—"

"I wish to buy my freedom, Sir."

6.

It wasn't that easy. Sir had flushed, had said "For God's sake!" had turned on his heel, and stalked away.

It was Little Miss who brought him around, defiantly and harshly—and in front of Andrew. For thirty years, no one had hesitated to talk in front of Andrew, whether the matter involved Andrew or not. He was only a robot.

She said, "Dad, why are you taking it as a personal affront? He'll still be here. He'll still be loyal. He can't help that. It's built in. All he wants is a form of words. He wants to be called free. Is that so terrible? Hasn't he earned it? Heavens, he and I have been talking about it for years."

"Talking about it for years, have you?"

"Yes, and over and over again, he postponed it for fear he would hurt you. I *made* him put it up to you."

"He doesn't know what freedom is. He's a robot."

"Dad, you don't know him. He's read everything in the library. I don't know what he feels inside but I don't know what *you* feel inside. When you talk to him you'll find he reacts to the various abstractions as you and I do, and what else counts? If someone else's reactions are like your own, what more can you ask for?"

"The law won't take that attitude," Sir said angrily. "See here, you!" He turned to Andrew with a deliberate grate in his voice. "I can't free you except by doing it legally, and if it gets into the courts, you not only won't get your freedom but the law will take official cognizance of your money. They'll tell you that a robot has no right to earn money. Is this rigmarole worth losing your money?"

"Freedom is without price, Sir," said Andrew. "Even the chance of freedom is worth the money."

7.

The court might also take the attitude that freedom was without price, and might decide that for no price, however great, could a robot buy its freedom.

The simple statement of the regional attorney who represented those who had brought a class action to oppose the freedom was this: The word "freedom" had no meaning when applied to a robot. Only a human being could be free.

He said it several times, when it seemed appropriate; slowly, with his hand coming down rhythmically on the desk before him to mark the words.

Little Miss asked permission to speak on behalf of Andrew. She was recognized by her full name, something Andrew had never heard pronounced before:

"Amanda Laura Martin Charney may approach the bench."

She said, "Thank you, your honor. I am not a lawyer and I don't know the proper way of phrasing things, but I hope you will listen to my meaning and ignore the words.

"Let's understand what it means to be free in Andrew's case. In some ways, he *is* free. I think it's at least twenty years since anyone in the Martin family gave him an order to do something that we felt he might not do of his own accord.

"But we can, if we wish, give him an order to do anything, couch it as harshly as we wish, because he is a machine that belongs to us. Why should we be in a position to do so, when he has served us so long, so faithfully, and earned so much money for us? He owes us nothing more. The debt is entirely on the other side.

"Even if we were legally forbidden to place Andrew in involuntary servitude, he would still serve us voluntarily. Making him free would be a trick of words only, but it would mean much to him. It would give him everything and cost us nothing."

For a moment the Judge seemed to be suppressing a smile. "I see your point, Mrs. Charney. The fact is that there is no binding law in this respect and no precedent. There is, however, the unspoken assumption that only a man can enjoy freedom. I can make new law here, subject to reversal in a higher court, but I cannot lightly run counter to that assumption. Let me address the robot. Andrew!"

"Yes, your honor."

It was the first time Andrew had spoken in court and the Judge seemed astonished for a moment at the human timbre of the voice. He said, "Why do you want to be free, Andrew? In what way will this matter to you?"

Andrew said, "Would you wish to be a slave, your honor?"

"But you are not a slave. You are a perfectly good robot, a genius of a robot I am given to understand, capable of an artistic expression that can be matched nowhere. What more can you do if you were free?"

"Perhaps no more than I do now, your honor, but with greater joy. It has been said in this courtroom that only a human being can be free. It seems to me that only someone who wishes for freedom can be free. I wish for freedom."

And it was that that cued the Judge. The crucial sentence in his decision was: "There is no right to deny freedom to any object with a mind advanced enough to grasp the concept and desire the state."

It was eventually upheld by the World Court.

8.

Sir remained displeased and his harsh voice made Andrew feel almost as though he were being short-circuited.

Sir said, "I don't want your damned money, Andrew. I'll take it only because you won't feel free otherwise. From now on, you can select your own jobs and do them as you please. I will give you no orders, except this one—that you do as you please. But I am still responsible for you; that's part of the court order. I hope you understand that."

Little Miss interrupted. "Don't be irascible, Dad. The

responsibility is no great chore. You know you won't have to do a thing. The Three Laws still hold."

"Then how is he free?"

Andrew said, "Are not human beings bound by their laws, Sir?"

Sir said, "I'm not going to argue." He left, and Andrew saw him only infrequently after that.

Little Miss came to see him frequently in the small house that had been built and made over for him. It had no kitchen, of course, nor bathroom facilities. It had just two rooms; one was a library and one was a combination storeroom and workroom. Andrew accepted many commissions and worked harder as a free robot than he ever had before, till the cost of the house was paid for and the structure legally transferred to him.

One day Little Sir came. . . . No, George! Little Sir had insisted on that after the court decision. "A free robot doesn't call anyone Little Sir," George had said. "I call you Andrew. You must call me George."

It was phrased as an order, so Andrew called him George—but Little Miss remained Little Miss.

The day George came alone, it was to say that Sir was dying. Little Miss was at the bedside but Sir wanted Andrew as well.

Sir's voice was quite strong, though he seemed unable to move much. He struggled to get his hand up. "Andrew," he said, "Andrew— Don't help me, George. I'm only dying; I'm not crippled. . . . Andrew, I'm glad you're free. I just wanted to tell you that."

Andrew did not know what to say. He had never been at the side of someone dying before, but he knew it was the human way of ceasing to function. It was an involuntary and irreversible dismantling, and Andrew did not know what to say that might be appropriate. He could only remain standing, absolutely silent, absolutely motionless.

When it was over, Little Miss said to him, "He may not have seemed friendly to you toward the end, Andrew, but he was old, you know, and it hurt him that you should want to be free."

And then Andrew found the words to say. He said, "I would never have been free without him, Little Miss."

9.

It was only after Sir's death that Andrew began to wear clothes. He began with an old pair of trousers at first, a pair that George had given him.

George was married now, and a lawyer. He had joined Feingold's firm. Old Feingold was long since dead but his daughter had carried on and eventually the firm's name became Feingold and Martin. It remained so even when the daughter retired and no Feingold took her place. At the time Andrew put on clothes for the first time, the Martin name had just been added to the firm.

George had tried not to smile, the first time Andrew put on the trousers, but to Andrew's eyes the smile was clearly there.

George showed Andrew how to manipulate the static charge so as to allow the trousers to open, wrap about his lower body, and move shut. George demonstrated on his own trousers, but Andrew was quite aware that it would take him awhile to duplicate that one flowing motion.

George said, "But why do you want trousers, Andrew? Your body is so beautifully functional it's a shame to cover it—especially when you needn't worry about either temperature control or modesty. And it doesn't cling properly, not on metal."

Andrew said, "Are not human bodies beautifully functional, George? Yet you cover yourselves."

"For warmth, for cleanliness, for protection, for decorativeness. None of that applies to you."

Andrew said, "I feel bare without clothes. I feel different, George."

"Different! Andrew, there are millions of robots on Earth now. In this region, according to the last census, there are almost as many robots as there are men."

"I know, George. There are robots doing every conceivable type of work."

"And none of them wear clothes."

"But none of them are free, George."

Little by little, Andrew added to the wardrobe. He was inhibited by George's smile and by the stares of the people who commissioned work.

He might be free, but there was built into him a carefully detailed program concerning his behavior toward people, and it was only by the tiniest steps that he dared advance. Open disapproval would set him back months.

Not everyone accepted Andrew as free. He was incapable of resenting that and yet there was a difficulty about his thinking process when he thought of it.

Most of all, he tended to avoid putting on clothes—or too many of them—when he thought Little Miss might come to visit him. She was old now and was often away in some warmer climate, but when she returned the first thing she did was visit him.

On one of her returns, George said ruefully, "She's got me, Andrew. I'll be running for the Legislature next year. Like grandfather, she says, like grandson."

"Like grandfather—" Andrew stopped, uncertain.

"I mean that I, George, the grandson, will be like Sir, the grandfather, who was in the Legislature once."

Andrew said, "It would be pleasant, George, if Sir were still—" He paused, for he did not want to say, "in working order." That seemed inappropriate.

"Alive," said George. "Yes, I think of the old monster now and then, too."

It was a conversation Andrew thought about. He had noticed his own incapacity in speech when talking with George. Somehow the language had changed since Andrew had come into being with an innate vocabulary.

Then, too, George used a colloquial speech, as Sir and Little Miss had not. Why should he have called Sir a monster when surely that word was not appropriate?

Nor could Andrew turn to his own books for guidance. They were old and most dealt with woodworking, with art, with furniture design. There were none on language, none on the way of human beings.

It was at that moment it seemed to him that he must seek the proper books; and as a free robot, he felt he must not ask George. He would go to town and use the library. It was a triumphant decision and he felt his electropotential grow distinctly higher until he had to throw in an impedance coil.

He put on a full costume, even including a shoulder chain of wood. He would have preferred the glitter plastic but George had said that wood was much more appropriate and that polished cedar was considerably more valuable as well.

He had placed a hundred feet between himself and the house before gathering resistance brought him to a halt. He shifted the impedance coil out of circuit, and when that did not seem to help enough, he returned to his home and on a piece of notepaper wrote neatly, "I have gone to the library," and placed it in clear view on his worktable.

10.

Andrew never quite got to the library. He had studied the map. He knew the route, but not the appearance of it. The actual landmarks did not resemble the symbols on the map and he would hesitate. Eventually he thought he must have somehow gone wrong, for everything looked strange.

He passed an occasional field robot, but at the time he decided he should ask his way, there were none in sight. A vehicle passed and did not stop. He stood irresolute, which meant calmly motionless, and then coming across the field toward him were two human beings.

He turned to face them, and they altered their course to meet him. A moment before, they had been talking loudly; he had heard their voices; but now they were silent. They had the look that Andrew associated with human uncertainty, and they were young, but not very young. Twenty perhaps? Andrew could never judge human age.

He said, "Would you describe to me the route to the town library, sirs?"

One of them, the taller of the two, whose tall hat lengthened him still farther, almost grotesquely, said, not to Andrew, but to the other, "It's a robot."

The other had a bulbous nose and heavy eyelids. He said, not to Andrew, but to the first, "It's wearing clothes."

The tall one snapped his fingers. "It's the free robot. They have a robot at the Martins who isn't owned by anybody. Why else would it be wearing clothes?"

"Ask it," said the one with the nose.

"Are you the Martin robot?" asked the tall one.

"I am Andrew Martin, sir," said Andrew.

"Good. Take off your clothes. Robots don't wear clothes." He said to the other, "That's disgusting. Look at him."

Andrew hesitated. He hadn't heard an order in that tone of voice in so long that his Second Law circuits had momentarily jammed.

The tall one said, "Take off your clothes. I order you."

Slowly, Andrew began to remove them.

"Just drop them," said the tall one.

The nose said, "If it doesn't belong to anyone, he could be ours as much as someone else's."

"Anyway," said the tall one, "who's to object to anything we do? We're not damaging property. . . . Stand on your head." That was to Andrew.

"The head is not meant—" began Andrew.

"That's an order. If you don't know how, try anyway."

Andrew hesitated again, then bent to put his head on the ground. He tried to lift his legs and fell, heavily.

The tall one said, "Just lie there." He said to the other, "We can take him apart. Ever take a robot apart?"

"Will he let us?"

"How can he stop us?"

There was no way Andrew could stop them, if they ordered him not to resist in a forceful enough manner. Second Law of obedience took precedence over the Third Law of self-preservation. In any case, he could not defend himself without possibly hurting them and that would mean breaking the First Law. At that thought, every motile unit contracted slightly and he quivered as he lay there.

The tall one walked over and pushed at him with his foot. "He's heavy. I think we'll need tools to do the job."

The nose said, "We could order him to take himself apart. It would be fun to watch him try."

"Yes," said the tall one thoughtfully, "but let's get him off the road. If someone comes along—"

It was too late. Someone had indeed come along and it was George. From where he lay, Andrew had seen him topping a small rise in the middle distance. He would have liked to signal him in some way, but the last order had been "Just lie there!"

George was running now and he arrived somewhat winded. The two young men stepped back a little and then waited thoughtfully.

George said anxiously, "Andrew, has something gone wrong?"

Andrew said, "I am well, George."

"Then stand up. . . . What happened to your clothes?"

The tall young man said, "That your robot, mac?"

George turned sharply. "He's no one's robot. What's been going on here?"

"We politely asked him to take his clothes off. What's that to you if you don't own him?"

George said, "What were they doing, Andrew?"

Andrew said, "It was their intention in some way to dismember me. They were about to move me to a quiet spot and order me to dismember myself."

George looked at the two and his chin trembled. The two young men retreated no further. They were smiling. The tall one said lightly, "What are you going to do, pudgy? Attack us?"

George said, "No. I don't have to. This robot has been with my family for over seventy years. He knows us and he values us more than he values anyone else. I am going to tell him that you two are threatening my life and that you plan to kill me. I will ask him to defend me. In choosing between me and you two, he will choose me. Do you know what will happen to you when he attacks you?"

The two were backing away slightly, looking uneasy.

George said sharply, "Andrew, I am in danger and about to come to harm from these young men. Move toward them!"

Andrew did so, and the two young men did not wait. They ran fleetly.

"All right, Andrew, relax," said George. He looked unstrung. He was far past the age where he could face the possibility of a dustup with one young man, let alone two.

Andrew said, "I couldn't have hurt them, George. I could see they were not attacking you."

"I didn't order you to attack them; I only told you to move toward them. Their own fears did the rest."

"How can they fear robots?"

"It's a disease of mankind, one of which it is not yet cured. But never mind that. What the devil are you doing here, Andrew? I was on the point of turning back and hiring a helicopter when I found you. How did you get it into your head to go to the library? I would have brought you any books you needed."

"I am a—" began Andrew.

"Free robot. Yes, yes. All right, what did you want in the library?"

"I want to know more about human beings, about the world, about everything. And about robots, George. I want to write a history about robots."

George said, "Well, let's walk home. . . . And pick up your clothes first. Andrew, there are a million books on robotics and all of them include histories of the science. The world is growing saturated not only with robots but with information about robots."

Andrew shook his head, a human gesture he had lately begun to make. "Not a history of robotics, George. A history of *robots,* by a robot. I want to explain how robots feel about what has happened since the first ones were allowed to work and live on Earth."

George's eyebrows lifted, but he said nothing in direct response.

11.

Little Miss was just past her eighty-third birthday, but there was nothing about her that was lacking in either energy or determination. She gestured with her cane oftener than she propped herself up with it.

She listened to the story in a fury of indignation. She said, "George, that's horrible. Who were those young ruffians?"

"I don't know. What difference does it make? In the end they did no damage."

"They might have. You're a lawyer, George, and if you're well off, it's entirely due to the talent of Andrew. It was the money *he* earned that is the foundation of everything we have. He provides the continuity for this family and I will *not* have him treated as a wind-up toy."

"What would you have me do, Mother?" asked George.

"I said you're a lawyer. Don't you listen? You set up a test case somehow, and you force the regional courts to declare for robot rights and get the Legislature to pass the necessary bills, and carry the whole thing to the World Court, if you have to. I'll be watching, George, and I'll tolerate no shirking."

She was serious, and what began as a way of soothing the fearsome old lady became an involved matter with enough legal entanglement to make it interesting. As senior partner of Feingold and Martin, George plotted strategy but left the actual work to his junior partners, with much of it a matter for his son, Paul, who was also a member of the firm and who reported dutifully nearly every day to his grandmother. She, in turn, discussed it every day with Andrew.

Andrew was deeply involved. His work on his book on robots was delayed again, as he pored over the legal arguments and even, at times, made very diffident suggestions.

He said, "George told me that day that human beings have always been afraid of robots. As long as they are, the courts and the legislatures are not likely to work hard on behalf of robots. Should there not be something done about public opinion?"

So while Paul stayed in court, George took to the public platform. It gave him the advantage of being informal and he even went so far sometimes as to wear the new, loose style of clothing which he called drapery. Paul said, "Just don't trip over it on stage, Dad."

George said despondently, "I'll try not to."

He addressed the annual convention of holo-news editors on one occasion and said, in part:

"If, by virtue of the Second Law, we can demand of any robot unlimited obedience in all respects not involving harm to a human being, then any human being, *any* human being, has a fearsome power over any robot, *any* robot. In particular, since Second Law supersedes Third

Law, *any* human being can use the law of obedience to overcome the law of self-protection. He can order any robot to damage itself or even destroy itself for any reason, or for no reason.

"Is this just? Would we treat an animal so? Even an inanimate object which has given us good service has a claim on our consideration. And a robot is not insensible; it is not an animal. It can think well enough to enable it to talk to us, reason with us, joke with us. Can we treat them as friends, can we work together with them, and not give them some of the fruit of that friendship, some of the benefit of co-working?

"If a man has the right to give a robot any order that does not involve harm to a human being, he should have the decency never to give a robot any order that involves harm to a robot, unless human safety absolutely requires it. With great power goes great responsibility, and if the robots have Three Laws to protect men, is it too much to ask that men have a law or two to protect robots?"

Andrew was right. It was the battle over public opinion that held the key to courts and Legislature and in the end a law passed which set up conditions under which robot-harming orders were forbidden. It was endlessly qualified and the punishments for violating the law were totally inadequate, but the principle was established. The final passage by the World Legislature came through on the day of Little Miss's death.

That was no coincidence. Little Miss held on to life desperately during the last debate and let go only when word of victory arrived. Her last smile was for Andrew. Her last words were: "You have been good to us, Andrew."

She died with her hand holding his, while her son and his wife and children remained at a respectful distance from both.

12.

Andrew waited patiently while the receptionist disappeared into the inner office. It might have used the holographic chatterbox, but unquestionably it was unmanned (or perhaps unroboted) by having to deal with another robot rather than with a human being.

Andrew passed the time revolving the matter in his mind. Could "unroboted" be used as an analogue of "unmanned," or had "unmanned" become a metaphoric term sufficiently divorced from its original literal meaning to be applied to robots—or to women for that matter?

Such problems came frequently as he worked on his book on robots. The trick of thinking out sentences to express all complexities had undoubtedly increased his vocabulary.

Occasionally, someone came into the room to stare at him and he did not try to avoid the glance. He looked at each calmly, and each in turn looked away.

Paul Martin finally came out. He looked surprised, or he would have if Andrew could have made out his expression with certainty. Paul had taken to wearing the heavy makeup that fashion was dictating for both sexes and though it made sharper and firmer the somewhat bland lines of his face, Andrew disapproved. He found that disapproving of human beings, as long as he did not express it verbally, did not make him very uneasy. He could even write the disapproval. He was sure it had not always been so.

Paul said, "Come in, Andrew. I'm sorry I made you wait but there was something I *had* to finish. Come in. You had said you wanted to talk to me, but I didn't know you meant here in town."

"If you are busy, Paul, I am prepared to continue to wait."

Paul glanced at the interplay of shifting shadows on

the dial on the wall that served as timepiece and said, "I can make some time. Did you come alone?"

"I hired an automatobile."

"Any trouble?" Paul asked, with more than a trace of anxiety.

"I wasn't expecting any. My rights are protected."

Paul looked the more anxious for that. "Andrew, I've explained that the law is unenforceable, at least under most conditions. . . . And if you insist on wearing clothes, you'll run into trouble eventually—just like that first time."

"And only time, Paul. I'm sorry you are displeased."

"Well, look at it this way; you are virtually a living legend, Andrew, and you are too valuable in many different ways for you to have any right to take chances with yourself. . . . How's the book coming?"

"I am approaching the end, Paul. The publisher is quite pleased."

"Good!"

"I don't know that he's necessarily pleased with the book as a book. I think he expects to sell many copies because it's written by a robot and it's that that pleases him."

"Only human, I'm afraid."

"I am not displeased. Let it sell for whatever reason since it will mean money and I can use some."

"Grandmother left you—"

"Little Miss was generous, and I'm sure I can count on the family to help me out further. But it is the royalties from the book on which I am counting to help me through the next step."

"What next step is that?"

"I wish to see the head of U. S. Robots and Mechanical Men, Inc. I have tried to make an appointment, but so far I have not been able to reach him. The corporation did not cooperate with me in the writing of the book, so I am not surprised, you understand."

Paul was clearly amused. "Cooperation is the last thing you can expect. They didn't cooperate with us in our great fight for robot rights. Quite the reverse and you can see why. Give a robot rights and people may not want to buy them."

"Nevertheless," said Andrew, "if you call them, you may obtain an interview for me."

"I'm no more popular with them than you are, Andrew."

"But perhaps you can hint that by seeing me they may head off a campaign by Feingold and Martin to strengthen the rights of robots further."

"Wouldn't that be a lie, Andrew?"

"Yes, Paul, and I can't tell one. That is why you must call."

"Ah, you can't lie, but you can urge me to tell a lie, is that it? You're getting more human all the time, Andrew."

13.

It was not easy to arrange, even with Paul's supposedly weighted name.

But it was finally carried through and, when it was, Harley Smythe-Robertson, who, on his mother's side, was descended from the original founder of the corporation and who had adopted the hyphenation to indicate it, looked remarkably unhappy. He was approaching retirement age and his entire tenure as president had been devoted to the matter of robot rights. His gray hair was plastered thinly over the top of his scalp, his face was not made up, and he eyed Andrew with brief hostility from time to time.

Andrew said, "Sir, nearly a century ago, I was told by a Merton Mansky of this corporation that the mathematics governing the plotting of the positronic pathways was far too complicated to permit of any but approximate solutions and that therefore my own capacities were not fully predictable."

"That was a century ago." Smythe-Robertson hesitated, then said icily, "*Sir*. It is true no longer. Our robots are made with precision now and are trained precisely to their jobs."

"Yes," said Paul, who had come along, as he said, to make sure that the corporation played fair, "with the result that my receptionist must be guided at every point once events depart from the conventional, however slightly."

Smythe-Robertson said, "You would be much more displeased if it were to improvise."

Andrew said, "Then you no longer manufacture robots like myself which are flexible and adaptable."

"No longer."

"The research I have done in connection with my book," said Andrew, "indicates that I am the oldest robot presently in active operation."

"The oldest presently," said Smythe-Robertson, "and the oldest ever. The oldest that will ever be. No robot is useful after the twenty-fifth year. They are called in and replaced with newer models."

"No robot *as presently manufactured* is useful after the twenty-fifth year," said Paul pleasantly. "Andrew is quite exceptional in this respect."

Andrew, adhering to the path he had marked out for himself, said, "As the oldest robot in the world and the most flexible, am I not unusual enough to merit special treatment from the company?"

"Not at all," said Smythe-Robertson freezingly. "Your unusualness is an embarrassment to the company. If you were on lease, instead of having been a sale outright through some mischance, you would long since have been replaced."

"But that is exactly the point," said Andrew. "I am a free robot and I own myself. Therefore I come to you and ask you to replace me. You cannot do this without the owner's consent. Nowadays, that consent is extorted as a condition of the lease, but in my time this did not happen."

Smythe-Robertson was looking both startled and puzzled, and for a moment there was silence. Andrew found himself staring at the holograph on the wall. It was a death mask of Susan Calvin, patron saint of all roboticists. She was dead nearly two centuries now, but as a result of writing his book Andrew knew her so well he could half persuade himself that he had met her in life.

Smythe-Robertson said, "How can I replace you for you? If I replace you as robot, how can I donate the new robot to you as owner since in the very act of replacement you cease to exist?" He smiled grimly.

"Not at all difficult," interposed Paul. "The seat of Andrew's personality is his positronic brain and it is the one part that cannot be replaced without creating a new robot. The positronic brain, therefore, is Andrew the owner. Every other part of the robotic body can be replaced without affecting the robot's personality, and those other parts are the brain's possessions. Andrew, I should say, wants to supply his brain with a new robotic body."

"That's right," said Andrew calmly. He turned to Smythe-Robertson. "You have manufactured androids, haven't you? Robots that have the outward appearance of humans complete to the texture of the skin?"

Smythe-Robertson said, "Yes, we have. They worked perfectly well, with their synthetic fibrous skins and tendons. There was virtually no metal anywhere except for the brain, yet they were nearly as tough as metal robots. They were tougher, weight for weight."

Paul looked interested. "I didn't know that. How many are on the market?"

"None," said Smythe-Robertson. "They were much more expensive than metal models and a market survey showed they would not be accepted. They looked too human."

Andrew said, "But the corporation retains its expertise, I assume. Since it does, I wish to request that I be replaced by an organic robot, an android."

Paul looked surprised. "Good Lord," he said.

Smythe-Robertson stiffened. "Quite impossible!"

"Why is it impossible?" asked Andrew. "I will pay any reasonable fee, of course."

Smythe-Robertson said, "We do not manufacture androids."

"You do not *choose* to manufacture androids," interposed Paul quickly. "That is not the same as being unable to manufacture them."

Smythe-Robertson said, "Nevertheless, the manufacture of androids is against public policy."

"There is no law against it," said Paul.

"Nevertheless, we do not manufacture them, and we will not."

Paul cleared his throat. "Mr. Smythe-Robertson," he said, "Andrew is a free robot who is under the purview of the law guaranteeing robot rights. You are aware of this, I take it?"

"Only too well."

"This robot, as a free robot, chooses to wear clothes. This results in his being frequently humiliated by thoughtless human beings despite the law against the humiliation of robots. It is difficult to prosecute vague offenses that don't meet with the general disapproval of those who must decide on guilt and innocence."

"U. S. Robots understood that from the start. Your father's firm unfortunately did not."

"My father is dead now," said Paul, "but what I see is that we have here a clear offense with a clear target."

"What are you talking about?" said Smythe-Robertson.

"My client, Andrew Martin—he has just become my client—is a free robot who is entitled to ask U. S. Robots and Mechanical Men, Inc., for the right of replacement, which the corporation supplies anyone who owns a robot for more than twenty-five years. In fact, the corporation insists on such replacement."

Paul was smiling and thoroughly at his ease. He went on, "The positronic brain of my client is the owner of the body of my client—which is certainly more than twenty-five years old. The positronic brain demands the replacement of the body and offers to pay any reasonable fee for an android body as that replacement. If you refuse the request, my client undergoes humiliation and we will sue.

"While public opinion would not ordinarily support the claim of a robot in such a case, may I remind you that U. S. Robots is not popular with the public generally. Even those who most use and profit from robots are suspicious of the corporation. This may be a hangover from the days when robots were widely feared. It may be resentment against the power and wealth of U.S. Robots which has a worldwide monopoly. Whatever the cause may be, the resentment exists and I think you will find that you would prefer not to withstand a lawsuit, particularly since my client is wealthy and will live for many more centuries and will have no reason to refrain from fighting the battle forever."

Smythe-Robertson had slowly reddened. "You are trying to force me to . . ."

"I force you to do nothing," said Paul. "If you wish to refuse to accede to my client's reasonable request, you may by all means do so and we will leave without another word. . . . But we will sue, as is certainly our right, and you will find that you will eventually lose."

Smythe-Robertson said, "Well—" and paused.

"I see that you are going to accede," said Paul. "You may hesitate but you will come to it in the end. Let me assure you, then, of one further point. If, in the process of transferring my client's positronic brain from his present body to an organic one, there is any damage, however slight, then I will never rest till I've nailed the corporation to the ground. I will, if necessary, take every possible step to mobilize public opinion against the corporation if one brain path of my client's platinum-iridium essence is scrambled." He turned to Andrew and said, "Do you agree to all this, Andrew?"

Andrew hesitated a full minute. It amounted to the

approval of lying, of blackmail, of the badgering and humiliation of a human being. But not physical harm, he told himself, not physical harm.

He managed at last to come out with a rather faint "Yes."

14.

It was like being constructed again. For days, then for weeks, finally for months, Andrew found himself not himself somehow, and the simplest actions kept giving rise to hesitation.

Paul was frantic. "They've damaged you, Andrew. We'll have to institute suit."

Andrew spoke very slowly. "You mustn't. You'll never be able to prove—something—m-m-m-m—"

"Malice?"

"Malice. Besides, I grow stronger, better. It's the tr-tr-tr—"

"Tremble?"

"Trauma. After all, there's never been such an op—op—op— before."

Andrew could feel his brain from the inside. No one else could. He knew he was well and during the months that it took him to learn full coordination and full positronic interplay, he spent hours before the mirror.

Not quite human! The face was stiff—too stiff—and the motions were too deliberate. They lacked the careless free flow of the human being, but perhaps that might come with time. At least he could wear clothes without the ridiculous anomaly of a metal face going along with it.

Eventually he said, "I will be going back to work."

Paul laughed and said, "That means you are well. What will you be doing? Another book?"

"No," said Andrew seriously. "I live too long for any one career to seize me by the throat and never let me go. There was a time when I was primarily an artist and

I can still turn to that. And there was a time when I was a historian and I can still turn to that. But now I wish to be a robobiologist."

"A robopsychologist, you mean."

"No. That would imply the study of positronic brains and at the moment I lack the desire to do that. A robobiologist, it seems to me, would be concerned with the working of the body attached to that brain."

"Wouldn't that be a roboticist?"

"A roboticist works with a metal body. I would be studying an organic humanoid body, of which I have the only one, as far as I know."

"You narrow your field," said Paul thoughtfully. "As an artist, all conception is yours; as a historian, you dealt chiefly with robots; as a robobiologist, you will deal with yourself."

Andrew nodded. "It would seem so."

Andrew had to start from the very beginning, for he knew nothing of ordinary biology, almost nothing of science. He became a familiar sight in the libraries, where he sat at the electronic indices for hours at a time, looking perfectly normal in clothes. Those few who knew he was a robot in no way interfered with him.

He built a laboratory in a room which he added to his house, and his library grew, too.

Years passed, and Paul came to him one day and said, "It's a pity you're no longer working on the history of robots. I understand U. S. Robots is adopting a radically new policy."

Paul had aged, and his deteriorating eyes had been replaced with photoptic cells. In that respect, he had drawn closer to Andrew. Andrew said, "What have they done?"

"They are manufacturing central computers, gigantic positronic brains, really, which communicate with anywhere from a dozen to a thousand robots by microwave. The robots themselves have no brains at all. They are the limbs of the gigantic brain, and the two are physically separate."

"Is that more efficient?"

"U. S. Robots claims it is. Smythe-Robertson established the new direction before he died, however, and it's my notion that it's a backlash at you. U. S. Robots is determined that they will make no robots that will give them the type of trouble you have, and for that reason they separate brain and body. The brain will have no body to wish changed; the body will have no brain to wish anything.

"It's amazing, Andrew," Paul went on, "the influence you have had on the history of robots. It was your artistry that encouraged U. S. Robots to make robots more precise and specialized; it was your freedom that resulted in the establishment of the principle of robotic rights; it was your insistence on an android body that made U. S. Robots switch to brain-body separation."

Andrew said, "I suppose in the end the corporation will produce one vast brain controlling several billion robotic bodies. All the eggs will be in one basket. Dangerous. Not proper at all."

"I think you're right," said Paul, "but I don't suspect it will come to pass for a century at least and I won't live to see it. In fact, I may not live to see next year."

"Paul!" said Andrew, in concern.

Paul shrugged. "We're mortal, Andrew. We're not like you. It doesn't matter too much, but it does make it important to assure you on one point. I'm the last of the human Martins. There are collaterals descended from my great-aunt, but they don't count. The money I control personally will be left to the trust in your name and as far as anyone can foresee the future, you will be economically secure."

"Unnecessary," said Andrew, with difficulty. In all this time, he could not get used to the deaths of the Martins.

Paul said, "Let's not argue. That's the way it's going to be. What are you working on?"

"I am designing a system for allowing androids—

myself—to gain energy from the combustion of hydrocarbons, rather than from atomic cells."

Paul raised his eyebrows. "So that they will breathe and eat?"

"Yes."

"How long have you been pushing in that direction?"

"For a long time now, but I think I have designed an adequate combustion chamber for catalyzed controlled breakdown."

"But why, Andrew? The atomic cell is surely infinitely better."

"In some ways, perhaps, but the atomic cell is inhuman."

15.

It took time, but Andrew had time. In the first place, he did not wish to do anything till Paul had died in peace.

With the death of the great-grandson of Sir, Andrew felt more nearly exposed to a hostile world and for that reason was the more determined to continue the path he had long ago chosen.

Yet he was not really alone. If a man had died, the firm of Feingold and Martin lived, for a corporation does not die any more than a robot does. The firm had its directions and it followed them soullessly. By way of the trust and through the law firm, Andrew continued to be wealthy. And in return for their own large annual retainer, Feingold and Martin involved themselves in the legal aspects of the new combustion chamber.

When the time came for Andrew to visit U. S. Robots and Mechanical Men, Inc., he did it alone. Once he had gone with Sir and once with Paul. This time, the third time, he was alone and manlike.

U. S. Robots had changed. The production plant had been shifted to a large space station, as had grown to be the case with more and more industries. With them had gone many robots. The Earth itself was becoming park-like, with its one-billion-person population stabilized and perhaps not more than thirty per cent of its at least equally large robot population independently brained.

The Director of Research was Alvin Magdescu, dark of complexion and hair, with a little pointed beard and wearing nothing above the waist but the breastband that fashion dictated. Andrew himself was well covered in the older fashion of several decades back.

Magdescu said, "I know you, of course, and I'm rather pleased to see you. You're our most notorious product and it's a pity old Smythe-Robertson was so set against you. We could have done a great deal with you."

"You still can," said Andrew.

"No, I don't think so. We're past the time. We've had robots on Earth for over a century, but that's changing. It will be back to space with them and those that stay here won't be brained."

"But there remains myself, and I stay on Earth."

"True, but there doesn't seem to be much of the robot about you. What new request have you?"

"To be still less a robot. Since I am so far organic, I wish an organic source of energy. I have here the plans—"

Magdescu did not hasten through them. He might have intended to at first, but he stiffened and grew intent. At one point he said, "This is remarkably ingenious. Who thought of all this?"

"I did," said Andrew.

Magdescu looked up at him sharply, then said, "It would amount to a major overhaul of your body, and an experimental one, since it has never been attempted before. I advise against it. Remain as you are."

Andrew's face had limited means of expression, but impatience showed plainly in his voice. "Dr. Magdescu, you miss the entire point. You have no choice but to accede to my request. If such devices can be built into my body, they can be built into human bodies as well.

The tendency to lengthen human life by prosthetic devices has already been remarked on. There are no devices better than the ones I have designed and am designing.

"As it happens, I control the patents by way of the firm of Feingold and Martin. We are quite capable of going into business for ourselves and of developing the kind of prosthetic devices that may end by producing human beings with many of the properties of robots. Your own business will then suffer.

"If, however, you operate on me now and agree to do so under similar circumstances in the future, you will receive permission to make use of the patents and control the technology of both robots and the prosthetization of human beings. The initial leasing will not be granted, of course, until after the first operation is completed successfully, and after enough time has passed to demonstrate that it is indeed successful." Andrew felt scarcely any First Law inhibition to the stern conditions he was setting a human being. He was learning to reason that what seemed like cruelty might, in the long run, be kindness.

Magdescu looked stunned. He said, "I'm not the one to decide something like this. That's a corporate decision that would take time."

"I can wait a reasonable time," said Andrew, "but only a reasonable time." And he thought with satisfaction that Paul himself could not have done it better.

16.

It took only a reasonable time, and the operation was a success.

Magdescu said, "I was very much against the operation, Andrew, but not for the reasons you might think. I was not in the least against the experiment, if it had been on someone else. I hated risking *your* positronic brain. Now that you have the positronic pathways interacting with simulated nerve pathways, it might be difficult to rescue the brain intact if the body went bad."

"I had every faith in the skill of the staff at U. S. Robots," said Andrew. "And I can eat now."

"Well, you can sip olive oil. It will mean occasional cleanings of the combustion chamber, as we have explained to you. Rather an uncomfortable touch, I should think."

"Perhaps, if I did not expect to go further. Self-cleaning is not impossible. In fact, I am working on a device that will deal with solid food that may be expected to contain incombustible fractions—indigestible matter, so to speak, that will have to be discarded."

"You would then have to develop an anus."

"The equivalent."

"What else, Andrew?"

"Everything else."

"Genitalia, too?"

"Insofar as they will fit my plans. My body is a canvas on which I intend to draw—"

Magdescu waited for the sentence to be completed, and when it seemed that it would not be, he completed it himself. "A man?"

"We shall see," said Andrew.

Magdescu said, "It's a puny ambition, Andrew. You're better than a man. You've gone downhill from the moment you opted for organicism."

"My brain has not suffered."

"No, it hasn't. I'll grant you that. But, Andrew, the whole new breakthrough in prosthetic devices made possible by your patents is being marketed under your name. You're recognized as the inventor and you're honored for it—as you are. Why play further games with your body?"

Andrew did not answer.

The honors came. He accepted membership in several learned societies, including one which was devoted to the new science he had established; the one he had called robobiology but had come to be termed prosthetology.

On the one hundred and fiftieth anniversary of his construction, there was a testimonial dinner given in his honor at U. S. Robots. If Andrew saw irony in this, he kept it to himself.

Alvin Magdescu came out of retirement to chair the dinner. He was himself ninety-four years old and was alive because he had prosthetized devices that, among other things, fulfilled the function of liver and kidneys. The dinner reached its climax when Magdescu, after a short and emotional talk, raised his glass to toast "the Sesquicentennial Robot."

Andrew had had the sinews of his face redesigned to the point where he could show a range of emotions, but he sat through all the ceremonies solemnly passive. He did not like to be a Sesquicentennial Robot.

17.

It was prosthetology that finally took Andrew off the Earth. In the decades that followed the celebration of the Sesquicentennial, the Moon had come to be a world more Earth-like than Earth in every respect but its gravitational pull and in its underground cities there was a fairly dense population.

Prosthetized devices there had to take the lesser gravity into account and Andrew spent five years on the Moon working with local prosthetologists to make the necessary adaptations. When not at his work, he wandered among the robot population, every one of which treated him with the robotic obsequiousness due a man.

He came back to an Earth that was humdrum and quiet in comparison and visited the offices of Feingold and Martin to announce his return.

The current head of the firm, Simon DeLong, was surprised. He said, "We had been told you were returning, Andrew" (he had almost said "Mr. Martin"), "but we were not expecting you till next week."

"I grew impatient," said Andrew brusquely. He was anxious to get to the point. "On the Moon, Simon, I was in charge of a research team of twenty human scientists. I gave orders that no one questioned. The Lunar robots deferred to me as they would to a human being. Why, then, am I not a human being?"

A wary look entered DeLong's eyes. He said, "My dear Andrew, as you have just explained, you are treated as a human being by both robots and human beings. You are therefore a human being *de facto*."

"To be a human being *de facto* is not enough. I want not only to be treated as one, but to be legally identified as one. I want to be a human being *de jure*."

"Now that is another matter," said DeLong. "There we would run into human prejudice and into the undoubted fact that however much you may be like a human being, you are *not* a human being."

"In what way not?" asked Andrew. "I have the shape of a human being and organs equivalent to those of a human being. My organs, in fact, are identical to some of those in a prosthetized human being. I have contributed artistically, literarily, and scientifically to human culture as much as any human being now alive. What more can one ask?"

"I myself would ask nothing more. The trouble is that it would take an act of the World Legislature to define you as a human being. Frankly, I wouldn't expect that to happen."

"To whom on the Legislature could I speak?"

"To the chairman of the Science and Technology Committee perhaps."

"Can you arrange a meeting?"

"But you scarcely need an intermediary In your position, you can—"

"No. *You* arrange it." (It didn't even occur to Andrew that he was giving a flat order to a human being. He had grown accustomed to that on the Moon.) "I want him to know that the firm of Feingold and Martin is backing me in this to the hilt."

"Well, now—"

"To the hilt, Simon. In one hundred and seventy-three years I have in one fashion or another contributed greatly to this firm. I have been under obligation to individual members of the firm in times past. I am not now. It is rather the other way around now and I am calling in my debts."

DeLong said, "I will do what I can."

18.

The chairman of the Science and Technology Committee was of the East Asian region and she was a woman. Her name was Chee Li-Hsing and her transparent garments (obscuring what she wanted obscured only by their dazzle) made her look plastic-wrapped.

She said, "I sympathize with your wish for full human rights. There have been times in history when segments of the human population fought for full human rights. What rights, however, can you possibly want that you do not have?"

"As simple a thing as my right to life. A robot can be dismantled at any time."

"A human being can be executed at any time."

"Execution can only follow due process of law. There is no trial needed for my dismantling. Only the word of a human being in authority is needed to end me. Besides—besides—" Andrew tried desperately to allow no sign of pleading, but his carefully designed tricks of human expression and tone of voice betrayed him here. "The truth is, I want to be a man. I have wanted it through six generations of human beings."

Li-Hsing looked up at him out of darkly sympathetic eyes. "The Legislature can pass a law declaring you one—they could pass a law declaring a stone statue to be defined as a man. Whether they will actually do so is, however, as likely in the first case as the second. Congresspeople are as human as the rest of the population and there is always that element of suspicion against robots."

"Even now?"

"Even now. We would all allow the fact that you have earned the prize of humanity and yet there would remain the fear of setting an undesirable precedent."

"What precedent? I am the only free robot, the only one of my type, and there will never be another. You may consult U. S. Robots."

" 'Never' is a long time, Andrew—or, if you prefer, Mr. Martin—since I will gladly give you my personal accolade as man. You will find that most Congresspeople will not be willing to set the precedent, no matter how meaningless such a precedent might be. Mr. Martin, you have my sympathy, but I cannot tell you to hope. Indeed—"

She sat back and her forehead wrinkled. "Indeed, if the issue grows too heated, there might well arise a certain sentiment, both inside the Legislature and outside, for that dismantling you mentioned. Doing away with you could turn out to be the easiest way of resolving the dilemma. Consider that before deciding to push matters."

Andrew said, "Will no one remember the technique of prosthetology, something that is almost entirely mine?"

"It may seem cruel, but they won't. Or if they do, it will be remembered against you. It will be said you did it only for yourself. It will be said it was part of a campaign to roboticize human beings, or to humanify robots; and in either case evil and vicious. You have never been part of a political hate campaign, Mr. Martin, and I tell you that you will be the object of vilification of a kind neither you nor I would credit and there would be people who'll believe it all. Mr. Martin, let your life be." She rose and, next to Andrew's seated figure, she seemed small and almost childlike.

Andrew said, "If I decide to fight for my humanity, will you be on my side?"

She thought, then said, "I will be—insofar as I can be. If at any time such a stand would appear to threaten my political future, I may have to abandon you, since it is not an issue I feel to be at the very root of my beliefs. I am trying to be honest with you."

"Thank you, and I will ask no more. I intend to fight this through whatever the consequences, and I will ask you for your help only for as long as you can give it."

19.

It was not a direct fight. Feingold and Martin counseled patience and Andrew muttered grimly that he had an endless supply of that. Feingold and Martin then entered on a campaign to narrow and restrict the area of combat.

They instituted a lawsuit denying the obligation to pay debts to an individual with a prosthetic heart on the grounds that the possession of a robotic organ removed humanity, and with it the constitutional rights of human beings.

They fought the matter skillfully and tenaciously, losing at every step but always in such a way that the decision was forced to be as broad as possible, and then carrying it by way of appeals to the World Court.

It took years, and millions of dollars.

When the final decision was handed down, DeLong held what amounted to a victory celebration over the legal loss. Andrew was, of course, present in the company offices on the occasion.

"We've done two things, Andrew," said DeLong, "both of which are good. First of all, we have established the fact that no number of artifacts in the human body causes it to cease being a human body. Secondly, we have engaged public opinion in the question in such a way as to put it fiercely on the side of a broad interpretation of humanity since there is not a human being in existence who does not hope for prosthetics if that will keep him alive."

"And do you think the Legislature will now grant me my humanity?" asked Andrew.

DeLong looked faintly uncomfortable. "As to that, I cannot be optimistic. There remains the one organ which the World Court has used as the criterion of humanity. Human beings have an organic cellular brain and robots have a platinum-iridium positronic brain if they have one at all—and you certainly have a positronic brain. . . . No, Andrew, don't get that look in your eye. We lack the knowledge to duplicate the work of a cellular brain in artificial structures close enough to the organic type to allow it to fall within the Court's decision. Not even you could do it."

"What ought we do, then?"

"Make the attempt, of course. Congresswoman Li-Hsing will be on our side and a growing number of other Congresspeople. The President will undoubtedly go along with a majority of the Legislature in this matter."

"Do we have a majority?"

"No, far from it. But we might get one if the public will allow its desire for a broad interpretation of humanity to extend to you. A small chance, I admit, but if you do not wish to give up, we must gamble for it."

"I do not wish to give up."

20.

Congresswoman Li-Hsing was considerably older than she had been when Andrew had first met her. Her transparent garments were long gone. Her hair was now close-cropped and her coverings were tubular. Yet still Andrew clung, as closely as he could within the limits of reasonable taste, to the style of clothing that had prevailed when he had first adopted clothing over a century before.

She said, "We've gone as far as we can, Andrew. We'll try once more after recess, but, to be honest, defeat is certain and the whole thing will have to be given up. All my most recent efforts have only earned me a certain defeat in the coming congressional campaign."

"I know," said Andrew, "and it distresses me. You said once you would abandon me if it came to that. Why have you not done so?"

"One can change one's mind, you know. Somehow, abandoning you became a higher price than I cared to pay for just one more term. As it is, I've been in the Legislature for over a quarter of a century. It's enough."

"Is there no way we can change minds, Chee?"

"We've changed all that are amenable to reason. The rest—the majority—cannot be moved from their emotional antipathies."

"Emotional antipathy is not a valid reason for voting one way or the other."

"I know that, Andrew, but they don't advance emotional antipathy as their reason."

Andrew said cautiously, "It all comes down to the brain, then, but must we leave it at the level of cells versus positrons? Is there no way of forcing a functional definition? Must we say that a brain is made of this or that? May we not say that a brain is something—anything—capable of a certain level of thought?"

"Won't work," said Li-Hsing. "Your brain is manmade, the human brain is not. Your brain is constructed, theirs developed. To any human being who is intent on keeping up the barrier between himself and a robot, those differences are a steel wall a mile high and a mile thick."

"If we could get at the source of their antipathy—the very source of—"

"After all your years," said Li-Hsing sadly, "you are still trying to reason out the human being. Poor Andrew, don't be angry, but it's the robot in you that drives you in that direction."

"I don't know," said Andrew. "If I could bring myself—"

1. (reprise)

If he could bring himself—

He had known for a long time it might come to that, and in the end he was at the surgeon's. He found one, skillful enough for the job at hand, which meant a robot surgeon, for no human surgeon could be trusted in this connection, either in ability or in intention.

The surgeon could not have performed the operation on a human being, so Andrew, after putting off the moment of decision with a sad line of questioning that reflected the turmoil within himself, put the First Law to one side by saying, "I, too, am a robot."

He then said, as firmly as he had learned to form the words even at human beings over these past decades, "I *order* you to carry through the operation on me."

In the absence of the First Law, an order so firmly given from one who looked so much like a man activated the Second Law sufficiently to carry the day.

21.

Andrew's feeling of weakness was, he was sure, quite imaginary. He had recovered from the operation. Nevertheless, he leaned, as unobtrusively as he could manage, against the wall. It would be entirely too revealing to sit.

Li-Hsing said, "The final vote will come this week, Andrew. I've been able to delay it no longer, and we must lose. . . . And that will be it, Andrew."

Andrew said, "I am grateful for your skill at delay. It

gave me the time I needed, and I took the gamble I had to."

"What gamble is this?" asked Li-Hsing with open concern.

"I couldn't tell you, or the people at Feingold and Martin. I was sure I would be stopped. See here, if it is the brain that is at issue, isn't the greatest difference of all the matter of immortality? Who really cares what a brain looks like or is built of or how it was formed? What matters is that brain cells die; *must* die. Even if every other organ in the body is maintained or replaced, the brain cells, which cannot be replaced without changing and therefore killing the personality, must eventually die.

"My own positronic pathways have lasted nearly two centuries without perceptible change and can last for centuries more. Isn't *that* the fundamental barrier? Human beings can tolerate an immortal robot, for it doesn't matter how long a machine lasts. They cannot tolerate an immortal human being, since their own mortality is endurable only so long as it is universal. And for that reason they won't make me a human being."

Li-Hsing said, "What is it you're leading up to, Andrew?"

"I have removed that problem. Decades ago, my positronic brain was connected to organic nerves. Now, one last operation has arranged that connection in such a way that slowly—quite slowly—the potential is being drained from my pathways."

Li-Hsing's finely wrinkled face showed no expression for a moment. Then her lips tightened. "Do you mean you've arranged to die, Andrew? You can't have. That violates the Third Law."

"No," said Andrew, "I have chosen between the death of my body and the death of my aspirations and desires. To have let my body live at the cost of the greater death is what would have violated the Third Law."

Li-Hsing seized his arm as though she were about to

shake him. She stopped herself. "Andrew, it won't work. Change it back."

"It can't be. Too much damage was done. I have a year to live—more or less. I will last through the two hundredth anniversary of my construction. I was weak enough to arrange that."

"How can it be worth it? Andrew, you're a fool."

"If it brings me humanity, that will be worth it. If it doesn't, it will bring an end to striving and that will be worth it, too."

And Li-Hsing did something that astonished herself. Quietly, she began to weep.

22.

It was odd how that last deed caught at the imagination of the world. All that Andrew had done before had not swayed them. But he had finally accepted even death to be human and the sacrifice was too great to be rejected.

The final ceremony was timed, quite deliberately, for the two hundredth anniversary. The World President was to sign the act and make it law and the ceremony would be visible on a global network and would be beamed to the Lunar state and even to the Martian colony.

Andrew was in a wheelchair. He could still walk, but only shakily.

With mankind watching, the World President said, "Fifty years ago, you were declared a Sesquicentennial Robot, Andrew." After a pause, and in a more solemn tone, he said, "Today we declare you a Bicentennial Man, Mr. Martin."

And Andrew, smiling, held out his hand to shake that of the President.

23.

Andrew's thoughts were slowly fading as he lay in bed.

Desperately he seized at them. Man! He was a man! He wanted that to be his last thought. He wanted to dissolve—die—with that.

He opened his eyes one more time and for one last time recognized Li-Hsing waiting solemnly. There were others, but those were only shadows, unrecognizable shadows. Only Li-Hsing stood out against the deepening gray. Slowly, inchingly, he held out his hand to her and very dimly and faintly felt her take it.

She was fading in his eyes, as the last of his thoughts trickled away.

But before she faded completely, one last fugitive thought came to him and rested for a moment on his mind before everything stopped.

"Little Miss," he whispered, too low to be heard.

Recommended Reading—1976

BRIAN W. ALDISS: "Appearance of Life," *Andromeda 1;* "Journey to the Heartland," *Universe 6.*

ALAN BRENNERT: "Jamie's Smile," *The Ides of Tomorrow;* "The Second Soul," *Galaxy,* March 1976.

RICHARD W. BROWN: "How You See It, How You Don't," *Amazing Science Fiction,* March 1976.

MICHAEL G. CONEY: "The Cinderella Machine," *Fantasy and Science Fiction,* August 1976.

RICHARD COWPER: "The Hertford Manuscript," *Fantasy and Science Fiction,* October 1976.

AVRAM DAVIDSON: "O Brave Old World!," *Beyond Time.*

URSULA K. LE GUIN: "The Diary of the Rose," *Future Power.*

GEORGE R. R. MARTIN: "A Beast for Norn," *Andromeda 1;* "In the House of the Worm," *The Ides of Tomorrow;* "This Tower of Ashes," *Analog Annual.*

ANDREW J. OFFUTT: "The Greenhouse Defect," *Stellar Short Novels.*

FRED SABERHAGEN: "Birthdays," *Galaxy,* March 1976.

BOB SHAW: "Skirmish on a Summer Morning," *Cosmic Kaleidoscope.*

ROBERT SHECKLEY: "In a Land of Clear Colors," *New Constellations;*

"The Never-Ending Western Movie," *Science Fiction Discoveries.*

JOHN SHIRLEY: "Under the Generator," *Universe 6.*

JAMES TIPTREE, JR.: "Houston, Houston, Do You Read?," *Aurora: Beyond Equality.*

STEVEN UTLEY: "Predators," *The Ides of Tomorrow.*

JOHN VARLEY: "Gotta Sing, Gotta Dance," *Galaxy,* July 1976;
"Overdrawn at the Memory Bank," *Galaxy,* May 1976.

JOAN D. VINGE: "Media Man," *Analog,* October 1976.

HOWARD WALDROP: "Mary Margaret Road-Grader," *Orbit 18.*

JAMES WHITE: "Custom Fitting," *Stellar #2.*

The Science Fiction Year

Charles N. Brown

Despite forecasts of gloom from science-fiction experts who felt the field had expanded much too quickly, 1976 seems to be another record year. The year isn't quite over as I write, so I have no exact figures, but the 1975 total of 890 books, new and reprint, will probably be beaten. The average price for both paperbacks and hardcovers also went up as usual: the average paperback price is now $1.60 and the hardcover average is slightly above $8.00.

The Science Fiction Book Club, Doubleday, Harper and Row and Berkley/Putnam continued to dominate the hardcover field in the United States, while Gollancz, and NEL did the same in England. The most prolific paperback publishers were Ballantine, DAW, ACE, and Berkley in the U.S. and Sphere, Orbit, and NEL in the United Kingdom.

Laser Books, which issued three titles per month in 1976, suspended publication in January 1977 to "evaluate" their sales figures. Laser had been seeking a wider market among adventure story readers and, after a year, discovered it didn't exist. Their sales figures and patterns of distribution indicated they were reaching the same audience sf books have always had. It wasn't large enough or unsophisticated enough for the Laser package, which was designed to sell as a product instead of as a specific book by a specific author. The magazine *Vertex,* which suspended publication in 1975, also tried to reach this mythical wider audience and failed. It seems clear that material packaged as science fiction sells to the existing sf audience—a fact that should be self-evident.

The 1976 *Locus* Poll showed that the average reader of science fiction was twenty-seven years old, a college student or graduate, started reading science fiction at age twelve, and spent nearly $10.00 per week on it. Only 20 percent of the sf audience was female. Science fiction was 70 percent of his or her pleasure (nontext-book) reading.

Several changes in publishing took place during 1976 which will affect science fiction. Ace Books was sold to Grosset and Dunlap and will be producing hardcover as well as paperback books; the new infusion of money may help a line which has gone downhill in the last five years. Dell Books became part of Doubleday, and Ballantine Books announced a new imprint, Del Rey Books, which will do six science-fiction or fantasy titles per month. The new imprint, edited by Judy-Lynn del Rey and Lester del Rey, will be the world's largest line specializing in science fiction.

The sf magazine field showed a number of changes in 1976, most for the better. The average circulation was up and several new magazines appeared or were announced. *Odyssey*, a large-size magazine marred by poor production, had two issues in 1976 before folding; the British magazine *Science Fiction Monthly* also ceased publication. But two new magazines appeared to take their place. *Isaac Asimov's Science Fiction Magazine* is a new digest size magazine which hopes to capitalize on Dr. Asimov's name and fame. *Galileo* is a large-size effort with no newsstand distribution. *Cosmos*, another large-size magazine, has been announced for 1977 publication. The two leading magazines, *Analog* and *Fantasy and Science Fiction,* continued to dominate the field. *Galaxy* skipped several issues and the other two, *Amazing* and *Fantastic*, dropped back to quarterly publication. *Analog* announced a price hike to $1.25 per issue and the other magazines will probably follow in due course.

Newsweek ran a special article on science fiction, written in its most sneering style, but *Publishers Weekly* made up for it by running a thoughtful issue devoted to the genre.

Academic interest in sf continued to grow, and the December 1976 meeting of the Modern Language Association featured a large number of science-fiction seminars. The Science Fiction Research Association held a successful conference in June 1976 with many sf authors present. The three academic journals about science fiction, *Extrapolation, Foundation*, and *Science Fiction Studies*, continued to publish. *Foundation,* the best of the three, features long autobiographical articles by authors and excellent critical reviews. *Science Fiction Studies* is written in heavy academic jargon and has a strong Marxist bias. *Extrapolation*, the oldest of the journals, is a mixture of the two.

The library reprint market continued to flourish in 1976. Gregg Press issued 29 new titles with introductions by some of the leading authors and critics in the field. Unlike their first series, this one consisted mostly of modern works. Hyperion Press, which started the science-fiction library reprint market, issued 19 more titles in both hardcover and paperback, concentrating on the early twentieth century. Avon/Equinox and NEL (United Kingdom) issued general series of classic reprints; the NEL "SF Master" series has critical introductions.

There were more translations of foreign sf in 1976 than ever before. DAW Books published most of them, including books from Russia, Germany, and France. Harper and Row did an American edition of a popular Japanese book, *Japan Sinks* by Sakyo Komatsu. Seabury gave us the latest translation of Polish author Stanislaw Lem, *The Star Diaries.* For a good sampler of European sf, try *The Best from the Rest of the World* edited by Donald A. Wollheim (Doubleday).

Noted sf author Edgar Pangborn died suddenly on February 1, 1976 of a heart attack. He was 66. Pangborn's most famous book, *Davy* (1964), is considered a science fiction classic. His earlier novel *A Mirror for Observers* (1954) won the International Fantasy Award. His output was small, but distinguished by smoothly written prose and incredibly sympathetic characterization. The postholocaust world of *Davy* forms the background for Pangborn's novels *The Company of Glory* (1974) and *The Judgment of Eve* (1966), and for a number of shorter works. His two non-sf books, *Wilderness of Spring* (1958) and *The Trial of Callista Blake* (1961) were critical successes.

Thomas Burnctt Swann, one of the leading fantasy authors, died of cancer on May 5, 1976. He was 47. Swann carved out a special niche all his own in the fantasy field: the retelling of classical myth with sympathetic humanized portrayals of minotaurs, dryads, fauns and other nonhuman characters. His first book, *Day of the Minotaur* (1966), was a Hugo nominee, as were many of his later books. He published eighteen books of fantasy, a handful of short stories, four collections of poetry, and six critical and biographical books.

Fritz Lang, the last of the famous early twentieth century German directors, died on August 2, 1976. He was 85. Lang made the classic science-fiction film *Metropolis* in 1926; it has enjoyed lasting popularity even though it's been shown outside Germany only in cut versions. His *Die Frau im Mond* (1929) was the first film attempt to use a realistic spaceship. His psychological thriller *M* (1931) introduced Peter Lorre to movie audiences. Lang fled Germany in 1933 and eventually settled in Los Angeles; he made many other films, but none had the impact of his early German classics.

Mary Gnaedinger, editor of *Famous Fantastic Mysteries* and *Fantastic Novels* from their beginning in 1939 to their demise in 1953, died on July 31, 1976 at the age of 78. The magazines started out reprinting fantasy material from the Munsey magazines *Argosy* and *All-Story*, but switched to reprinting fantasy and science-fiction books in 1943. A run of the magazines today is both highly prized and highly priced.

Daniel F. Galouye, science-fiction author and newspaperman, died on September 7, 1976 after a long illness. He was 56. Galouye started writing in 1952 and published over sixty stories in sf magazines. His first novel, *Dark Universe* (1961), was an immediate success and a Hugo nominee. He published four other novels and two collections of short stories.

The 1976 Nebula Awards were presented on April 10 at the Century Plaza Hotel in Los Angeles. Winners were: Best Novel: *The Forever War* by Joe Haldeman; Best Novella: "Home is the Hangman" by Roger Zelazny; Best Novelette: "San Diego Lightfoot Sue" by Tom Reamy; Best Short Story: "Catch That Zeppelin" by Fritz Leiber; Best Dramatic Writing: *Young Frankenstein* by Mel Brooks and Gene Wilder. Jack Williamson won the Grand Master Award.

The 1976 World Science Fiction Convention was held September 2–6 in Kansas City, Missouri. Two thousand six hundred members attended. Robert A. Heinlein was Professional Guest of Honor and George Barr was Fan Guest of Honor. There were panels, speeches, readings, parties, movies, and general socializing. The winners of the 1976 Hugo Awards were: Best Novel: *The Forever War* by Joe Haldeman; Best Novella: "Home is the Hangman" by Roger Zelazny; Best Novelette: "The Borderland of Sol" by Larry Niven; Best Short Story: "Catch That Zeppelin" by Fritz Leiber; Best Professional Editor: Ben Bova of *Analog*; Best Professional Artist: Frank Kelly Freas; Best Dramatic Presentation: *A Boy and his Dog*; Best Fanzine: *Locus* edited by Charles and Dena Brown; Best Fan

Artist: Tim Kirk; Best Fan Writer: Richard Geis. The John W. Campbell Award for best new writer was won by Tom Reamy.

The First World Science Fiction Writers' Conference was held in Dublin, Ireland, September 24–26, 1976. Writers were present from Britain, Ireland, America, Germany, and Hungary. There were talks on translation, creativity, criticism, and the problems of publishing. An international sf writers' organization was proposed.

Two science-fiction novels, *Imperial Earth* by Arthur C. Clarke and *Children of Dune* by Frank Herbert, made the best-seller lists during 1976. Publishers' payments for paperback rights to novels by at least five other sf authors further reflected the commercial popularity of the genre: Ben Bova, Robert Silverberg, Frederik Pohl, George R. R. Martin, and Joe Haldeman all sold paperback rights to new books for advances in excess of $30,000. Joe Haldeman set the record with *Mindbridge,* which went for $100,000.

Coming events worth noting:

Allen & Unwin have announced Autumn 1977 publication for *The Silmarillion* by J. R. R. Tolkien, which has been edited for publication by Tolkien's son, Christopher.

The 1977 World Science Fiction Convention will be held in Miami Beach, Florida, September 2–5, 1977. Jack Williamson will be Professional Guest of Honor, Robert A. Madle the Fan Guest of Honor; Robert Silverberg will be toastmaster. For information on membership, write: Suncon, Box 3427, Cherry Hill, NJ 08034.

The 1978 World SF Convention will be in Phoenix, Arizona, August 31–September 4, 1978. Harlan Ellison will be Professional Guest of Honor, Bill Bowers the Fan Guest of Honor; the toastmaster will be F. M. Busby. For information on membership, write: Iguanacon, Box 1072, Phoenix, AZ 85001

Charles N. Brown coedits Locus, the Newspaper of the Science Fiction Field. *Copies are 60 cents each, subscriptions twelve issues for $6.00, payable to Locus Publications, P. O. Box 3938, San Francisco, CA 94119.*